The Praise Keeps Rollin' In . . .

Pumpkin Roll

"*Pumpkin Roll* **is tightly plotted, with twists, turns, and pinches in just the right places,** and it's obvious Josi takes the recipes just as seriously as she does the story. Complete with expert character development, unique premise, and polished voice, *Pumpkin Roll* is a thumping good read!"

—Luisa Perkins, author of *The Book of Jer3miah* and *Despirited*

"*Pumpkin Roll* is different from the other books in the series, and while the others have their tense moments, **this had me downright nervous and spooked.** During the climax, I kept shaking my head, saying, 'No way this is happening.' Five out of five stars for this one. I could not stop reading."

—Mindy Holt, www.ldswomensbookreview.com

Blackberry Crumble

"*Blackberry Crumble* **offers up a thrilling murder mystery!** Most people are not who they appear to be. I can't give away the really shadowy characters or the killer, but there is a killer—and this killer means business!"

—Gabi Kupitz

"**Josi Kilpack is an absolute master** at leading you to believe you have everything figured out, only to have the rug pulled out from under you with the turn of a page. *Blackberry Crumble* is a delightful mystery with wonderful characters and a white-knuckle ending that'll leave you begging for more."

—Gregg Luke, author of *Blink of an Eye*

Key Lime Pie

"I had a great time following the ever-delightful Sadie as she ate and sleuthed her way through **nerve-racking twists and turns and nail-biting suspense.**"

—Melanie Jacobsen, author of *The List* and *Not My Type*,
http://www.readandwritestuff.blogspot.com/

Devil's Food Cake

"Josi Kilpack whips up **another tasty mystery where startling twists and delightful humor mix** in a confection as delicious as Sadie Hoffmiller's devil's food cake."

—Stephanie Black, three-time winner of the Whitney Award for Mystery/Suspense

English Trifle

"*English Trifle* **is an excellent read** and will be enjoyed by teens and adults of either gender. The characters are interesting, the plot is carefully crafted, and the setting has an authentic feel."

—Jennie Hansen, *Meridian Magazine*

Lemon Tart

"**The novel has a bit of everything. It's a mystery, a cookbook, a low-key romance and a dead-on depiction of life.** . . . That may sound like a hodgepodge. It's not. It works. Kilpack blends it all together and cooks it up until it has the taste of, well . . . of a tangy lemon tart."

—Jerry Johnston, *Deseret News*

BANANA SPLIT

OTHER BOOKS BY JOSI S. KILPACK

CULINARY MYSTERIES

Her Good Name
Sheep's Clothing
Unsung Lullaby

Lemon Tart
English Trifle
Devil's Food Cake
Key Lime Pie
Blackberry Crumble
Pumpkin Roll
Tres Leches Cupcakes (coming Fall 2012)

Banana Split recipes

Island Teriyaki Chicken	17
Fish Tacos	83
Macadamia Nut Pancakes with Coconut Syrup	117
Sweet Hawaiian Dinner Rolls	123
Green Bean Bow Tie Salad	156
Banana Splits: Pineapple Topping, Great-Grandma Jensen's Caramel Sauce, and Laree's Hot Fudge	163
Sadie's Sassy Grilled Pineapple	175
Spam-Fried Rice	240
Slow-Cooked Kalua Pig	305
Aloha Cookies	359

Download a free PDF of all the recipes in this book at
josiskilpack.com or shadowmountain.com

BANANA SPLIT

A CULINARY MYSTERY

Josi S. Kilpack

SHADOW
MOUNTAIN

Visit us at ShadowMountain.com

Library of Congress Cataloging-in-Publication Data
Kilpack, Josi S., author.
Banana split / Josi S. Kilpack.
      pages cm
    Summary: Sadie Hoffmiller needs some time to rest, and where better than in beautiful Hawaii? But when Sadie finds herself entangled—literally—with a body, she is forced to face the compounding fears that are making her life so difficult to live. Her determination to focus on her healing soon takes a backseat, however, when she meets the son of the woman whose body she discovered and decides to help him.
    ISBN 978-1-60908-903-0 (paperbound)
    1. Hoffmiller, Sadie (Fictitious character)—Fiction. 2. Cooks—Fiction. 3. Hawaii—Fiction. I. Title.
    PS3561.I412B36 2012
    813'.54—dc23   2011043912

Printed in the United States of America
R. R. Donnelley, Crawfordsville, IN

10   9   8   7   6   5   4   3   2   1

To Lee, who rolls with me along the tides of life
and reminds me to feel the sun on my face

CHAPTER 1

"You snorkel before?"

Sadie looked up from adjusting her life jacket. Konnie was the last woman, other than herself, still in the small boat that had taken them to where the snorkeling was *nani*—Sadie hoped nani meant *wonderful* and not *deadly*.

"Years ago," Sadie said. "In Waikiki, when my children were younger."

"I'm not sure that even counts," Konnie said with a tinkling laugh. Her wide smile fit perfectly on her round face. Her black hair was in one long braid down her back. "Everyone knows O'ahu has the worst snorkeling in the islands. Kaua'i is amazing. Lots of beautiful coral."

"I can't wait," Sadie said, but her tone was flat. She was still trying to figure out why she'd come today. She didn't like boats or sand or swimsuits, and she wondered if she'd accepted Konnie's invitation simply because she'd refused most of the other invites Konnie had extended on behalf of the Blue Muumuus, a group of local older women similar to the Red Hat Society Sadie had seen in her hometown of Garrison, Colorado.

"The weather is perfect today," Konnie continued. "And the tide is just right. You won't believe the variety of fish you'll be able to see."

Sadie nodded, peering over the side of the boat with trepidation. The water was clear enough that she could make out the shape of the coral beneath the shifting surf, and she shivered, thinking about that hidden, undersea world. Coming to Kaua'i was supposed to cure the anxiety that had overwhelmed her after what had happened in Boston, but despite spending three months in a tropical paradise, Sadie was no better off than she'd been before. Only more isolated.

When Sadie had come to Hawai'i with her children ten years ago, she hadn't been a big fan of being in the ocean, but the displeasure she'd felt then was nothing like what she felt now. Sadie swallowed her fear and forced a smile, determined not to let her anxiety get the best of her in front of the woman who was trying so hard to be her friend.

Konnie lived a few houses away from the condominium complex where Sadie was staying, and she didn't care that Sadie was a *haole*—Caucasian—or *malihini*—a newcomer—to an island not always welcoming to mainlanders. Konnie was big and loud and wonderful in every way, which Sadie found a little bit scary. Well, everything seemed a little bit scary to Sadie right now.

"You ready?" Konnie asked.

"It'll be fun," Sadie lied. They were about a quarter mile off the north shore near Anahola. The drive from the inland town of Puhi, where Sadie was staying, would have been beautiful if Sadie had been able to focus. But she wasn't used to leaving her condo these days and felt nervous whenever she stepped out the door.

"I'm going in," Konnie said, getting to her feet and causing the small fishing boat to rock back and forth. Sadie forgot to breathe until Konnie sat her voluptuous self on the side of the boat and the rocking evened out. "You can lower yourself in if you'd rather not jump."

A moment later, Konnie put on her mask and fell backward over the side just like an islander who had spent half her life in the ocean—which was exactly what she was. The ensuing wave caused by Konnie's splash made the boat rock more than ever, and Sadie clung to the side with both hands. Konnie surfaced and yelled at her to jump in. "One of the tour companies brings tourists out here around noon—times a wastin'."

Sadie nodded, hoping to appear confident as she sat on the side of the boat and let her flippered-feet dangle over the side. The water was the perfect temperature—not too cold, not too warm. She chose the side of the boat opposite her companions—Konnie and the five other members of the Blue Muumuus—so that if she freaked out once she hit the water, the boat would hide her from their view. Though she recognized her anxiety, so far she'd avoided the actual panic attacks she'd studied up on. But if ever there was a day for all that to change, it was this one.

"You're okay," Sadie said to herself under her breath, eyeing the water and keeping her breathing even as she double-checked the clasps of her life jacket. She was the only woman who had chosen to wear one. "You'll be just fine. You can do this."

She looked over her shoulder, where six backs bobbed in the water; the snorkeling tubes looked as though they were poking out of six heads of dark hair. The stillness of the bodies bothered her, and she turned away, pulling on her mask and putting the mouthpiece of the snorkel in place. Another deep breath filled her with just enough courage to finally plunge into the water.

She hadn't considered that the snorkel would fill with water, and her first attempt at breathing was salty and wet. She headed for the surface and spat out the mouthpiece and the water, coughing and sputtering. Her heart raced, and she felt a wave of nausea as she gripped her life jacket with both hands and went to work convincing herself she wasn't drowning.

After taking a minute to get her bearings, and berating herself for being so dramatic, she replaced the salty mouthpiece of the snorkel and practiced breathing for another minute. Maybe two. Or four.

Konnie rounded the boat, her mask still on while her snorkel lay awkwardly against her left ear. "You okay?"

Sadie gave her a thumbs-up, bit down on her snorkel, took a deep breath, and put her face in the water.

The coral reef was full of fascinating shapes, colors, and textures. She'd been warned that the brain-shaped coral was alive and therefore not to be touched—not that she wanted to touch it. The water was clear enough that no detail of the scene below her was lost. A school of yellow tangs darted beneath her.

It's beautiful, she told herself even as she felt her heart rate increasing. *Ethereal. Amazing.* And yet her lungs struggled to draw a breath as she watched a parrot fish lazily swimming a few feet away as though she weren't there. But she *was* there. She was in their world, trying to appreciate the resplendence while battling the fact that their world was completely creepy! Some of these things around her were probably poisonous, and there were certainly unseen creatures lurking at the bottom, ready to pull her to the depths and never let her go. She'd seen *Jaws.*

After twenty seconds, she had to lift her face out of the water. Deep relaxing breaths didn't help when they were inhaled through a snorkel. Konnie was nowhere in sight, and Sadie couldn't subdue her growing terror. With her head lifted, she was more aware of her feet dangling deeper in the water and closer to those unseen, bottom-dwelling creatures. She tried to pull her feet up, but would that really deter the monsters lurking beneath her? She'd also seen that movie about the surfer who had had her arm bitten off by a shark. What did Sadie look like from the bottom of the sea?

Sadie spat out the mouthpiece and tried to inhale, but it was as though her mouth were no longer connected to her lungs. She couldn't get the air in. Why not? What was wrong with her?

She headed for the boat, knowing she had to get out of the water. Now. Once she reached the side, however, she couldn't figure out how to get in. The rim was too high for her to grab onto. Her gasps were ragged and noisy, making it sound like she was drowning even though her head was out of the water. She couldn't see any of the Blue Muumuus.

What if she passed out in the ocean? Would the fish eat her before anyone discovered she was gone?

You are being ridiculous, she told herself, ripping off her mask in hopes it would help her breathe. She clutched at her life jacket and closed her eyes, trying to pretend she was simply resting on a punctured water bed. After a full minute, her lungs opened up again. She took long, deep breaths and tried to clear her head. She felt oxygen returning to her brain as her body relaxed.

Then something touched her foot, and her eyes flew open in panic. She began thrashing toward the shore.

She had to get out of the water!

That the boat was *right there* or that Konnie or the other women would certainly have helped her get in it didn't cross her mind until she was crawling onto the sand, coughing and spitting up water, her lungs and arms burning from her desperate swim to shore.

The sand turned from wet to dry as she crawled out of the

ocean; the shore was littered with sticks, rocks, and broken shells left behind by the tide. This wasn't one of the groomed beaches like they had in Florida, where machines cleaned up the shoreline before the tourists woke up. This beach was natural and messy, and the sand stuck to her wet skin. Something cut her knee, reminding her that she should stand up. But she didn't want to do anything that would slow down her escape.

Finally, she collapsed, the bulky life jacket keeping her face out of the sand while she once again focused on breathing like a normal human being. It felt like forever before she felt safe. Her thoughts turned to how she would apologize to her new friends, who probably thought she was absolutely bonkers. She wasn't so sure they weren't right.

The nightmares that had plagued Sadie after her trip to Boston had led to insomnia and too many late-night infomercials that had provided her with more kitchen gadgets and exercise equipment than she could ever use. When her friend Gayle, her son, Shawn, her daughter, Breanna, and her boyfriend, Pete, had sat her down for an intervention, they told her she needed to get away for a little while. Unwind. Relax. At the time, she'd been optimistic about the change of environment—who wouldn't want to go to Hawai'i?

But, though she was no longer ordering useless items off QVC, she still stayed inside most of the time, and the only people she interacted with were the Blue Muumuus every few weeks. She slept through the afternoons and was awake most of the night, double-checking the locks at regular intervals.

The only other time she left the condo was to do her job cleaning the additional seven condos in the complex that were rented out by the week. Housekeeping in Hawai'i was very different from housekeeping at home—sand got everywhere, and mildew was a constant battle. It was good to have something to do, though, and the cleaning job was her way of paying rent to her friend Tanya, who owned the complex but preferred her husband's ranch in Arizona this time of year.

It was because of Tanya that Konnie even knew Sadie had moved in. Konnie had said any friend of Tanya's was a friend of hers, but Sadie couldn't help feeling like she was a burden all the same. The women, all of them grandmothers—*tutus* in Hawaiian—were very nice, but Sadie had yet to really feel like she was a part of their group.

"I need help," she admitted out loud as water dripped off her long hair. She had grown it out past her shoulders, longer than it had been in decades. Before leaving Garrison, she'd had her stylist lighten it, in hopes that she'd have more fun as a blonde, but she hadn't kept up the color, and it had faded to a brassy grayish-yellow. Two inches of gray roots had grown out since her arrival. The climate seemed to accelerate how fast her hair grew, and she lacked the courage to go to a salon full of strangers. Most days, she tied her hair back with a bandana and avoided mirrors, blaming her lack of style on the humidity.

Her senses refocused, and she could hear the incessantly pounding waves. The admission that whatever she was dealing with was more than she could handle on her own washed over her and filled her with both fear and relief.

"I need help," she said again, wondering if it would be more powerful a second time she said it. It was. She *did* need help, and she needed it soon. Things had happened to her, scary things that had obviously taken their toll on her mental health. She needed to get back to who she was; she needed to feel whole again. Though she talked to her family and friends on a regular basis, she'd kept how bad things were to herself. She didn't want them to worry. What would they say if they knew the truth?

She flipped onto her back, staring up at the blue, blue sky and wondering how her life had become so dark. Optimism had always been Sadie's foundation. It had gotten her through her husband's death more than twenty years ago. It had helped her raise her two children by herself. But in the wake of what had happened in Boston, she'd lost her confidence, and her world had been spinning out of control ever since.

Getting to her feet, she yanked off her flippers and looked out at the water that appeared so innocent now that she wasn't in it. The Blue Muumuus were back in the boat, heading toward the shore, and she felt overwhelmed by embarrassment and shame, while grateful she wouldn't have to consider swimming back to them. They had been so kind to her, and she had so little to give back. Now she'd ruined their adventure.

Konnie waved her arms, and Sadie waved back to indicate she was all right. The saltwater was beginning to dry the sand to her skin, making her feel like a big worn-out piece of sandpaper. The cut on her knee stung; she'd need to wash it out with freshwater.

A small boat dock had been built into the rocks along the beach, and Sadie headed toward it with a flipper in each hand. The floating dock moved gently beneath her feet when she stepped on it, and she froze for a moment, afraid she might fall in.

Konnie pointed the boat toward the dock, and Sadie walked slowly down the weathered boards, dreading the explanation of her bolt to the shore. What could she tell them other than the truth? *Hi, my name is Sadie, and I'm losing my mind. Congratulations on winning front-row tickets to the show!*

When she reached the end of the dock, Sadie waited for the

boat like a penitent child. Watching the water lap against the sides of the wood that was green with moss and other sea life gave Sadie the chills. Long strands of dark seaweed flowed alongside, like the hair of a mermaid from some long-ago fairy tale. Sadie watched it move, fluid and graceful, and tried to draw calmness from its easy motion.

After a few seconds, however, she realized the seaweed was black, not green. Despite her misgivings, she bent down to get a closer look into the water and was soon on her knees, peering at the underside of the dock where what she thought was seaweed was actually hair connected to a human head.

Scrambling to her feet as fresh panic descended like a hammer, she screamed for help at the same moment that she lost her balance, dropped the flippers, and plunged headlong into the sea that had already claimed one victim.

Chapter 2

"It sounds like you've had quite a trauma."

Sadie shredded Kleenex in her lap and nodded at Dr. McKay, her new psychiatrist. Trauma sounded like too mild a word to describe what it had been like to discover the body and then fall on top of it in the water. She hadn't cried about it yet. The tissues were simply for her nerves, and they were not helping as much as she'd hoped.

Dr. McKay consulted the file in front of him. "What happened after you fell in?"

The question transported her back to that moment last week—six days to be exact—when the water had closed over her head. Wild with panic, Sadie had accidently kicked the body, dislodging it from the dock. The body had then floated upward with her. During Sadie's frantic attempt to get away, her fingers had become entangled in the dark hair, catching her like a net and causing her to pull the body with her as she retreated from the dock toward open water.

She looked at her hands in her lap; she could still feel the hair wound around her fingers. The same deadening panic she'd felt while trying to get away from the corpse pressed in upon her in the small office and rendered her frozen and overwhelmed as she tried to stay in *this* moment, not that one. The cut on her knee and the bumps and scrapes she'd suffered from falling into the ocean and then being pulled over the side of the boat were healing, but the things in her head had only gotten worse.

Dr. McKay said something about post-traumatic stress disorder and how it could mentally transport a person back to the moment of the incident, igniting the fight-or-flight feelings that had occurred at the time of the trauma.

"I thought that was something soldiers got at war," Sadie said. She certainly wasn't a soldier—she wasn't any kind of hero. When had she ever *saved* anyone? No, she always entered the story after the horrible things had already happened.

"That's where PTSD gets most of its attention, but it certainly isn't reserved only for war-time trauma—it can happen anytime someone encounters something psychologically overwhelming."

Sadie tried to listen to his words but she could still feel the soft impact of her feet against the bloated body as she'd finally untangled herself from the hair and kicked frantically toward the boat heading toward her. By the time the Blue Muumuus got her calm enough to talk coherently, Sadie had lost all perspective on where she was and what had happened. When her first words were about someone by the dock trying to kill her, they had shared a look that communicated their wonder of why they had invited this unstable haole on their snorkeling trip in the first place. But then Konnie had leaned out of the boat, peering toward the dock.

A moment later, she was screaming too.

What happened next was anyone's guess—Sadie certainly didn't remember it, other than she'd been taken to the hospital for an assessment; the Blue Muumuus thought she'd been hurt in the fall.

The doctors had kept her overnight and then gave her some pills to help her sleep and arranged for her to meet with someone to "work things out in her head." Enter Dr. McKay.

"So don't expect an instantaneous recovery," Dr. McKay said, bringing her back to the present. "It can take time to repair the psychological injury from such an event, which is what we will work on." He flipped through the papers in her file and paused to read something else. "It says here you'll be in Kaua'i until the end of April, is that right? Three more weeks?"

"I fly home on the twenty-second."

"So you'll be back home in time for Easter—that's nice."

Sadie nodded.

"Do you have plans for the holiday? Time with family, perhaps?"

"My children are spending Easter with me and my boyfriend, Pete, plus his children and their families." It would be the first time their children would meet one another. She felt more capable of building a replica of the Eiffel Tower out of cheese doodles than successfully pulling off the holiday gathering. It had seemed like such a worthy goal three months ago—the perfect reentry into a life that felt like someone else's, now that she'd been gone so long.

"That sounds like something to look forward to," he said, smiling in a way that made him look a little like Mr. Rogers but with glasses and a Hawaiian shirt.

"I really need to be doing better than this when I go home."

"I understand. I can work in three visits a week during the remainder of your stay. That gives us at least six more visits—maybe as many as nine. I think we can make a lot of progress in that amount of time."

"Okay," she said. "So, I just come to you and talk about it and this will go away?" Maybe she'd be bright and shiny and new by the time she returned to Garrison. She hoped so, but she didn't really believe it.

"I certainly can't make guarantees, but we'll process things together, and as your thoughts are cleared up, it will start to make sense."

"Sense?" Sadie repeated. "Really?"

"Well, a kind of sense."

"How is that possible?"

He smiled. "One step at a time," he said. He looked down at his papers again. "Do you know much about the woman whose body you found?"

"She was a drug addict." Sadie stared at the floor. She felt her throat thicken but refused to give in to the emotion. She preferred numbness. "She'd been missing for a week before anyone reported she was gone."

"That's very sad," Dr. McKay said.

Very sad? Sadie repeated in her head. She was paying this guy a hundred bucks an hour for *very sad?*

"I'm curious," Dr. McKay continued, his tone of voice changing. "What kind of support system do *you* have, Sadie?" He lifted another paper to read the one underneath. "Colorado is a long way from here."

"I have good support," Sadie said. "I have a good relationship with my children, Breanna and Shawn. And Pete—he's my boyfriend." She felt a little silly saying it like that. She wasn't a teenager after all.

"You've talked to them about this?"

Sadie shifted in her chair and settled on a shrug. Of course she hadn't talked to them about this. "My cell phone went dead while I was in the hospital, and I've been sleeping a lot since I got released."

She shredded more Kleenex. "But I sent them all e-mails yesterday telling them I was fine. My friend Gayle will be coming to stay with me for the last week of my visit—I'll tell her before then."

"I wonder why you're not comfortable confiding in her now, or in any of the rest of your friends and family," Dr. McKay said. She chose not to answer. He allowed the silence for nearly a minute then mentioned something about the cathartic healing that talking to her loved ones could invite.

"I'd like to give you a couple of prescriptions," he said when he finished. "One's an antidepressant for you to take on a daily basis; based on your intake evaluation from the hospital, I think it would be helpful. The other medication will give you a kind of quick fix when your anxiety peaks. Are you open to that?"

She nodded. The pills the hospital had given her to help her sleep had run out. Having another medicinal lifeline was certainly welcome.

Dr. McKay also trained her to breathe in a way that would help calm herself down—drawing in a breath while counting, then exhaling it to the same count. Sadie practiced it with him; it seemed elementary.

When her hour was up, Sadie gave him a sheepish "thank you" and agreed with Dr. McKay when he reminded her that this would be a process and that they would go at her pace. As Sadie left the office, she wondered if she would go to her next appointment on Thursday. She didn't want to, and yet she *did* want to get better. It was just hard to think that talking to him would really give her what she needed.

The trip home was a blur of anxiety and attempts to keep from completely freaking out. If not for feeling desperate to get the prescriptions filled, she'd have gone straight home, but she tried to see it as a small miracle that she'd gone into the grocery store, waited in line at the pharmacy counter, and ordered the medicine to be brought to her house that afternoon, all without screaming.

When she walked passed Konnie's house, less than a block away from the condo, she held her breath, then winced when Konnie called her name from the doorway. Luckily, Konnie was just leaving. She only had enough time to hand over a Tupperware of shoyu chicken and rice that Sadie could heat up for dinner. The chicken was from last night, Konnie explained, but would reheat well in the oven at 200 degrees for an hour. Sadie thanked her and then practically ran home, holding the Tupperware with both hands.

Inside the condo, she turned the lock three times to make sure it was secure. "One, two, three." Then she hurried to the back sliding door and made sure it was locked too, just in case. "One, two, three."

All the drapes were pulled, and she tugged at the curtains above the kitchen sink to smother a sliver of sunlight that was sneaking through. She took a deep breath, telling herself that she was safe now—she didn't have to leave the condo for two more days . . . assuming she'd keep that appointment with Dr. McKay. Did she feel better for having gone to the first appointment? She couldn't tell, and so she stopped thinking about it all together.

The Cap'n Crunch cereal Sadie had had for breakfast while watching M*A*S*H reruns at noon had worn off, but the chicken would take too long. She put it in the fridge and opened the freezer to survey her options. Turkey pot pie or a bean and beef burrito. She'd fallen so far from the woman she once was.

The Sadie she used to be cooked everything from scratch, both for nutritional reasons and because she loved to cook. The Sadie she used to be wasn't afraid of leaving her home, in fact she kept herself very busy outside of her own four walls. The Sadie she used to be was strong and capable and self-assured.

This new Sadie was a rather pathetic version of the woman she'd been six months ago. It would be nice to blame the changes on having found a body in the ocean last week, but she'd been spiraling for months. Every day she hoped the next day would be the day something changed. Tomorrow, she'd have energy, motivation, and purpose. Tomorrow, she'd rediscover the woman she used to be. But tomorrow wasn't today, and so *this* Sadie pulled a burrito out of the freezer and dropped the frozen brick onto a microwave-safe plate.

It wasn't until she removed the burrito from the microwave two minutes later that she noticed the light blinking on the answering machine. Like everything else in the condo, the phone hadn't been updated in fifteen years. Her cute little notebook computer and cheap printer were the most modern things here, but Sadie liked that she knew how to work everything. Only a few people had the direct number to the condo though, and she pushed the button while adding a dollop of sour cream to her lunch.

"Hey, Mom, it's me," Shawn's voice said. "I got your e-mail but haven't talked to you for a while. I'm hoping that's 'cause you've taken up surfing. Call me when you get a second."

Sadie smiled sadly. Shawn was such a good boy, and though she didn't think he was struggling as much as she was, Boston had taken its toll on him as well. The old Sadie would have known how to help him. Instead, she worried his burdens would be too much for her to handle along with her own. Maybe he sensed the same thing. Their conversations had become rather shallow. She missed her boy and the relationship they used to have, but she didn't know how to fix it.

The next message started playing, and her mood fell even more. "Sadie, it's Pete." His voice was open and even—a tone she'd come to hate because it meant he was playing police detective with her. "I talked to the Kaua'i police and am wondering why you didn't tell me what happened. Call me, okay?"

She looked at the phone and felt her stomach drop. Pete had talked to the Kaua'i police before Sadie had left for Hawai'i, asking them to keep an eye on her. She didn't really know if the police had done so or not—she'd hadn't met any cops until last week—but it had been sweet of Pete to go to the trouble. Either they had informed him of what had happened or he had called them to check up on her. She should probably be grateful it took six days for him to find out, but now she would have to come up with an explanation. Would Pete buy the argument that she'd taken it in stride and therefore didn't feel it was important enough to talk about?

The thought of being so flippant brought back the moment when her hand had pushed at the arm of the dead body. The skin had felt slimy, and the memory of it made Sadie wince. She clenched her eyes shut, and sweat broke out on her forehead.

Go away, she commanded the memories. *Leave me alone.*

Island Teriyaki Chicken

1 cup soy sauce (Aloha brand is best)
1 cup white sugar
1 cup water
3 cloves garlic
1 teaspoon ground ginger (more to taste), or a 1-inch piece of ginger root
2 pounds boneless, skinless chicken breasts, or 3 pounds any type bone-in chicken

Twenty-four hours before serving, combine everything but the chicken in a saucepan and bring to a boil on medium-high heat. Boil one minute. If grilling chicken, reserve ½ cup of sauce. If using chicken breasts, tenderize the meat. Combine sauce and chicken in a zip-top bag or airtight container. Allow to marinate in the refrigerator overnight. (For a quick-cook method, you can skip marinating, but the flavor of the meat won't be as strong.)

To Bake: Arrange chicken breasts and marinade in 9x13 pan. Cover pan with foil. Bake at 350 degrees for 40 minutes.

To Grill: Discard marinade. Grill chicken on medium-high heat until cooked through. Use reserved sauce to enhance grilled chicken as desired.

Slow-Cooker Method: Combine everything in a slow cooker and cook on low heat for 8 hours. If using ginger root, remove root after 5 hours.

Serve with white rice.

Serves 6.

Note: To make shoyu chicken, a Hawaiian version of teriyaki chicken, add the following ingredients to the marinade, then follow the rest of the directions as stated:

1 teaspoon black pepper
½ teaspoon oregano
up to 1 teaspoon crushed red pepper flakes
up to 1 teaspoon paprika
up to 1 teaspoon cayenne pepper

CHAPTER 3

Sadie was unable to get up the courage to call Pete back before he called again an hour later. It was tempting not to answer the phone, but she wasn't sure she could handle the guilt of making him worry even more. She answered on the third ring.

"Hey there," she said in a chipper tone, wishing she could fake it for the duration of their call.

"Sadie," he said, obviously relieved. "Are you alright?"

What followed was twenty minutes of Sadie trying her best to communicate what had happened in a perfectly logical way and Pete pretending to be calm even though she knew he was upset. Whether "upset" translated into being angry with her, she couldn't be sure. It was clear, though, that they both knew she should have told him, and he was hurt that she hadn't.

"Um, how did you find out?" Sadie asked.

"I guess it took a while for them to match you up with the woman I'd asked them to keep an eye out for. An Officer Wington made the connection; he called me to get some history about you. He thought I already knew about the body."

Sadie shrank inside from the accusation. "I'm sorry. It's just been so . . . much. I didn't know how to tell anyone."

He paused, and Sadie wondered what it was he wasn't saying. "Maybe it's time for you to come back to Garrison," Pete finally said. "I don't think this has worked out so well."

Sadie had mixed feelings about the suggestion. On the one hand, sleeping in her own bed and having her friends around sounded wonderful. But going home would mean having to reformulate her life there. The Senior Center would expect her to help run their fundraiser, the Red Cross would be planning a new summer blood drive, and there was the hospital's fun run, the Latham Club summer picnic, and the church food drive. The old Sadie had always been busy with, involved in, and necessary to all those events. Was *that* Sadie still here? Hiding in some dark corner of her mind? Or had she disappeared completely? The Sadie of today didn't feel at all like that woman.

"Sadie?"

"Oh, yes, I'm here," Sadie said. "Um, did you ask me something?"

"I offered to get you a plane ticket home."

"I promised Tanya I'd stay through the twenty-second, and Gayle's already bought her ticket to come visit for the last week."

"You didn't tell either of them what's happened, though, did you?" Pete said. "If you did, I've no doubt they'd both understand why you need to come home right now. Gayle would be the first one to tell you so, and Tanya can hire someone else to clean the condos, like she did before you got there."

Sadie didn't know what to say. He was right, they would understand, but she didn't want to go home yet and didn't know how to say it. They were both silent for a full five seconds until Pete spoke again. "Unless there's another reason you don't want to leave. Are you involving yourself in the investigation?"

"No," Sadie said quickly, a little horrified by the idea. "Not one bit. I haven't talked to the police since giving my statement, and I want nothing to do with it. I just . . . I don't feel like myself, Pete," she admitted, embarrassed to say it out loud but remembering what Dr. McKay had said about using the support system she had. "And the thought of living the life I used to live is a little overwhelming."

"Why didn't you tell me when it happened, Sadie?" he asked in a soft and vulnerable tone. He was no longer Detective Cunningham. He was just Pete—the man who loved her.

Sadie felt tears well up in her eyes, and she leaned back against the bamboo chair she'd pulled next to the kitchen counter when she'd answered the phone. "I didn't want you to worry about me."

"I've worried about you every day since I took you to the airport," Pete said. "And I've *missed* you every day. Come home to me, Sadie. Let's go about this another way. I know a good therapist, she can help you—"

"I'm already seeing a therapist," Sadie interrupted. "I have appointments with him up until I leave."

"How's it going?"

"Okay, I guess," she said, shrugging despite being alone. "It's strange. It's not just about what happened last week that's giving me trouble, it's everything. Boston. Miami. The . . . the threat."

"To have . . . *this* happen on top of everything else has got to be . . . awful."

His tenderness triggered more emotion which Sadie continued to push down. She was touched by his validation, and his understanding encouraged her to be even more open. "I really want to return home *better* than this, Pete. I think Dr. McKay can help me with that if I finish my stay here."

"Okay," he said. His tender voice washed through her. "Then what *can* I do to help?"

"I don't know," Sadie said, grateful to know she had him in her corner. "Pray for me?"

Pete managed a dry laugh. "Of course. What else?"

"I really don't know," she said. "This feels like something I have to fix, and I'm trying, I really am." But was she? Yes, she'd kept her appointment with Dr. McKay today, but she hadn't been as forthcoming with him as she could have been. She'd come to Kaua'i to heal in the first place, but she hadn't been healing. She'd been hiding and marinating in all that had happened leading up to this. Would she have kept doing that if not for having become entangled—literally—with the body beneath the dock?

"Can we talk like this every day?" Pete asked. "Open and honest. I'm not going to judge you, Sadie, but I want to feel like we trust one another."

"Yes," Sadie said, touched by his sincere concern for her. "And I do trust you, Pete. I'm sorry."

"It's okay," he assured her. "Everyone hits a wall, so to speak, when they're dealing with things like what you're going through. I've seen it over and over again within the departments where I've worked. I've taken administrative leave myself when things were just too much. I also know how easy it is to get stuck in it, and I want to make sure you know I'm here for you."

"I know that," Sadie said. "I'll write it on a sticky note and put it on the fridge in case I ever forget again."

Pete chuckled, then went quiet. "Do you want to talk about the body you found?"

Whatever warm feelings had developed between them ran cold. "No," Sadie said. "I really don't." Since Pete had talked to the Kaua'i police, he likely knew more than she did, but she wasn't the tiniest bit tempted to ask him for details.

"If you ever do want to talk about it, I'm here, alright?"

"I know," Sadie said. "And I'll keep going to my therapy appointments. I expect to be doing a lot better by the time I get home."

"I'm glad Gayle's coming to see you—is it next week?"

"Yes," Sadie said. "A week from Saturday. We have the same flight home on the twenty-second."

"But you haven't talked to her about what happened?"

Sadie squirmed, and when she didn't answer, Pete continued. "You need to talk to her. I ran into her a couple of days ago, and she said you hadn't been returning her calls either."

The heavy feeling of regret and embarrassment increased in Sadie's belly. She felt horrible about making things hard for the people she loved. Gayle had arranged her vacation time from work to come to Kaua'i, and yet she had no idea what she'd be walking into when she arrived.

"I'll talk to her," Sadie said.

"Good. I'm sorry this happened to you, Sadie. I know homicide detectives who haven't dealt with as many bodies as you have in the last year and a half." He laughed, but the humor was lost on Sadie as the comment struck a tender cord.

Magnet for Murder, flashed through Sadie's mind, and she wondered, not for the first time, if she attracted these horrible things. If so, was she somehow to blame for them happening in the first place?

For a while she'd actually felt she had some kind of divine gift—that God had somehow placed her on a path to help solve these cases. But there was no way to know if the truth would have been discovered another way. And then Boston changed everything.

Pete was talking again, but she'd missed what he was saying and mentally returned in time to hear him promise to call her tomorrow. "I'm in North Carolina for the rest of the week."

"Oh, right, you have that gun conference."

"Ballistics and forensic technology," Pete clarified.

"That's what I meant."

Pete laughed. "I won't be available all the time, but call me if you need anything. If I can answer, I will; if I don't, leave a message, and I'll call you back as soon as I can, okay?"

"Okay."

"And charge your cell phone," he said.

"I will," Sadie agreed with a nod. *Where is my cell phone?*

"And Sadie?"

"Yes?"

"I love you."

Tears sprang to her eyes. "You must," Sadie said, emotion rendering her voice a whisper. "I love you too."

"Everything will be okay," he said. "I'm counting the days until I see you again, okay?"

"Thank you," Sadie said, pushing back her emotions. Any emotion was too much right now, even the good kind.

They finished the call, and Sadie sat in her dim apartment, pondering what he'd said and what she'd realized. In less than three weeks, she would *have* to go back home. Healed or not. She needed to use that time to get better.

Following her decisive thoughts, Sadie went on a search for her cell phone and found it in a bathroom drawer. Who knew what it was doing there. She plugged her phone into the charger, then went to the sliding glass door facing the common courtyard shared by all the condominiums. She opened the vertical blinds, squinting at the bright sunshine. She'd been in Hawai'i of all places for three full months, but she was as pale as though she'd made it through another Rocky Mountain winter. Wasn't vitamin D important for neurological health?

"Sunshine every day," she said out loud, then turned to find some paper so she could make a list of her newly realized goals. Her gaze landed on the half-eaten burrito she'd called lunch, and it brought to mind a second goal. "Fruit every day." She hadn't had so much as a banana in more than a week. She wrote down the first two goals and added a third: "Talk to Pete every day." It was only three things—three small things—but writing them down made her feel empowered and gave her a new focus. She smiled.

She tore the paper out of the notebook and secured it to the fridge with a magnet shaped like the sun, which seemed apropos.

Doing her own grocery shopping would be a step in the right direction, but she felt unable to take on that task right away, so she called the local market and placed an order for mangos and a pineapple to be delivered along with her prescriptions. On a whim, she also ordered a brownie mix, then felt overwhelmed by the thought of having so much preparation-needy food in the house.

Baby steps, she told herself, taking a breath and recognizing that after three months of waiting for change, *making* change happen wouldn't be easy. But she had Dr. McKay and Pete and brownies. She was heading in the right direction.

Then there was a knock at her door and all of her self-assurance disappeared. Her hand went to her throat, she forgot to breathe, and the first thought that immediately came to mind was that she should hide.

CHAPTER 4

Sadie approached the door on her tiptoes, careful not to make a sound. There was no way the delivery from the market had arrived already. Konnie was the only other person who ever came to her condo, but she knocked four times in a quick rhythm. Plus Konnie had already checked in on Sadie today.

It could be one of the renters for the other condos, but why knock on Sadie's door? The rental company that supervised the condos preferred e-mail communication, which was fine with her. Now and then she would see one of the renters in the common area, but they assumed she was renting too and weren't looking to make life-long friends while on vacation.

When Sadie reached the door, she pressed her eye against the peephole, glad that she'd kept the curtains closed over the front windows. She could see the small square porch and the sandalwood shrub dotted with pink blossoms on the left side. Whoever was out there was standing too far to the right for her to get a full view of them. Was that on purpose?

If her visitor didn't have the courtesy to stand in the center of the porch, she couldn't be expected to open the door, right? As she justified her silence, she saw an arm raise up. She watched the entire movement but still jumped when it knocked on the door again. Pulling back, she shook her head at her reaction but didn't open the door. Instead she pressed her eye against the peephole one more time. The visitor had shifted, and she could see it was a child. A young boy—maybe twelve years old. He had big brown eyes, and his long black hair was pulled into a messy ponytail at the base of his head. He didn't have native features, exactly, and was therefore probably *hapa*—mixed race. He kept looking over his shoulder.

It was one thing to hide from a salesperson, but a little boy? After taking a deep breath, Sadie latched the swing bolt and pulled open the door so that she could look out through the four-inch gap. The boy immediately straightened up when he saw her.

"Hello?" she asked.

"Aloha," he said, managing a slight wave before wiping his hand on the side of his shorts. He wore red flip-flops—what they called rubber slippahs on the island. "Um, I'm looking for Sadie Hoffmiller."

"Why?"

"I need to talk to her."

"About what?"

"Um, is she there?"

"I'm Sadie," she said, wondering why he hadn't assumed as much.

"You are?" he asked in disbelief. "You're so old."

It took work to keep her tone even. "What can I help you with?" Sadie said.

"Oh, um—" He looked over his shoulder. Was he hiding from someone? Sadie could relate to that fear. "Can I come in? I won't take anything."

Take anything? That right there should have been a bright red flag, waving back and forth in front of her face, and yet, despite all the reasons not to, she told him to hang on a minute. She closed the door, undid the latch, and opened the door all the way to allow him entry.

"Come on in," she said, standing to the side. He was only too eager to enter and looked around the room once she shut the door behind him. Was he scoping out the place to see if there was anything valuable? There wasn't, really, but just having someone else in the house made her uncomfortable. It was her only sanctuary, and she'd allowed it to be breached. Only Konnie had ever been inside her condo, and that was because she wouldn't take no for an answer.

"Have a seat if you'd like," Sadie said, waving the boy toward the futon against the wall and across from the TV.

He sat on the very edge of the futon and tried to bounce, but the cushion was pretty solid. Sadie sat in the rattan chair to the side of the futon and looked at him expectantly, trying to summon the persona of a welcoming hostess. She couldn't make it work, however, and so she simply spoke her mind. "You already know who I am. What's your name?"

"Charlie," he said.

"Well, nice to meet you, Charlie. What can I help you with?"

He twisted so he could get something out of the right front pocket of his shorts. His clothes were not new, and he smelled like a little boy who'd just come in from a humid afternoon. Sadie hadn't smelled that in a long time and felt a flash of nostalgia for the days when she'd had to bribe Shawn to take a shower. This little boy, Charlie, wasn't all that different from what Shawn had been a decade ago. Charlie was smaller and not as dark-skinned, but the similarities tugged at her heart, which made her even more uncomfortable.

Charlie removed a folded piece of paper from his pocket and

opened it up, smoothing it out on his lap. It was the grayish newsprint paper her students had used back when she taught school—cheap, soft, and thin. He cleared his throat very official-like. "I read about you in the paper," he said, glancing up at her quickly.

"I was in the paper?" Sadie asked, her heart instantly racing.

"Yes," the boy said, looking at her eagerly. "Because you knew my mom."

Sadie's attention snapped back to him. "Your mom?" she said, having a hard time processing the idea.

"Noelani Pouhu," the boy said.

"I'm sorry," Sadie said, shaking her head. "I don't know anyone by that name." And yet something niggled that she'd heard the name before.

"The newspaper said you—you were with her," he said, his voice quiet, almost reverent. "Up by Anahola."

Sadie's mouth went dry.

Noelani.

She *had* heard the name before, and the realization of who he was talking about brought back the stark memory of pushing away a water-bloated body. Instantly her sweat glands reacted, and she focused on taking deep breaths.

"She was a mother?" Sadie's head tingled and her throat thickened. "I didn't know that." She'd purposely avoided learning about the woman for this very reason. It was easier to think of her as simply a body, although Sadie was ashamed to admit that even to herself. "How did you find me?"

"I read about you in the paper and then heard the police talking. They said you was staying at a condo in Puhi on Valley Street, and the guy in the other one"—he pointed his thumb over his shoulder,

29

technically in the direction of the street but she knew he was trying to tell her which condo—"said you was probably in this one."

He put all that together himself? If he could do it, anyone could. She wasn't safe here anymore.

He looked back at the paper and smoothed it out again. "I just wanted to ask you some questions about her."

Sadie held her shaking hands together in her lap and swallowed. "You don't want to know anything about that, I promise," she said.

"Everybody says she was high, but she wasn't doing drugs no more so—"

Sadie stood up, cutting him off and wringing her hands as though the hair—Noelani's hair—was still wrapped around them. "Look, I'm really, *really* sorry about your mom. I can't even . . ." She paused for breath, trying to keep her anxiety at bay, but images of that day in the water flashed in her mind and she wasn't sure how much longer she could focus. For the first time, she pictured some kind of tattoo on the woman's forearm. She hadn't remembered that before, and she wished she hadn't remembered it now. She didn't want to think about this anymore. "I'm so sorry," she said again. "But I didn't know her. I only . . . found her, and I don't know anything else."

"You weren't her friend?"

"No." Sadie shook her head, surprised by the question. "I'd never seen her before."

He pulled his eyebrows together and looked back at the paper in his lap. "But I thought . . . I thought you must have been with her."

Sadie's confusion overrode her anxiety for a moment. Why would he think that? Had the newspaper insinuated something like that? "No," she said. "I didn't know her, and I don't know anything about her now. I didn't even know she had a son." Her voice cracked.

Charlie pursed his lips together, and she noticed his face darken. Embarrassment? Disappointment? A moment later, his shoulders slumped forward, and he hung his head, staring into his lap.

Sadie sat back down in her chair, unsure what to do. Was he crying? Should she comfort him? She could *imagine* herself sitting next to him on the futon and pulling him into a hug, but she couldn't move. She didn't want to touch him. Just as she couldn't have an in-depth conversation with her son about what had happened in Boston, she couldn't bear the responsibility of trying to comfort this little boy.

"I'm sorry I can't help," Sadie said, feeling bad about how much she wanted him to leave. She wondered when her prescriptions would be delivered. She had a feeling she'd need the anxiety one very soon.

Charlie sniffed and wiped his eyes.

She felt horrible, but she really couldn't help him. She didn't have anything to give. "Can I call someone to come get you?"

He sniffed again and stood up, moving for the door. The paper from his pocket was crumpled in his hand.

She stood, too. "Wait," she said, though she didn't move. "Let me call someone, uh—Who . . . who do you live with?" What a horrible thing to ask him!

"I don't live with nobody," he said loudly as he grabbed the doorknob and pulled it open.

"No one?" Sadie asked, taking a nervous step toward him. "Now, that can't—"

He ran outside without looking back. She hurried after him but stopped at the threshold as though it had a force field keeping her inside.

"Wait," she called, but it was halfhearted. She couldn't help this little boy? She was *that* messed up? "Wait," she said again, but it was a whisper.

Charlie disappeared around the corner, and a moment later she couldn't even hear the sound of his footsteps on the street. She raised a shaking hand to her mouth, then closed and locked the door. One, two, three.

She was a mother!

Sadie's heart continued to shudder in the wake of what she'd just learned, and she rested her back against the door and brought her hands to her face.

Just a body.

Just a body.

Oh, please, can't it just have been a body?

But she'd never been very good at fooling herself. A sob rose in her chest, though she tried to push it down. She pictured Charlie in her mind, a sad little boy trying to find out what had happened to his mother. Piecing together enough little details to track down Sadie in hopes of getting answers no one else would give him. Believing *Sadie* was the one person who could help him. But she wasn't. She couldn't help herself let alone anyone else. Another sob followed the first, and finally, she gave in, feeling her face contort behind her hands as she gave in to the tears she'd been holding back for what felt like years.

It wasn't a body.

The woman was a real person who'd been living a real life.

Noelani Pouhu.

Sadie would never forget that again.

CHAPTER 5

Not long after Sadie's meltdown, there was another knock at the door that instigated the same panic. It turned out to be Reg, the delivery boy from the market. She knew she looked a sight with her swollen eyes, but he was too polite to say anything. She gave him a generous tip and put the perishables in the fridge before turning on the TV in search of some distraction. The anxiety and emotion had passed, but she still felt jumpy, so she took one of the pills Dr. McKay had prescribed for the anxiety in hopes the medicine would chase the last of her undone-ness away.

Sometime during the first or second episode of *Wizards of Waverly Place,* Sadie fell asleep. When she woke up, there was an infomercial on. She turned off the television, knowing she was not strong enough to resist. She felt heavy and thick as she sat up and blinked into the darkness. She hadn't had any lights on when she'd collapsed on the futon, so the house was dark and silent.

Dr. McKay hadn't said the anxiety medication would help her sleep, but she certainly wasn't complaining about that particular side effect. She'd sleep twenty hours a day if she could. She continued to sit on the futon, hoping her brain would wake up more fully if she didn't rush it. Eventually, Charlie came to mind. She could only hope he'd been lying about not having a home. Pre-teen boys were prone to exaggeration, and he'd been upset. Surely he wasn't truly on his own. Then again, his mother *was* dead.

Dead.

The word made her shiver, and she saw another flash of the body—Noelani Pouhu—in the water, but only a flash this time. Thank goodness. Sadie entertained the idea of somehow checking up on Charlie, finding out who was taking care of him, but that was only a flash too. Trying to find information about Charlie would be a step into a world she felt ill prepared to enter.

She rubbed her arms and wrapped them around herself despite the thickness of the night's humidity. Even with central air conditioning, she always felt slightly sticky, no matter the time of day, but she'd heard that humidity helped prevent wrinkles, so it was a trade-off she could live with. A glance at the VCR clock made it easier to decide against making any phone calls about Charlie. It was two o'clock in the morning. She'd slept for hours and still had hours and hours of night left to go. What time had she fallen asleep? Four o'clock in the afternoon? Had she really slept for ten hours? Maybe next time she'd take half a pill, assuming she wouldn't want to sleep that long.

Sadie turned on the lamp beside the futon, then stood up to turn on the kitchen lights as well. Immediately, she noticed that the blinds over the sliding glass door were still open. Her heart began to race. She moved toward them, intent in closing herself in again, but then she wondered if this was an opportunity to prove herself stronger than she felt.

After a moment of contemplation, she turned her back on the open blinds and returned to the kitchen area—determined to be brave. Her stomach growled, so she put the shoyu chicken and rice

Konnie had given her into a covered dish and put it in the oven, heating it to 200 degrees, just like Konnie had said. Then she spied the brownie mix she'd ordered on impulse and remembered the quote she had on her fridge at home: "Chocolate makes everything better." She increased the oven temperature to 350 degrees and made a note to keep an eye on the chicken to make sure it didn't dry out.

Mixing the eggs into the brownie batter and sliding the pan into the oven was both familiar and new, but as the smell of baking chocolate filled the air, Sadie felt lighter, a little bit more herself than she had before. She ignored the sliding glass door completely.

She'd come to enjoy watching old movies at night when she couldn't sleep, and Tanya had an extensive collection. She chose *The Searchers* and put the tape into the VCR. It wasn't that Tanya couldn't afford to update the condo, there was just no reason to do so when it was all so very functional. Sadie's condo was the smallest— only one bedroom—and was therefore the least rentable, which made it a perfect maid's quarters, and it was where Tanya stayed when she and her husband came each summer. The outdated technology wasn't a problem for them, so they didn't bother changing anything.

Listening to the Duke and Jeffrey Hunter was like having old friends come for a visit, and Sadie felt herself relax even more. She removed the chicken and rice from the oven after twenty minutes and began straightening up while it cooled.

She scraped the burrito from that afternoon into the garbage, washed the plate and the brownie preparation dishes, wiped down the counter, and swept the tiled floor. Then she put about half of the chicken and rice on a plate and sat down at the kitchen table. It was really good, and though she considered asking Konnie for the recipe, she was embarrassed to do so for reasons she didn't entirely understand.

She looked outside again as she pushed the chair underneath the kitchen table, her plate and fork in hand. The blinds were still open but everything on the other side of the glass was dark. A sudden thought entered her mind that she should go out there. It would be healing; it would prove she was getting stronger. The timer dinged, and she jumped, shaking her head with embarrassment as she turned to the oven. She removed the brownies, placing them on the stove top to cool since she didn't have a cooling rack.

Five minutes later, she pulled the blinds back from the sliding glass door, causing a pileup of the vertical slats on the far left side. She stood there challenging herself to open the door—to face her fears.

The sound of the door sliding along its track was soft and fluid, but as soon as it was open, the outside sounds filtered in with the coolness of the night. The croak of the coqui frogs that infested the islands sounded like loud, creepy crickets, but she could handle it. Someone's dog was barking. No people sounds. "Nothing to be afraid of," she whispered to herself.

She stepped out onto her little square of concrete patio, scanning for the huge centipedes that always gave her the willies and ignoring the two darting geckos poised on the stucco above the sliding glass door as she slid it shut. She could tolerate the lizards because they kept down the even more distasteful bug population.

I'm outside, she told herself, trying to pump herself up as she looked at each of the patios belonging to the other seven condos. Three of them were rented out this week, but all the windows were dark. It was close to three o'clock in the morning after all. Only the jungle and Sadie were awake. The heat had dissipated somewhat, and a breeze raised goose bumps on her arms—or chicken skin, as Konnie would say. She tried to rub the bumps away and wondered if it was really the breeze creating the reaction.

She waited for the panic to descend. She thought about returning to Garrison in a few weeks. Did she want to return to a state of healing and strength? If so, then she needed to meet new challenges and prove herself capable of such things. *You're safe here,* she told herself. *And it's a beautiful night.*

A gentle wind tousled the palm fronds overhead. The stars were vibrant, and a quarter moon looked crisp in the ink-colored sky. Sadie began walking along the black lava rock path that connected the patios and encircled the pool and common barbeque area in the center. Everything looked fine. One of the renters had hung a swimsuit on the turning clothesline near the pool, and the same wind that played amid the foliage of the trees moved the swimsuit gently back and forth. The showerhead near the pool dripped water onto the brick-lined drain area. Drip, drip, drip.

She studied every detail, having memorized what belonged and what didn't and assuring herself that everything was as it should be. The longer she walked around the courtyard, the more victorious she felt. She'd left her condo in the middle of the night. That was progress!

She was almost back to her own patio when she heard something behind her, a rustle that didn't coincide with the wind. She froze at the same time she internally screamed at herself to run. Instead, she turned and looked behind her.

Be strong, she told herself. *Know what you're up against instead of reacting to nameless fear.*

The slightest possibility that someone *might* be out there with her was too easy a seed to plant—a seed that would then grow all night long until it was the Venus flytrap Audrey from *Little Shop of Horrors* and gobble her up. She was determined to make it through the night without panicking.

An avocado tree with tall winding branches stood a few feet off the path and seemed to be the location of the mystery sound. Sadie had harvested several avocados over the last few months and knew the tree well, which helped give her the courage to approach it. Her eyes traveled upward as she neared the trunk, and she was all but convinced the noise had been nothing but a bird when she noticed the outline of a shoe. No, a flip-flop—a small red rubber slippah. Again she was prompted to run, and yet she recognized the flip-flop even though her anxiety prompted her to think it belonged to someone far more sinister.

"Charlie?" she asked quietly.

Nothing moved, and she took a step closer to the tree. When she was below the branches, she could make out the shape of his silhouette as he stared down at her. It was creepy, seeing him outlined against the tree and the stars beyond the leaves, but she didn't feel panic setting in. Maybe it was a lingering effect of the medication.

"What are you doing here?" Sadie snapped, her fear translating into anger even though she knew this boy had no idea what his unexpected appearance had cost her. He just stared at her, not saying a word in his defense. Sadie reminded herself that he was a little boy who'd lost his mother.

She was careful to soften her tone before she continued. "It's the middle of the night, Charlie. Surely someone is missing you."

He didn't answer again, and Sadie let out a breath, realizing with amazement that her lingering fear went with it. This boy posed no threat to her, and he must be uncomfortable up there. As her eyes adjusted, she could see he'd taken one of the renters' beach towels and put it between himself and the branch he was sitting on.

"Should I call the police?" she asked.

He shook his head quickly, his eyes wide. His reaction left no doubt that Sadie *should* call the police, and yet . . . this boy pulled at her heart. What if he didn't have anywhere to go? What if he really was on his own?

"Are you hungry?" she asked.

He hesitated but after a moment, nodded.

"I have some chicken and rice, and I made brownies," she said. "They're just a mix, so it's nothing special, but I really shouldn't eat the whole pan myself. Do you think you could help me?"

He didn't speak or nod or anything, but he did start climbing down from the tree. Sadie felt something unfamiliar in her chest, a kind of peace or comfort. Charlie dropped to the ground a few feet away from her, still regarding her carefully and clutching the towel.

"Go put that back where you found it," Sadie said. He did as she said, taking the time to smooth out the towel on the back of a chair by the pool. He knew how to take care of things. When he headed back toward her, she turned to the condo, allowing him to follow her. It wasn't until she opened the door for him and smiled as he passed her that she realized what this new feeling was. And it wasn't really new at all, just forgotten. It had been a very long time since Sadie had given much of anything to anyone else. The anxiety she'd been living with had wrapped itself around her so tightly that there'd been no room left for reaching out to anyone else. The fear was still there, pressing against her chest as she shut and locked the sliding glass door—one, two, three—but maybe the stranglehold was a little less than it had been. Maybe reaching out to help someone else was some kind of cure for her own disease.

"Have a seat," she said, feeling the forgotten role of hostess fall over her shoulders like a superhero cape. "Let's get some real food in you before we serve up the brownies."

CHAPTER 6

Sadie slid a plate of the remaining shoyu chicken and rice in front of Charlie before sitting down opposite him at the table. He didn't thank her with words, but the fervor with which he ate clearly communicated his appreciation and hunger. Sadie wished she could take credit—it was always rewarding to see someone enjoy something she'd made herself—but she had no ownership in anything placed before him tonight.

"So," Sadie said after he'd taken a few bites. Though he was hungry now, she could tell by his overall physique that he wasn't malnourished. "How old are you, Charlie?"

"Just made eleven," he said with his mouth full.

"Fifth or sixth grade?" Sadie asked.

"Fifth."

"I used to teach school. Second grade though."

He said nothing and kept eating.

Sadie wanted to ask where he went to school and who he lived with but since those types of questions had not met with success in their earlier conversation, she tried a different approach. "I'm sure sorry about your mom. I wish I did know her, so I could help you."

"You're sure you aren't her friend?" Charlie asked, looking at her with a doubtful expression.

Sadie shook her head. "Why do you think I was her friend?"

He smashed a piece of rice with his thumb. "You was the only person in the paper and then the police was talking about you when they talked to CeeCee."

"Who's CeeCee?"

He took another bite instead of answering. He was almost finished eating so Sadie hurried to get him a brownie and a glass of milk. She'd dealt with kids from hard family situations before—such as a mother addicted to drugs—and knew they were often quite wary of questions. The food seemed to help keep him open.

"What was your mom like?" Sadie asked as she set two plates of brownies on the table. He immediately abandoned the last few bites of his dinner in favor of the dessert. Big surprise.

"She's real pretty," he said quickly. Sadie noted his use of the present tense and the way a light jumped into his eyes. He loved his mother. Sadie wondered what their relationship had been like. All she knew about Noelani was that she was a drug addict. Had Charlie been living with her? Who was CeeCee?

"Was she nice too?"

Charlie nodded, but his smile faded and he looked back at the plate as he lifted the brownie. There was so much in his head, Sadie could almost feel his thoughts wanting to burst out. But life had taught him to be careful—she could sense that too—and she didn't dare betray the little bit of trust he'd given her by pushing too much. He reminded her of the feral cats on the island that would eat your food, but never really let you get close.

"Have you always lived on Kaua'i?" Sadie asked.

"No," he said, shaking his head and taking a bite, a big one. "We lived in Honolulu when I was little," he said after he swallowed.

Sadie had to smile. He was only eleven; being little wasn't that long ago. She lifted her own brownie and took a bite out of one corner. It wasn't bad—for a mix. "Do you like it here?"

He shrugged. "I guess." He took another bite.

"Why did you come to Kaua'i?"

"'Cause my mom did," he said, though he eyed her carefully. She was asking too many personal questions.

"How's that brownie?" Sadie asked.

"*Ono.*"

Sadie smiled; she knew *ono* meant good, or delicious in this context. "Would you like another one?"

He nodded quickly, and Sadie served him another brownie, hoping she could get more information from him before his stomach realized how full he was. She waited almost a minute, finishing her own brownie, and then pushed forward again.

"When you and I first met, you said that your mom wasn't doing drugs."

Charlie looked up quickly, instantly defensive. "She wasn't. She's been clean 'cause the judge told her she has to if she's gonna get me back."

Ah. So he was in foster care of some sort but expected to go back with his mom. For an instant, Sadie wondered what it would feel like to have things change so sharply, so quickly. It wasn't that hard to imagine. She remembered the feeling of coming home to two young children after Neil had been pronounced dead at the hospital from a massive heart attack. And then, a decade later, her brother had called to tell her their mother had been killed in a car accident. A year and a half ago, Sadie's neighbor had been found murdered in the field behind her home. Sadie had experienced her share of those turns of fate that gave you whiplash and shook up your future like a snow globe. But she'd been an adult when all of those things happened, not a child.

"You think the police are wrong about how she died?"

He nodded. "She don't take drugs no more, and sometimes people lie." He looked up at Sadie with a guarded, yet eager, expression. Like he wanted to make sure she was listening. "Even cops lie sometimes. You can't trust nobody."

Sadie winced inside and leaned back in her chair, feeling overwhelmed by the hurt inside this little boy and remembering why she had been so hesitant to involve herself earlier. It was hard to feel what other people were feeling.

"Who do you live with now, Charlie? CeeCee?"

"I already told you I don't live nowhere."

"So you're homeless?" Sadie asked. "You live on the streets?"

He nodded, but Sadie could see that, for all his toughness, he wasn't that hard or neglected. His fingernails were trimmed, and the slippahs were still shiny, they were so new. She glanced at the wall clock near the phone. It was nearly four o'clock in the morning, and while she knew she would have to call the police at some point, she wished she could have more time with Charlie first.

Calling the police would drag Sadie even further into this "situation," and the anticipation of giving another statement landed like a block of ice in her chest. She gripped the edges of the table, trying to come up with another solution, but there wasn't one. She would have to explain everything to the police, and they'd probably be suspicious as to why Charlie had come to her. She'd done so well with Charlie here—she'd barely felt any fear or anxiety—but now she closed her eyes and swallowed, trying to get hold of herself. When she opened her eyes a few moments later, Charlie was looking at her, a little fear mixed in with the confused look on his face.

"I'll be right back," Sadie said, forcing a smile as she quickly stood up from the table and headed for her bedroom. She closed the door and sat on her bed, bracing her elbows on her knees and holding her head in her hands as she fought for control over her emotions and fears that ran like wild animals these days. After almost a minute, she was able to draw a deep breath and accept that she hadn't done anything wrong and therefore didn't need to be afraid of getting in trouble. Maybe she should call Pete to talk her through this—but wouldn't he be proud of her if she handled it on her own? Wouldn't she be proud of herself? Finally she stood up and went to the bedroom door. It had been a few minutes, but she tried to take pride in the fact that she had faced her fear and made a rational decision. It was an accomplishment.

She didn't want to risk upsetting Charlie by telling him she was calling the police. Maybe she could try again to get him to talk about where he was staying. Maybe she could get his okay to talk to this CeeCee person, or get him to agree that calling the police was the best choice for both of them. Creating a safe environment was the first step in having an important conversation, so she forced a smile and lifted her chin, hoping she could approach this in a way that wouldn't make Charlie feel threatened.

She took another deep breath as she rounded the corner into the kitchen. "So, I'm wondering if . . ."

Charlie's chair was empty.

Her wallet was lying open on the table.

Charlie had left the sliding glass door open when he'd made a run for it.

CHAPTER 7

What had seemed like a break in the cloud cover was instantly overcast again. Sadie locked the sliding glass door—one, two, three—and closed all the blinds. Then she spent an hour sitting in the living room, trying to decide what to do, battling wave after wave of self-recrimination.

The clouds in her head made it hard to come up with a new plan. It wasn't until the night was turning into early morning gray that Sadie called Pete on her freshly charged cell phone. North Carolina was five hours ahead, but Pete didn't answer. She was leaving a message when he called back on the other line.

"What's wrong?" he asked in a panic when she clicked over to answer his call. Sadie couldn't even think about trying to calm him down, instead she rushed to tell him what had happened.

"What are you going do?" Pete asked when she finished. She knew the calm in his voice was forced.

"I don't know," Sadie said, glad that Pete hadn't automatically given her marching orders. "The police will think I'm a nutcase for having waited so long to call them." She glanced at the clock. It had been more than two hours since she'd first invited Charlie inside. Not to mention his first visit had been a full fourteen hours ago.

Pete didn't argue, and she deflated a little bit. She'd hoped he'd reassure her that she'd done the reasonable thing, but she knew she hadn't been thinking straight.

"I don't want to call the police," she finally admitted rather than dancing around it with other excuses. "This poor kid has already faced so much, and I don't want to get him in trouble. He took less than a hundred dollars."

"The amount doesn't really matter, and to not make him accountable doesn't help him in the long run," Pete said. "I understand you're sympathetic toward his situation, but are your sympathies in his best interest? Calling the police will help them find him and get him back to his caregivers."

Caregivers. Not family. Sadie leaned forward, holding the phone to her ear while covering her eyes with her hand. "Why didn't I take my wallet into the bedroom with me?" she groaned, remembering how she'd put it on the counter after paying Reg for the groceries yesterday afternoon. "I feel like I set him up."

"You didn't," Pete assured her. "He's the one who ultimately made the choice. What does an eleven year old need with that much money?"

"I don't know," Sadie said. "I feel so awful for him. He's just a little boy, and he's hurting so much, Pete."

They were both silent for several seconds. "Do you want to help him, Sadie?"

"Yes," she said, knowing where this was going. "I just don't know that the police will be the help he needs, and I don't want to get myself involved. It will look so strange to them that he came to me."

"Not that strange," Pete said. "He's looking for connections, and you're connected to the last bit of information everyone knows about his mother. He's obviously streetwise, and he *did* find you, so it mustn't have been that hard."

That made her feel a little better, but it didn't silence her fears. "There was a family who lived a few blocks north of me in Garrison," Sadie said, sitting up straight and pausing for a breath that she hoped would even out her emotions. "The Hadfields. They did foster care for years. When a kid ran away, which happened from time to time, the kids were automatically sent to detention. Wherever Charlie's living right now, it's all he has. If I turn him in to the police, he could lose that, and he already has so many disadvantages."

Pete let out a heavy sigh. "He's young enough that they might not react so harshly; they'll consider his age and circumstances. Look, I explained to Officer Wington that you might want more information—that was before all this happened with Charlie—but I thought, in time, you might need to know more about the woman you found. Maybe now's a good time."

"You can't guarantee that the police will go easy on him," Sadie said, choosing to ignore the part about Officer Wington being willing to give her details of a case she didn't want.

"I want to leave this up to you, Sadie, but I don't know that I can't *not* inform the Kaua'i police. I have certain obligations, and we both know that if something happens to that boy, neither you nor I would be able to live with ourselves."

Anger and frustration battled inside Sadie; she knew Pete was right. Hot tears rose in her eyes. "I don't want to make things harder for anyone," she said, her voice wobbling. "This is exactly why I stayed away from the case, why I didn't want any part of it." Tears rolled down her cheeks, and she wiped at them quickly. After having given in to the emotion after Charlie's first visit, she couldn't seem to go back to holding it in anymore. The more involved she became, the more overwhelmed she felt—as though her head might explode at any moment due to too much information, too much stress, too much inability to cope.

"I'm sorry, Sadie," Pete said. "I'm so sorry."

Sadie took a shuddering breath, berating herself for being so fragile and glad she hadn't mentioned her exploding-head fear out loud. She really was losing her mind. "I don't know what to do," she whispered.

"Do you want me to call the police for you?"

"It won't change anything," Sadie said. "Except make them wonder why I didn't call them myself." She'd look weak and scared. Wait, she *was* weak and scared. Still, she dreaded having to talk to the police. Wasn't there another option? "If he is in foster care, he'd have a caseworker assigned to him, right?"

"Yes," Pete said, obviously trying to figure out where she was going with this.

"What if I talked to *them* instead of to the police? Maybe Charlie wouldn't get in trouble that way."

"It's not a bad idea," Pete said. "They'd still likely have to report it, but they might be able to help you with the process. I think I can have someone back in Garrison find out who's working Charlie's case. I just . . . need to tread carefully."

"I'm sorry," Sadie said quietly, knowing it was a risk every time he used his official position to help her find information. "I didn't want any of this to happen."

"I know," Pete said sweetly. "And you haven't done anything wrong. We just need to deal with the situation as best we can, okay?"

Sadie agreed, and Pete said he'd call her as soon as he had the information. Sadie hung up the phone and sat down heavily on the futon. Why was this happening to her? Again?

Though she hadn't immersed herself in the Hawaiian culture, she knew that the local people tended to be superstitious. They believed in ghosts and curses. Sadie was finding it harder and harder to believe she wasn't cursed. These awful situations kept finding her, haunting her. Were they slowly imprisoning her, too?

She waited by the phone for half an hour before she forced herself to get off the futon. She had hoped Pete would be able to find the information quickly, but she knew he was in the middle of his conference. He'd probably run out of a class to talk to her in the first place; she felt so high-maintenance.

Charlie's empty plate stood as proof that she hadn't dreamed up the events of last night, but it was a small comfort. It would be much easier if it had been a figment of her imagination.

She put the plate in the sink and wrung out a washcloth to wipe down the table. When she turned to the table, though, she noticed something on the floor next to the chair where Charlie had been sitting. At first she thought it was a sock, but within a couple steps, she realized it was a crumpled piece of paper. A beat later she realized what it was—the paper from Charlie's pocket that afternoon.

She hurried over, pulling out the chair so she could reach down and pick up the paper. Taking a deep breath, she sat down at the table and unfolded the soft paper carefully, as though it might turn to dust if she handled it roughly. There were six questions, written in sloppy, little-boy handwriting.

1. How did you no Mom?
2. Did you tell any lie to the polise?
3 Does Mom have a new boyfrend?

4. Was Mom taking drugs when you was with her?
5. Did Mom say anything about me?
6. When is Mom coming back?

Sadie closed her eyes to regain her composure, but the words were still blurry when she opened her eyes and read the list again. She imagined Charlie sitting somewhere, a pencil in hand as he planned out his interview with Sadie, someone he thought had the answers to these questions. The fifth question put her interaction with Charlie into a different focus, and Sadie stared at it for several seconds.

She reviewed everything she knew about this little boy: independent, determined, smart, reserved, hurting, and . . . loyal to his mother. Why had he come here, really? Why would he come to talk to someone he thought was a friend of his mother? At eleven years old, he didn't know what closure meant. At fifty-seven, she wasn't sure she did either. He wouldn't know that finding answers could make him feel better. She thought over the few things he'd said about his mother: "She's real pretty" and "She doesn't use drugs anymore." Not she *was* pretty; she *didn't* use drugs.

Sadie touched the words of the fifth question: "Did Mom say anything about me?" She let out a breath. Poor Charlie.

The last question on his list seemed to support the fact that Charlie wasn't looking for information *about* his mom, he was looking *for* his mom.

A minute later, Sadie found herself facing her computer screen, still black since she didn't dare touch the keyboard and wake it up yet. She stared at it for a long time, not sure she was entirely ready for this. She thought about what Pete had said: "What are you going to do?" She wanted to help Charlie, but anything she did, like everything she'd already done, could not be undone. Was she strong enough to step into this situation? Could she get out of it if it got to be too much?

The longer she sat there, the more the fear built up in her chest and the more frozen she became in her insecurities. This was so much bigger than she was. She closed the computer, but her brain wouldn't calm down. She'd already slept through the evening and most of the night and now the sun was almost up. She went into the kitchen, thinking she'd clean until she was really tired. Instead, her eyes landed on the list of goals she'd posted on the fridge.

Go outside every day.
Eat fruit every day.
Talk to Pete every day.

She stared at the words and knew she was missing something. If she wanted to get stronger, if she wanted to be less afraid of the world around her, she needed to be proactive. She reached for a pen, adding one more goal to the list.

Do something brave every day.

Sadie looked at those words, breathed them in and rolled them around like a fine pearl. She had tracked down thugs, faced off against murderers, fought for justice and won. *That* Sadie couldn't be too far away. There had to be a way to find her again.

Sadie went to her computer, sat down, opened a browser window, and typed in the words "Noelani Pouhu Kaua'i." Her finger hovered over the mouse button for a few seconds before she initiated the fateful click. She paused for a moment to ensure her head wasn't exploding, and then scanned the information the search had brought up.

It had begun.

CHAPTER 8

The current information on the local news sites about Noelani's death consisted of two articles about the discovery of her body—one article included Sadie's name as the person who'd found her—and an obituary that brought more tears to Sadie's eyes and made her wish she hadn't started this search. Why was this so hard?

But she was trying to be brave, and Charlie was still out there somewhere, so she clicked on some of the websites she had once used for her investigation company, which she'd completely abandoned since coming to Kaua'i. It took less than an hour for Sadie to find everything on public record about Noelani Pouhu, which she copied into a Word document and organized chronologically. It wasn't happy information. Noelani had had three drug-related arrests over the last four years. Her employer at the time of the most recent arrest—two years ago—was a strip club in Honolulu. She'd lost custody of Charlie after that last arrest and had been sentenced to seven months in jail. She'd moved to Kaua'i after her release, but Charlie had said he moved to Kaua'i "'cause his mom did." That seemed strange if he were in state custody.

Noelani's Facebook profile listed her employment as a dancer and entertainer—that matched the strip club job. She had at-tended Punahou High School in Honolulu but didn't post a gradu-ation year—perhaps she'd dropped out. Charlie had been born when she was seventeen so that was a reasonable hypothesis. She hadn't attended college, and her top three music choices were Dave Matthews, The Fray, and IZ. Sadie had become familiar with the Kaua'i-born singer Israel Kamakawiwo'ole known as IZ. Posters of his album covers—many of them featuring the 700-pound musician—were posted all over the island despite the fact that he'd been dead for more than a decade. Sadie had heard his version of "Somewhere over the Rainbow" before coming to Hawai'i, but had become famil-iar with his other work since her arrival. Sharing the love of his mu-sic with Noelani made Sadie feel connected to the woman in some small way. Noelani didn't list any books, but had liked several movies Sadie had never seen, including *Fight Club* and *Shutter Island*.

Sadie clicked on the photo section and got her first look at the real Noelani, rather than the bloated version from her nightmares. Most of the pictures showed the hollow face of an addict, often look-ing stoned or drunk as she attempted to smile at the camera during a party. There were a few pictures from the strip club where she'd worked; they were equally unfortunate, and Sadie didn't spend much time on them. But then Sadie found a picture of Noelani with a younger version of Charlie—he was missing his two front teeth—at a beach. She looked healthy and happy with a bright smile on her face as she hugged her boy to her chest and looked into the camera. The tattoo Sadie had remembered was a dragonfly on her forearm.

In the photo, Noelani looked like any other young mother bonded to her son. A very different woman from the one in the party photos that made up the majority of her images. Sadie couldn't help but wonder which one of the pictures represented the true Noelani.

Was she more addict than mother, or was it the other way around? Charlie wanted to believe that Noelani had left the emaciated shoulders and thinning hair behind her, and for his sake, Sadie wanted to believe it too. But was that reasonable?

Sadie printed off the picture of Noelani and Charlie together and taped it to the wall above the desk. Her personal opinions about some of the ways Noelani had lived her life were secondary to the facts that, for whatever reason, God had made her Charlie's mother and that Charlie loved her. Sadie would need to keep that perspective if she moved forward.

If.

She still wasn't fully committed and found herself wishing for a way out almost as much as she wished for that golden nugget of information that would push her over the fence once and for all. She stood up from the computer and poured herself some cereal while she thought about her options. Neither option—pursuing it or leaving it alone—felt right.

Pete called her just after seven o'clock in the morning Hawai'i time. "I'm between workshops but I wanted to give you an update. I have someone back in Garrison looking into the social worker overseeing Charlie's case," he said, "but I wanted to make sure you understood that once you talk to the caseworker, you can't control what they do with the information. Do you feel up to this?"

Pete didn't know Sadie had spent the last two hours researching Noelani. He didn't know that a picture of a healthy Noelani and a happy Charlie had been staring at her for almost half an hour. He didn't know the battle taking place in Sadie's mind. But he knew what it meant to do the right thing, and he knew what Sadie was capable of doing. That he'd done what he'd done so far, and then left it up to her, was a huge vote of confidence. But Sadie still had to make a decision. She sat down in front of her computer and looked at the picture again.

"I would like to talk to the caseworker," Sadie said, accepting that she couldn't turn away from this now. "I . . . I can do this."

"Okay then," he said. "I've thought this over and, while I can let it play out for the rest of the day, I'll have to call the Kaua'i police tomorrow morning if you're unable to make headway with the caseworker. I hope you can understand my position."

"I understand," Sadie said even though it bothered her. But he had responsibilities she didn't have, and she didn't want him to put his job at risk. He'd done that several times in the past, and she dreaded that one day his helping her would get him into serious trouble.

"I'll send you the caseworker information as soon as I get it, okay? I've got a full afternoon and won't be available much, but I'll see that you get it."

"Okay," Sadie said. "Thank you, Pete."

They said their good-byes. Sadie hoped she hadn't distracted him too much. She wished she could do this on her own, and yet she was so grateful for both his help and his support.

After hanging up the phone, Sadie went into the kitchen and picked up Charlie's list. Sitting in her kitchen, with the sun lighting up her windows, Sadie read Charlie's words again. His questions were a glimpse into his place in this situation and what he needed to know if there was hope of him finding peace.

Peace.

Was it really possible?

With the last few months as an example, Sadie had a hard time feeling much faith in that. For herself. Or for Charlie. But he was young, and her heart broke. There *had* to be hope for him.

A moment later, she went to her bedroom and opened the top

drawer where she'd hidden all the papers and things from her hospital stay. Shuffling through the papers, she found the card she'd been looking for—a card given to her by the officer who'd taken her statement once she'd been capable of talking about finding Noelani's body.

Pete had told Officer Wington she might call but it was nerve-racking to think about it. What if she accidentally told him about Charlie being at her condo? What if she didn't accidentally tell them anything, but they found out about it later? And yet, Officer Wington was Sadie's best bet at finding the information she needed. When she saw his e-mail address on the card, she felt even better and hurried back to her computer where she sent him a message, asking for an update on Noelani's case.

Her head didn't explode. Bells and whistles didn't even go off inside her brain. In fact, she felt the tiniest recognition inside herself of empowerment, confidence, and—dare she say it?—optimism. Did this little jolt mean she was doing the right thing? Gosh, she hoped so!

Now that she'd started, what came next?

She took comfort knowing that it would probably be awhile before Officer Wington got back to her, giving her time to accept the choice she'd made to contact him. However, her cell phone rang within two minutes. The number matched the one on Officer Wington's card, and her heart, which had begun to calm, sped right back up again.

Sadie took a deep breath, pulled all her courage from the dark corners of her mind as though sweeping together dust bunnies long-ignored, and answered the phone, hoping she sounded braver than she felt.

"This is Officer Wington," he said after she said hello. He sounded very official, with a deep voice that graveled when he spoke. "I just got your e-mail."

CHAPTER 9

"Yes, um, hi, uh, thanks for calling," Sadie said, wiping her sweaty hands on her leg. Notes! She needed to take notes. With one hand holding the cell phone to her ear, she rummaged in the cupboard for a notebook and pen.

"Sure," Officer Wington said. "Detective Cunningham had said you might call. Your e-mail said you have some questions about Ms. Pouhu."

"Um, yes," Sadie said. "I'm, uh, trying to get a little closure on the situation and wondered what you guys had learned about what happened to her." Enough with the um-ing and uh-ing! She took a deep breath, channeling herself into this moment.

Officer Wington sighed. "Unfortunately, we haven't learned much. She left work early the night of Saturday, March 17, and no one has come forward to report seeing her after that."

"No one?"

"No," Officer Wington repeated.

"Um, did anything about her . . . body give any clues as to what happened?"

"You mean the cause of death? I'm afraid that's still undetermined.

The autopsy reports have been sent to forensics, and the toxicology reports will still be a few more weeks, possibly longer."

"Undetermined? I guess I assumed she'd drowned." When she had said clues, she'd meant things like a book of matches from a nightclub she'd been at—but then that wouldn't have lasted in the ocean.

"Or she was already dead before she entered the water," Officer Wington added. "Again, the autopsy reports are under review right now to determine a conclusive cause of death. Once a body's been in water a certain period of time, you can't tell if the water in the lungs actually caused their death."

"When I was in the hospital, someone told me she was a drug addict."

"That's what brought her to Kaua'i—a rehab facility in Waimea."

"But she was from O'ahu originally, right? Why did she stay here after rehab?"

"She indicated to me that she came to Kaua'i with the intent to stay in order to keep a distance from the places where she'd lived and used. After rehab, she became active in a local church and got a job. She also has a son in state custody and was working toward reunification."

The obituary had mentioned Noelani's church, but Sadie's attention was caught by his first words. "You spoke to her? You knew her?"

"I met her a few months ago in connection to another case, unrelated to this one as far as we can tell."

What case? There wasn't anything on public record, meaning Noelani hadn't been arrested. Something had put her in arm's reach of the law. But what?

"However," Officer Wington continued, "when we searched her

things, we found marijuana, which was a violation of her parole and leads us to the possibility that she may have discovered the drug scene here on Kaua'i. The fact that no one has come forward to admit having been with her when she died is another indication that she could have been using again. Are you familiar with the terms 'body dump' or 'party drop'?"

"No," Sadie said. "What is it?"

"Sometimes when a group of people are using drugs and someone ODs, they panic and drop the body somewhere. In a person's car, on the side of the road, or, if they happen to be on an island, such as this one, they'll sometimes throw the body in the ocean. Dumping the body is the best way to avoid an investigation because there's typically very little evidence to tie the body back to anyone else involved. There was no obvious cause of death, which leaves us with that theory until we get the reports back."

"Oh," Sadie said. The thought of people just dumping the body of a friend made Sadie slightly sick to her stomach, but she shook herself out of it.

"We typically don't get much information about the circumstances leading to the death, since coming forward puts the people involved at risk of facing significant charges."

It made sense, in a really horrendous way. "Do you know *when* she died? Was it the last night anyone saw her?" Sadie asked, realizing she hadn't been taking notes. She quickly scribbled a few words—*unknown cause of death, former case, Waimea rehab, body dump, party drop.*

"We think so. The medical examiner estimates she was in the water several days, but it's hard to calculate exactly how long."

"Who was the last person to see her?"

"A coworker Ms. Pouhu called to cover her shift at the motel where she worked. Ms. Pouhu said she'd be back in a couple of hours. No one saw her again, at least no one who's willing to say so."

"Where did she work?"

"Sand and Sea Motel in Kalaheo. She had temporary housing there as well but, we understand, was looking for an apartment, which can be difficult to find on the island."

Sadie wrote furiously.

"And I guess you don't know why she was so far from Kalaheo that night."

"She'd borrowed a car from the employee who covered for her at work, but it was found off the Kuhio highway the next morning with an empty gas tank. It was impounded, and the owner recovered it the following day."

"So, you think she ran out of gas, went to a party, and over-dosed?"

"Or someone tried to return the car and ran it dry," he said. "Most overdose victims die alone in a back room where they've been left to sleep it off. When the people she was with realized she was dead, they likely took her to the beach and threw her in, probably thinking she'd be washed out with the tide. We think she got caught under the dock before low tide took her out to sea. Otherwise, she likely would have washed up on the beach."

Sadie didn't realize until he stopped speaking that she'd frozen some time during his recitation of the facts. She'd asked for them, but hearing the details put her right back at the dock. It was all she could do to push away the pictures in her mind; she couldn't even take notes because her hands were shaking. But she knew she couldn't waste this opportunity to get information, and she forced herself to pay attention.

"We didn't connect Ms. Pouhu to the car until she was officially reported missing almost a week later."

Sadie had heard that part before and frowned. "Do you know why it took so long for her disappearance to be reported?"

"From talking to her associates, they assumed she'd relapsed and would either show up eventually or go back to O'ahu."

"So they weren't very worried about her," Sadie summarized. Maybe Noelani had been a loner and no one knew her very well. "And phone records? Did she have a cell phone that showed who she called that night?"

"The last call she made from her cell phone was to the employee who covered her shift and loaned her the car," Officer Wington said. "And none of the other numbers have opened up a new lead."

"Who was the employee?"

"That's beyond the scope of information I can give you, Mrs. Hoffmiller."

"Of course, I'm sorry," she said, flushing slightly even though his reprimand was mild.

"I've given you more detail than I normally would," he said, "but Detective Cunningham indicated that being open with you would be helpful for your situation."

"It is helpful," Sadie said, liking that Pete thought she was strong enough to handle it, even if she was still unsure. "I appreciate it very much."

"Is there anything else?"

"Yes, just a few more things. How's her son doing?"

"I'm sure it's been difficult for him," Officer Wington said. "All of my communication goes through the caseworker."

Sadie felt her chin quiver slightly as she wrote "Charlie" on the paper, with a frowny face next to it. She hurried to the next topic.

"I guess they can't do a funeral if they're still doing tests and things."

"The testing is merely done on tissue samples. The actual body was released earlier this week. Her ashes were scattered as part of the memorial service yesterday morning."

"Oh," Sadie said, both surprised and disappointed. "I didn't realize she'd been cremated." Wasn't that unwise in an open case? What if something was discovered in the autopsy reports and the body needed to be exhumed for verification? Wait . . . the memorial service was *yesterday?* That meant Charlie had come to see her just hours afterward. He'd been at the service, listening to people say farewell to his mother, and remained unconvinced that she was gone.

"Common practice on the islands and far less expensive. Is there anything else?"

He was clearly ready to get on with the rest of his day, and she couldn't think of anything else to ask. "No, thank you," she finally said. *Mahalo* was the Hawaiian word for thank you, but she always felt out of place when she said it. "I appreciate your taking the time to talk to me."

"Of course," the officer said. "I hope things go well for you, Mrs. Hoffmiller. I'm sure it's hard to think that what happened to you that day was a good thing, but at least it allowed Ms. Pouhu to be found."

It *was* hard to think that Sadie's trauma was a positive thing, but what if Noelani had never been found? What if she'd just disappeared? That's what Charlie thought had happened—that his mom had left—and he thought he might be able to find her again.

Sadie caught herself before she voiced her fears that Charlie didn't believe his mother was dead. Mentioning Charlie would open up everything that had happened with him—everything she didn't want to talk to the police about. Heat washed through her at the near slip. "Thank you so much," she said instead. She was suddenly eager to get off the phone in case she didn't catch herself the next time she was tempted to talk about Charlie.

"You're welcome."

After hanging up the phone, Sadie stared at her notes, fighting the resurgence of frightening memories. She circled the note she'd made about Noelani having met with Officer Wington about a different case. She also circled "tide" and "party drop," then she leaned back and looked at the visual of those details that stood out to her the most. Once she'd done that, she was left with the question that kept coming back to her over and over again.

What are you going to do about it?

CHAPTER 10

The discussion with Officer Wington convinced Sadie that talking with the social worker was the best choice for her to make. But she couldn't do anything until she heard back from Pete. She tried not to think about the fact that if things ever got back to Officer Wington, he would know she'd hidden information from him. Maybe she *should* have told him what had happened with Charlie . . . but what if that meant Charlie lost the only home and hope he had right now? It felt like too big a risk to take, but she still reviewed what she'd learned and what she could have done differently a hundred times.

She showered and changed into long khaki shorts and a light cotton T-shirt instead of a fresh muumuu because she was trying to prepare herself mentally in case she needed to meet with the social worker overseeing Charlie's case face to face. When she looked at herself in the mirror, though, she wanted to cry. Was that really her? Sarah Diane Wright Hoffmiller? The shorts were too big and the T-shirt hung limp on her shoulders. She really needed a new bra, and her legs were downright pasty. Her hair had grown out past her shoulders, but was gray at the roots with half-a-dozen shades of grayish-yellow between that and the ends which were split and frizzy. The humidity played havoc with her natural curl, making her head one big hair ball. Nothing about the reflection staring back at her said to the world "I've got something to offer!"

Not only did her clothes look bad, but they were uncomfortable too. She had worn muumuus almost exclusively since her first few weeks in the islands, and the stiff fabric of the shorts felt constricting. She'd thought of dressing differently as dressing up, but she looked and felt awful, so she changed into a short blue-and-white muumuu—the one she wore when she went out with the Blue Muumuus—with a little ruffle just below the knee.

Before coming to Hawai'i, she'd thought muumuus the unattractive equivalent of a housedress someone would wear on the mainland—i.e., frumpsville. But here, it was different. They were bright and comfortable, and it was socially acceptable to wear them nearly everywhere. The muumuu was an improvement the moment she put it on, and she felt like her old self again . . . or was it her new self? Then she wet her hair and pulled it into a bun at the top of her head. It didn't hide the mess of color, but it helped camouflage it somewhat and would keep the hair off her neck. Makeup wasn't even worth considering—the heat and humidity would make it an oily mess within an hour—but she did put on some SPF 15 moisturizer and a pale pink lip gloss with sparkles in it that caught the light.

She was staring at the woman in the mirror, still not sure she knew who she was, when her cell phone rang from the bedroom. For an instant, she was tempted to let it go to voice mail—she'd done that many times over the last several weeks—but then she remembered Pete was going to call with the social worker's number. She hurried to the phone, then paused when she saw that it wasn't Pete. It was Gayle.

Sadie bit her lip, realizing she hadn't talked to Gayle like she'd promised Pete she would. Right now seemed like such horrible timing, but she couldn't justify putting it off. She took a breath as she brought the phone to her ear and sat down on the edge of her bed.

"Hi, Gayle," Sadie said, remembering her goal to be brave every day. Since writing it down, she'd already had many opportunities to test her resolve. This was one more challenge she had to face.

"Sadie," Gayle said, sounding a bit surprised that Sadie had answered. "How are you doing?"

Sadie considered the list of assurances she could use to explain herself and put Gayle at ease. However, there were more reasons not to do that than supporting justifications to keep pretending everything was okay. "Actually," she said, feeling nervous and hating it, "things have been a little rough."

"Really? What's going on?"

Sadie took a breath and laid it all out there.

"Oh. Wow," Gayle said when Sadie finally ran out of words. Sadie braced herself for the inevitable "Why didn't you tell me?" comment, but instead, Gayle shored up her best friend status and said, "I'm so sorry this happened to you."

"So am I," Sadie said. She then told Gayle about the therapist and about Charlie coming over. "I'm feeling all . . . mixed up about everything. Pete's trying to find the social worker. I feel so anxious and driven and scared. It's confusing." She left out that she also felt incredibly vulnerable.

"I struggled with anxiety after my divorce," Gayle said, sounding embarrassed. "I look back now and can see there was some depression mixed in, but it was awful, not being able to trust your reactions to things, being afraid and not knowing why, not being able to see ahead or make sense of things that happened."

Sadie's throat thickened, and she nodded before realizing Gayle couldn't see her. "I've never felt like this before," she confided. "I've always been a strong person."

"You're still strong," Gayle said. "Anxiety doesn't make you less than what you are at your core, but it's really hard to see *you* amid everything else that's going on. And coming up with coping mechanisms to deal with it just compounds things."

"Coping mechanisms?" Sadie repeated.

"Things that protect you from the anxiety," Gayle clarified. "Like not going out as much to avoid things that seem scary, or drinking too much, or getting angry so no one can see you're so scared—things like that."

Sadie automatically listed the coping mechanisms she'd developed to avoid her own anxiety—not making friends, not being honest with the people who cared about her, and isolating herself. She hadn't seen them as things she was doing to avoid scary situations that would trigger her anxiety, but with Gayle's definition fresh in her ears, she could see them for what they were.

"I'm so sorry you're facing it," Gayle added after a pause.

"But you got better?" Sadie asked, needing hope.

"I did," Gayle said. "For the most part. I still have moments, but I know how to deal with them now, and I know why they're really there. And, believe it or not, I think I'm stronger because of that period of time; I learned how to confront hard things in new ways. I had a good therapist and some great friends."

"I didn't even know," Sadie said, feeling bad she hadn't been one of those great friends. She hadn't even noticed.

"No one knew, other than my kids and my sister," Gayle said. "But that doesn't mean great friends didn't help me all the same. You were always my cheerleader, even if you just thought I was devastated that Harold left me like he did. My friends helped me have some-where to go, and they let me be angry, which I needed to be, and they let me see that there was still life to be lived."

Sadie nearly asked why Gayle hadn't told her about it—maybe she could have helped more—but she already knew the answer. It was the same reason why Sadie had kept things to herself: embar-rassment, fear of rejection, not feeling capable of carrying the burden of knowledge for someone else who would then worry.

They talked until Gayle arrived at her office; she'd called Sadie while she drove back from lunch. "I'll call you later, okay?" she said.

Sadie thanked her, and they ended the call. A few minutes later, her phone rang again. It was Gayle, and Sadie furrowed her brow, wondering what Gayle had forgotten to say.

"I thought you were at work," Sadie said.

"I was, I mean, I am." Gayle took a quick breath. "I'm just gonna throw this out there, and I already know what your automatic an-swer will be so just don't say it right away, okay? Just think about it for a minute."

Sadie braced herself. "O-kay."

"I told you how Denny's niece, Barb, has been training with me for a few weeks, right?" Denny was Dr. Lithgo to everyone else and the best optometrist in Garrison. Gayle had managed the front desk and optical center of his practice for almost sixteen years.

"Yes, that's why you could take your vacation and visit me next week," Sadie said. Barb was going to be running the new optical of-fice in Sterling when it opened in May. Dr. Lithgo was bringing on a new doctor who would split time with him at both locations. Sadie's heart stilled for a moment as she considered that maybe Gayle couldn't come, that something had happened and Barb couldn't cover for her after all.

"Right," Gayle said. "The opening for the Sterling office has been delayed, again, which means she's going to be in the office with me for an additional three weeks. We'll be lucky to get it open by Memorial Day at the rate things are going."

"I'm sorry," Sadie said. When she'd talked to Gayle almost two weeks ago, the conversation had been full of complaints about Barb, who had just started her training. Gayle liked to rule her own roost and was irritated by the younger woman being underfoot within her domain.

"It's okay," Gayle said quickly. "The thing is, I have, like, two months of vacation stacked up and no reason to stay here now that Barb knows how to do everything. What if I came out there sooner? Stayed two weeks instead of one. I could use the break."

Sadie blinked. "Uh . . ."

"I know your automatic reaction is to say no," Gayle said in a rush. "That's why I want you to think about the responsibility you'd be taking upon yourself to deny me the chance to come out there when I have coverage at the office and I am in such *desperate* need of a vacation. I mean we've already established that you're dealing with a lot of pressure right now. Do you really feel capable of carrying the burden of denying me an extra couple of weeks in paradise along with everything else?"

"Are you using my anxiety issues to manipulate me into agreeing to have you come?" The banter felt good, though. Really good. Sadie knew she was safe with Gayle.

"I'm not sure I'd say it quite like that."

"How would you say it, then, if I gave you a second chance?"

"Um." Even though Gayle was thousands of miles away, Sadie knew she was biting her lip and twisting a lock of her red hair between her fingers. "Okay," Gayle said, gearing up for a second attempt. "Please let me come," she begged. "Did I tell you that Barb is a size four and every day talks about how she needs to lose weight? She doesn't even look like a grown woman. If she needs to lose weight, what does she think when she looks at me?"

Gayle had never apologized for being a full-figured woman. It helped that her figure, full though it may be, was amazing. Still, skinny women who whined about their weight had always rubbed her the wrong way. "She's making me crazy, Sadie. If that's not enough to convince you I need a longer vacation, it's been raining for three weeks out here. Sadie, spring is being held hostage, I swear, and I am going crazy. And did I mention that I found out George wears a toupee?"

"No," Sadie breathed, a smile hovering around her lips.

"Yes!" Gayle said. "We were on the couch, watching a movie, and I started running my fingers through what I *thought* was his hair, and he tried to stop me. I thought he was being playful and . . ." She made a shuddering sound. "I managed to avoid him for a few days, but then he confronted me on my way to my car after work. I told him how I feel about fake hair, and he had the gall to call me shallow. Me! I have depth, Sadie, but that doesn't mean I'm going to settle for a man lacking in self-confidence, oh no it does not! I think I had already taken great strides by dating a man named George in the first place, but there has to be a line drawn somewhere."

Sadie put a hand over her mouth to keep from laughing out loud.

"*Please* let me come sooner," Gayle said. "It will solve all my problems, and maybe help you out too. *Please*. If you need some time to think about it, that's okay. I can call you after work or something."

"Can you even change your tickets?" Sadie asked.

"I'm sure I can. One of my clients works part-time for Delta, and he helped me when my aunt Grace's funeral was bumped back a few days to give her son time to come home from Iraq. Barb and I are stepping all over each another, and now that the Sterling office is being delayed, she's going to be underfoot even longer. The office will be fine—better, even, without Barb and me racing to answer the phone at the same time. I just need you to tell me you want me to come sooner than we planned and to stay longer. I can take care of everything but that."

Did Sadie want her to come? Her instant reaction was to feel bad at having Gayle go to such expense, time, and money to fix Sadie. Though veiled as a solution to all Gayle's problems, Sadie knew this was really Gayle coming to the rescue. She wasn't used to playing the damsel in distress role, but Gayle had told her not to go with the automatic answer. What, then, was Sadie's second answer?

"Like I said," Gayle continued when Sadie didn't say anything. There were trace amounts of defeat in her tone. "You can take your time to think about it. I'm really not trying to put you on the spot or—"

"Yes," Sadie cut in.

"Yes?" Gayle repeated, her tone rising. "Really?" she practically squeaked.

"Yes," Sadie said with a laugh, though it quickly fizzled. "But, you have to know that I'm . . . different."

"I know," Gayle said in a motherly way. "And I understand."

"And I'm looking into the life of the woman I found." Saying it out loud was hard. Really hard.

"Ohhh," Gayle said.

Sadie heard a warning of caution coming and hurried to cut Gayle off. "I know that, based on my history and what's going on with me right now, it might not seem like the smartest thing to do, but I just . . . I have to make sure Charlie's okay. I have to answer those questions about his mom."

"No, I get it," Gayle said, and her voice was calm, sweet and sincere.

Did she get it? Sadie wondered. *Could she?*

"I can be your wingman, okay? I'm not going to get in the way, I promise."

"I can't wait to see you," Sadie said, feeling a smile pulling at her cheeks. "It's so beautiful here. Thank you, Gayle."

"Thank *you*," Gayle said quickly. "You haven't met Barb and you haven't seen George's toupee so you can't adequately appreciate what you're saving me from. I'll let you know the details as I get them worked out, okay?"

Sadie said good-bye and hung up, her stomach churning with emotion. Guilt? Fear? Vulnerability? She didn't know what it stemmed from, but it wasn't any more uncomfortable than her usual discomfort. And then she smiled. Gayle was coming! Discomfort aside, she would have a friend here. Not just any friend—her best friend who understood, at least to an extent, what Sadie was dealing with. Maybe Gayle could help her connect back to the Sadie she'd been when she left Garrison. What would it be like to not be alone anymore? It had been so long that she wasn't sure she knew how to feel about having companionship, but it did feel good, and good was . . . good.

Less than fifteen minutes later, she received a text message from Pete with the name and phone number of the social worker based in Lihue who had been assigned to Charlie's case: Tate Olie. After the contact information, Pete had added a note:

I'll call when I have some time. Good luck.

She'd need it. Things were coming together faster than she expected, and she feared that at some point it would all crash over her like a wave in the impact zone—lethal to many an unsuspecting surfer who was unfamiliar with what lurked beneath the waves. For now, though, she was still paddling out to sea, in hopes of finding that perfect wave that would bring her in unscathed.

CHAPTER 11

S adie paced back and forth for ten full minutes, trying to work up the confidence to contact Charlie's caseworker at the Department of Human Services. This was going to be a long journey if she had to put so much thought into every single thing she did. She read Charlie's list again before folding it back up and stuffing it in her shoulder bag. Then she sat down at the kitchen table, took a breath, and called Mr. Olie's office.

When the receptionist answered, Sadie asked for Mr. Olie and was immediately transferred to his voice mail. She left a message, saying it was urgent, then hung up and stared at her phone, willing it to ring before she lost her nerve. The seconds ticked by. Pete's comment about her having one day to figure this out echoed louder and louder in her head.

She mopped the floor, which took all of eight minutes—making it a total of twenty minutes since she'd left her voice mail.

She called the office a second time and was, again, sent to his voice mail, which she hung up on before calling the office again, knowing she was making a pest of herself. "I need to talk to Mr. Olie," she said when the receptionist answered for the third time.

"I can transfer you to—"

"I'm sorry," Sadie said, surprised with the snappy tone she managed despite feeling bad for being difficult. "I already left a message, and he hasn't called me back. I really need to talk to him."

"Mr. Olie is in meetings this morning," the receptionist said, sounding annoyed instead of sympathetic. "I'm sure he'll return your call as soon as he can."

Sadie pursed her lips, trying to think of what she could say to make this woman understand.

"Aloha," the woman said curtly and hung up before Sadie came up with anything. She didn't know all the rules, but she was pretty sure "Aloha" wasn't supposed to be said like that.

Sadie closed her eyes and took a breath, telling herself that she wasn't out of line. Once Mr. Olie and the receptionist knew what she was calling about, they would understand. The next logical step hovered in her brain for a moment before she acknowledged it—go to his office.

Even though she'd considered the possibility of having to meet with the social worker in person, going to his office uninvited was something she'd rather avoid. Yet, she knew from experience that meetings were almost always more effective face-to-face than over the phone. And she didn't have time to wait for him to call her back. The receptionist said he had meetings; what if Sadie was waiting for him when he got out of them?

Sadie went to her computer, squared her shoulders, and set about figuring out how to get to Lihue—she didn't have a car here. She'd taken the bus into town a few times when she first arrived in Puhi, but it had been weeks since she'd done it, and she'd thrown away the bus schedule. The tightness in her chest grew incrementally as she looked up the bus routes online and mapped out the closest stop to the Department of Human Services office.

Taking the bus. Finding the office. Meeting with a stranger. Putting her nose into business that wasn't her own. It all felt like too much and she had to take a break, choosing to walk around the pool a few times to calm herself down. Even after that, it took the promise to herself that she'd get a shave ice—not *shaved* like she'd called it the first time; for whatever reason, Hawaiians dropped the "d" on the end of the word—as a reward for being brave. She'd had the tasty treat during one of the outings with Konnie and the Blue Muumuus where she'd learned that the best shave ice had ice cream on the bottom and sweetened condensed milk drizzled on top. The promise of enjoying another shave ice got her out the door and down the block to the bus stop with almost fifteen minutes to spare. That, and she was worried that if she missed this bus, she wouldn't have the courage to try again.

By the time the bus arrived, tiny gray hairs that had been tight against her head had begun to pop up like daisies. The morning cool had vanished. She was sweaty and chanting "I can do this, I can do this, I can do this," under her breath even though she knew it made her look like a crazy person hanging around a bus stop. Not that she wasn't crazy, but it was too bad she couldn't pretend otherwise anymore. All she had to do was give her information to the social worker, and then she could wash her hands of it completely. Right?

If only she believed it could possibly be that easy.

The bus ride was uneventful, and when she arrived at the address Pete had texted her, she asked to speak to Mr. Olie without telling the receptionist she'd already called that morning. She was told to take a seat in the waiting room. She did so and listened to the hum of office machinery and muted conversations as people came and went, busy and necessary. The sound of purpose.

Despite being in an air-conditioned office, Sadie continued to sweat as her stress level kept rising. The tiny Asian receptionist with turquoise feather earrings that matched her eye shadow left the desk several times, and each time she returned, Sadie was hopeful she'd have an answer but the receptionist never even looked in her direction.

A heavyset, older Hawaiian man came toward her at one point when the receptionist had stepped away from her desk, and Sadie straightened, hoping he was Mr. Olie coming out to greet her, but he barely glanced at her before pushing through the doors.

After fifteen minutes, Sadie approached the desk again to remind the receptionist she was still waiting. "It's really important," Sadie said.

"I'll call his office again," the receptionist said, then looked pointedly at Sadie.

Sadie returned to her seat, completely intimidated by the tiny woman. Only when Sadie was out of earshot did the receptionist dial a number on the phone. A moment later, the receptionist left her desk and moved down one of the hallways. When she returned, she motioned for Sadie to come forward, which Sadie did, perhaps a little too eagerly.

"I guess Mr. Olie already left," the receptionist told her.

"For lunch?" Sadie asked, disappointed. "When will he be back?"

"He's *pau*."

"*Pau?*" Sadie had heard the word before, but wasn't sure what it meant.

"Finished. Done. Gone for the day," the receptionist said, seemingly irritated that Sadie didn't understand pidgin. "Mr. Olie is only in the office half a day a few times a week. Shall I take a message for him?"

"I already left a message on his voice mail," Sadie said, feeling confused and unable to adjust her plans as quickly as she should. "He didn't call me back, and so I came down to talk to him."

The receptionist looked at Sadie appraisingly and narrowed her eyes slightly. "You called earlier, didn't you?"

Sadie nodded and hated that it made her feel as though she were confessing to something she'd done wrong. She was trying to do something right, and it wasn't going very well. "I really needed to talk to him. It's important."

"I can make you an appointment for tomorrow," the receptionist said, looking at the computer in front of her which, presumably, held a calendar. She clicked a few keys. "Oh, wait, I guess he's not back until Friday."

Sadie shook her head. That wouldn't work. She only had today. "I'll have to think about it," she said, not sure how to proceed.

The receptionist gave Sadie an exasperated look and blinked once, slowly. "He only has a few possible appointment times, and he likes to have his schedule first thing in the morning. Even if he was coming back this afternoon, he probably wouldn't see you."

"I'm sorry," Sadie said. "I'm just . . . I just need to think."

She returned to her chair, leaned her elbows on her knees, and put her head in her hands, trying to think of her options. She could go to Officer Wington instead of Mr. Olie, but then she'd have to explain why she didn't tell him about Charlie when they had spoken on the phone that morning.

She could make an appointment with Mr. Olie for Friday and beg Pete for another two days, but that would put Pete in a difficult position, not to mention that it could keep Charlie in danger for two more days.

Sadie knew the chances of finding Mr. Olie's home number was slim; most social workers and therapists weren't listed in local directories. She had access to different databanks of information thanks to her private investigation business and could probably track Mr. Olie down at home. How would he respond to that, though?

There was the tiniest spark of excitement when she thought about the investigative techniques she already knew and the subsequent thrill of discovery that would follow if she used them, but the fear that wrapped around that excitement was something she'd never felt when she was doing her PI work back in Colorado. Things had changed so much since then.

She was plotting out her strategy, wishing she'd brought a notebook so she could organize her thoughts, when a hippie-looking woman with long brown hair and a flowing purple skirt came out of one of the offices and approached the receptionist. Her blue top did not match her skirt. She wore a flower behind her right ear, which traditionally meant she was single, but Sadie knew not all women paid attention to tradition.

"Tate didn't leave already, did he?" the hippie-looking woman asked.

Tate? Wasn't that Mr. Olie's first name? Sadie double-checked Pete's text message. Yep, his first name was Tate.

The receptionist flicked a look at Sadie, who studied her phone intently so it wouldn't seem as though she was eavesdropping. "Yes, just a bit ago," the receptionist said.

"How long?" the woman asked, looking at her watch. "I told him I needed him to sign this petition before he left so I can submit it to Judge Hander today."

"He's been gone at least ten minutes," the receptionist said, but she'd lowered her voice as though not wanting Sadie to overhear. The only man Sadie had seen leave the office was the Hawaiian man. Was that Mr. Olie? Olie didn't sound very Hawaiian, but it was probably short for Oliewaikiakahakoo.

The woman let out a heavy sigh. "I swear he leaves just as I get going for the day. Did he say if he was stopping at Poko's for lunch today? Maybe I can catch up with him and—"

"Um, I don't know where he was going," the receptionist cut in. She flicked another telling look in Sadie's direction.

Sadie kept her expression blank, but smiled inside as she felt old instincts kicking in. She knew she was making the receptionist nervous, so instead of hanging around for details, she left the office and leaned against the wall outside the main doors. If the hippie woman didn't try to catch up with Tate, Sadie would be no worse off than she already was. But if she did decide to hunt him down, Sadie would have an unsuspecting guide.

Her instincts weren't as rusty as she feared. Within a minute, the hippie woman came out of the building, not even looking at Sadie as she passed her by. Sadie waited a few seconds and then followed after her. On the street, the woman waved at someone she knew, then jaywalked. Sadie followed at a discreet distance as the woman turned one corner and then the next, before cutting through an alley and ending at an outdoor restaurant. Sadie would never have known it existed if she hadn't been led there. It was as though the thatch-covered pavilion had been built in someone's backyard. The hand-carved sign under the thatched roof said "Poko's" but it couldn't have been seen from either of the nearby streets, which seemed like a poor marketing plan for any business. That said, the ten or so tables were at least half full at 11:30 on a Wednesday, so people obviously knew how to find it, probably locals. Maybe that was the point.

Sadie hung back as the hippie woman walked through the gap in the split-rail gate surrounding the cement pad that made up the floor of the restaurant, but kept her view clear as the woman approached the same Hawaiian man Sadie had seen leaving the office earlier. He sat alone at a table on the far side of the restaurant, away from the other occupied tables. A few plates of food were laid out in front of him.

As the woman slid into a seat across from him, she moved one of his plates away in order to put the papers she'd brought in front of him. She was talking fast, but Sadie wasn't close enough to hear what she was saying. The man hadn't smiled at Sadie when he had passed her in the waiting area, and he wasn't smiling now as he wiped his hands on his shorts and used the woman's proffered pen to sign the papers. When he finished, he nodded at her, swapping the papers for his plate and returning his attention to his food.

The hippie woman stood and hurried out the way she'd come in, looking pleased with herself. Sadie admired her confidence; she didn't seem the least bit bothered that Mr. Olie hadn't said a single word. Sadie would have felt horrible about that, like she'd done something wrong even though he was the one who'd left the office without signing the paperwork.

Sadie waited until the purple skirt disappeared around the corner before entering the open-air restaurant. Ceiling fans spun overhead, providing a hint of a breeze while tiny birds hopped between the chairs, foraging for crumbs. A young, petite waitress was flirting with the cook on the other side of the counter, laughing coyly and not paying attention to her new customer, which was fine with Sadie. IZ's song "Kaleohano" played over the speakers. Sadie liked that one and hoped it was a sign of good luck for her upcoming interaction with this man she found wholly intimidating.

Interrupting someone while they were eating was never a good idea, and yet Sadie didn't feel she had much of a choice. Mr. Olie's unwelcoming energy certainly didn't help her nerves as she approached the table. What if he berated her? What if he wasn't someone she should trust after all? Then she remembered her call to Officer Wington. He'd responded because she'd claimed to be looking for closure—which wasn't necessarily an untruth—and she wondered if perhaps Mr. Olie would be more open to helping her if she used the same approach.

She stood by his table, waiting for him to look up at her. He didn't. Instead he took a few bites of what looked like mashed sweet potatoes.

"Are you Mr. Olie?" she asked after a few more seconds, and bites.

He didn't answer her, just glanced up with an expression that told her he did not appreciate the interruption.

She wished she had another option. She didn't sit, but took a breath and laid out her purpose for being here—to get closure on the death of Noelani Pouhu.

Not one part of her explanation caused any kind of reaction from the man eating at the table. He pushed away the plate of sweet potatoes and pulled another plate in front of him, picking up a corn tortilla out of a covered dish and using the other ingredients on the plate—fish, lettuce, tomatoes, and mangoes—to make a taco. After adding the toppings, he squeezed a quarter of a lime over the finished taco. Sadie hadn't ever eaten fish tacos—they sounded strange compared to the ground beef with taco seasoning she was familiar with—but it looked delicious, and she felt the stirrings of the old Sadie's habit of recreating recipes roll over in its sleep.

He'd finished his first taco when she finished the condensed version of who she was and why she was bothering him. After she stopped talking, he looked up without lifting his head as though checking to make sure she was done.

"I just want to know more about Noelani," Sadie said, shifting under the discomfort of the information she'd left out—Charlie. She didn't feel ready yet to mention him, not until she better understood this man. She hadn't expected him to be so stoic and uninterested. Weren't social workers supposed to be . . . well, social?

"I didn't know her that well," Mr. Olie said as he began wrapping another taco. "I don't think I'm the person that's going to make you feel better about this."

Fish Tacos

Cilantro Sauce
¼ cup mayonnaise
2 tablespoons cilantro, chopped
1 tablespoon lime juice
1 clove garlic, minced or pressed
1 teaspoon water
1 teaspoon white sugar
⅛ teaspoon cumin

Fish
1½ pounds white fish cut into 1-inch cubes (halibut, cod, roughy, snapper, perch, swai)
2 tablespoons chopped cilantro
½ cup pineapple juice

1 tablespoon butter
1 clove of garlic, minced or pressed
¼ teaspoon white or black pepper
¼ teaspoon cumin
¼ teaspoon salt
Zest of one lime
Flour or corn tortillas, warmed

Toppings
Shredded lettuce or cabbage
Diced tomatoes
2 mangoes, cut into slices (mangoes make all the difference)
Avocados or guacamole (optional)
Freshly squeezed lime juice (optional)

In a small bowl, mix all the ingredients for the cilantro sauce. Set aside.

Cut up fish and put into a small glass or plastic (anything non-metal) bowl. Add cilantro and pineapple juice. Set aside. (For a tangier version, soak fish in 2 tablespoons lime juice instead of pineapple juice.)

In a frying pan, melt butter on medium-high heat. Add garlic and sauté for 1 minute. Add spices and sauté for 30 seconds. Drain the pineapple juice (or lime juice) from the fish. Add drained fish to butter and spices. Sauté for 2 minutes, stirring constantly. Add lime zest. Cook an additional 3 to 4 minutes, stirring constantly until fish begins to flake apart. Remove from heat.

To prepare tacos, place a large spoonful of cooked fish in the center of a warm tortilla. Add toppings as desired. Top with cilantro sauce. Add lime juice, if desired. Roll up and eat.

Makes approximately 8 tacos.

CHAPTER 12

"I don't expect anything will make me feel better," Sadie said. "I just want . . . understanding."

He harrumphed and then waved at the chair across the table. Sadie felt a flutter of victory. He was inviting her to sit. That was a good sign! Maybe IZ's aloha spirit was rubbing off on this man too.

Once she sat down, Mr. Olie stared at her, and she was surprised by his anger. Not the aloha she was hoping for. Was he angry about what had happened to Noelani, or was he angry with Sadie for interrupting him?

"Understanding is a worthless pursuit. Understanding Noelani Pouhu is even more so."

Definitely angry at or about Noelani.

"I just have a few questions," Sadie said, feeling a rush of courage as she reviewed what she knew about Noelani's situation and put her questions in order of priority. She had a feeling Mr. Olie wasn't going to tolerate a long discussion.

He let out a breath, giving in, and nodded quickly, as if saying "Let's get this over with." He went back to his meal.

"I understand Noelani lost custody of her son on O'ahu two

years ago, then transferred here for rehab after her release. Her son was transferred to a foster home here too, right? To Kaua'i?"

He nodded, but only once.

"It seems as though the state was working hard for them to reunite. I imagine it can't be easy to change jurisdictions."

"It isn't," he said. "But there were special circumstances."

"Can I ask what those special circumstances were?" Sadie felt a tremor of excitement at the prospect of figuring something out.

"No, you can't," he said, sounding offended. Her excitement died instantly.

"Okay," Sadie said, trying to rebuild the confidence this man was shattering one word at a time. "Can you tell me if she and her son were close to being reunited?"

She held her breath, sure he was about to have her thrown out of the restaurant. Instead, he took another bite of his taco, chewed, swallowed, and then spoke.

"Last month the judge gave her ninety days to get an apartment. If she had her own place by that time, her son could be returned to her for a probationary period of time," Mr. Olie said, rerolling his taco, but not lifting it for another bite. "All she had to do was find a place to live and pass her weekly drug screens. I thought she was on her way, but I was wrong. What else do you want to know?"

"Um," Sadie said. She hadn't thought of another question, and his intense stare made it hard for her to think clearly. "What was she like?"

His eyes narrowed slightly, and Sadie had the distinct impression he was disappointed in her question. It confused her. "What was she like?" he repeated.

Sadie nodded. "What was she like with her son? Did they have a good relationship?"

"They seemed to."

"Oh, um, good," Sadie said. "Do you think she was still using drugs?"

"She'd passed all her screenings since coming to Kaua'i," Mr. Olie said. "She got a full-time job at the motel a few months ago and was getting closer to reunification every day. But she wound up dead in the ocean so something went wrong."

He seemed to have the same opinion Officer Wington did—that Noelani's death was drug-related despite no conclusive evidence. Before Sadie could figure out another question, Mr. Olie continued.

"I had a heart attack five years ago and took early retirement," he said, taking the conversation in a totally different direction. "I returned to work three years ago, part-time, and decided to make every case count. I fought harder than anyone else would for my clients. Reuniting families was my specialty and the best part of my job. I had the seniority to handpick my cases, and in time, people brought me cases they thought I would really sink my teeth into. I've had an impressive record. Noelani's situation was unique, and the department worked hard to help her make a go with this. They even let her leave O'ahu and transferred her son to Kaua'i in the name of reunification—*ohana*—family. I was the perfect guy for the job.

"As of six months ago, I had three of these types of cases I was working, and they were all looking good. The first family consisted of a single mother—a widow who'd turned to prescription pain medication after her husband died—and her three kids. Grandmother had taken over guardianship of the kids so Mom could go to rehab without her kids going into foster care. She completed treatment and was working on getting a job while living with her mother and the kids as they reestablished their relationships.

"We were days away from Mom taking back guardianship of her

children when she came into my office, high as a kite, wanting to sign away her parental rights. I did everything I could to convince her that it wasn't the right decision—I even made her wait two days before I'd let her sign—but she came back—sober—and signed her kids away. Then she hopped a plane for the Big Island to meet up with some tweeker she'd met online. Grandma was diagnosed with colon cancer two weeks later.

"So, I've got three kids—ages ten, twelve, and fourteen. Their father is dead, they were abandoned by their mother, and they are about to lose their grandmother, and I don't have anywhere to send them. They're native, which means they require a special foster home, and I don't have any homes that have room for three siblings. Last night, the fourteen-year-old was arrested for public intoxication, and I can't help but wonder who's going to raise *her* children one day."

"I'm so sorry," Sadie said, reflecting on how much hurt he witnessed through his work. She could hear both anger and exhaustion in his voice.

"The other family was a mom, a dad, and two preteen daughters; haoles who'd come from California so Dad could surf now that he was off parole for aggravated assault. He decided to grow his own weed instead of getting a real job, got caught, went to jail, the house fell apart, Mom was arrested for check fraud, yada yada yada. But they were devastated when the kids were put into temporary placement, and they worked hard to get their lives back on track, which happened in January.

"This last Valentine's Day, Dad got drunk and beat Mom unconscious. The two girls are now in two different temporary homes because I don't have a home that will take sisters in their age bracket. We're all waiting to see if Mom, who's been in a rehab facility due to the significant injuries she sustained from the beating—including neurological damage—will ever be able to care for them again." He looked past Sadie for a moment before bringing his gaze back to her.

"My third case was Noelani Pouhu and her son, and it was feeling like a slam dunk, especially compared to those other two. Noelani took every class we offered, she toed the line to perfection, passed every drug screen, involved herself in a church and her community; she really seemed to step up." He took a breath before going back to his meal. He took a bite, and then a long drink of his Coke.

"I can't imagine what that's like to see those things up close," Sadie said when he didn't comment further. What else could she say? "I'm sorry."

He grunted and kept eating.

Sadie waited a full minute, expecting him to break the awkward silence. He didn't. She finally felt she had no choice but to do it herself. "When did you last see Charlie?"

His chewing slowed, and he looked up at her. "How do you know his name?"

Sadie felt her cheeks flush. "I, uh, talked to the police this morning." But she didn't think they had actually told her his name. She hurried to continue. "Have you talked to him since his mother was found?"

Mr. Olie's wide shoulders went up as he took a deep breath, then he put his fork and knife on the edge of his plate and glared at her until Sadie felt herself shrinking beneath his gaze. He'd softened during his monologue, but his anger was back now. It was all Sadie could do not to excuse herself and flee for home.

"What do you want from me? I can't give you peace about Noelani, and I can't give you hope for Charlie's future. He's a ward of the state now, and he very likely is highly traumatized by all of this because I promised him—*promised* him—that he and his mother would be a family." He paused long enough for his words to sink in. "I can't make you feel better about what happened to you or to Noelani. She was an addict, but I thought she had it in her to beat the statistics. I believed her when she said she would do anything to get her son back. I was wrong."

"What if it wasn't an overdose?" Sadie said. "The police said the toxicology reports were—"

"It was drugs," he cut in. "I spoke to her the day before she took off. She'd petitioned for more visitation hours, and the judge had awarded them so I gave her a call. She turned the conversation to her frustrations with the apartment requirements we put on her: no roommates, certain areas were off limits, biweekly home visits for the first month. The waiting list for low-income housing was two years long, and she couldn't afford much. She argued that we were making it too hard on her, said we didn't really want them together. I got sharp with her—we'd just doubled her visitation hours, after all—but she hung up on me. I had a meeting with her and my supervisor the next Thursday for a drug test and to see where she was at with her housing situation. I hoped she'd be calmer by then. I got a call Wednesday night that she hadn't shown up for her weekly visitation with Charlie. I made some calls over the next couple of days, which is how I realized she'd been missing for almost a week."

"And you thought she'd gone back to the drug scene."

"Parents who want their kids back don't let anything get in their way. Her frustration was building, and she was seeing that this wasn't going to be easy—and it wouldn't get easier. That she hit her limit and went back to the drugs she'd been using since she was thirteen years old isn't a stretch. I've seen it happen a thousand times. She knew she had a screening on Thursday. Failing it would be failing everything. She'd lose every bit of progress she'd made."

Sadie blinked. She wanted to make her point again that there was nothing conclusive, but the way he said it made the explanation about drugs sound so plausible. He had far more experience with this type of thing than she did, and so did the police. Who was she to question their judgment of the situation?

Mr. Olie shrugged, resigned. "I've been a social worker for almost thirty years. I've tried to make a difference, but with the rise of hard drugs on the islands, the bureaucracy which has me doing more paperwork than face-to-face meetings with my clients, and the disintegration of overall values of people has worn me out. How can I swim against a current like that? Why do I put myself in the middle of helpless situations? The fact is that I thought I was helping Noelani, and I didn't help her after all. I certainly didn't help Charlie."

"I think you helped her," Sadie said, keeping her voice soft and, she hoped, nonthreatening. "Charlie saw his mother clean before she died. Maybe it doesn't seem like much compared to what he lost, but one day he'll have that to reflect on. One day he'll know she was trying."

"She'd been clean before," Mr. Olie said. "For up to a year one time, but she never lasted, and while it was nice for Charlie to see his mom clean, one day he'll also know they found marijuana in her stuff. He'll know that the one thing she had to do to get him back was stay clean and she couldn't do it. He'll know it wasn't worth it for her."

"But she *was* clean," Sadie insisted. "For a while. Charlie has good memories of that—certainly that has to count for something."

"It won't be enough," Mr. Olie said, shaking his head. "It never is."

There was something in his statement that held a question.

"Sometimes it is, isn't it? You've done this for so many years—don't you see successes too?"

He immediately looked away, confirming that Sadie had hit a nerve.

"Doesn't Charlie still have a chance? Isn't there hope for him?"

Mr. Olie sat back in his chair, glaring at her as he crossed his arms over his expansive chest. "What do you want from me?" he asked again. For the first time since they'd met, Sadie could see how broken he was. It hadn't been his anger she felt after all. He felt like a failure, he felt used up, but there was something in the look he gave her that said he was also looking for hope of his own.

CHAPTER 13

I don't know what I want from you," Sadie finally admitted once she realized that, despite all the reasons for him not to, he'd made himself vulnerable to her. She looked at the table and considered her options, and then looked up, ready to make herself vulnerable too. "Charlie found me," she admitted, her words cramming together as though in a hurry to get out before she changed her mind. "Yesterday. He showed up at my condo in Puhi with this list of questions about his mother." She pulled the list out of her shoulder bag and placed the folded paper on the table between them. "I was going to call the police, but I left him alone and when I came back, he was gone."

Mr. Olie glanced at the paper, his thick eyebrows pulled together, but didn't reach for it.

She wondered if he was afraid to read it, afraid of becoming emotionally involved in whatever the list contained. Sadie couldn't blame him. She'd read it, and she couldn't let go of it now.

"He took all the cash from my wallet, but I don't want to get him in trouble. I haven't told the police because I'm afraid they'll take him out of his foster home—that happened to a foster family I know in Colorado—so I came to you instead. The police don't seem to be actively investigating his mother's death, and I don't think Charlie believes his mom is really dead, and I'm just . . . I don't know what I want or what I'm looking for except that it feels like something isn't right, and maybe if I can answer these questions for Charlie I can help make it a little less wrong."

She stopped for a breath, but when she opened her mouth to continue she realized she'd already said too much. Mr. Olie was looking at her as though she were something confusing, something untrustworthy, and Sadie felt her heart racing at having allowed herself to become so vulnerable. She snatched the list back and shoved it in her bag, wondering if this was how Charlie had felt when she'd told him she had no answers for him. And hadn't Mr. Olie already made it clear that he'd made up his mind about Noelani? He didn't *want* to believe anything different.

"I'm sorry I interrupted your lunch," she said quickly as she stood and tried to keep her back straight. She knew she should look him in the eye, leave a strong impression, but she didn't feel strong anymore and so she kept her eyes on the floor. She felt ridiculous. "Sorry," she mumbled again as she stepped away from the table.

She gripped the strap of her bag that hung across her chest and hurried toward the street, wondering why she'd come at all. She needed to get back home. She had to wind around some other buildings before she got to the sidewalk, but once there, she realized she'd lost her bearings. Where was she? Where was the nearest bus stop? She dug in her bag for the bus schedule, then checked her watch to see that she had twenty minutes until the next bus came to the Rice Shopping Center stop where she'd originally gotten off. Could she hold on to her sanity for twenty minutes? Wait, then she'd have the bus ride and the walk home—she'd have to hold on to her sanity a little longer. And she didn't know where the Rice stop was from here.

Her hands started to shake, and she swallowed again. She started walking, looking for a landmark that would tell her how to get back to the bus stop. She felt as though everyone were wondering who she was and what she was doing. She had to look as out of place as she felt right now. What if Mr. Olie went to the police with what she'd told him? She hadn't emphasized that Charlie was away from his foster home the way she should have. Would Mr. Olie follow up on it? Should she go to the police now that Mr. Olie hadn't responded the way she'd expected he would? She'd been so sure contacting him was the best choice.

She reached the corner of the block and turned in a slow circle, trying to figure out where she was and holding back frustrated tears. She had no business trying to do any of this.

An awning a few blocks down the street looked like it might be familiar, but as Sadie stepped off the curb, a dark truck pulled in front of her. She stepped back quickly, gasping at what felt like a close call even though she was at least four feet away from any real danger.

The passenger side window rolled down, and Mr. Olie leaned across the seat. "Where you headed?"

"Puhi," she said after a moment. Lifting up the bus schedule, she added, "I got turned around and don't know where my stop is."

He pulled the door release and pushed it open. "Maybe we have a little more to say to one another."

Sadie looked at the open door, questioning whether or not she was safe, but realized she didn't feel any safer on the streets of Lihue. And she was too tired and overwhelmed to turn down a helping hand. She sat down in the passenger seat and pulled the door shut with a snap.

"Thank you," she said sheepishly, feeling like a child.

He nodded, then checked his blind spot before pulling into traffic, giving the two-fingered "shaka" wave to another car that let him in. Sadie tried to relax, but kept clenching the strap of her bag nervously. She waited for Mr. Olie to start the conversation, but he didn't. Maybe he was taking his time because he was sorting out his own thoughts.

"There's a stop," Sadie said, recognizing one she'd passed on her way into town.

"I'll drop you off in Puhi," he said.

"Oh. Okay." She tried not to admit to feeling a little freaked out, but she *was* a little freaked out.

"What's your name?" he asked as he pulled onto the Kaumualii Highway toward Puhi.

"Sadie Hoffmiller," she said, not remembering whether she'd introduced herself at the restaurant. Before Kaua'i she would have been certain she had—she was always well mannered—but so many things had fallen by the wayside lately.

"Where are you staying?"

"The Coral Coast Condos."

"On Valley Street?"

Sadie turned to look at him. "You know it?"

"Kaua'i is not a big island, and I've visited homes in every neighborhood at some time or another."

"Oh," Sadie said, shifting uncomfortably. "Do you live in Lihue?"

"I'll check in on Charlie," Mr. Olie said instead of answering her question. "How much money did he take?"

"Not quite a hundred dollars."

"Do you want it back?"

"No," she said quickly, thrilled to know Mr. Olie was going to do something to help her. "I don't care about that; I just want to make sure he's okay."

He was looking forward, still burdened and tired, but thoughtful too. "Before Charlie was removed from his mother's care, he was on his own a lot, and sometimes she didn't buy food. He's continued to struggle with the impulse to steal and hoard since being in foster care. It's something we're working on, but I would rather use this as a means to find him better help than getting the police involved. If you're not planning on pressing charges, I think I can get this worked out without having to risk him being sent to detention— which is the next step if this ends up on his record. He already ran once, and it's only because he's in one of my best homes that they allowed him back."

"Thank you for checking on him," Sadie said. "I feel awful for what he's been through."

"I do too," he said. "He doesn't deserve the life he's been handed."

Sadie nodded and wondered if Mr. Olie was going to say more, but he remained silent. Sadie followed his lead.

When they reached Puhi, she asked if he would drop her off by the local market instead of at her condo a few blocks further west. Mr. Olie pulled over at the corner of the small business district. She thanked him as she stepped away from the car. She expected him to say something more, but he just nodded his head again. She shut the door, and a moment later, he pulled back into the street, disappearing around a bend in the road.

Well, that was interesting, she thought.

Sadie adjusted her bag as her phone dinged to alert her to an incoming text message. It was from Gayle.

I land in Honolulu at 8:00 am Friday. Kaua'i by 10:30. Will send more info later.

Sadie texted back a smiley face, but then she caught her reflection in a storefront window. She was so different from the woman Gayle had said good-bye to in Garrison three months ago. Sadie raised a hand to her head, where a thousand little hairs had come out of her bun and corkscrewed around her face. She didn't want Gayle to see her like this.

She stopped walking and looked at the shops around her on the main street of Puhi. She hadn't noticed the sign for The Salon before, but now she moved forward and looked at a paper sign in the window that said "Walk-ins Welcome."

There is no way I can let Gayle see what I've allowed myself to become, she told herself. With that in mind, she took a deep breath and pulled open the door.

CHAPTER 14

Even though Sadie had made the conscious decision to go into the salon, she realized that part of her hoped they wouldn't be able to help her so she could feel good about the *idea* but not have to follow through. Fortunately—or unfortunately depending on the perspective she took from any one moment to the next—a Filipina stylist by the name of Lou was just finishing up a trim and could help Sadie right away.

"I was planning to go home early," Lou said as she put some gel in the hair of the woman sitting in front of her. "But all I've got is my no-good boyfriend waiting for me so I may as well stay and earn some rent money."

Lou was open and friendly, and Sadie tried not to be terrified of her. Two other hairdressers and a nail tech were bustling around the salon and chatting with their customers. One conversation was in a language Sadie didn't recognize, maybe Filipino since both women seemed to be of that ethnicity; she hoped they weren't talking about her. It had been a long time since she'd been around so many busy people, and she found their energy surprising.

"So, you want it colored?" Lou asked after Sadie took a seat in the chair facing the mirror. She took Sadie's hair out of the bun; it looked even worse than she remembered it. Lou ran her fingers through the jagged curls, her fingers catching where the split ends tangled together.

"I want whatever will fix it," Sadie said.

The stylist rubbed a section of hair between her fingers. "Blonde?"

"An attempt," Sadie said, embarrassed. "It looked nice for the first two weeks."

"It always does," Lou said, still smiling as she appraised Sadie carefully. "Blonde is a tricky color, though. Requires maintenance, yeah?"

Sadie nodded. The salon smelled like acetone and perm solution, zinging her nose, which wasn't used to such aromas.

"How do you feel about giving into the gray?" Lou touched the two inches of grown-out roots that connected Sadie's brassy-ash-colored blonde to her scalp.

"I've never thought about it." Sadie had always equated gray hair with old women, and yet she knew a handful of women her age who had transitioned to all gray and looked amazing. Pam Sandival from the library committee had gone gray in her late twenties, and never colored it a single day. Now, in her early fifties, her hair was snowy white and beautiful. Then there was Paula Deen—she was a knockout, too. "Wouldn't you have to cut off all the color? I don't want it that short." Short hair would make her look like a man, she was certain, and that wasn't a look she was going for.

"We can blend it with some other colors while you grow it out so you can keep some length, then work with it until the transition is complete."

Sadie had forgotten to mention she'd only be in Kaua'i for another month.

"If I trim it up, maybe to about here"—Lou lifted the last couple of inches of Sadie's hair off her neck, so that the bulk of her hair was to her chin—"and put in some fun, choppy layers that would give you some sass without taking you all the way to punk, I could weave in some brown, black, and platinum. That would give you a more gradual change toward your regular gray." She dropped the hair and inspected the roots again. "You have really healthy hair, and it's not thinning. With the right product, we could control your curl just enough to keep it full without being too . . . amplified, if you know what I mean."

"Really?" Sadie said, looking at herself and wishing she could see the vision this girl had.

"Gray's all the thing right now, anyway, and you can always go back, to, uh, blonde if you don't like it, but, honestly, I think you can pull off gray better than most." She ran her fingers through Sadie's hair again. It was strange to be touched after so much isolation. "You've got great texture and tone, and with a little training on how to style your hair here on the island, I think you'd be really happy."

Sadie looked at herself in the mirror, really looked, and made peace with the idea of bringing a little more of the real Sadie to the surface. She imagined the cut Lou was suggesting, and then imagined people seeing her looking that way. Her goals stuck to the fridge at the condo came to mind again: *Do something brave every day.* She'd already done many brave things today, what was one more?

"Let's do it," Sadie said, smiling widely at the stylist's reflection in the mirror, excited to become the woman Lou saw.

Lou gave her a little shoulder hug from behind. "Ono," she said with a sharp nod and a bright smile.

Lou headed to the back of the salon as one nail customer left and another one came in, a haole like Sadie. The other two stylists started talking about a mutual friend whose husband had left her for reasons undisclosed. A beauty shop always seemed a hotbed of female gossip. The stylists discussed several motives but eventually concluded it had to be another woman. The man had always been a dog. Their clients agreed, and they moved to the next topic—the drug-seeking helicopters that kept waking up one of the women's children during nap time.

"So a farmer grows a few *pakalolo* plants to make up for the shortfall with his mango trees," one of the stylists said as she pulled a lock of hair up from her client's head and snipped off the ends. "The *aupuni* need to legalize it and get it over with."

True, Sadie had been a hermit, but she was still aware of the relaxed attitude many people had toward marijuana here on Kaua'i. Kids wore T-shirts with the big green leaf, and many cars sported green-and-yellow bumper stickers that read "2450 steps closer to legal!" referring to bill 2450 that had reduced possession of small amounts of marijuana from a misdemeanor to a civil infraction. Sadie wondered if the amount of the drug found in Noelani's things was within that limit. Would a civil offense have impeded her reunification with Charlie?

"Ah, but to make it legal will bring every pothead from the mainland to our beaches—our neighborhoods." The other woman shook her foil-wrapped head. "People who need it can get their blue cards; no one else should be messing with it. It's *pilikia.*"

Sadie didn't know what pilikia meant, but she had a Hawaiian dictionary at the condo and hoped she'd remember the word long enough to look it up. She had her own opinions on the topic of legalizing marijuana, but she was a malihini, and it wasn't really any of her business so she let the words move around her, educating her on the community she was sort of a part of.

"Those cards are a great start," the nail technician inserted, filing her client's nails in a rhythmic pattern as she shook her head. "My nephew has that Crohn's disease, got himself a card to deal with the pain and now he can hold a job."

"Well, my neighbor has a card too," the foil-headed lady said. "And he beats his wife when he's high. His two sons toke up with him, now that it's legal to do so. I say double the helicopters and draw a hard line—no drugs on Kaua'i. We have the best beaches in the world and the beauty of Mount Wai'ale'ale. What do we need drugs to improve for us?"

"Oh," the first stylist said with a laugh, "you are not paying attention. Fort Street gets closer every day, sistah, and a little pot at the end of the day is nothing compared to the things happening on this island. It's ridiculous that the government gives a blue card, but makes people buy from a corner dealer. They support the very thing they say they are working against. If pot were legal, they could spend the time and the money to find the *real* drug dealers—the ones who are seducing our children with their meth every single day. Instead, we arrest single moms and out-of-work farmers for trying to put bread on the table." She shook her head and clucked her tongue. "The real pilikia slides right past the KPD."

"All right," Lou said as she reappeared from the back, balancing three plastic bowls in her hands and taking Sadie's attention away from the discussion. Lou carefully transferred the bowls to the counter before pulling out a stack of foil papers from a drawer and arranging them the way she wanted them.

"This is going to be great," Lou said, flashing Sadie a bright smile. "I just love working with brave women."

Brave. The word washed through Sadie, bringing with it hope that she could be a brave woman again. As Lou started brushing the color on Sadie's hair and folding over the foils, Sadie allowed herself to look at her successes today. She'd learned about Noelani, and she'd found Mr. Olie and passed on what she knew about Charlie. She'd agreed to have Gayle come, and she was getting her hair done for the first time in months.

She let the pride wash over her as she redirected Lou's questions about herself back to Lou's life instead. It worked, and before she knew it, Sadie was hearing all about how Lou met her boyfriend who, though he drove her crazy with his lack of motivation to work, was the love of her life—*ke aloha o ku'u ola.* Sadie listened to Lou talk, concentrated on her breathing, and watched herself be transformed.

CHAPTER 15

Sadie kept catching her reflection in the windows of the shops she passed on her way to the market two hours later. It was difficult to trust her own judgment, but she thought she really liked what Lou had done. The colors she'd woven in worked well together and gave Sadie a kind of salt-and-pepper look that blended into the existing gray of her roots and darkened on the way to her ends, which Lou had showed her how to flip out. Her hair was layered and felt light on her head, and yet the cut gave her a fullness that seemed to balance out her body. Lou had also sold Sadie $30 worth of product that would allow her to do the same thing herself, but Sadie was doubtful it would look as good as when Lou did it.

It was nearly four o'clock, and she hadn't eaten since her bowl of cereal that morning—and the shoyu chicken and rice in the middle of the night—so at the market, Sadie filled her basket with things she hadn't wanted to commit herself to before now. She added flour and sugar to her list, having decided to make macadamia nut pancakes with Tanya's coconut syrup for dinner. It was one of half a dozen recipes Tanya had taped to the inside of her kitchen cabinets for easy reference. Sadie had made the meal once, when she had first arrived, and enjoyed it, but then things had gotten dark, and even pancakes felt like too much work. But she was brave today. And hungry.

She was also exhausted. By the time she got home, her feet were dragging, and she was having a hard time holding onto the motivation to put effort into anything, let alone cooking, which was unfamiliar to her these days. In hopes of getting a second wind, Sadie read through the recipe and put the coconut milk in a strainer over a bowl to get it ready to make into syrup.

However, the second wind she'd hoped for didn't materialize, and when Pete called, she was relieved to be able to sit on the futon with her cell phone and tell him all about Officer Wington, Mr. Olie, and her hair. He was relieved with her progress, and though he didn't say it out loud, she felt that he was okay with her not calling the police. It would be a few weeks before she'd know what he thought about her hair.

"Good work," Pete said. "You had a very productive day."

"I did," Sadie said, unable to hide her own smile of satisfaction. "And even though it was kind of scary, it was really good. Thank you for your help. I couldn't have done it without a cheering section and you finding Mr. Olie for me."

"I'm glad I could help from so far away," he said. "I'm jealous that it's Gayle coming out and not me."

"Oh," Sadie said, touched, but slightly horrified by the thought. "You're not ready for me. I still have some work to do."

Pete chuckled. "I'll have you any way I can get you."

Sadie felt her cheeks heat up. Pete must have caught the unintended implication too because he cleared his throat and changed the subject. "What next?" he asked.

"Well," Sadie said, happy to follow his lead, "I think I want to talk to the employee who loaned Noelani the car that night. She also attended a church in Kalaheo, so maybe I could talk to her minister after my appointment with Dr. McKay tomorrow."

"Sounds like another full day, then."

"Yes," Sadie agreed. "Brimming. In a good way, I hope."

"You sound tired."

"I'm exhausted," Sadie admitted. "At least I earned my exhaustion today, though."

"I'm proud of you," Pete said. "You did some good today."

"Thanks," Sadie said, letting the compliment wash over her.

"I'll let you get some rest, okay?"

He must have forgotten it was only four thirty in the afternoon in Hawai'i. She needed to be on a normal sleep schedule before Gayle arrived, so she was determined to stay up until at least nine o'clock.

"But we'll talk again tomorrow, and if you need me for any reason, don't hesitate to call, okay?"

"Okay."

They said their gooey-sweet good-byes, and Sadie put the phone on the end table before deciding to rest her eyes for a minute. Okay, ten minutes. Maybe twenty.

The sound of someone knocking at the door caused her to bolt upright. *What time is it?* She hurried to the door, pulling it open before she had time to think about being anxious about a visitor.

Mr. Olie filled the porch, and Sadie stopped in silent surprise. "Mr. Olie," she said once she remembered her manners. "Um, hi."

He nodded his head in response, but didn't offer anything more.

"Would you like to come in?" Sadie asked. She still didn't know what time it was but the shadows outside were growing dark as they prepared for sunset. Seven o'clock? Maybe eight?

He shook his head and let out a breath, his large hands shoved into the front pockets of his Bermuda shorts that still showed some grease stains from his fish tacos at lunch. "I dropped in on Charlie's foster home."

"Was he there?" Sadie said eagerly.

Mr. Olie nodded. "He was at school, but came home while I was there."

"Oh, thank goodness," Sadie said, letting out a breath. Charlie was home. He was safe.

Mr. Olie continued. "I told his foster mom that someone thought they'd seen him somewhere on Tuesday, and she said he had come home after the memorial service and had stayed home the rest of the day."

Sadie felt heat well up in her chest. Did Mr. Olie think she was lying about Charlie having come to Puhi? "He was here," she defended. "Right here. I fed him some shoyu chicken and he left his list."

"His foster mother was lying to me," Mr. Olie said. "It was a normal visit until I mentioned that afternoon, and then she was nervous and fidgety. When Charlie came home, she hurried me out the door. I've done this a long time; I know when I'm being lied to. CeeCee has never been dishonest with me before."

CeeCee, Sadie noted in her mind. She was Charlie's foster mother, the one the police had been talking to when Charlie had overheard Sadie's name.

Sadie remembered that Mr. Olie had referred to Charlie's foster home as one of his best homes. She thought about the two other cases he'd told her about, how discouraging they'd been. How hopeless he'd felt.

"I'm sorry," Sadie said, unsure of what else she could say.

"I have an idea," Mr. Olie said.

"Oh?"

"Why don't you talk to her?"

"Oh, uh . . ." Sadie glanced around as though she might see an excuse why she couldn't do that. It was an automatic response she'd honed well over the months she'd made up reasons why she couldn't go out with Konnie and the Blue Muumuus. But she caught herself this time. She'd wanted to answer Charlie's questions, and it was silly to assume the pursuit of those answers wouldn't raise a few more questions along the way. "Why me?"

"I didn't paint her into a corner or confront her with what you've told me, but I think you can get her to tell you the truth. Will you do it?"

Sadie wanted to say no. But she also wanted to help Charlie, and Mr. Olie was asking her to help him do that. *Be brave.* "Can I have a few minutes to put together something to eat? All I had was cereal this morning, and I'm starving." And she needed a little time to absorb the unexpected request.

Mr. Olie's face lit up, showing the most animation Sadie had ever seen from him before. It startled her, and she found herself reflexively closing the door a little as though to protect her from something she didn't understand. "Any chance you have enough to share?"

Sadie relaxed and felt another link to the Sadie she had once been fall into place. Feeding people, sharing what she had with someone else, was something familiar.

"I certainly do," she said, standing to the side of the door and pulling it wide open. "And I'd love the company."

CHAPTER 16

M r. Olie had left his shoes at the door, an island tradition Sadie had forgotten about since she had so few visitors and was a visitor to other people's homes even less. Like, never. Once he'd taken a seat at the kitchen table, Sadie offered him a Pop Tart for the sake of time. His face fell. "That's what you meant when you said you were going to make something?"

"Well, no, I was going to make macadamia nut pancakes with coconut syrup, but I didn't know if there was time."

His expression brightened immediately and he nodded quickly. "There's time. Charlie isn't going anywhere."

"It'll take me about fifteen minutes," Sadie warned, glancing at the clock to see what time it was: 7:02.

"That's fine," he said. "Home-cooked food is worth waiting for."

Sadie began assembling the ingredients she needed. Tanya had a pancake recipe, but Sadie was partial to her own so she made it instead, adding the vanilla extract and the nuts.

"I eat out a lot," he said out of the blue.

Sadie gave him a sympathetic smile, wondering if part of the reason for his gruff personality was because he was lonely. He didn't wear a wedding ring, and he didn't talk like someone with a lot of close connections. That was too bad. At the same time, if he weren't so prickly, maybe he'd have a wife or a girlfriend who'd cook for him. Life was funny that way.

He looked at his large hands clasped together on the tabletop. "Could I look at Charlie's list?"

"Sure," Sadie said, wiping her hands on her muumuu and heading toward her bag to retrieve it. He looked over the list and asked Sadie about Charlie's visit, which she relayed to him in detail as she mixed the batter in a bowl and brought the syrup to a boil on the stove. It was a relief to tell someone. Not that Pete and Gayle didn't count, but to tell someone who knew Charlie was different. She worried Mr. Olie would question why she didn't go after Charlie when he left the first time, but he didn't ask. Just listened.

When she finished, she asked about his visit with Charlie's foster mother, CeeCee, hoping Mr. Olie would be as open with her as she'd been with him.

He paused and then said that he'd driven straight to the foster home after dropping her off in Puhi earlier in the day. That meant the foster home was south of Puhi. She wondered if it was in Kalaheo, where Noelani had lived and worked.

"CeeCee asked me about permanent placement again."

"Again?" Sadie asked. The first pancakes were cooking on the griddle, but she was out of practice arranging the order of what she cooked, and the syrup wasn't ready yet. It was a novice mistake that annoyed her.

"CeeCee and her husband, Yogi, have fostered boys for almost twenty years; they've also adopted four of the boys they fostered. Yogi passed away six years ago. CeeCee continues to foster and does a wonderful job—always in compliance, very loving, and yet strong enough to properly guide the children in her home. All four of her boys are grown and doing well—two are married with children of their own, another one is in the military. She's as good as they come, and Charlie's been a good fit with her. She told me a few months ago that if things didn't work out with Noelani, she wanted to look into adopting Charlie." He paused, watching hungrily as Sadie flipped the pancakes. They smelled absolutely wonderful.

After a few seconds, she looked at him with an expectant expression, and he shook himself out of his scent-induced stupor. Sadie took pride in having created it, but she still wanted to hear the rest of what he had to say.

"When the family court gave Noelani ninety days, I told CeeCee about it in person because I knew it would be hard for her. She was supportive of reunification, which she knows is the first priority of DHS, but now Noelani's gone, and she's apparently still interested in pursuing the possibility of adoption."

"Which is probably why she lied to you about him being gone. She didn't want to endanger her chances." Sadie hoped that CeeCee wanting to adopt Charlie hadn't played some part in Noelani's death. It was a horrible thought.

She stirred the syrup, relieved that it was thickening up nicely. Thank goodness she'd drained the coconut milk before lying on the couch.

Mr. Olie nodded, but he was watching Sadie carefully as she moved the pancakes from the griddle onto two plates. She topped both of them with the hot, white syrup and slid one plate in front of Mr. Olie and the other in front of the seat across from him.

"Mahalo," he said as he cut a bite from his pancake. He put the first syrup-dripping bite into his mouth and chewed it slowly, as if savoring every moment.

Sadie sat down and smiled as she cut a bite of her own. It felt good to see someone enjoy her food again. It had been a long time, not counting Charlie. The food she'd served him had consisted of brownies from a mix and the chicken and rice Konnie had cooked—nothing that inspired a lot of pride.

Sadie got up to put a new batch of pancakes on the griddle, and then they both ate in silence for a few minutes. She got up to turn the pancakes and then again to remove them from the griddle. She put the syrup on a trivet on the table and the extra pancakes on a plate in the center. Mr. Olie put three more pancakes on his plate as soon as he finished his first serving.

Sadie waited until he started slowing down before talking again. The old Sadie would never interrupt someone's moment of joyful eating. When he asked for a glass of milk, however, she was embarrassed not to have thought of it first. She got the milk from the fridge and filled a glass, which he drained half of in a single swallow. She topped off his glass and poured herself one of her own before putting the milk back in the fridge.

"What makes you think Charlie's foster mom will tell me the truth?" she asked.

"You're a woman. You're not government. You're safe."

"I'm malihini. I'm haole. I'm . . . anxious."

"It's our best bet," he said, resting his fork and knife on the edges of his plate. "Look, if Charlie ran and CeeCee didn't report it, she knows she's in big trouble, and so is Charlie. She could lose her certification. Charlie will go to detention if that happens, probably on O'ahu, and the hard things he's dealing with will get a whole lot worse. Right now there's still a good chance she'll be able to adopt Charlie."

"Except that she lied to the social worker who would be a key person in recommending the adoption take place, right?"

"I've been doing this a long time," Mr. Olie said. "The letter of the law isn't always the right choice, but she won't take the chance of trusting me *not* to follow the rules because I have the power to stop the adoption completely."

"So, if I get the information from her, you won't write her up or whatever you would do?"

"That depends on what happened, and why she lied. I need to understand her motives . . . without also putting myself at risk of being taken off her case."

"For not reporting what you know."

"What she would *know* I know," he clarified. "By not confiding in me, she doesn't know I'm aware of what's going on, and I don't worry about her going around me."

"To your superiors," Sadie said, filling in the blanks.

Mr. Olie nodded.

She held his eyes for a minute. "Why trust me? You don't even know me."

"You didn't call the police about Charlie, and you came to Lihue to talk to me. I think our goals are aligned. We both want to know Charlie's safe and ensure that he stays that way. I need to know why CeeCee lied to me in order to properly assess the situation, but I can't ask her myself."

Sadie nodded, but found it difficult to swallow her bite of pancake. She'd talked to a lot of different types of people over the last year and a half as she pieced together different mysteries. She knew how to do it, and she had rarely been nervous in the past, surely she could do it again. She took a deep breath and lifted her head, determined to appear confident and capable, even if internally she questioned both of those things.

"Can I ask one more question?"

Though he didn't nod, he didn't tell her no either.

"What were the special circumstances that brought Noelani and Charlie to Kaua'i?"

He looked down at his plate and took a bite before he answered. "You already know Charlie was removed from his mother's care two years ago when she was arrested. Her brother was the only local relative DHS felt was capable of caring for him, so Charlie went to live with him while she served her time. Six months into the placement, a few weeks before Noelani was going to be released, the brother was arrested for child abuse."

"Against Charlie?" Sadie said, a lump in her throat.

"Some," he said. "Mostly his own boy, but Charlie got a fair amount as well. A neighbor had called the caseworker months earlier, but she didn't follow up the way she should have. She had almost twice the cases she should have been carrying at the time. Charlie was put in foster care after his uncle's arrest. Due to the circumstances of Noelani's arrest and parole, Charlie couldn't be returned to her custody immediately upon her release. She was determined to get her son back, however, and the state made some accommodations because of what had happened with her brother. We had a very specific set of guidelines and timelines that would put her and Charlie back together again—including rehab, parenting classes, gainful employment, and community involvement. The state felt that having her and Charlie both come to Kaua'i and work with a new caseworker—me—and a new judge would create a better environment for her to meet the goals we set before her."

Sadie tried to hide her surprise at the flood of information. It felt like wonderful progress in regard to their relationship. "Are those circumstances part of why you're giving CeeCee the benefit of the doubt and working so hard to figure out what happened?"

Mr. Olie nodded. "It doesn't happen very often," he said. "But in this situation, the state of Hawai'i really hurt Charlie and, in the process, Noelani too. I worked hard to try to rebuild that trust, and now Charlie's the only one left to make things up to."

"Officer Wington, the officer I talked to this morning, said something about having met Noelani before all this happened. Do you know what that was about?"

Mr. Olie bobbed his head. "A few months after she finished rehab, a guy she'd gone through the program with was picked up for distribution. He tried to finger some of the other people from the rehab as his accomplices. Noelani was one of them, and, because of her history, she was considered a person of interest for awhile. In the end, the guy recanted and admitted he'd named those people he'd had conflicts with. I guess Noelani had turned him in for stashing beer in his room during treatment. She had nothing to do with the drug deals."

"I see," Sadie said. "Was she upset they questioned her?"

"Very. She wasn't very trusting of police, or anyone in authority really, and that certainly didn't help. I hope the officer you spoke to didn't imply she had some involvement in that."

"No," Sadie said. "He just mentioned he knew her before is all. I wondered why."

They were both quiet for a few seconds, then Sadie pulled her confidence together, took a deep breath and offered a smile as Mr. Olie leaned back in his chair and fully enjoyed his final bite.

"I'm ready when you are," she said.

Macadamia Nut Pancakes with Coconut Syrup

2 cups all-purpose flour
1/3 cup sugar
2 teaspoons baking powder
1 teaspoon baking soda
1/2 teaspoon salt
2 cups buttermilk or sour milk
1/3 cup vegetable oil
2 eggs
1 teaspoon vanilla
1/2 cup macadamia nuts, chopped

Coconut Syrup
1 (14-ounce) can of coconut milk
1/2 cup white sugar
1/4 teaspoon sea salt
1/2 teaspoon vanilla

Heat griddle or frying pan to medium-high heat. Combine all dry ingredients in one bowl, whisk together. Add wet ingredients and stir together to form a batter, adding more flour or water to get the right consistency. Add nuts, and mix to combine. Spray heated griddle or frying pan with nonstick spray, or lightly brush with butter or vegetable oil. Drop batter by one-third cup portions onto hot, greased pan. Cook 2 to 3 minutes or until edges of pancakes are dry. Turn pancakes and cook 1 to 2 additional minutes, or until cooked through. Remove to a plate and butter immediately.

To make syrup, strain coconut solids from the coconut milk. Save 1/2 cup of the resulting coconut water and combine with sugar in a small saucepan over medium-high heat. Bring to a boil. Simmer about 5 minutes, or until mixture begins to thicken. Add coconut solids and simmer another 2 to 3 minutes, until mixture is combined and smooth.

Add sea salt and vanilla. Stir to combine flavors. Serve over hot, buttered pancakes. (You can also use traditional maple syrup with macadamia nut pancakes.)

Serves 6.

Note: For a thicker syrup, make a slurry from 1 teaspoon cornstarch and 1 tablespoon coconut water, add with solids.

Note: Add 1 ripe mashed banana to batter for Banana Macadamia Nut Pancakes.

CHAPTER 17

Kalaheo was bigger than Puhi, but not close to a larger town like Lihue was, thus a bit more self-sustaining. Where was the motel where Noelani lived and worked? Did she and Charlie see each other often? Was being able to be in the same town part of the special conditions of their situation with DHS?

Mr. Olie dropped Sadie off at a street corner and pointed to a café where they'd meet when she finished. She looked at the two-story cement apartment building on the right, painted bright blue. The white railing on the stairs and the balcony was pockmarked with rust. Power lines hung heavily across the street, connecting to a ramshackle hut across from the apartments that was surrounded by a weathered wooden fence. A couple of chickens pecked at the dirt, and Sadie reviewed the instructions Mr. Olie had given her when he dropped her off a block away. *First yellow house on the right after the two-story blue apartments.*

It took another minute to reach the foster home, and Sadie inhaled the heavy scent in the air—sweet, fruity, but yeasty too. She couldn't be certain it was coming from Charlie's foster home, but in case it was, she wished she was coming on behalf of a more social visit. It smelled delicious.

Sadie walked up the somewhat overgrown flagstone path. It was a nice plantation-style home painted bright yellow with green trim. Two rocking chairs sat on a large wraparound wooden deck. A hedge skirted the property, and hibiscus bushes lined the front of the house while Mount Wai'ale'ale rose behind it. Yellow flowers with red centers, called Hula Girls, were scattered here and there around the yard and matched the house, further emphasizing the cheery look of the home.

A tiny rooster came around the corner of the house, one of the thousands of feral animals on the island. Without natural predators, chickens, goats, wild pigs, and cat populations were out of control. Tanya had a trapping company that took care of the cats around the condos—spaying or neutering them before rereleasing them—and Sadie hadn't had any run-ins with the pigs or goats since she stayed away from the mountains. She didn't mind the chickens, though; they were kind of cute. This one had a rust-colored head, black body, and a cream-colored tail that arched nearly to the ground. Classy . . . for poultry, anyway.

Sadie walked up the concrete steps. A twelve-inch plastic butterfly was mounted on the front door beside a nameplate that read "Kahuali." Sadie knocked on the door before taking a step back. She took a deep breath, planning how she was going to go about this, anticipating the reaction of Charlie's foster mother, and praying for a little help in knowing exactly how to move forward. Her goal was simple—find out why CeeCee Kahuali had lied to the social worker who considered her one of his best foster homes. No problem, right?

All her words stuck in her throat, however, when the door opened and none other than Charlie himself looked up at her, his wide eyes going even wider as Sadie blinked at him. They stared at each other for a few seconds until Sadie found her voice.

"Charlie?" she breathed. "Uh, how—"

"Who is it, Charlie?"

The woman's voice pulled Sadie's attention away from Charlie, and she looked up as a top-heavy woman wearing an apron over a tank top and casual knee-length skirt approached from behind him. She was older than Sadie had expected, possibly older than Sadie herself, and was drying her hands on a dish towel as she approached them. When she arrived at the door, she placed one hand on Charlie's shoulder like any mother would. She was an over-tanned Caucasian with somewhat frizzy bottle-blonde hair, mostly covered by a turquoise bandana that matched her skirt. She had green eyes and pronounced crow's feet when she smiled, revealing a gap between her two front teeth that was very Lauren Bacall, island-style.

"Aloha," she said, inclining her head slightly.

"Aloha," Sadie replied automatically.

"Can I help you?"

"Uh," Sadie hedged, trying to remember why she was there. "I, uh, wondered if I could talk to you for a few minutes." She tried to ignore Charlie's expression of fear. Her heart tightened. Was her coming here going to get him in trouble? What if she did or said something that made everything worse? Then again, maybe he needed to get in trouble. Just not too much. Her discomfort seemed to pull her anxiety out of hiding. She didn't know how to move forward; it all felt so awkward.

A buzzer went off from somewhere behind them, and CeeCee stepped forward to wave Sadie inside. "Oh, those are my rolls. I've got a big order due for a wedding in the morning, and I'm in a rush to get them baked up. Wait here for a minute, will you?"

That explained the heavenly aroma from the street; Sadie realized it was even stronger now that she was inside. CeeCee reached around Sadie, ushering her in as she did so, and shut the door before heading toward the back of the house. Sadie could see an outdoor kitchen through the screen door at the back—common in Hawai'i to keep from overheating the house. There was a pile of shoes and rubber slippahs by the door, and Sadie slipped off her own.

"Have a seat," CeeCee called over her shoulder. "Charlie, will you get her a drink, dear?"

Charlie, however, had backed up as though intent on disappearing. Sadie honed in on him as soon as they were alone, and at her look, he slipped down the hallway. She automatically headed in his direction. He entered a room, and she didn't hesitate to follow him. Her building anxiety about this meeting, culminating with the shock of seeing Charlie, had her reeling and unsure of what to do, which meant she couldn't control her feelings as well as she liked. She was suddenly mad and didn't fully understand why. She'd come here in hopes of helping him, yet right now she just wanted to put him in time out.

Charlie stood in the middle of a bedroom, looking terrified of her as she put her hands on her hips and stared him down from the doorway.

"I think you have something to say to me, young man," she said sharply, trying to control the feelings churning inside of her, but finding it difficult to sort through them all. Was she more upset about the money than she realized? Or was this some new coping mechanism that masked her anxiety with anger?

He stood there, looking scared, and then his eyes darted to the right at the same time someone on far side of the room cleared his throat.

Sweet Hawaiian Dinner Rolls

4 to 5 cups of all-purpose flour, divided
⅓ cup sugar
2 tablespoons dry milk
1 tablespoon instant yeast (To use regular yeast, reduce pineapple
    juice to 1 cup and add yeast to ½ cup warm water. Add proofed
    yeast with other liquids.)
1 teaspoon salt
1½ cups pineapple juice, heated
3 tablespoons butter
2 tablespoons honey
1 egg
1½ teaspoons vanilla

Preheat oven to 150 degrees (or as low as it will go). Mix
one-half of the flour and the rest of the dry ingredients in a mixing
bowl. In a saucepan, heat pineapple juice until warm, but not hot.
Add butter and honey to warmed pineapple juice. Stir until butter is
melted and honey is incorporated. Add to dry ingredients. Add egg
and vanilla. Mix everything until smooth.

Add remaining flour a little at a time until dough is tacky but
does not stick to fingers when touched. Knead 5 minutes. Form dough
into balls (a little larger than a golf ball) and place 1-inch apart on
greased jelly roll pan. Turn off oven. Cover rolls with a dish towel
and put pan of rolls into still-warm oven. Allow rolls to rise 40
minutes or until just doubled. Leave rolls in the oven, but remove
towel and turn heat to 350 degrees. Bake 15 to 20 minutes or
until rolls are a golden brown. Immediately brush tops with butter.

Note: For a lighter roll, allow to rise the first time right after
kneading, still in mixing bowl. Follow the directions here for the
second (shaped) rise.

CHAPTER 18

Sadie's head turned toward the throat-clearer in slow motion, and her heart seemed to stop for at least two full seconds. The old Sadie might have a quick explanation for why she'd followed a boy down the hallway of his own house and confronted him in his bedroom but the new Sadie had nothing.

When her eyes met those of the other person in the room, she relaxed a little bit. Instead of an intimidating man with immense shoulders and glowering eyes—like Mr. Olie—she was face-to-face with a small, thin man, at least part Asian, she guessed, with a sparse mustache and closely cropped hair that spiked up into one of those short Mohawks that were all the rage. He wore board shorts and a gray surf shop T-shirt with the sleeves cut off.

"Um, hi," the man said in a tone that bespoke of suspension of his judgment. At least for now. "Can I, um, help you?"

Sadie dropped her hands from her hips as the stance felt superfluous all of a sudden. She scrambled for an explanation but realized there was nothing to tell but the truth. "My name is Sadie Hoffmiller. Who are you?"

"Who are *you?*" he countered, crossing his arms over his chest with a lot more confidence than Sadie would have liked. Clearly, he wasn't intimidated by her. This would be much easier if he was.

Seeing as how she was in someone else's house and had just chased a little boy down the hallway, Sadie felt she had no choice but to cut to the chase in order to justify her actions. "Charlie robbed me."

The man's eyebrows went up, and his head snapped toward Charlie, who looked suddenly trapped. "What?"

His surprise gave Sadie the confidence she needed, and she decided to answer before Charlie could put any kind of spin on it. "I won't give details until I know who you are. Otherwise, this is between Charlie and me."

The man looked at her. "I'm Charlie's brother, Nat."

"Brother?" Sadie asked, looking between the two of them again. Nat's features were sharp and dark, nothing like Charlie's softer ones. Nat didn't look anything like CeeCee either.

"Foster brother," Nat clarified.

But that didn't help. Nat had a small build, but he was most definitely in his twenties. "Aren't you a little old to be in foster care?"

Nat's jaw tensed, and she cringed. She hadn't meant to insult him.

"I'm one of CeeCee's adopted sons—there's four of us. That makes me Charlie's foster brother."

Oh. Sadie cleared her throat and remembered Mr. Olie giving her the status of CeeCee's sons—all grown, two married with kids, one in the military, and . . . Nat, she supposed.

He raised his eyebrows at her, reminding her that it was her turn to explain her side of things.

"Charlie came to my house on Tuesday, looking for information about his mother. I told him I didn't have what he was looking for, and . . . he stole almost a hundred dollars from my wallet."

"Is that true?" Nat snapped at Charlie. "That's where you went?"

Charlie looked between Sadie and Nat, and Sadie felt her protective instincts rising at the increased look of fear on the little boy's face.

"I'm not here to get him in trouble," she quickly amended, gratified to have an admission that Charlie *had* been gone. That was a step toward the information Mr. Olie needed her to get.

Nat looked back at her. "Why else would you be here? If he stole from you, he—"

Sadie turned to Charlie, not wanting the conversation to go this direction. "I came here because I was worried about you," she said to him, though her tone still sounded angry. She was going to have to work on that. "And I didn't want to get you in trouble by going to the police before I talked to your foster mother about what happened. When did you come back?"

"This morning," he mumbled, looking at the ground.

"And your foster mother wasn't angry?"

He shrugged and glanced at Nat. Sadie did too and saw a guilty expression in Nat's eyes before he looked away. Sadie knew a shared secret when she saw one. "She doesn't know, does she?" Yet CeeCee had still lied to Mr. Olie; Sadie wondered why.

"Where's the money, Charlie?" Nat asked, looking at Charlie and answering her question without saying a word in direct response.

"Um, I, uh, don't know."

"You don't know?" Nat and Sadie said in unison. They shared a quick glance, and Sadie inclined her chin, indicating for Nat to continue . . . for now.

"I lost it," Charlie said.

Nat cocked his head to the side, giving Charlie a look that said he wasn't buying it. "You lost a hundred dollars."

Charlie nodded, but Sadie had no doubt he was lying.

"We'll talk about that later." Nat moved toward a desk in the room that must be his—the room was too clean and too grown up to be Charlie's. He fumbled in a drawer before pulling out a wallet. "I'll make him pay me back."

"I don't care about the money," Sadie said. She quickly heard her own words and looked hard at Charlie. "Although what you did was wrong."

He looked at the floor again, and Sadie turned back to Nat. "But I want to know what's going on. Why was Charlie alone?"

"It wasn't Nat's fault," Charlie said. He shrugged and cast a nervous glance at Nat. "He just took me fishing."

"You weren't fishing from my avocado tree at three o'clock in the morning," Sadie said, staring at both boys. The situation had reached the point where it was completely appropriate for her to put her hands back on her hips, but she didn't. It felt a little too postured now.

Nat tried to look away, but Sadie had perfected her stare through two dozen second-grade classes and two children of her own. Finally, Nat crumpled and looked at Charlie. "Go see if *Makuahine* needs any help. I'll be there in a minute." Sadie had heard the word makuahine before and knew it meant mother.

Charlie didn't jump to action, showing that he was more interested in what was happening here, but Nat gave Charlie a look that didn't allow argument, and the boy slinked away. Nat waited a few seconds, then closed the door and faced Sadie. "It would be helpful if you wouldn't pull CeeCee into this," he said evenly. "It will not help things."

"I'm not so sure," Sadie said, making no promises. "An eleven-year-old boy has no right being left alone, especially at night."

"He was in my care," Nat said, then after considering his own words added. "Mostly."

Sadie raised her eyebrows, and Nat sighed before glancing quickly at the door. Sadie didn't want to be interrupted either but knew it was only a matter of time before CeeCee realized Sadie wasn't waiting in the living room. This was an explanation she couldn't step away from, however.

Nat started talking. "Charlie went to his mom's memorial service Tuesday morning. He didn't want to go to school afterward, but CeeCee had a catering job so I stayed with him. Within half an hour of coming home, I caught him trying to sneak out. I took him into town for a shave ice, and he told me he was planning to go look for his mom."

"So he doesn't think she's dead," Sadie said, feeling validated in her hypothesis.

Nat shook his head. "He's used to her being gone—she's been gone for a lot of his life—but he'd never considered that they wouldn't be together again. Because of the condition of the . . . body, there was no way he could see her, and so he was left having to take the word of a whole bunch of people he doesn't trust. After I talked to him, I called CeeCee and said we were going fishing, but I told him we were going to go to Anahola, where his mom was found, and have our own ceremony. I had hoped it would help him let go. Release his demons."

Sadie thought it was a sweet gesture that had obviously gone awry. "How did he end up in Puhi?"

"We stopped there to buy a lei we could take out to where his mother had been found. There's a flower stand off the highway."

"I know it," Sadie said. She used to walk the mile or so to the stand every few days and talk to the old man, Leloy, who ran the shop with his grandsons. They did the picking while he sold the flowers and the leis he made during the day. She hadn't been there in more than six weeks.

"Did he talk to the old man?" She could imagine him confirming to Charlie where she lived if Charlie had had the gumption to ask for her by name. The towns on Kaua'i were all so small, a few thousand people in each village, if that. Leloy knew everyone in Puhi.

Nat pulled his eyebrows together, then nodded. "I had to take a phone call so I gave him the money for the flowers and stayed in the car. We got back in the car, but then Charlie said he needed to use the bathroom. We stopped at a gas station a couple of blocks later."

"Sid's Texaco," Sadie said with a nod. Right up the street. "That's when he ran off?"

Nat nodded again.

Sadie smiled. "I live a few blocks down from Sid's. What time was this?"

"Around three thirty."

Sadie nodded. "That's about right."

"I waited there for an hour, thinking he'd come back. When he didn't, I spent the rest of the day looking for him, panicking. I called Mom and told her I'd have him home in time for school the next day. She has enough to worry about right now, and I knew she'd get in trouble if his disappearance was reported. I looked everywhere, and then, about six in the morning, when I'd finally given up, I found him walking alongside the highway on his way back to Kalaheo."

"He'd been out of your care for fourteen hours," Sadie said. "That's a very long time."

"I know," Nat said, "but I knew what could happen if I reported him. He's a good kid, but he can be sneaky too. It would have killed CeeCee to know he'd run away again. He did it once before, soon after placement. I couldn't tell her or anyone else until I knew for sure. I was so relieved when I found him and figured he'd had his own . . . aloha for his mother. Sometimes people need solitude."

"You didn't ask him where he'd gone?"

"No. He's becoming a *kane*; I can respect that."

Sadie had seen the word "kane" on many a bathroom door with a stick man below it so she knew what it meant. "He's eleven," she reminded him. "He's not ready to become a man. What if something had happened to him? What if I wasn't who I am, and he'd been turned into the police, or hurt? He could have been taken away from the only family he has left." And yet even as Sadie delivered the lecture, she was glad she hadn't called the police either. She didn't know what Charlie felt for his foster mother, but she sensed he had a bond with Nat.

"You don't think that's exactly what I was thinking?" Nat countered. "I was relieved when I found him. He promised he wouldn't leave again."

There was still the issue of CeeCee telling Mr. Olie that Charlie had been home all day Tuesday. But to ask that would be admitting that Sadie was here on Mr. Olie's orders.

"Your mother didn't ask about the trip?"

"Not details, no," Nat said. "It's been an overwhelming time for her. She's worried about Charlie, busy with her work. She wants what's best for him, really."

Sadie nodded, but knew she still needed to talk to CeeCee.

"He came to you about his mother?" Nat asked.

Sadie nodded. "He must have misunderstood the context of my name in an article. I'd never met her while she was . . . alive."

"What?" he asked, looking a bit stunned. This must be a painful thing to discuss.

"I found her body."

Nat's eyes went wide. The room went silent.

"Why did you really come here? You said you didn't want the money back," Nat asked, once he'd absorbed what Sadie had said.

"I wanted to make sure Charlie was okay," Sadie said. It was the truth. "And . . . I want to help him, if I can." That was true too. "He had a list of questions he left at my house, and I thought that, maybe, if I could answer those, he'd find some peace."

"No one knows what happened to his mom," Nat said. "Last I heard, the police didn't have any leads."

"I know," Sadie said. "But sometimes they miss things, and this isn't really about the police so much as it's about Charlie. I just wanted to help him, and I'm glad to know he has people who care about him."

"That's the help Charlie needs most right now—recognizing how good he has it," Nat said. "He only came to Kaua'i because she did—because the judge wanted them together again. Now that she's gone, everything's changed for him." He pointed to himself. "I can see what he has here, with us. We love him, and we want him here. I can also see that his mother would never have been able to give him this much stability, but he can only mourn what he hoped for. When we got home this morning, CeeCee let him sleep until lunch, then took him to school. He seems to be feeling better, at least as much as he can be."

"Why?" Sadie asked. "Why is he feeling better? I didn't have answers for him."

Nat shrugged, shaking his head and looking troubled.

"Nat?" a woman's voice called from outside the room. CeeCee.

His eyebrows went up, and he began looking around just as his mother pushed open the bedroom door.

Sadie tried to force a smile as her cheeks heated up with embarrassment. She'd been found with a young man behind the closed door of a bedroom. How humiliating.

CeeCee wasn't impressed either. "What are you doing in here?" she asked Sadie, looking at her with justifiable concern, deep lines on her forehead.

"Uh," Sadie said, struggling for an explanation.

"She was interested in ordering some rolls and maybe a cake for her daughter's wedding," Nat said.

"Oh," CeeCee said, though she still looked confused. Sadie didn't blame her; she was confused too. "Why is she in here, then?"

"I was showing her the new flier I made up, yeah?" He grabbed a paper off the printer by the computer and handed it to Sadie.

CeeCee looked at Sadie, still doubtful. "Your daughter's getting married?"

"Well, yes, actually," Sadie said. Breanna *was* getting married, never mind that the wedding was going to take place in either Colorado or England, not Hawai'i.

CeeCee immediately smiled and all doubt and confusion disappeared. "Well, then you've got to try one of my Hawaiian rolls, fresh out of the oven." She grabbed Sadie's hand and pulled her toward the bedroom door.

Sadie glanced over her shoulder, and Nat attempted a smile. He didn't follow her, didn't rescue her at all. Sadie fell in step behind

CeeCee who started explaining how she'd worked in the bakery of a hotel for years before she'd retired after her husband died and now she ran a small catering company with select items—her specialties—from her home. "Keeps my hands in the dough," CeeCee said once they arrived in the kitchen and she'd ordered Sadie into a seat.

She pulled a hot roll off the pan, tossing it from hand to hand to cool it slightly as she continued to talk about her catering. Sadie nodded when appropriate, commented when the time was right, and thoroughly enjoyed the roll, but she didn't get to see Charlie again.

CHAPTER 19

It was almost an hour later before Sadie left with CeeCee's number written on the back of the flyer and two more sweet rolls wrapped in a paper towel. She hurried down the street toward the café where she was meeting Mr. Olie. She hoped the rolls would be an adequate peace offering. It was dark, and the jungle bug sounds that always increased at night made her jumpy.

It was a relief when she turned the corner and saw the café. She picked up the pace, almost getting run over by a guy on a bike who called her a "stupid haole." She apologized as he disappeared around the corner, but she didn't think he heard it. She felt better for having said she was sorry, though, even if he'd insulted her.

Mr. Olie was not happy about how long she'd taken, and, without a word, he drained his coffee cup, refolded the paper he'd been reading, and got up from the booth. Sadie followed him to his truck. She offered up the rolls, and he took them with a grunt, placing them on the seat between them in the truck. Once they were on their way back to Puhi, she filled him in on what had happened.

"You didn't talk to CeeCee about Charlie being gone?" he asked.

Sadie felt the accusation of his question. It was the one thing she had been supposed to do, and she hadn't done it.

"I didn't get the chance," she said. "But I still got the information you wanted, right? We know where Charlie was."

"Nat's not even supposed to be living there," Mr. Olie said.

The comment sent a tremor down her spine as she realized how easily she'd believed what Nat had told her. Was he not trustworthy? "Why not?"

"It's not that big a deal," Mr. Olie said, perhaps hearing the concern in her voice. "It's just that CeeCee's supposed to notify me if anyone else lives in the house. Nat moved up to Hanalei about a year ago; I didn't know he was back. CeeCee's a certified foster parent, but Nat isn't trained through the state to act as a caretaker. For Charlie to be in Nat's care violates her agreements."

"That must be why she lied to you, then," Sadie said. "Because she knew he wasn't certified. From what Nat said, she really wants Charlie to stay—like you said before—and I think she's working hard to ensure he can. I don't feel like there was anything . . . sinister behind it."

Mr. Olie nodded. Did that mean he wouldn't write up CeeCee?

"Nat and Charlie seem to be pretty close," Sadie said. "It might be good to have a male figure in his life to help with the transition. When my husband died, my brother filled that role for my son, and I've always been so grateful he was there for Shawn. I don't think I could have given Shawn what he needed, but Jack did. It was a blessing."

Mr. Olie nodded once, sharp, and returned to his customary thoughtful silence.

Sadie didn't want to let her thoughts turn to the dark spectrum of things, but CeeCee letting Nat live there without approval couldn't be ignored. CeeCee had a good reputation with Mr. Olie—what would motivate her to put that in danger? She must have been in a full-on panic when Mr. Olie had dropped in for a surprise visit and asked about Charlie being out and about on Tuesday. *Was she hiding something?* Sadie wondered. It seemed impossible. CeeCee appeared to be kind and open. But what if Charlie wasn't as safe there as Sadie wanted to believe? What if that household wasn't a good place for him? The thought was depressing. Where else could he go?

Beyond her questions was a truth that sat like a stone in Sadie's stomach—if Noelani were still alive, CeeCee would not be able to adopt Charlie.

"Did CeeCee and Noelani know each other?" Sadie asked.

Mr. Olie nodded. "Noelani had visitation rights. She would pick up Charlie and drop him off."

"Did they talk, ever? I mean, did CeeCee know where Noelani lived and worked? Did they get along?"

Mr. Olie was quiet, and Sadie tensed as she considered the thoughts her questions must be raising in his own mind. He didn't answer her, and she couldn't decide if she was grateful for that. Maybe she didn't want to know. The idea that Charlie wasn't safe where he was, that the one hope for his future wasn't so hopeful, was an awful consideration. She could only imagine that for the man who was inextricably involved in this situation, it was even worse.

Sadie spent the rest of the drive waiting for Mr. Olie to talk to her, but he didn't. It wasn't until she started recognizing landmarks indicating they were close to Puhi that she realized she'd pulled off the meeting with barely a ripple in her emotional state. She hadn't freaked out. She hadn't failed to get the information. Sure, her mind had blanked a time or two, but her fear going into the meeting was that she wouldn't be able to get what Mr. Olie needed. But she had, and despite Mr. Olie's lukewarm reception of what she'd discovered, and despite the concern Sadie had about the circumstances involving Charlie's foster family, she felt a bubbling pride at having achieved her purpose.

A few minutes later, Mr. Olie pulled up in front of her condo, and she got out of the truck.

"Well, I hope I helped," Sadie said, holding the door open.

"Yeah," he answered, sounding distracted. "Me too."

Sadie shut the door and frowned as Mr. Olie drove off. She really wanted to like him, and she did feel sympathy for his discouragement, but other than answering some of her questions and graciously enjoying her food, he wasn't very nice. Had he always been like that, she wondered, or was his current personality a result of the hard times he'd had of late? Maybe with his past health issues and disappointing work situation he'd given up on making room for the niceties of life. If that were true, it was a shame.

When Sadie entered her condo, she flipped on the lights and finished cleaning up the mess leftover from making pancakes. She'd learned the hard way that leaving any food out invited bugs—ants, cockroaches, and anything else that crawled—so she'd already rinsed everything out, but her dishes still needed to be washed.

It was somewhat shocking that after so many days of such little texture, today could be so full. She'd done Internet research on Noelani, talked to the officer overseeing her case, met Mr. Olie, gotten her hair fixed, met CeeCee and Nat, and seen that Charlie was okay.

Sadie's thoughts turned to CeeCee. She seemed like a kind woman. She was also a good homemaker, if a bit cluttery with knick-knacks and cheap artwork on the wall. She loved her children—foster and adopted—and had an entire wall in her living room brimming with pictures of the boys she'd cared for. *And* she was a great cook. Sadie wanted to like her. Wanted to trust her. Wanted to believe she was a bright light in Charlie's life. Could she believe in those good things? At least for now?

CHAPTER 20

Sadie didn't fall asleep until after midnight despite feeling utterly exhausted. She had to get her circadian rhythm in order before Gayle came. She got up at nine the next morning, however, and spent a few hours cleaning up unit number five—a new family would be checking in that afternoon. Afterward, she took a shower and wrestled with her hair, trying to make it look as good as Lou had—impossible—made some more pancakes for lunch—delicious—and tried to do some basic research information on Nat and CeeCee. Unfortunately, like many people in Hawai'i, they both went by nicknames, and she couldn't find anything.

Sadie made it to Dr. McKay's office with far less anxiety than she'd felt last time. She didn't know how much to tell him, if anything at all. Would telling him what she'd done get Charlie or Mr. Olie in trouble? Could she talk about her goal to answer Charlie's questions without actually talking about *him*? Maybe she should have canceled, but that worried her too. She'd felt better after her first appointment with Dr. McKay, and she knew both Pete and Gayle would be concerned if she canceled, so here she was, shredding Kleenex for the second time in a week.

Dr. McKay asked how she was. She gave a basic answer, and he looked at her for a few seconds.

"You got your hair done," he said. "It looks nice."

Sadie raised a hand to her hair, unable not to smile about the compliment. He was the first person who'd noticed, and she wondered if maybe, as a psychiatrist, he'd had special training on identifying these types of details—it certainly didn't come naturally for the typical man. "Thank you." Would Pete have noticed her hair, she wondered?

"What prompted the change?"

"I was feeling better, and, well, my friend Gayle is coming to visit tomorrow. I couldn't let her see me so undone."

"Your friend is coming," Dr. McKay said. "Tell me about that."

It was the perfect topic to discuss—safe—and Sadie was able to relax as she explained the plans they'd made. Dr. McKay helped her identify some things that might be difficult—Gayle seeing her anxiety up close, not having so much personal space—and they discussed what Sadie could do to deal with those situations. Dr. McKay offered to talk to Gayle if Sadie felt it would be helpful. Sadie hoped that wouldn't be necessary, but it felt good to have an option should she need it. He asked if she'd told her family about what had happened, and she explained that she'd talked to Pete every day, but her daughter was on a trip to Africa, studying wildebeest migration, and Shawn had enough on his plate. Dr. McKay didn't question her choice to not tell Shawn, and she was grateful for that.

"How are the nightmares?"

"Better," Sadie said, surprised by her own answer. But they *had* been better the last couple of nights. The realization was kind of exciting, and she decided to attempt to explore it with Dr. McKay. "I started learning about Noelani—the woman whose body I found."

He raised his eyebrows. "You did?"

She nodded, and before she knew it, she was downloading what she'd learned. She had plenty to say without bringing up Charlie. "Even though the toxicology reports won't be ready for weeks, everyone assumes Noelani overdosed simply because there isn't any other obvious cause of death."

"That bothers you?"

"Yes," Sadie said. "What if she didn't? What if something else happened, but her past has led to people making assumptions that then are reflected within the investigation. If foul play occurred, the police might miss it if they're so sure it was drugs."

"Foul play," Dr. McKay repeated, still in his neutral position. "What made you jump to that possibility?"

Sadie thought about that and realized there were other possible causes for Noelani's death other than an overdose or murder. Suicide. An accident. She considered Dr. McKay for a moment before she dared admit why she hadn't thought of those things. "I'm a magnet for murder," she said.

Dr. McKay raised his eyebrows. "And why would you say that?"

It wasn't as difficult as she thought it would be to tell him about her history. He made her feel comfortable and safe, and when she admitted the continual fear she had that her involvement was somehow connected to these incidents, he seemed to understand why she would feel that way.

"I wonder why you take on so much responsibility for these things that have happened," he said when she finished.

"Well, I lived almost fifty-six years without ever coming face-to-face with a murderer, or a murder victim for that matter. In the last year and a half, my life has become overrun with both, and now someone wants to kill *me*. It's hard to come up with another explanation other than the fact that something about me is . . . inviting these horrible things."

"Does there have to be an explanation?"

Sadie pulled her eyebrows together. "What do you mean?"

"I mean, do you have to have a solid answer? Does it have to be your fault or not be your fault? Could it be that events are happening around you that other people might ignore, but you have an interest and ability that draws you in? Maybe for the first fifty-six years of your life you were interested in other things, and then that changed."

Sadie blinked. It was a completely new idea. A totally different perspective. She thought back over the cases she'd been involved in. Hadn't she chosen to try to figure out what the police were missing when her neighbor Anne wound up dead in the field behind her house? There had been at least a hundred people present when the gun went off at the library fundraiser, but she had been the only one who put herself into the middle of things. In Oregon, she'd actually been hired to find answers.

Dr. McKay was watching her, and she blinked again. "I hadn't thought about it that way. But you're right, I've always had the option to not become involved." She thought on that vein a little longer, then tilted her head and looked strongly at her therapist. "So, perhaps what I should be trying to figure out is why I can't seem to stay away."

Dr. McKay nodded and smiled, making her feel like the teacher's pet. His glance flickered behind her, where she knew a clock hung on the wall. "We're out of time today, so we'll have to work on that next week. Before we finish, though, I want to leave you with one thought."

Sadie nodded, eager to hear what he had to say.

"One of the aspects of anxiety and depression is that the person becomes very self-focused," he said.

Sadie felt instant shame.

"It's not right or wrong, Sadie, it's simply something that can happen. The funny thing about anxiety and depression is that the more you think about it, the more focused on it you become and the bigger part of your life it takes over. My suggestion for you is to look for ways to get outside of yourself a little more. I think learning about Noelani is a good start. And you seem to be feeling better, right?"

"Yes," Sadie said, but she was thinking about everything she'd done that she hadn't told Dr. McKay about—Charlie's list and helping Mr. Olie. It made her feel bad to have not included her therapist in those things, and yet she also felt a boost of confidence that she'd already started on a path he was now recommending.

"Good," Dr. McKay said, smiling. "Keep those things in mind. Be careful of being too hard on yourself, and good luck with your friend." He reached into his shirt pocket and pulled out a card. "This has my cell number. If you need me before our next visit on Monday, give me a call, okay?"

CHAPTER 21

It was invigorating to feel as though everything she'd done was conscious rather than accidental or somehow fated. She'd made choices, and they had led her in certain directions that hadn't always been positive, but right now she was safe from the threat that had followed her since Boston. She was on a tropical island in the middle of the Pacific Ocean. She had changed her cell phone number, e-mail, and used her Facebook account only to read other people's statuses—she hadn't updated her own in months. Only a handful of people knew where she was. The hiding place she'd chosen had worked. Circumstances hadn't changed from a week or a month ago, but something inside her had. Empowerment? Was that the word for it?

Sadie let herself into her condo and locked the door. One, two, three. Then she pulled out Charlie's list. She could maintain control of this, she could stop whenever she wanted to, but she might also be able to do some good, and doing something for someone else might be the key to her own healing. Come Monday, she might have a much more interesting discussion with Dr. McKay.

She immediately went to her computer and opened up a new

document, typing notes as quickly as she could remember them. After she'd dumped all the info onto the page, she organized it into what she'd learned from whom and then took a few minutes to type out all the questions she had. They were extensive and a little overwhelming. She had hoped to hear from Mr. Olie, but realized she hadn't given him her number except on the voice mail she'd left yesterday morning, before they'd met. Maybe tomorrow she'd call his office and see if he had any kind of update. She called Pete and talked to him about her day, and by the time she was finished, she was energized enough to go to Kalaheo.

Pete had suggested she stay the night at the motel where Noelani had worked in Kalaheo so she'd have time to talk to the people Noelani had worked with and wouldn't have to try to find a way back to Puhi if she stayed late. Sadie thought it was a great idea, and it took all of five minutes to pack her laptop, an extra muumuu, and a change of underclothes. She folded the stack of papers she'd printed off—articles, Noelani's obituary, and the photo of Noelani and Charlie—and threw them in along with her deodorant almost as an afterthought. Everything fit easily in her shoulder bag, and for an instant she considered how the old Sadie would pack everything she could possibly imagine needing while she was away. She'd have lists and maps, and she'd have triple-checked everything. Should she be doing that now? Considering every contingency? After another moment of contemplation, however, she pushed the thought aside—just thinking about it made her tired. And how often had she actually used the space blanket or fabric scissors?

She took a deep breath. Stood. Squared her shoulders and called a cab. By the time it arrived, her anxiety was creeping up on her but being dropped off at the Sand and Sea Motel in Kalaheo reaffirmed her decision was the right one—doing something seemed to make all the difference.

The single-level white stucco motel looked recently updated due to the bright, still shiny, teal trim. The horseshoe-shaped building opened to the street, but a black wrought-iron fence created a barrier between the street and the courtyard, a pool, and a few lawn chairs. On one end of the building, a vacancy sign glowed in the window and, above the door, a sign said OFFICE. It wasn't a large motel, and it looked like it could use some more TLC, but it was likely affordable, and that counted for something. She looked up at the sign fifteen feet off the ground where the name of the motel was written in big bubbly letters, a generic pink hibiscus flower in the lower corner. The changeable marquee beneath the custom sign offered rooms with free Wi-Fi for the lowest rates in town. Sadie paid the cab driver, then headed into the office.

A young haole with long blonde hair pulled back into a ponytail smiled at her from the other side of the desk. "Can I help you?"

Sadie asked for a room, and the young woman—Ashley—searched around the counter until she found a paper for Sadie to fill out. Then she fiddled with the computer, but seemed frustrated with whatever she saw on the screen. It took several attempts before she successfully charged Sadie's card; she'd have be sure to check and make sure it wasn't charged four times.

"When did you start working here?" she asked when Ashley handed back her card.

The girl's face reddened, contrasting with the green-and-white Hawaiian shirt she wore. "Is it that obvious?" she said, attempting a laugh.

Sadie smiled. "You're doing great, but learning curves are really intense sometimes."

"No kidding," Ashley said, smiling at Sadie with bright white teeth that matched the broken shell necklace around her neck. "So of course the computer froze on me, and the people in eighteen were playing the TV so loud that nineteen called to complain." She took a deep breath, raised her shoulders, and then lowered them.

"Tomorrow will be easier," Sadie said, offering a commiserating smile. "Are you from Kaua'i?"

"Just moved here," Ashley said with a nod. "My cousin has lived here for a few years and needed a roommate." She handed Sadie some papers. "Just fill out this top paper with your phone number and local address, if you have one."

"Sure," Sadie said. She started filling in the information. "So, did you know Noelani?" she asked, hoping it sounded casual.

"Who?"

"Noelani Pouhu—she used to work here."

The girl looked confused, then her face fell. "Oh, the girl who died?"

CHAPTER 22

Yeah, so sad," Ashley said, making a pouty face. "I guess she was a druggy or something. Did I remind you about the continental breakfast? It's from seven to ten here in the lobby. Totally free." She smiled again.

Sadie nodded. "Thanks," she said, pondering the fact that this girl was likely Noelani's replacement. She finished filling out the paperwork and handed it back. She couldn't think of anything else to ask so she headed to her room—number nine, far away from the blaring TV of eighteen, for which Sadie was grateful.

She unpacked her meager supplies, mostly because she didn't like knowing she had undies in her shoulder bag, then went back to the front desk and asked Ashley if she knew where the Fellowship of Kaua'i Christian Church was located; the church had been mentioned by name in Noelani's obituary. Ashley didn't know, but she looked it up on the computer.

"It's not too far," she said as she printed off a map and handed it to Sadie.

It was less than a five-minute walk to get there, and when she arrived, Sadie was pretty sure the motel was back-to-back with the church, or at least close; she hadn't had to cross any streets, any-way. It was nice the church was so convenient, and she wondered if Noelani had chosen to attend the church because it was close to the motel or to work at the motel because it was close to the church.

The church building was one big square of white stucco with angled walls on the ends that led the eye upward to the large cross on top of the building. Beside the recessed doorway was black letter-ing that said Fellowship of Kaua'i Christian. The name didn't quite roll off the tongue, but it communicated its nondenominational Christian base well enough.

Sadie crossed the small parking lot—nearly full this time of eve-ning, which surprised her—and started up the wide sidewalk toward the front doors of the church. Before she reached the steps, however, she heard laughter from the back of the building and changed her course, following a narrow sidewalk around the south side of the building. The laughter and voices got louder.

While the church may have been all business out front, it was a party in the back—literally. A volleyball net had been set up in the middle of a large, grassy area, and a dozen teenagers and young adults hit a beach ball back and forth over the net. Adults were seated at some picnic tables in the shade of some twelve-foot palm trees, enjoying what looked like a hot dog dinner while a handful of little kids played on a swing set off to the side.

"*Aloha ahiahi.*"

The middle-aged man who'd addressed her as he approached wasn't exceptionally tall, under six feet, and wore a red Hawaiian shirt and khaki shorts; she'd seen the outfit so many times it seemed as though it were practically a uniform on the island. He had a puka shell necklace around his neck, and his teeth looked too white against his overly tanned face. He gripped her hand and leaned in to kiss her on the cheek. Despite being on the island for three months, Sadie still wasn't used to the affectionate greetings some of the locals gave so freely. He straightened and moved his hand to the small of her back, guiding her toward a table of food near the church.

"You're just in time," he said. "As soon as that game's over"—he nodded toward the nets—"those boys will make short work of these leftovers, yeah? We better get you served up before they start viewing you as competition."

A teenage boy in a white T-shirt and black-and-yellow board shorts dove for the beach ball and face planted into the grass instead, eliciting a burst of laughter from everyone, including her host. They reached the buffet while Sadie was still trying to keep up with the conversation, and he put a plate in her hands. "Macaroni salad and fruit?"

"Oh, um, I wasn't really invited to this," Sadie said, finally finding her voice as he began serving her. "I just came to talk to Pastor Darryl."

"At your service," he said, flashing her another smile as he put a scoop of macaroni salad on her plate. "But I wasn't kidding about the circling sharks." He nodded toward the game again. "We'll get you fixed up, and then we can make proper introductions, yeah?"

"Yeah," Sadie said, nodding. It made so much sense for her to eat at a party she hadn't been invited to when he said it like that. "Um, thanks."

"*He mea iki,*" he said. Sadie could only assume that meant "You're welcome."

The hot dogs were in a roasting pan at the end of the table, and he let Sadie choose her own toppings, even though he was the one who put everything else on her plate. The hot dogs were bright red—Konnie called them sunburned—but delicious.

Within a few minutes of her arrival, Sadie was seated opposite Pastor Darryl in a pair of functional vinyl chairs and commenting on how delicious the green bean pasta salad was. It was different from the typical mayonnaise-based salads she was used to, and although Sadie might have added black olives or maybe some finely diced red onion, it was very good.

"That," he said, grinning proudly, "is my wife's contribution to tonight's luau. Bets is an amazing cook—*lani*."

"She is," Sadie agreed after swallowing. She followed his gaze across the yard to a beautiful woman talking with an older couple. She had smooth brown skin, big brown eyes, and wavy hair that was piled on top of her head, a few tendrils framing her face. "Is that your wife?" she asked, pointing.

If anything, Pastor Darryl's smile got wider and prouder. "Sure is. She's the kind of *wahine* that makes men believe in soul mates."

"She's beautiful."

"She is," Pastor Darryl agreed. "I suppose I should formally introduce myself. I'm Pastor Darryl Earlhart, shepherd of this fold, and I'm very pleased to meet you."

"I'm Sadie Hoffmiller," she said, reaching her hand across to shake his even though they'd already been through the ritual greeting.

"Pleased to meet you, Sadie. You're not *kama'aina*, yeah?" he said.

"No, I'm not local," she said. Kama'aina was a word she'd heard a lot. "I've been here a few months, and I'll be going back to Colorado soon."

"Well, I'm sorry I didn't meet you when you first arrived, but I'm glad to know you for the duration of your trip. You said you came to speak to me; what can I help you with?"

The reminder of her reason for being there cast a pall on the sunny exchange they'd had so far, but Sadie had only to picture Charlie in her mind before recommitting to her motives. She took one more bite of the salad, then laid down her fork. "I'm afraid that I'm here to discuss a difficult subject," she said by way of preparing him.

"I'm a pastor," he said without losing his smile. "Difficult subjects are my specialty. Which one brought you here?"

"Noelani Pouhu," Sadie said and watched his eyes jump and his smile falter.

He leaned back in his chair and rested his hands lightly on his thighs. "Noelani," he said almost reverently. "She was a dear *makamaka*, and we miss her very much."

"I understand she was active in your church."

He nodded. "Very active, very involved. And with such a powerful spirit. How did you know her?"

"I didn't," Sadie said, looking down and reminding herself why she was there. "I . . . I found her in the ocean after she died."

Pastor Darryl paused, then leaned forward, putting his hand on Sadie's forearm, which she found uncomfortable. "Oh, dear sister, I am sorry. That must have been an awful experience for you."

"It was," Sadie said, blocking out the memories that tried to intrude. She'd controlled her anxiety so well the last couple of days. She needed to keep herself present, and yet she could feel the slight tingling in the back of her neck.

"And now you're looking for closure? For purpose in this tragedy?"

His hand was still on her arm, and she wished he'd let go. She wasn't used to having people touch her, let alone a man in such a familiar way. "Sort of. I'm also trying to put the pieces together for her son."

His eyebrows pulled together. "You know Charlie?"

"A little," Sadie explained, having already decided not to keep too many secrets in hopes he would do the same. "I hoped that talking to the people who were her friends might fill in some of the blanks. For Charlie, of course. Can you tell me when you last saw her?"

"A couple of days before she disappeared," he said, then waved toward the crowd. "At a gathering like this. We do it every Thursday night. She came only for a short time; she worked early the next morning."

"Do you know what happened the night she disappeared?"

Pastor Darryl shook his head and leaned back in his chair. "I'm afraid what happened to her that night is a mystery for me as well as for everyone else," he said. "I know that she was supposed to be at work and she called someone to finish her shift. That's the last anyone saw or heard from her."

"What did you think happened?" Sadie asked. "Before her . . . body was found?"

"Noelani was a recovering addict facing hard times," he said, shrugging slightly and looking sad. "When she didn't finish her shift and no one heard from her, I assumed she'd relapsed."

"Is there anything specific that makes you think that? Had she said she was tempted to go back?"

"She was always tempted," Pastor Darryl said. "Every day, every hour. Drugs had been her best friend for a very long time."

"But she'd been clean for two years, right?"

"And still dreaming of using at night," he said, smiling compassionately. "She and I spoke of it often those last few weeks; she had a great fear of not being able to stay away. As hard as it might be for us to understand, drugs were the one thing in her life that had never abandoned her, and she didn't quite feel like herself without them."

"Would you be surprised, then, if the reports were to come back showing she hadn't used drugs that night?"

"Is that what the police concluded?" Pastor Darryl said, leaning forward slightly and sounding genuinely surprised.

"No, the reports will take several weeks. I'm just curious."

"Well," he said, taking a thoughtful breath. After a moment he nodded and leaned back again. "It would be surprising to me to learn that drugs weren't a factor. She was really struggling." He paused. "Sometimes the trials we face are of our own making, poor choices that bounce back on us—Noelani had many of those in her life. Other times our trials come out of the blue and are something we truly don't deserve to experience. And yet, we have to cope with both types of *he mau pilikia, hihia*. Are you a woman of faith?"

"I am," Sadie said, though it had felt thin of late.

"Then you know there is only One who can heal us, only one Great Physician who can succor our souls, regardless of which type of trial we face."

Sadie nodded, but had to look away. His faith was hard to look at, like staring at the sun. And Sadie wasn't sure she was ready to discuss her feelings on the subject of faith and God's healing. She brought the subject back around to her purpose. "You don't have any idea who Noelani could have been with that night?"

He shook his head. "Creating a new social group is key for recovery, and it's one of the things our fellowship gave to her. Those were the only associates of hers that I knew."

"How did she find your congregation?" Sadie asked. "I understand she was a fairly recent resident of Kaua'i."

"Our fellowship supports an outreach program in Lihue, and Bets and I conduct weekly meetings of faith with music and scripture."

"Outreach?" Sadie said. "Is that like rehab?"

"It's a place of transition from rehabilitation to independence. Noelani moved there after finishing her inpatient program in Waimea. Bets and I met her when she began coming to the meetings we hold at the outreach. She was quiet at first; it takes time for an addict to trust anyone, let alone a God they can't see. When she was ready to leave the outreach program, we helped her find a new life." His expression grew sad, and he looked at the ground for a moment, his eyes shiny with unshed tears. "How grateful I am to know of a plan that extends beyond this one. I firmly believe that we were able to help prepare her for whatever she may be experiencing now. That she knew God before she met Him is a remarkable gift. I don't judge her for what may have happened that cut her earthly existence short," he said, sounding sincere. "She'll be missed either way, and we'll always be grateful to have known her."

"Hey, there, sweetie."

They both looked up as Bets perched on the arm of Pastor Darryl's cream-colored vinyl lawn chair and draped an arm over his shoulders before leaning in for a kiss. She was lovely up close, but Sadie could see the lines around her eyes and the texture of her skin that gave away her age—mid-forties, probably about the same as the good pastor. When Bets lifted her head from kissing her husband, she smiled at Sadie.

"Aloha," she said, nodding slightly. "I'm Bets Earlhart."

"Sadie Hoffmiller." She reached out to shake Bets's long tapered fingers. No acrylic nails, no manicure, just beautifully natural.

Bets barely pressed Sadie's fingers before withdrawing her hand.

"We've been talking about Noelani," Pastor Darryl said.

Something flashed behind Bets's eyes, so quick and so subtle that a less keen observer wouldn't have noticed it. But despite being out of practice, Sadie *was* a keen observer and she *did* notice. Bets's smile faded appropriately in proportion to the sad topic, but she also stiffened a little bit. Defensive, maybe? Nervous?

"I understand you and your husband helped her a great deal," Sadie said. "Were the two of you friends?"

"Absolutely," Bets said, her face perfectly polite. "Sisters really, in Christ."

Sadie had a hard time believing her.

Green Bean Bow Tie Salad

3 Roma tomatoes, diced (the riper the better)
1½ tablespoons balsamic vinegar
1½ tablespoons olive oil
2 teaspoons dried basil
1 teaspoon sea salt
3 cups dry bow tie pasta
2 cups fresh green beans, ends removed and broken into 1-inch
    pieces

Combine diced tomatoes, vinegar, olive oil, basil, and sea salt in a bowl. Set aside. In a large pan, heat 1 quart of salted water to boiling. Add pasta, stirring to separate as it cooks. Boil pasta for 5 minutes. Add green beans and boil 6 more minutes, or until pasta is tender. Drain pasta and beans in a colander and return to cooking pot. Add tomato-vinegar mixture while pasta and beans are still hot. Stir together. Adjust seasoning as needed. Transfer salad to serving bowl. Serve warm or at room temperature. Chill leftovers.

Note: To spice it up, add ½ cup diced red onion and/or black olives to the tomato-vinegar mixture. Also, ½ cup crisp bacon, diced, makes the salad even more fabulous.

CHAPTER 23

I t must have been very difficult when you learned of her death," Sadie said, watching Bets closely.

"It was awful," Bets said, her voice low. She fiddled with the collar of her husband's shirt, smoothing it down and not meeting Sadie's eyes. "But I find peace in knowing that she was saved through grace."

"Yes, that is a powerful balm," Sadie said.

"To make the wounded whole," Pastor Darryl added. "'For all have sinned and fall short of the glory of God, and are justified freely by His grace through the redemption that came by Christ Jesus.'"

"P.D.," someone called out, causing all three of them to turn toward the volleyball game. "Jana had to go home, and we're short a member. Come help us out, brah. We're three points from winning this thing!"

Immediate protests rose from the opposing team, but Pastor Darryl—or P.D.—was all smiles as he unwound himself from his wife and stood, raising his hands above his head as though already claiming victory. "'And behold, I am with you always, to the end of the age.'"

He stopped by Sadie's chair and placed his hand on her arm again. He was a very touchy-feely man. "Will you stay so we can visit some more after I show these kids who's the *kahuna*?"

"Sure," Sadie said with a smile. Even though he made her a little uncomfortable, he was really quite charming. He gave her a thumbs-up and headed into the fray. Sadie watched Bets watch her husband for a few seconds until she turned back to Sadie, not looking as comfortable without her husband there.

"Well, I better get to work on serving the dessert."

Sadie instantly got to her feet. "Can I help? I've been known to be rather handy in the kitchen."

"Oh, uh, sure," Bets said in a tone that clearly said she'd rather do it herself. Sadie took it at face value. "If you'll just follow me."

Sadie followed her through the back door of the church, which opened into a small foyer with two chairs on one side and a phone on the wall between them. At the end of the foyer was a hallway that stretched in both directions. Bets turned left, and Sadie followed her through the first door on the left and into a utilitarian kitchen with gold-sparkle-embedded Formica countertops and a worn linoleum floor. It smelled like chocolate, and Sadie felt her mouth begin to water.

On the wall across from the door was a scripture written in elegant lettering: "Blessed are those who hunger and thirst after righteousness, for they shall be satisfied." It wasn't the King James translation, but Sadie recognized it as one of the beatitudes given by Jesus during the Sermon on the Mount. The design of the lettering, full of wispy curls and elegant flourishes, only amplified the beautiful meaning of the words. The border done with scrollwork and flowers further enhanced the good news of the scriptural passage.

"This is lovely," Sadie said, approaching the words that took up most of the wall. She'd assumed it was the vinyl lettering so popular back in Colorado, but when she got close, she realized it was paint. "Someone hand painted this?"

Bets didn't answer, and Sadie looked at her in time to catch the humble smile.

"You did this?"

Bets shrugged.

"You're a woman of many talents," Sadie said, moving toward the stainless steel island in the center of the room. "I already sampled your cooking, and you're an artist as well." She waved toward the wall. "It's extraordinary."

"Thank you," Bets said, inclining her head. She retrieved an ice cream scoop from a drawer, and though Sadie wasn't done admiring the mural, she could tell Bets was uncomfortable with the attention so she let it go.

Bets opened the fridge and pulled out a jar of maraschino cherries and a three-pack of canned whipping cream. She set everything on the counter and lifted the lid of a slow cooker, increasing the smell of chocolate that Sadie had noted upon entering the room.

"What's for dessert?" Sadie asked.

"Banana splits. It's a congregational favorite."

"You made the hot fudge from scratch?"

Bets shrugged as though it was no big deal. "The slow cooker keeps it warm. There's caramel and pineapple topping too." She waved toward two metal bowls on the counter. "I got them out of the fridge earlier so they wouldn't be cold."

"Sounds delicious," Sadie said. "What can I help with?"

"I just need to get everything ready to go before we take it outside," Bets said, unplugging the hot fudge. "Could you stir the caramel and pineapple toppings?" She pulled open a drawer and handed Sadie two spoons.

"Sure," Sadie said, glad Bets was letting her do something. "So how long have you and Pastor Darryl been married?"

"Just over sixteen years," Bets said, opening a cupboard beside the stove and removing a serving tray. She put the cherries and the whipping cream on the tray, then moved around the kitchen, gathering plastic spoons, bowls, and napkins from various cupboards and drawers.

Sadie removed the plastic wrap from the caramel—also homemade, she guessed—and began to stir it smooth. "Was he already the pastor when you two met?"

"He was a youth pastor," Bets said, pulling open the freezer where two gallons of vanilla ice cream lay waiting. "I'd moved to Kalaheo and met up with him through a fellowship meeting here. When Pastor Hani moved back to the Big Island, Darryl was asked to serve in his place." She shrugged. "We got married right here about six months after he took over the congregation, and we've been serving together ever since."

"That's wonderful," Sadie said, glad that Bets seemed to be softening up a little. "I love hearing people's stories. God is a clever matchmaker."

"Yes, He certainly is," Bets said, giving Sadie another dazzling smile. She had the longest eyelashes Sadie had ever seen, and if not for the fact that Sadie couldn't identify any makeup on the woman, she'd have been sure they were fake. But nothing about Bets seemed phony in any way. She had natural fingernails, wore no jewelry except a simple wedding band, and yet there was an unease with herself that Sadie couldn't figure out.

"Do you have children?" Sadie asked by way of keeping the

conversation going. She deemed the caramel smooth as silk and moved on to the pineapple.

An instant veil descended over Bets's face, and Sadie mentally kicked herself. Of all people, Sadie knew the cutting edge of that question, having been asked it a thousand times herself and having felt the sting over and over again. She hurried to undo the damage before Bets had to come up with a polite reply. "I'm sorry," she said. "That's none of my business."

"No, it's fine," Bets said, but it was forced, and she was suddenly busy organizing all the toppings onto the tray. She grabbed a bowl of chopped nuts from the fridge. "We haven't been blessed with children of our own, but caring for so many of God's children in ways that He cannot eases the longing."

"I'm sure," Sadie said, still feeling horrible. "I wasn't able to have biological children," she blurted out, feeling the desperate need to explain her comments somehow.

"Biological?"

"We adopted."

Bets's smile remained forced. "That's wonderful." She didn't expand on why she and Darryl hadn't adopted, and Sadie kicked herself again.

Bets returned to the toppings while Sadie shook her head and decided to change the subject. "Your husband was telling me you two met Noelani through the outreach program."

Bets nodded but added nothing more.

"I assume she joined your congregation after she left the outreach program?"

"Yes."

"How long ago did she leave outreach?"

"About seven months," she said, all business. "Will you grab the tray so we can take everything out?" She picked up the slow cooker and turned toward the door.

Sadie nodded and picked up the tray, following Bets to the backyard. The volleyball game had adjourned, and, just as Pastor Darryl had predicted, the leftover hot dogs and salads were being consumed by the famished athletes who laughed and ate in clusters here and there throughout the yard. Sadie quickly estimated there were nearly forty people at the luau.

They were a few steps from the buffet table when Bets's step faltered slightly. Sadie would have steadied her if her hands hadn't been full, but Bets quickly recovered and kept moving toward the table. Sadie scanned the ground for a possible hazard that could have caused Bets to trip so she'd be certain to avoid it, but there wasn't anything obvious. Thank goodness Bets hadn't spilled the hot fudge. That would have been tragic!

When Sadie looked up, however, she saw something else that might explain Bets's misstep. Pastor Darryl was standing about fifteen yards away from everyone else, holding both hands of a young woman and staring at her face intently. They stood very close to each another, perhaps only a foot apart, their clasped hands at chest level between them.

The woman said something and smiled, causing him to squeeze her hands and smile back at her. If not for the fact that they were surrounded by people, chief among them Pastor Darryl's wife, Sadie would have described the scene as intimate. She'd no sooner thought that than he pulled the woman into an embrace—a very close embrace—wrapping his arms around her back and holding her tight as she did the same, resting her cheek against his shoulder and closing her eyes.

Sadie averted her gaze and looked to Bets, who was watching

the embrace in quick glances as she set down the hot fudge. Her mouth was drawn tightly and her posture was stiff, despite trying to pretend not to notice, or so it seemed.

"Bets," Sadie said, coming up beside her. "Are you all right?"

Bets looked up, her cheeks darkened with embarrassment. "Thank you," she said, smiling as she adjusted Sadie's tray on the table. "I appreciate your help."

Sadie nodded toward the embracing couple, but didn't say anything.

"He's a pastor," Bets said, though her tone sounded too defensive to be trusted completely. "It's his job to offer comfort to members of the fellowship. Could you get the ice cream please?"

Sadie nodded and headed back toward the kitchen, wondering if Pastor Darryl had ever offered the same kind of comfort to Noelani. It would explain the shadow that had crossed Bets's face each time Sadie had said Noelani's name. Sadie didn't want to think it could also explain Noelani's dive into the ocean that had taken her life, but once the thought had popped up, it wouldn't go away.

Banana Splits

Pineapple Topping
4 tablespoons butter
1 (20-ounce) can crushed pineapple, drained
⅓ cup sugar
¼ teaspoon salt

Melt butter in small saucepan on medium-high heat. Add pineapple. Mix well. Add sugar and salt. Bring to a boil while stirring continually. Stir until thickened. Allow to cool.

Great-Grandma Jensen's Caramel Sauce

1 cup brown sugar
1 cup corn syrup
½ cup butter (or margarine)
¼ teaspoon salt

Mix all ingredients in a small saucepan. Bring to a boil over high heat and boil for exactly one minute. (The longer it boils, the thicker the sauce will become.)

Laree's Hot Fudge

½ cup butter
2 cups sugar
¼ cup cocoa powder
1 (15-ounce) can evaporated milk
1 teaspoon vanilla
¼ cup flour

Combine butter, sugar, and cocoa powder in a 2-quart saucepan on medium heat, stirring consistently until butter is melted. It will be very thick and chunky. Add milk gradually, stirring constantly until smooth. Add vanilla and flour. Bring to a boil, then remove from heat. Mixture will thicken as it cools. Serve while sauce is still warm. (You can keep the hot fudge warm in a slow cooker set on the lowest heat setting.) Store leftovers in the refrigerator.

CHAPTER 24

S adie ended up staying at the party until nine o'clock—much later than she'd expected. After dessert, a teenage girl suggested playing a game she called Banana Split. After the girl began explaining the rules to the group, Sadie realized it was the same concept as the game she knew as Fruit Salad. Enough chairs were set in a circle for everyone playing, except for one person who stood in the middle. Everyone sitting in the circle silently chose one of the five toppings Bets had offered for the banana splits—hot fudge, caramel, pineapple, nuts, or cherries. When the person in the middle called out a topping, those in the circle who had chosen that topping in their mind had to run for a new seat while the person in the middle tried to get there first. Whoever missed out on claiming a seat was now "It."

The girl was having a hard time describing the game, and no one except Sadie seemed to understand what she was trying to say. As soon as Sadie mentioned her familiarity with the game, Pastor Darryl made her cocaptain with the girl, who looked relieved to have the help and quickly sat down, making Sadie "It" for the first round.

Standing in front of the group was hard at first; she kept clearing her throat and having to consciously calm herself. She tried to take Dr. McKay's advice and not focus on the anxiety she felt. By the end of the first round—she'd made sure to get a seat—she was barely aware of her discomfort. Still, she didn't choose a topping for most of the game, not wanting to fight for a seat, but enjoyed the energy of the group all the same. She noticed Bets didn't participate either. There was a chance she simply never chose the same topping the person in the middle called out, but Sadie sensed it wasn't that. She sat there smiling and clapping from time to time, but still apart somehow. Lonely?

The woman Pastor Darryl had been embracing, however, was very into the game. She wrestled seats away from the teenagers and laughed and teased constantly. Her name was Mandi, and she was always in the middle of the action. After a few rounds, Sadie noticed that whenever a seat next to Pastor Darryl emptied, Mandi ran for it, even if she hadn't immediately stood when the topping was called out. She wouldn't exit the spot until he jumped up in pursuit of another seat himself. Because of her strategy, she and Pastor Darryl sat next to one another through most of the game. He often had his arm around her shoulders, though he put his arm around the shoulders of anyone who ended up next to him. Sadie tried to pay attention to whether Bets was watching them like she was, but she couldn't be certain.

By the time kids finally started heading for home in the cars parked out front or on the bikes leaned against the back wall of the church, Sadie couldn't remember when she'd had such a good time. Certainly not for several months; before coming to Kaua'i, for sure.

"I'm delighted you could join us," Pastor Darryl said when Sadie headed for the chair where she'd left her bag. "You fit in as though you've always been one of us."

Sadie smiled as she put the strap of her bag over her head, adjusting her bag so it rested against her hip. He put a hand on her arm, and she was glad to have noticed that he was equally touchy with everyone in his congregation. Consistency had to count for something, but she, personally, wasn't comfortable with it.

"I appreciate you working so hard to make me feel a part of the group," she said, moving away casually so that he dropped his hand. "I didn't mean to stay so long."

"We don't usually go this late," he said, waving toward the moon rising in the night sky. "We meet every week as an opportunity for the youth to have a wholesome activity. Today was especially *nani*, though. Maybe you were good luck."

Sadie shook her head. "You're a charming man," she said, only hearing the accusation in her own mind.

"All in the name of God," he assured her.

A yawn snuck up on her, but she tried to hide it behind her hand then frowned apologetically when he took note.

"We wore you out and didn't finish our conversation about Noelani."

"That's okay," Sadie said, smiling in hopes of assuring him that it really was all right. In fact, maybe it was optimal. Bets had avoided her after Sadie had spotlighted the embrace between Pastor Darryl and Mandi, but maybe she'd be more open tomorrow. "I'm actually staying in Kalaheo tonight. Perhaps I could come over in the morning and we could talk some more?"

"Are you staying with a friend here in town?"

"No," Sadie said, shaking her head. "At a motel."

"We have a guest room at our apartment that I'd invite you to use," Pastor Darryl said, waving toward the square cinder block house located adjacent to the church. "But I'm afraid Sister Mandi's staying there until she finds a more permanent place."

Mandi lives here? Wow. Sadie tried to hide her surprise and quickly scanned the yard until she saw Bets and Mandi talking with another woman on the other side of the yard. At some point in the evening, Bets must have gone inside because she wore a pink sweater—more like a big knitted scarf with sleeves—in the cool night air. As in the game, Bets seemed a quiet participant in the conversation taking place, while Mandi and the other woman did most of the talking. Bets couldn't be comfortable having Mandi under her roof. Never mind what she said about it being her husband's job to comfort the members of the congregation, her body language betrayed the discomfort Sadie believed she wouldn't easily put into words.

"That's all right," Sadie said. "I've already got a room at the Sand and Sea Motel. I understand Noelani worked there."

"She did," Pastor Darryl said with a nod, his expression a bit more somber. "God bless her."

"Well, I ought to get going," Sadie said, peering into the dark night around her. There were lights on buildings and such, and she could only hope they would light up the street enough that she could get back to the motel without having a panic attack. Maybe she'd run. Had she brought her pepper spray, or was it back at the condo?

"Let me drive you," Pastor Darryl said. "There's actually a trail that cuts through the back way, but it's not well lit at night." He gestured toward a low-growing hedge around the back of the property. Sadie could make out a gap in the bushes, but was grateful for the ride and thanked him for the offer. She really didn't feel up to running.

"Let me get the keys to the Jeep," he said.

He left Sadie and jogged across the lawn. As he passed Bets, he took hold of her hand and leaned in, presumably to tell her where he was going. Her eyes immediately snapped to Sadie, and although Bets's smile didn't falter, Sadie recognized the tightness behind it.

Wanting to keep things good between the two of them, Sadie hurried over to Bets as Pastor Darryl disappeared into the apartment. The other woman said good-bye, and Bets and Mandi hugged her. Mandi followed Darryl inside. Bets looked after them a little too long before turning toward Sadie.

"Darryl says he's driving you over to the Sand and Sea."

Sadie nodded. She considered asking Bets to drive her in place of Pastor Darryl, for propriety sake, but then realized that would leave Pastor Darryl alone with Mandi. She felt bad for having such torrid thoughts, but felt sure she wasn't the only one entertaining them.

"There are other places to stay," Bets said.

Interesting that she would point that out, Sadie thought. "I might as well stay there, though, and ask about Noelani in the morning. I'm trying to put together some pieces."

"Pieces of what?" Bets asked. She began moving toward the tables, and Sadie followed her. They began clearing empty bowls in tandem and dumping the trash into a large black garbage can set next to the tables.

"What happened to her," Sadie said. "The police have such little information, and I'm hoping to find some answers that will help her son."

"Charlie's a sweet boy," Bets said, smiling sadly.

"You know him?"

"Noelani brought him with her sometimes. He was surprisingly well-behaved for a boy with such a difficult childhood."

"Difficult childhood?"

"His mother was an addict." There was an unexpected sharpness in her words, but she sensed Bets heard it too because the next words she spoke were softer. "Children of addicts wear the scars all their life."

Sadie suspected Bets was talking about herself. She began putting the nearly empty bowls of toppings back on the tray she'd used to bring them out. She tapped the leftover hot fudge from the serving spoon while considering how best to continue the conversation.

"How's Charlie doing?" Bets asked before Sadie came up with anything to say. "I didn't get a chance to talk to him at the memorial service."

"I think he's really struggling," Sadie said, placing the sticky spoon on the tray where Bets had placed the other utensils. "It's a hard situation for adults to make sense of, let alone a little boy who doesn't understand everything. I'm not sure he's accepted that she's really dead."

"Oh?" Bets said, a strange, forced casualness in her tone that Sadie couldn't figure out. "Why do you think that?"

"Just some things he's said," Sadie said, thinking of what Nat had told her about Charlie being used to Noelani not being in his life. "Like you said, the life he had with her before was chaotic, and I wonder if he thinks she may have just left again, rather than died. And he wasn't able to see her, of course."

"So, you're trying to prove to him she's dead? Maybe it's better for him to keep his fantasies. Reality isn't always what it's cracked up to be."

The comment surprised Sadie. Why would an adult want a child to believe a lie? She knew from experience that people often said the most important things when they thought no one was taking notes.

"I imagine that believing his mother might come back could have a significant negative impact on his ability to embrace his new future," Sadie said carefully.

"If her body hadn't been found, he'd have had no choice. Time would then lead to acceptance as he got older."

"That's possible," Sadie said with a nod, wondering again at the strange comment and what it could mean. "But her body *was* found."

Bets nodded, but her smile was even more forced. She picked up the tray, and Sadie grabbed the slow cooker. The ends of Bets's pink sweater swayed as she headed toward the church.

"You'd mentioned earlier that Noelani had been a part of your congregation for seven months," Sadie said, trying to milk the conversation for all it was worth. "But she didn't start working at the motel until a few months ago, right? Where did she live in between the outreach program and the motel?"

"She stayed with us for a few months before she found a job at the motel."

Ah, the plot thickened like the hot fudge Sadie was holding. "She didn't have a job when she lived here?"

"Full-time work is hard to find on the island due to so many malihini willing to do whatever it takes to stay here. She was waitressing part-time but needed better employment. The full-time position with housing at the motel was a blessing." They reached the kitchen and put their loads on the counter.

"Did you guys help her find the job at the motel?" The connecting path between the locations spoke of some kind of association.

"It just worked out," Bets said, putting the dirty utensils in the sink. "God's hands."

"Of course," Sadie said. For a moment, she put herself in Bets's position—dedicated to the church, a faithful believer, married to a man who, while he obviously adored her, was demonstrative with other women. How would Sadie tolerate other women living in her house? The answer was instant. She wouldn't tolerate it at all. Why did Bets? She was beautiful and talented and kind, which in Sadie's mind should equate to having enough confidence to not put up with such a . . . demeaning and unwise situation.

Sadie was spared having to fill the silence as Pastor Darryl appeared in the doorway, jingling a ring of keys in one hand.

"There you are," he said, grinning broadly as he crossed the floor into the kitchen. He leaned in to kiss Bets on the cheek before he draped his arm over Sadie's shoulder. "Don't wait up," he said.

Sadie felt her face flush at his comment, but he laughed, and Bets smiled as though that were a typical joke between them. Sadie wanted to kick him in the shins.

Instead, she thanked Bets one last time, holding the other woman's eyes for a second longer than normal, trying to communicate that she didn't fault her for being uncomfortable with her husband's actions. Whether or not Bets received the message, Sadie couldn't be sure. When she looked over her shoulder as they exited, Bets was holding the edges of her sweater around herself as she watched them leave, a concerned expression on her face.

"So the Sand and Sea by way of Hattie's?" Pastor Darryl said, holding open the back door of the church for her. "Hattie's serves the best grilled pineapple. I'm not certain, but I think they put Tabasco sauce in the marinade."

"Cayenne pepper, probably," Sadie said automatically. "At least that's how I've made it before. It goes really well with barbequed pork chops."

"Ah, you're a foodie like my Bets," he said with a grin as he hurried a step ahead of her in order to open the door of the Jeep.

"Thank you," Sadie said, acknowledging his chivalry as she climbed into the passenger seat, smoothing the skirt of her muumuu beneath her.

Pastor Darryl hurried around to the driver's side, climbed in, and started up the engine. "So, Hattie's?" he said again.

"I couldn't eat a thing," Sadie said, vastly uncomfortable with the idea of sitting across a table from this man and surprised by his offer. "You've already fed me too well."

He draped his arm over the back of her seat as he drove, and she felt herself tense. She'd considered herself as someone far away from his standard of women, but now she wasn't so sure. The thought no sooner entered her mind than she discarded it, embarrassed to be thinking that at all.

"I'd like to get to know you a little better," he said. "Learn more about where you've come from and where you see yourself going."

Holy cow, could he be any more creepy? "There's really not much to say," Sadie said, wanting to remind him that she wasn't going to be a long-term member of his flock and therefore getting to know her wasn't necessary. She *did* want to talk to him, but not under such casual circumstances, and late at night with just the two of them was far too casual for her comfort level. She would feel more secure with daylight at the very least. "And I'm quite tired. But thank you for the offer, and your hospitality tonight, and the ride to the motel. Perhaps I can come back tomorrow and we can finish our discussion about Noelani with you and your *wife*."

He nodded, still smiling, and removed his arm from her seat in order to use both hands to steer the car around the corner. A few seconds later, he pulled up in front of the motel. Judging by the lights in the windows, only half a dozen rooms were rented out. The vacancy sign still flashed in the window. Sadie reached for the door handle, but Pastor Darryl grabbed her other hand, keeping her in the Jeep. For a moment, Sadie couldn't breathe. Was he detaining her?

When he spoke, his voice was soft as a whisper, and she looked from his hand holding hers to his bowed head. "May the Holy Spirit be your guide, and may God whisper peace and comfort to your troubled soul, Sister Sadie." He looked up and smiled at her. "If there is any way I can be of assistance, all you need do is ask." He let go of her hand in order to reach into the pocket of his Hawaiian shirt and pull out a business card—just as Dr. McKay had done that afternoon—handing it to her across the seat.

She took the card and read his name and cell phone number. Along the bottom of the card was the scripture "Joined together in the same mind and in the same judgment. 1 Corinthians 1:10."

"Thank you," Sadie said.

"Just come by the church in the morning. I'm usually in my office from nine until one."

"I'll plan on it." Sadie opened the door of the Jeep and let herself out. "Thanks again."

He nodded and waited until she waved to him from the door of her room before he tapped his horn and did a U-turn on the street. Seconds later, Sadie let herself into her room and locked the door—one, two, three—flipped the swing bolt, and checked the window locks. Secure in her room, she turned on the TV for company and stayed up far too late updating her notes on her computer and doing searches on Pastor Darryl Earlhart and his wife.

She didn't have Bets's full name until she tracked down the details of their marriage certificate: Elizabeth Leilani Iliona Earlhart. She was listed as a resident of Kaua'i at the time of the marriage sixteen years earlier. Most of what she'd done since that time was church and community related—selfless, necessary roles that improved the world she lived in. It was hard to believe Bets could have had anything to do with what had happened to Noelani, but there had been some tension there, Sadie was sure of it. She wrote down some questions she wanted to ask Bets and Pastor Darryl the next day, before Gayle arrived. The more she learned, the more information she'd have for Gayle to help her process.

Sadie's Sassy Grilled Pineapple

1 teaspoon honey
3 tablespoons melted butter or balsamic vinegar
Dash of cayenne pepper
1 fresh pineapple, peeled, cored, and sliced into ¾-inch thick rings
Dash of salt

Combine the honey, butter or vinegar, and cayenne pepper in a large zip-top bag. Add pineapple slices and allow to marinate for at least 1 hour.

Grill 4 to 5 minutes, turning halfway through, on cleaned and lightly oiled grill. Serve warm.

Notes: If using canned, sliced pineapple, dry rings on a paper towel before marinating. You can also thread 1-inch chunks of fresh or canned pineapple onto metal skewers or soaked bamboo skewers instead of grilling pineapple rings. (Most grocery stores will core the pineapple for you if you ask a produce employee.) Pineapple can also be broiled in the oven on the middle rack for 15 minutes, turning halfway through.

CHAPTER 25

Sadie slept until seven o'clock Friday morning, but once she woke up, she was strangely energized rather than exhausted by the events of the previous day. She took a shower, and then fought with her hair until accepting the fact that even if she couldn't get it to look like it had when Lou styled it, it looked much better than it had before she'd gone to the salon.

She put on the clean muumuu she'd brought—a light pink with baby blue hibiscus—and adjusted the elasticized ruffle around the neck. Braver women would pull the ruffle down around their shoulders for a saucier look, but Sadie had bought it for the length and the flattering cut that dipped in just enough at the waist to show she had a figure. The featherlight cotton hit her just below the knee, and once it was on, she wouldn't think about it for the rest of the day, it was that comfortable.

Before leaving, she straightened her room and put Charlie's list on top of the pile of papers she'd collected so far. She smiled, liking the list being in its rightful place—on top because it was the most important . . . even though she hadn't actually answered anything yet.

Mount Wai'ale'ale was considered the rainiest place in the world, and, as usual, the sidewalk was wet with the remnants of the nightly rain. The moisture would be gone within the hour, Sadie guessed, evaporating back into the sky and adding to the humidity. She loved how the world here seemed to be washed clean every night to start bright and shiny each morning. She knew it was another aspect of Kaua'i she would miss once she returned home.

The continental breakfast in the office of the motel consisted of prepackaged Danishes, orange juice, and bananas. There was a different girl behind the front desk this morning, dark skinned and dark haired, but wearing the same kind of green-and-white aloha shirt that Ashley had worn the night before. Sadie held her breath until she reached the counter and read "Kiki" on the girl's name tag. Hopefully she knew Noelani better than Ashley had.

A couple was looking through a display of brochures, so Sadie took her time with breakfast and didn't approach Kiki until the couple had left. Once alone, Sadie wanted to dive right in with her questions, but she took her time and chatted with Kiki about the weather and fun things to do in the area before working her way into a conversation about Noelani.

Kiki immediately looked at the desk, suddenly busy with straightening stacks of papers.

"Were you friends with her?" Sadie pushed.

Kiki nodded, looking toward the front doors as though hoping someone would come in and interrupt them.

"What can you tell me about her?" Sadie asked. "I'm just trying to get a better picture of who she was."

Kiki stopped going through the files, but didn't face Sadie. "I really can't talk about her."

A man and his son came in, grabbed breakfast, and left after asking Kiki about the nearest Redbox. As soon as they were gone, Sadie picked up right where she'd left off; Kiki was back at the desk.

"Why can't you talk about it? Is it upsetting?"

Kiki shook her head, then stopped and turned to face Sadie. For the first time, Sadie noticed Kiki was pregnant—five or six months, Sadie would guess. She had a small frame so it was an obvious baby bump. "Well, yes, it is sad, but . . . well . . ."

Sadie offered up her softest, most trustworthy smile. "Yes?"

Kiki glanced at the door behind Sadie then said, "The owner asked those of us who knew Noelani not to talk to anyone about her. It's bad for morale."

"I certainly won't tell him anything you tell me."

"I'm sorry," Kiki said, putting her hands on her belly. "I really need this job."

Sadie's arguments fizzled as her protective side took over. She came up with another idea. "What's the owner's name?"

"Jim," Kiki said, pointing to a plaque on the wall that honored a James Bartley for outstanding service back in 1999. A quick glance at the office with the curling wallpaper by the door, faded teal curtains beside the window, and the pressed wood furniture made Sadie think 1999 might have been the last good year the motel had had.

"Maybe I'll talk to him." She hadn't meant it to sound like a threat, but the way Kiki's eyes went wide she realized it could sound like one. "I certainly won't say anything about having talked to you. I'll just pretend to have gone to him in the first place. What time does he come in?"

For a few seconds, Kiki seemed to go back and forth on what to do, but finally she told Sadie that Jim was at the expedition office— a separate building next to the motel where he kept the boat he used for tourist groups. He was taking a group out at nine thirty and would be getting ready for the outing right now.

"Thank you," Sadie said. "I would still like to talk to you about Noelani. Could I talk to you when you finish your shift?"

"Sure," Kiki said, but her voice was hollow. "I'm not off until two, and then I have class at three thirty at the community college. I'll have to figure out a good time."

Sadie gave Kiki her cell number, which Kiki put into her phone before stashing it under the desk. "Call me with a time and place," Sadie said. "I really appreciate it."

The garage was next to the motel on the east side, set back from the road, but still easily found. A sign above the door read BARTLEY EXPEDITIONS. Jim Bartley was apparently an entrepreneur within numerous vertical industries of the tourist trade.

Just before letting herself in, Sadie's phone signaled that she'd received a text message.

Kaua'i flight lands at 10:13. Can't wait to see you!

Sadie's stomach flipped with suppressed nerves, and she leaned her back against the metal pre-fab building as she took a deep breath. Gayle's arrival was getting closer every minute, and she took a moment to reply.

See you soon!

Seconds later, she let herself into the small waiting area. A chest-level counter created a barrier between where she stood and an orange metal door she presumed led to the shop taking up most of the building. The waiting room was utilitarian, with posters on the wall featuring the underwater reefs surrounding Kaua'i as well as the

Na Pali cliffs on the north side. The pictures triggered her anxiety, so she ignored them and approached the counter to tap the bell sitting there. "Hello?"

The shop door opened and a man came through. He was tall, with brown outgrown hair, light brown skin, a slight belly pressing against the blue cotton of his sleeveless shirt, and blue eyes. His eyebrows were thick, as were his arms. "Can I help you?" His tone was brusque and his expression intense.

"Um, yes," Sadie said. "I wanted to talk to Jim Bartley."

"I'm Jim. What do you need?"

"I'm trying to learn more about Noelani Pouhu," Sadie said, already feeling him dismissing her. "I understand she worked for you."

His hard expression turned even harder. "I'm busy," he said, then turned and disappeared through the shop door.

Sadie waited, hoping he'd realize how rude he'd been and come back. He didn't. After a few seconds, she took a breath and headed for the door herself. People could be so difficult sometimes.

She let herself into the shop and looked around. There was a wall full of accessories—life jackets, paddles, fishing gear, nets, and a few kayaks. Another wall had a long counter built into it, covered with tools and other odds and ends. In the center of the garage was a fishing boat—not too different than the ones some of her neighbors owned for weekend water skiing trips on North Sterling Reservoir. Jim's boat was off-white due to age, with an open bow and a covered helm. A thick orange stripe wrapped around the entire vessel. She could see Jim Bartley's shoulder at the back of the boat where he seemed to be working on the motor.

"I just have a few questions," she said as she moved toward him. "You can keep working."

He glanced up at her, still irritated, then went back to whatever he was doing.

"You with the police?" Jim asked, twisting something a little tighter.

"No," Sadie said. "Just myself."

"So what's Noelani to a haole like you?"

She chose to assume he wasn't using the term in a derogatory manner, though that was giving him an awful lot of credit. "I found her body," Sadie said, using the excuse automatically since it had proved itself effective in other discussions. "In the ocean last week. It's been a little haunting, and I'm hoping to find some closure by learning more about her."

He glanced up at her again, an annoyed expression in his eyes, before going back to his engine. When he didn't say anything else, she chose to assume he was okay with her reason for being here. At least, he hadn't told her to leave yet.

Sadie cleared her throat, wishing she wasn't so nervous. "So, did you know her?"

"I was her boss. Of course I knew her."

"And she lived at the motel, right?"

"Yes." He moved to the counter and rummaged in a toolbox for something.

Sadie waited until he came back and the subsequent metal on metal sounds had stopped before she continued.

"You knew about her history? The drug abuse?"

"Yes."

"Did you think she was using again? I mean, toward the end?"

"Yes," he said, standing up and pushing his long hair off his face. If not for his sour expression, and overgrown eyebrows in need of a good tweezing, he'd have been handsome.

"What made you think she was using?"

"She was late for work that last week, not very talkative, agitated." He shrugged and threw the wrench he'd been holding into the toolbox. Sadie jumped when it hit the other tools. "And then the cops found drugs when they searched her stuff. Hard to explain that away."

"I heard about that," Sadie said, admitting it was a pretty good indication of what everyone assumed, that Noelani was using again. "Who found it?"

"I don't know," he said, all but rolling his eyes in contempt. "The cops."

"I understand it was more than a week after she disappeared before she was found. Did you keep all her things in her room until the police contacted you?"

"No," he said, but he seemed a little defensive. "Once she missed her Sunday shift I had her things packed up and put in storage. I assumed she'd hit me up for her last paycheck at some point. When the police showed up instead, I gave her stuff to them. When they found drugs, they did a more thorough search of the room she'd stayed in, but they didn't find anything else."

There was so much casualness about marijuana on the island, Sadie wondered why it was such a big deal for Noelani to have it. "Do you know why she was having a hard time the last little while?"

"Doesn't matter," Jim said quickly. "She should have kept her personal problems to herself."

"What personal problems?"

He gave her a hard look. "All of them."

He started throwing life jackets into the boat, but he still hadn't told her to leave so she didn't. She'd have to get a sense of what was upsetting Noelani from other people; she wasn't going to get it from this guy. "When did you last see her?" she asked.

"A week and a half before she washed up. That Saturday night," he said. "She was scheduled to work until six the next morning. I checked in just after shift change—at ten—and she said everything was fine."

"Did you know she called someone to work for her?"

"No, and I'd have fired her for it if she'd come back. All scheduling goes through me, and she knew it."

Harsh, seeing as how she was dead. "You said she was late for work that week."

"She said her phone died, so her alarm hadn't woken her up." He seemed to scoff at the idea—like he'd never overslept in his life.

"Had she missed other shifts?"

"No, but I'd already had to switch the schedule when she got visitation with her kid that day."

"That day? That Saturday she disappeared?" Had Noelani seen Charlie *that* day? No one had told her that. Sadie hurried to move on, though, while he was in the mood to answer questions.

"Did the employee who covered for her know why Noelani needed to leave?"

"She didn't give Kiki a reason."

Ah, so it was Kiki who had covered the shift. Hadn't the police said that Noelani had borrowed a coworker's car? Kiki's car? That made Kiki even more interesting.

"Did Kiki get written up for covering without your permission?"

He looked up at her and nodded. "Yeah, she did. One more and she's outta here too."

Sadie nodded, wishing she didn't *have* to talk to Kiki, but she did. "I understand Noelani was part of Pastor Darryl's congregation at Fellowship of Kaua'i Christian."

He grunted and narrowed his eyes. "Don't you mean his harem?"

Sadie felt an inner jolt at the word.

Jim must have liked her reaction because when he went back to work on the engine, he was oozing arrogance. "Have you met the sheik, then?"

"I've met Pastor Darryl," Sadie said. It was all she could do not to lecture Jim on the importance of using kind words for people. Then again, she was curious as to why he'd reached such a dramatic conclusion—a conclusion that wasn't *completely* incongruent to Sadie's concerns about Pastor Darryl. "He seems like a nice enough man."

"Oh, he's *real* nice," Jim said. "Especially to the ladies. When did you meet him? Was he *fellowshipping?*"

"I met him at a social last night," Sadie said, cautious. This man's hardness made her uncomfortable.

"Ah, his weekly mix-and-mingle. Does it every Thursday night. So, tell me, how many men did you see at that party?"

"There were men," Sadie said, but other than the teenage boys playing volleyball, there had been maybe only one or two.

"They were likely there for the women too," Jim said. He moved around the boat, collecting fishing gear from the walls and counters, and Sadie found herself following him so she could hear what he was saying. "Pastor Darryl has a *special* place in his heart for women of every kind: the single mother, the former *female* addict, the young widow. And women flock to him like hummingbirds to a feeder."

"Has Pastor Darryl taken his relationship further than it should have been with these women?" Sadie felt bad even asking the question; it made her feel disloyal to Pastor Darryl and Bets before she realized that her loyalty was supposed to be toward Charlie. That loyalty had grown to include his mother, but no one else.

"Everybody knows he's a womanizer," Jim said almost flippantly.

"Gossip isn't the same as knowledge."

Jim looked at her with a bored expression. "Believe me, I've got insider knowledge on the way he works. As for Noelani, there were at least a dozen times I saw him coming or going from the motel during the time she worked here. I live here," he said, pointing upward.

Sadie looked at the ceiling and noticed for the first time a stairway built into one side of the shop that ended at a single metal door. She deduced that there was an apartment above the shop. An apartment that would look out over the motel.

"Pastor Darryl came at night?" Sadie asked, trying to be sure she didn't misinterpret him.

"During the day as well." He threw a few more life jackets into the boat. "Here's the thing about that guy, he hides behind his collar—figuratively speaking—and any time he's questioned, he asserts his position as a man of the cloth and expects all of us to bow down and worship him."

"Did you ever confront him?"

"Yeah, the last time I saw him at the motel was about a week or so before Noelani took off. She was doing housekeeping that day, and he was following her from room to room while she cleaned. I asked him to leave, and he explained that Noelani was going through a difficult time and he was counseling her. I told him to shove off, that he could find another motel to peddle his services."

Sadie felt her cheeks heat up at the inference. "He didn't come back?"

"No," he said, crossing his arms over his chest and looking

pleased with himself. "He didn't. He knows better than to go head-to-head with me."

Sadie hoped the allegations weren't true, but there were only so many explanations for closeting yourself with a pretty young woman. Why wouldn't he counsel with her at the church?

"I understand Noelani was looking for an apartment. Did that bother you?"

"Nope," he said. "She was my employee, lady. I didn't have any kind of emotional bond with her."

Obviously, Sadie thought. "Do you offer housing to all of your employees?"

He narrowed his eyes at her, but she held his gaze without wavering in the slightest. "I let her live here for Bets. She deserved to catch a break, for all the good it did."

CHAPTER 26

"Bets?" Sadie repeated. She hadn't seen that coming.

Jim walked past her and lifted the fishing poles over the side of the boat and onto the seats. "Noelani had been staying in their spare room for a couple months when Bets begged me to give Noelani a job and a place to stay at the motel. She couldn't take it anymore and"—he shrugged and climbed into the boat, organizing the gear he'd thrown in—"I couldn't tell her no. I gave up a room—$350 a week potential, mind you—in hopes of giving Bets a break. Of course, within the month, another lonely heart had moved into the good pastor's apartment, but I'd done what I could."

"Did Noelani live at the motel for free?" Sadie had known Jim all of ten minutes, but he didn't strike her as all that charitable . . . except toward Bets, perhaps.

"She worked an additional ten hours a week in trade—which was a heck of a deal." He looked at her hard as if daring her to disagree. She didn't dare.

"Pastor Darryl seems to really love his wife," Sadie said, unable to discount the tenderness she'd seen between them even though she wondered at the soft spot Jim seemed to have for Bets as well. "I saw them together, and they seem very close."

"Sure," Jim said, a sardonic smile on his face. "No one trusts a single pastor."

She didn't know Pastor Darryl well, but was hesitant to take Jim's view of him.

"Look," he said before she could respond. "The fact that I can't stand her husband isn't something I want thrown in Bets's face, okay?"

"I won't say anything to her," Sadie said. "But why does she put up with it, do you think? I mean, she's beautiful and talented and . . . I guess I just can't wrap my head around why she'd go to all the trouble to move Noelani out, but then let another woman move in."

Jim looked away. "I gave up trying to figure out women a long time ago. Something keeps her there, but there's always hope that one day she'll look around and realize she can do better."

Sadie wanted to ask if Jim thought he was the "better" he was alluding to, but he wouldn't tell her that.

"Do you feel better now?" he asked, interrupting her thoughts. "Have you got your closure and all that?"

"Maybe, but I still have a few more questions," Sadie said. "Is there anyone you can think of who might have wanted to get rid of Noelani?"

He looked up sharply. "Get rid of her?" he questioned. "She doped up and fell off a cliff."

"You're so sure?"

He looked at her with narrowed eyes. "What are you suggesting?"

Sadie shrugged. "I don't know. Someone suggested suicide."

"I didn't say she walked off a cliff by accident," he said, still looking at her closely. "But *you* don't think it was suicide, do you?"

Sadie shifted her feet. "I have no idea. That's what I'm trying to figure out."

"You think someone did something to her."

Sadie opened her mouth to deny it, but why? "It's possible," she said. She wanted to ask him about the gag order he'd given his employees, but she couldn't figure out how to say it without getting Kiki in trouble for having told her about it in the first place. Jim had been surprisingly open about Noelani, which seemed contradictory to the threats he'd made to Kiki. "Sometimes things aren't as they seem. I'm not convinced she overdosed. Could I talk to your other employees—"

"Everyone else thinks she shot up too much and keeled over," he said, sounding almost frustrated with Sadie's point of view.

Not everyone, Sadie thought, picturing Charlie in her mind. "I just feel like there are a lot of details no one knows, which is why I wondered if I could have your blessing to talk to your employees— especially Kiki since she's the one who covered for Noelani that night."

"Kiki told everything to the police last week."

"I'm not the police."

His eyes narrowed. "Which makes me wonder what you're doing here. This isn't about closure."

"Have you ever discovered a dead body?" Sadie asked, squaring her shoulders and not giving into the quivering she felt as the interview began to wear on her. "I'd just like to talk to as many people as possible in hopes of getting a better picture of Noelani, that's all."

He continued to stare at her, and she shifted her weight from one foot to another. After a few seconds, he started cleaning up his tools. "I've got a business to run, and Noelani's cost me enough time and trouble as it is."

"I just want to talk to them and see—"

"No," he said, closing a hatch where he'd thrown the life jackets. "You talk to them and they're fired. Understand? How's that for closure?"

CHAPTER 27

Sadie still needed to talk to Pastor Darryl and Bets, but suddenly Jim seemed a more interesting candidate. He'd given her walking papers and refused her access to his employees. Why? And he was so mean. Mean toward Noelani, mean to Sadie. Was he hiding something? Trying to intimidate her? It was working—she was totally intimidated—but that wouldn't stop her.

Once she got back to her motel room, she closed her eyes to try to ebb the growing frustration she felt. She wished Gayle were there already. It wasn't even nine in the morning.

With a deep exhale, she raised a hand to her eyes and tried to come up with a new plan. Should she try to talk to Kiki despite Jim telling her it would put Kiki's job at risk? Would he really fire her? Probably. He had written her up for taking Noelani's shift that night.

Sadie crossed the room to her laptop that she'd set up on the small desk and flipped it open before sitting down and taking a breath she hoped would help dispel the tightness in her chest. Writing things down always helped her sort through her thoughts.

The floor lamp next to the desk wasn't very bright, and the overhead light from the sink at the back of the unit was too far away to be effective, so Sadie opened up the drapes over the window by the front door to let in some natural light in hopes of avoiding eye strain. The window gave a nice view of the pool and the surrounding gardens, which were somewhat overgrown, but pretty nonetheless.

She'd been typing out her thoughts and observations, her anxiety calming in the process, when someone passed her window, casting a shadow over her computer screen. Sadie looked into the mirror over the desk just in time to catch a glimpse of long dark hair and the flip of a pink skirt. She paused, then jumped up and hurried to the window. It had only been a flash, but the woman had looked like Bets.

The window only gave her a limited view, so Sadie opened the door and peered out in time to see another flash of hair and pink as the woman entered the motel office. Sadie doubted Bets had come for the continental breakfast and didn't hesitate to follow her, quick-stepping to the office, where she peeked through the floor-length window beside the door. She squinted through the glass in time to see Bets disappear into Jim's office, where the door immediately closed behind her. What was she doing here? Then again, Jim and Bets were close enough for him to help her with her marital problems. Was Jim in the office too?

Sadie was pondering this when she caught Kiki watching her from inside the office. She smiled, embarrassed to be caught. Kiki looked worried. Sadie gave a little wave and then walked past the office door, picturing in her mind where Jim's office was in relation to the rest of the motel. Though the building was horseshoe-shaped, there were a few open walkways that led to the back, and one was located near the office. It wasn't hard to cut through the corridor and backtrack enough to find the single window, complete with teal curtains similar to those in the front office, on the back side of the building right where Jim's office should be. The window was open, typical for the cool mornings.

Sadie looked around quickly to ensure she was alone before ducking down and walking, half crouched, to the window where she could hear the murmur of voices. She slid right up underneath the window before raising up as far as she could without her head peeking over the sill. Whoever was talking was female; she could only assume it was Bets. A hedge blocked Sadie from being seen from the street but it wouldn't protect her from anyone who came from the other direction.

"I can't believe you're asking me to do this again," Jim suddenly said, his deeper tones carrying much easier than his companion's. "It didn't do any good the last time."

Again? Last time?

Bets spoke again, but Sadie couldn't hear anything more than perhaps a pleading in her tone of voice. As Sadie listened, though, the voice came closer. Bets must be pacing around the room. As Bets came closer to the window, Sadie was able to hear what she was saying.

"She used to work in a dental office, Jim. She'd be good at managing the desk, and we both know you need the help."

"I need a housekeeper, not a desk girl."

"Mandi's overqualified for housekeeping," Bets said. "Can't the new girl do housekeeping?"

Mandi?

"Don't you mean she *won't* do housekeeping?" he asked. "She'll live off you but won't lower herself to being a maid?"

"She'd do a good job," Bets said in a pouty tone.

Silence.

"Jim, please," Bets said softly.

"Even if I offered her the job, she'd only take it because it would mean she could stay close to him," Jim countered. "Too close. It won't solve your problem, Bets, just like it didn't last time. You know I want to help you, but this won't fix it."

It was all coming together. Bets had come to Jim for help with Noelani; now she had another woman to get out of her house. Was it a coincidence that with Noelani gone, Bets thought she had somewhere for Mandi to go?

"We just need some time together, alone," Bets said. Her voice started moving away again, and Sadie leaned toward the window in hopes of hearing it as long as possible. "I'm sure that . . ."

Biscuits, Sadie thought when Bets's voice turned back to soft murmuring tones.

"I'll tell you what," Jim said, interrupting her a few seconds later. "Why don't *you* move into the motel? That will send a message he might actually listen to."

"Jim," she said, back in range. From the tone of Bets's voice, Sadie wondered if that was an offer he'd made before.

"Look," Jim said, sounding frustrated. "I've got a charter in ten minutes, and the boat's not ready yet thanks to some busybody hijacking my morning about your husband's *last* girlfriend."

It had been so long since someone had called Sadie a busybody that she almost forgot it was an insult. Bets said something Sadie couldn't hear.

"She said she's trying to figure out what happened to Noelani," he said. "I checked out the video from last night, and she talked to Ashley and then Kiki this morning. I told Kiki she's not allowed to say a word."

Bets murmured something.

"Of course not, and I told her to leave, but not before I figured out she didn't know anything. She's just fishing."

Bets spoke again, but her voice was coming closer, and Sadie strained to hear what she was saying.

"—want everything about that woman to go away."

Was she talking about Sadie or Noelani?

"What if she's undercover or something?" Bets asked.

"She's not," Jim said confidently.

The silence in the office increased Sadie's tension, and she leaned forward until her ear touched the cool stone of the building. Why would Bets worry about the police asking questions unless she had something to hide?

"I just want to forget any of it happened," she said again.

"She thinks someone knocked off Noelani," Jim said.

"What?" Bets asked, the panic in her voice taking Sadie off guard. "Why would she think that?"

"We didn't get to that part," Jim said.

"Why can't she just go away?" Bets said, a hint of emotion in her voice.

"She'll be gone soon," Jim said. "Checkout is at eleven."

"I wasn't talking about her," Bets said. "I meant Noelani. What does it take to get her out of my life?"

Silence fell, and Sadie didn't dare breathe for fear of being over-heard.

"I'd be careful who you say that kind of thing to," Jim said. "And maybe you should—"

A hand clamped around Sadie's arm, and she jumped and gasped simultaneously, hitting her head against the windowsill in the process. There was no way Jim and Bets hadn't heard her. She didn't get a chance to see who'd grabbed her before she was pulled around the corner. The hand on her arm released her as she stumbled to a stop, and she turned to look into Kiki's face for a quick second before the girl slid a card into the lock of the room they were closest to. She pushed open the door, pulled Sadie inside with her, and closed the door.

"Wait here for five minutes, then leave. Check out as soon as you can. Jim will only make this harder for both of us if you stick around. I'll call you when I can, and I'll tell you what I know."

Sadie opened her mouth to reply, but Kiki had already darted out the door, letting it slowly close behind her and leaving Sadie alone in a darkened motel room.

CHAPTER 28

Sadie followed Kiki's advice and waited exactly five minutes—which was about how long it took for her heart rate and breathing to return to normal. After peering outside and making sure the coast was clear, Sadie left the room and hurried to her own door. Only when she got there, she realized she'd left her key inside her room when she'd gone after Bets.

Biscuits!

There was nothing to do but get a new key, so she headed toward the office, hoping Jim wouldn't be there. She let out a breath when she walked in to find him talking to Kiki behind the counter. Didn't he have a charter?

They both went quiet when Sadie entered. Jim glared at her; Kiki's jaw tightened. The door to his office was open, showing the room was empty. Bets must have left while Sadie was waiting those five minutes.

"I locked myself out of my room," Sadie said. "Could I get a new key?"

"Do you have your ID?" Jim asked, crossing his arms over his chest and looking smug.

"No, I left my bag—and my key—inside the room."

"We can't issue a new key without ID."

Kiki looked from him to Sadie in surprise but took a step backward, physically distancing herself from the confrontation.

"You know who I am," Sadie said evenly.

He shrugged. "It's policy. Sorry. We can't issue a new key without ID to prove you're the registered guest on record."

Sadie narrowed her eyes at him and looked at Kiki, who was looking at something on the desk. The girl tucked her hair behind her ear with forced casualness. She would be no help. Sadie took a deep breath, and when she spoke again, her voice was sincerely humble. "Please let me into my room, Mr. Bartley."

"Like I said, without ID, I can't issue a key." He couldn't have looked more pleased with himself.

"Look," Sadie said, leveling him with an annoyed stare. He knew she'd been listening in on his conversation with Bets. That was the only explanation. He knew and he was punishing her for it. "Just let me get my things, and I'll get out of your hair."

Jim made an exaggerated effort to look at his watch. "Oh, look at the time. I've got a charter. I'll see you this afternoon."

Sadie's blood began to boil. "You're seriously going to keep me out of my own room? Checkout is at eleven. I'll . . . I'll call the police."

"Go for it," he said. "But they'll have to wait for me to get back from the charter to tell my side of it." He turned to Kiki. "You are not authorized to let her into her room or to make her a new key. Tell the police they have to wait for me *if* she calls them, but I bet she doesn't want them to know she's been asking about Noelani. We'll figure this out when I get back."

He headed for the main door. Sadie was taken off guard by his assessment of her not wanting to call the police, which was dead-on. But she had to get in her room; her phone and computer were in there. The only thing she could think to do was follow him out. He walked fast, and she had to almost jog to keep up with him, her slippahs slapping the sidewalk. "You can't do this!" she yelled at him.

"Sure I can," he said over his shoulder. "I own the motel. What's more, any employee you talk to for any reason will be fired—that's what I was explaining to Kiki just now. She'll be passing that message on to the employee who takes over for her at two o'clock. I'd hate to fire them over something stupid *you* do. Gainful employment can be hard to find around here."

Sadie stopped walking, realizing that a power struggle with him would never work. When he noticed she wasn't following him, he faced her, looking pleased with himself.

"You must be really afraid of what I'm going to find out," she said.

His eyes narrowed, but he raised his chin in defiance.

"Go ahead," she said, growling low in her throat and shooing him toward the gate. "Go do your little charter and then come back and see what's happened while you were gone." She turned on her heel, heading back toward the office.

She wanted to look back—she really, really wanted to—but she didn't. Instead she marched past the main office and stopped at her room, looking at the lock. She'd read up about apps that could copy the IP address of an electronic lock and disable it long enough for her to get inside, but she'd never tried it. Her phone was in the room anyway. She sighed. Even if this was a traditional lock, she'd left both her pick gun and her manual pick set at the condo, which she had locked up tight, anxious about her safety. The keys to the condo were in her bag. She was locked out of everything.

"This is ridiculous," she muttered. She found herself staring at the main office and took a deep breath to center her thoughts. Gayle's flight landed in an hour; how would she know where to go? Sadie had assumed she'd be able to communicate with her when she got in.

"Ridiculous," Sadie muttered again as she tried to figure out the back way Bets had used to get to the church. However, she got all turned around and eventually had to go back to the motel, out front, and walk to the church the same way she had the night before. She needed to call Gayle and leave a message for her to meet her at the motel. And she needed to call Pete to find out if she could call the police about what Jim had just done without having to divulge what she was doing there. Would they really make her wait until Jim got back before they would let her get her things? The sun was up, and the heat was rising with every minute. Surely Pastor Darryl would let her use the phone to call Gayle and Pete, though it was an overseas call.

Sadie had just reached the parking lot of the church when she saw a little boy slip inside the double doors of the church. A familiar little boy.

Charlie?

The surprise of seeing him caused her to jolt to a stop and forget all about stupid-head Jim Bartley—well, almost. It wasn't yet ten in the morning, and her day had been hijacked for the second time.

CHAPTER 29

Sadie hurried across the parking lot and carefully opened the front doors of the church so as not to make a sound. She tiptoed across the threshold onto the white marbled floor of the foyer, quickly surmising she was alone. Everything was white—floor, walls, ceiling—except for the colored light that shined through a stained glass window set high above the door. The way the light played on the marble was beautiful, but Sadie didn't have time to fully appreciate it. She didn't hear the slap of slippahs in the hallway, so she moved toward the double doors directly across the foyer area, assuming they led into the chapel area. She pulled the door open carefully.

Her eyes were immediately drawn to the dark-haired boy in a light blue shirt and khaki shorts walking purposefully down the aisle. The chapel was mostly white as well, but with dark red upholstery on the cushions and black trim on the top of the pews. Simple and striking at the same time. At the front of the room was a large black cross set against the wall—the only adornment in the room. Sadie used her fingertips to allow the door to close gently behind her and noted the sound of the air conditioner that created a good amount of white noise.

At the front of the chapel was a raised platform the width of the room and about twenty feet deep with a pulpit pushed to the right. Sadie imagined the stage area would fit a Christian band or choir quite nicely; that kind of thing was popular in some churches, or so Shawn had told her after attending one with a roommate.

Charlie climbed the stairs to the stage, intent on reaching the cross on the back wall. The bottom of the cross came to his waist, and Sadie noticed a paper or envelope in his hand. As she watched, he lifted the paper, held it with both hands for a moment, then folded it in half and seemed to feed it into the bottom of the cross. A moment later, he stepped back, his hands empty.

Sadie felt her eyebrows raise. What had just happened? She'd no sooner thought it, however, than Charlie turned around. In the moment before he realized she was there, she saw peace and confidence in his expression. Whatever he'd just done had brought him some kind of comfort.

"Hi, Charlie," Sadie said, quietly. It felt appropriate to speak softly in this room.

Charlie froze and stared at her, looking scared and ready to run, except that she was blocking the only exit. Actually, there was a door set into the other side of the room, near the stage, but it was closed, and she wasn't sure Charlie had noticed it since it seemed to be designed to blend into the wall.

Rather than confront him about what he was doing here and why he wasn't in school, Sadie walked about a third of the way down the aisle and sat on the end of one of the pews. She shifted her gaze from him to the cross and said a little prayer for help to know what to do with this sad little boy.

She didn't say anything else to Charlie, but could feel him waiting for her to. After almost a minute, Charlie walked off the stage and headed down the aisle. Sadie purposely kept her eyes on the cross but could see him getting closer and closer, edging to the far side as though she might jump out and grab him. He passed her, but she still didn't speak, though she questioned her judgment. Should she stop him? If she wanted him to trust her, she couldn't take a position of offense. He needed to come to her and that would only happen if she presented herself as trustworthy.

She waited for the sound of the doors being opened, but didn't hear anything. The air conditioner kept up a steady hum, though she thought she'd hear the door over the white noise since she was listening so intently. Almost another full minute passed in utter silence before she heard him slide into the pew behind her. She contained the smile that pulled at the edges of her mouth, but just barely.

"It's sure peaceful here," Sadie said, when she couldn't stand the silence anymore.

Charlie didn't answer.

"Do you come here a lot?" she asked after several seconds passed.

"Every day," a man answered, causing Sadie to startle and turn quickly in her seat.

Pastor Darryl grinned at her with his bright white teeth.

She looked past him, her face hot with embarrassment, but Charlie wasn't there. She looked back at Pastor Darryl and cleared her throat. "I, uh . . . thought you were someone else," she said, feeling ridiculous.

"Who, I wonder?" Pastor Darryl said, still teasing her.

"Never mind," Sadie said. She glanced at the door again. How had Charlie left so quietly?

"My next appointment isn't for thirty minutes, so your timing is exceptional. Why don't we take this into my office?"

Sadie followed him down the aisle, casting one last look around the chapel, before going through the hidden door by the stage area. The door led into a small office decorated in neutral shades of browns. Nice, but simple. Fitting for his position. There was another door on an adjacent wall that she assumed led to the hallway. Probably so he didn't have to go through the chapel to get to his office. Instead of sitting behind his desk, Pastor Darryl sat in one of the upholstered chairs across from it and indicated for her to do the same in the other chair. When she sat, their knees were nearly touching.

"So," he said. "Where would you like to start?"

Sadie didn't even know. What was it she'd wanted to learn from him? Why was she here? Thoughts about her locked motel room and Charlie's surprising appearance followed by his even more surprising disappearance twisted up in her mind until she couldn't find a way to fit Pastor Darryl into her thoughts. She needed to call Pete, and she needed to leave a message for Gayle. Should she tell Pastor Darryl his wife was meeting with Jim Bartley behind closed doors?

"I want to understand Noelani," Sadie said as though from rote memory. "Can you just tell me about her?"

He smiled, kind and understanding, before launching into what he knew of Noelani's past. Sadie's notes were in her room, so she tried to concentrate on what he said. Most of it she'd heard before from her own searches or from Mr. Olie, though she liked Pastor Darryl's compassionate version. It was difficult to think of him having an affair with Noelani, but Jim's inference and Bets's insecurity were hard to ignore. She didn't have a clue how to bring it up, however, so she listened and nodded and tried to think of what she needed from Pastor Darryl that no one else could give her.

"I understand she was having a difficult time the last few weeks,"

Sadie said, remembering that Jim had said Darryl had been following Noelani around the motel. "You were counseling with her?"

Pastor Darryl inclined his head. "It's common for recovering addicts to confront what sent them to their addiction in the first place once they find themselves in a safe place. She'd had a lot of feelings coming up and was struggling to cope with them appropriately."

"Appropriately?"

"She was used to turning to drugs or alcohol to numb those feelings, and now she was trying to sort them out, to deal with the pain, forgive, and learn from past mistakes and traumas she hadn't faced before."

"You sound like a psychiatrist," Sadie said.

"Just a spokesperson of God's love who believes in Christ's promise to bear our burdens, if we ask."

Sadie nodded. "Did it help? Talking to you?"

"I think so. Or at least I thought so. One day she'd seem fine, and the next day she was sullen. As reuniting with Charlie drew closer, she seemed to be more and more connected to everything that had happened that took him from her in the first place. It's a difficult process."

"You last saw her at the social Thursday night, right? How was she?"

He pondered and let out a breath. "She was upset."

"About what?"

"She was working toward getting Charlie back, but the state's requirements were difficult for her to meet. She'd been looking for an apartment but couldn't find anything she could afford. The state wouldn't let her have a roommate, and she had to avoid certain areas that had a bad reputation. She felt as though she wouldn't be able to do it." Pastor Darryl looked at the floor. "The last thing she said to me that night was that she didn't know if it was worth it. She felt like she was working so hard only to have to keep working even harder. She'd need two jobs to pay for her own place, which meant she'd never see Charlie anyway."

"She said it wasn't worth it?" Sadie's heart sank. It was getting harder and harder to be optimistic that something else had happened other than the former junkie using again.

"She said maybe he was better off where he was."

It broke Sadie's heart to hear that, and she hoped Charlie would never know his mother had said it. "What did you say?"

"I assured her that God had chosen her to be Charlie's mother for a reason and that she owed it to both of them to fight for that role. I told her God would help her if she did everything she could do first. She needed to have faith."

"And then she was gone."

Pastor Darryl nodded. "Don't misunderstand me when I say that I believe what I said to her, Sister Sadie. I believe God creates a way for us, but He is not a God of force. He couldn't make Noelani have faith in Him or herself. She had to have that, and sadly she was struggling to believe it. When we parted that night, I made her promise to call me if she needed to talk, any time. I never spoke to her again." He looked over Sadie's head. "After she was found and the police began investigating her death, they told me she'd called my phone, but I wasn't available, and she didn't leave a message."

"But she tried to call you," Sadie said. That felt like hope.

"She tried," he repeated. "I admit I feel guilty for not being there for her. I wonder what I could have changed if I'd been there to answer her call." He looked at a clock mounted above the door. "I'm afraid I'm about out of time, Sister Sadie."

"Me too," she said automatically, trying to process everything he'd said. "Thank you for talking with me."

"Sure thing," Pastor Darryl said as they stood. He placed his hand on the small of her back as they walked toward the door that led to the hall instead of the chapel. She tried to walk faster, so that his hand would fall away, but he kept pace with her. He really did seem like a kind man, but his constant physicality, if not conscious, still seemed to be inviting something—some kind of connection that Sadie wasn't sure was right. That thought reminded her of something else.

He pulled open his office door, and Sadie turned toward him, stepping away so he couldn't put his hand on her shoulder or arm. "Was Noelani seeing anyone?"

"I don't think so," he said. "She was cautious with men. I think that made it hard for her to open up to me right away. When we spoke about such things, she said she didn't plan on being in a relationship for a long time—the only men she had room for in her life right then were God and Charlie."

Sadie smiled. She liked that thought very much. "What can you tell me about Jim Bartley?"

Pastor Darryl's smile fell. "Have you spoken to him already?"

Sadie nodded.

"What did he tell you that has you asking me about him?"

"He doesn't seem to think very highly of you," she said, then cringed because she hadn't planned on saying something so negative.

Pastor Darryl's jaw tightened. "Believe it or not, we were friends once. We worked together with the same outreach program Noelani came through. The Sand and Sea employed some of the people who chose to attend my congregation; we had a very symbiotic relationship."

"That *is* hard to believe," Sadie said carefully. "What happened?"

"His wife left him and took her boys from her previous marriage with her when she went," Pastor Darryl said, pushing his hands into his pockets. "Jim hasn't been the same since. He quit the outreach, cut all ties to us, and stopped hiring members of the congregation."

"But he hired Noelani," Sadie said.

"Yes," Pastor Darryl agreed. "He did. I'd hoped that perhaps that meant there would be some healing between us, maybe the start of working together again, but it hasn't come to that."

"What about Bets?" Sadie asked. "Has she maintained a . . . friendship with Jim?"

"Bets is friends with everyone," Pastor Darryl said, but Sadie didn't think his smile was entirely sincere. "I'm afraid I'm out of time, Sister Sadie. Sorry."

"That's okay," Sadie hurried to assure him, hating the change of mood. "Thank you for your time."

"You're welcome," he said. "I hope you find some peace about Noelani. Though her death is tragic, I've no doubt she is in a place of comfort and love now."

Sadie nodded. "I believe that too."

Pastor Darryl smiled. "Thank you for your faith, Sister Sadie," he said. "*Metetaloko.*"

He shut the office door, him on the inside, her on the outside. Sadie shook her head, questioning the wisdom of having confronted him like that. She walked down the hallway until she reached the foyer she'd been in last night when she'd come in with Bets. The phone on the wall reminded her that she'd come to the church in order to call Pete. And Gayle, who would be here soon. Should she also call Mr. Olie and tell him about having seen Charlie?

Thinking of Charlie made her remember the strange action

she'd seen at the cross—the disappearing note. Rather than picking up the phone, she followed the curving hallway until she reached the chapel doors on the other side. Surely it would only take a minute to figure it out.

CHAPTER 30

The chapel was empty, and Sadie hurried down the aisle and onto the stage, her eyes trained on the cross on the wall. She scanned the area as she got closer, looking for the note in case Charlie had just dropped it. When she was about a foot or so away from the wall, she stopped and leaned forward, staring at the very bottom of the cross, where the edge of the black wood met up with the stark white walls. She reached forward and felt with her fingers the slot she wasn't sure her eyes were really seeing. It was the same width as the cross and therefore perfectly hidden beneath it. Her fingers probed the smooth edges of the cut in the wall, and she wondered what it was for. She knelt in front of it and tried to look into the opening, but it was too dark on the other side. What was it here for? Where did it go?

She stood up and stared at the wall itself. What was behind it? She'd been in Pastor Darryl's office, but that was to the right side of the chapel, not the back. There must be a room behind this wall. She hurried back down the aisle and exited the doors into the white marble foyer. The hallway that ran parallel to the chapel ended at a door, and Sadie felt her heart rate increasing. Pastor Darryl's office didn't have a door at the back of it, so this must be the way in. It was the only explanation she could think of—that the paper Charlie had put into the slot went into this room somehow.

There was a light switch to the right of the door, and Sadie flipped it, watching the gap beneath the door illuminate, proving the switch controlled the light within the room. She reached for the doorknob, hoping against hope that it would be unlocked, then frowned when the knob didn't turn in her hand. But the knob had a keyhole. Probably a basic five tumbler residential lock that would keep most people out. Sadie, however, was not most people and simple interior door locks were her specialty. She'd picked her own at home a hundred times during her training, which was self-taught, mostly, with some help from YouTube.

If only she'd brought her pick set. A paper clip or a bobby pin could torque the plug, and another one could push on the pins until they reached the shear line. But she didn't have a paper clip or a bobby pin. She'd need to find something else.

She looked around and listened to the silence of the church. Would someone find her trying to break into this room? Was it fair to put her curiosity ahead of her responsibility to call Mr. Olie about Charlie, or her need to get Pete's advice, or tell Gayle where she was? But she didn't know if she'd get this opportunity again. Certainly she wasn't the only one who knew about the slot and this room. If she didn't get to it first, she might never know what it was Charlie had put in there.

She hurried to the kitchen and began going through drawers, keeping an open mind as she looked for the tools she'd need to get past the lock. Her search yielded a wire whisk and an ice pick. The ice pick could brace the plug, and if she could detach the wires of the whisk, they could possibly fit into the lock and push up against the pins. Whether it would be strong enough to lift the pins up to the shear line, she couldn't be certain, but it was worth a try, and she didn't have any other ideas. Pete had once called this type of improvising "a kitchen hack." She'd never actually done it and was a little excited by the prospect.

She hated breaking a perfectly sound cooking utensil, but she had thrown out enough whisks in her day to know how easily the wires were to pull out of the casing. She wrapped her hand in the skirt of her muumuu for friction purposes; all it took was a good yank to pull out one of the wires. She followed the wire to the other end, yanked, and it too came right out. She did it again, so that she had two curved wires for her purposes, just in case.

She put the now-disabled whisk back in the drawer, making a note to replace it as soon as she could, then she opened the door slowly and peeked down the hall toward Pastor Darryl's office. She couldn't tell if he was still in there, so she hurried back to the locked door on the opposite side of the church while straightening out the wires and holding the ice pick under her arm.

When she arrived at the locked door, she flipped on the light switch to ensure the interior would be illuminated once she got in. She squinted at the keyhole before holding the wires in her teeth so she could manipulate the ice pick. She wanted to hold the plug still, but with enough tension so she could turn it. Once she felt she had sufficient tension, she removed one of the wires from her teeth and slid it into the lock with her free hand, twisting the pick and prodding with the wire until she felt the first pin shift, then, nearly a minute later, the second.

While she'd watched videos of people who could pick a lock in fifteen seconds or less—there were actually competitions held all over the world—she always took a long time. But she was patient, and after two full minutes of shifting and pushing, sweat trickling down her back from the constant pressure she had to keep on the plug, she finally felt the plug shift. She quickly turned the knob and pulled the door open. She was in—but she only allowed herself to enjoy the triumph for a moment. There was work to do.

The narrow room was storage of some kind, stacked to the ceiling with cardboard and Rubbermaid boxes. Thick black marker labeled the boxes with notes like THE CREATION and NATIVITY. The boxes were stacked along the walls, allowing a walkway between them that turned to the right about six feet in.

Sadie put her tools on the floor and closed the door most of the way behind her. She didn't want it gaping open in case someone came by, but she didn't like the idea of closing herself in either. She moved forward and was instantly confronted with thick musty heat; this room wasn't well ventilated.

At the bend at the back of the narrow room, Sadie leaned forward to peer around the corner. There were more boxes and an artificial Christmas tree—did they do Christmas trees on the islands? The room was only about six feet wide and darker in the back. If there was a light fixture for this area, the bulb had either burnt out or there was another switch Sadie couldn't find. She *could* see, however, thanks to a very small ray of light toward the end of the back corridor that she followed as though it were the northern star. Her skin prickled with sweat. Possibly from her growing anticipation as well as the heat, she couldn't be sure.

As she continued forward from the bend in the room, five feet, then ten, the stacks of boxes became shorter—less convenient to get out of the room, she assumed—until she reached the last ten feet of the room. It was empty except for a blue Rubbermaid tub with no lid pushed up against the wall beneath the narrow cut that let in the tiny slice of light.

Sadie felt her excitement rise as she reached the box and looked inside it, counting at least a dozen notes scattered along the bottom of the plastic bin. A few were sealed inside of envelopes, but the rest were folded-over papers. Sadie knelt next to the box, wondering what the notes were for. She reached in for a paper that was on top of the rest; maybe that meant it was the most recent. She unfolded the plain white paper but had to lean over the box and hold the note next to the light to see what it said. As soon as she opened it, she knew it was an adult's handwriting—not Charlie's—but she read it anyway.

Please bless that my sister's psoriasis might be healed.

Your child,

D. Halakimaki Koto

Sadie refolded the letter and put it on the floor beside her. Was this some kind of prayer box? She'd known people to write out their prayers and bury them or burn them, and she'd read a book where people stuck the papers into a wall in their garden, kind of like the Wailing Wall. The next note, also written by an adult, had a much more disturbing prayer.

Please bless him to know how much I love him and that leaving his wife is not a sin when she's already been untrue to their vows. I feel that you've led me to him. Help him see that.

In faith,

ACR

It took some . . . gumption to pray for something like that. Sadie set the note with the first one, feeling guilty for reading people's prayers that were certainly meant to be private. She wondered what happened to the notes once they came through the wall. Did Pastor Darryl read them?

She reached in again and, this time, looked for the clues that might point out Charlie's note to her. One note wasn't folded perfectly, and it was written on the same newsprint paper as the list he'd left at Sadie's house. A bead of sweat began trailing down the side of her face, and she wiped it away before reaching into the tub for the note.

She unfolded it and had to squint due to the fact that it was written in pencil, like the list of questions.

Dear God,
Mom says you can help make stuff come tru.
Help me find my mom and make her not to do
drugs.
                              Charlie Pouhu

Sadie's breath caught, and she read it again, holding back the emotion that was close to the surface. While there was nothing earth-shattering in the note, there was a quality of desperation that worried Sadie. Charlie was reaching out to anyone he thought could possibly help him. What if he decided no one would? Would he take it on his own shoulders to find a woman who couldn't be found?

After reading the prayer the second time, she folded it back up, then folded it one more time and tucked it into the only pocket she had—her bra. It was trashy, she knew that, but she needed to keep it safe. It was time to call Mr. Olie, but as she turned, she saw the prayers she'd left out of the box. She picked them up and threw them back in the bin. After cleaning up her mess, she hurried toward the door, hoping she wouldn't end up having to leave another message for Mr. Olie. She should have asked him for his direct number last night.

She was almost to the bend in the room when the room went black. She stumbled to a stop in the near-darkness, blinking quickly before rushing toward the doorway.

She was just turning the corner when the door shut, quick and quiet—but not slammed. Sadie hesitated for a millisecond, then hurried forward and grabbed the doorknob, which didn't move in her hand.

CHAPTER 31

Sadie shook the doorknob as though that would work before remembering that there was a thumb lock on the inside. She turned the lock before twisting the handle and pushing, but something was obstructing the door. Another bead of sweat trailed down the side of her head, and she told herself to think reasonably even as panic started setting in. Who would barricade her in? Why? How would she get out? What if she *couldn't* get out? What if there were rats in here? Or cockroaches? How long would the oxygen last? Her heart rate increased, and her sweat glands kicked into hyperdrive. Before she knew it, she was banging on the door.

"Let me out!" she yelled, smacking the door with the palms of her hands. "Please, let me out!"

The voice in her head told her that whoever locked her in wasn't about to let her out just because she asked, but the rest of her was in a full-on panic that kept her screaming and banging, pleading to be let out, rattling the door in hopes that whatever was in the way of the door would move. Getting out was the only thing she could think about. Maybe Pastor Darryl would hear her—he had to hear her, didn't he? He'd said he had an appointment, but maybe he hadn't left yet.

She kept yelling and pounding, then felt her way back to the wall with the prayer slot and banged and yelled there. No one came. She started crying, begging for someone to please let her out. The palms of her hands stung and her fingertips tingled. She felt light-headed. Still she didn't stop. The only relief she could imagine was getting out of the room, and the only way to get out was to get the attention of someone capable. She was not capable.

She went back to the door—the only exit—and pounded on the wood in vain. She was entirely helpless. The feeling wrapped her up tight until she was gasping for air, her pleas just above a whisper. Her arms ached, and she fell against a wall of boxes as she lost her balance. The boxes teetered, and she tried to look up at them in the darkness but then had to grab onto them for stability when the blackness spun around her. The boxes steadied, and she lowered herself to the floor with her hands over her head, her chest heaving as she tried to draw a breath.

Sitting helped dispel the dizziness, but her head felt wobbly on her shoulders. She held it still with both hands, rocking gently back and forth as she tried to catch her breath. No one was coming to save her. No one was letting her out. The fear was an avalanche falling over her, and she thought of the pills Dr. McKay had given her. Pills that were safely stored in her bag in the motel room she'd been banned from, literally.

Dr. McKay's breathing exercises came to mind, and she tried to draw a full breath but couldn't do it. She tried again, counting to two with the inhale and again with the exhale. Then she counted to three—in and out—increasing the length of each breath until she reached eight, which was as high as she'd ever been.

The feeling returned to her fingers, though her palms still throbbed, and she wiped at her eyes and nose with the hem of her muumuu, something she knew she wouldn't do under any other circumstances. She kept breathing and told herself she was alive, that she was uninjured, and that she needed to be calm in order to think logically about what to do next. Eventually, her pulse slowed, and she could breathe through her nose instead of having to gasp air through her open mouth. The nausea lessened, and she didn't feel so shaky.

You're safe, she told herself. *You're alive. You've been locked in a room before and survived.*

Yes, and there'd been a dead body with her last time.

Panic descended again and soon she could barely breathe, but she forced herself to be calm, using the breathing exercises again and trying not to think about the anxiety.

But it was dark, and she was hot and someone had shut her in a small room. Who? Pastor Darryl? Bets? Did she know Sadie had been listening to her conversation with Jim? Had Jim left on his charter yet? She was pretty sure he had, but he'd love to lock her up if he had the chance. Could it have been Charlie? He was capable, but why would he do it? And yet, amid trying to figure out who had done this to her, there was something . . . positive to the fact that she'd been locked in and life as she knew it hadn't come to an end. At least not yet.

She finally stood, able to make out the faintest lines of boxes from the light coming in around the edges of the door. Without a rescuer, she had to figure out how to get out of there by herself. She could think of two options off the top of her head: find a way to push away whatever was barricading the door or take advantage of the wall the prayer slot was on and break through the drywall. What she wouldn't give for a headlamp to better see her way around in here!

She decided to start with the option of removing the barricade, if she could. It seemed reasonable that one of the foyer chairs had been wedged between the doorknob and the floor, keeping the door closed. If she could push something against the legs of the chair, maybe she could release the tension and push the door open. She was sure she'd seen it work on TV. Then again, toxicology reports came back in thirty minutes on TV—sometimes during the time it took for a commercial break. Still, unjamming the door was the better option and the least destructive. To make it work, though, she would need something long enough to reach the legs of the chair and thin enough to fit under the door. And she had to find it in the dark.

The first thing she tried was a lid from one of the Rubbermaid tubs. It was too thick to fit under the door. Then she emptied out one of the cardboard boxes that happened to be full of papers of some kind and folded the box flat. It wasn't strong enough to do the job and kept buckling when she tried. After hitting the chair legs half a dozen times from every angle she could manage on her hands and knees, sweat was dripping down her face.

With the cardboard option a failure, Sadie had no choice but to start going through tubs in search of an object that would work. A yardstick would be perfect, but people kept yardsticks in hall closets that were easy to access, not in Rubbermaid boxes stacked to the ceiling. After going through four different tubs and searching by the sense of touch alone, she sat on the ground for a break, fanning herself with a piece of poster board she'd found in one of the boxes and trying not to let the anxiety overtake her. It still sat on her chest like a cat waiting to pounce. Someone would come check out the church at some point, right? Someone would notice the chair and investigate, right?

She kept fanning and focusing on her breathing, gearing up for another search of the boxes before she'd have to turn to plan B and start looking for something to break through the drywall. As she pushed herself to her feet, she muttered a prayer. "Please get me out of here," she said. It was on the tip of her tongue to promise she'd go back to Puhi and forget all about this when she caught sight of a shadow of movement beneath the door.

"Help me!" she yelled, scrambling over the contents of the boxes on her way to the door. "Let me out of here!"

She went quiet, waiting for someone to answer her, but she heard nothing, and it caused her heart to race even more. Anyone but the person who'd locked her in would have responded to her screams. She dropped to her hands and knees and put her face on the floor in hopes of being able to see the shoes of whoever was out there.

Something thin and white slid underneath the door, causing her to inhale sharply and scramble backward as though it were a grenade. She collided with the piles of unidentified stuff on the floor and was immediately tangled up in some kind of cloth. Nothing exploded, though. She was trying to untangle herself from whatever costume had gotten the better of her when she heard a scrape from outside the door. Immediately she jumped to her feet, put her shoulder against the door, and grabbed the knob. She turned and pushed for the hundredth time. This time, however, the door flew open, Sadie with it.

She burst into the hallway and tried to catch herself but wasn't able to stop her momentum as she crashed into the heavy wooden chair set a few inches past the door. She fell on it, then over it, and cracked her head against it as she tumbled onto the white marble of the floor. Once she came to a stop, she blinked at the ceiling. She tried to get up despite the stars in her eyes, and, staying crouched in a defensive stance, she looked around the hallway for whoever had let her out.

"I know you're here," she yelled, certain her captor was still within hearing range. She crept silently down the hall toward the foyer. The closest door was on her right and she opened it quickly, jumping inside with a "ki-ya" in hopes of taking someone by surprise. The room was empty, and she pushed her sweaty hair out of her eyes as she returned to the hallway, first peering around the doorway before she made herself fully visible—and vulnerable.

The next classroom was also empty, as was the foyer and the chapel, though she didn't take time to check the pews. She was breathing hard when she returned to the foyer and accepted that whoever had let her out—probably the same person who'd barricaded her in—had made their getaway. Then she remembered the object that had been slid under the door.

She returned to the storage room, the door gaping open and the chair haphazardly blocking the entrance. Her hip and head were throbbing, and she winced as she reached up to touch the tender spot on her shoulder that had seen far too many ungraceful falls like this one. She pulled the chair from the doorway and regarded the scene with suspicion. She flipped on the light to illuminate the inside of her recent prison.

The floor was covered with a messy pile of box contents, papers and cloth scattered in no order at all. She began flinging things here and there, trying to find what had come under the door while also looking over her shoulder to make sure no one was going to lock her in again.

She could only think the object was a note of some kind, but when she moved away an armful of costumes, she saw the small white rectangle near the stacks of tubs on the left side. She approached it cautiously. She looked over her shoulder again before she picked up the rectangle and turned it in her hand. Her breath caught. She knew exactly what it was—the only thing it could be. Her room key.

CHAPTER 32

Sadie knew she should check out the rest of the church. She should see if Pastor Darryl was there—if he was, and hadn't helped her, he was definitely in on this. She should also check if Bets was home and see if she could get a feel for the possibility that she was involved in the situation too. If Sadie wanted to figure out who had done this to her, scoping the scene of the crime was essential. It was basic investigation stuff and yet, as she stood in the stark white foyer and looked down the hallway that curved around the chapel, Sadie couldn't make her feet move. She knew what she should do— what the old Sadie would do—but *she* couldn't make herself do it. While she'd survived the storage room, the ordeal had exhausted her, and all she could think about was the deal she'd made with herself before she started: if it got to be too much, she'd stop.

It was a relief to remember that promise, and without looking back at the closet behind her, she let herself out the front doors of the church. She passed no one on her way through the parking lot to the sidewalk, which she followed around the block to the motel. The plastic key card cut into her palm, she was holding it so tight, as she tried to decide if someone was helping her by giving her the key or not. It was all so confusing.

Only Kiki and Jim knew she was locked out of her room and, therefore, in need of a key. Did that mean the person who locked her in also knew she needed her room key? Did that mean it was Kiki or Jim? Or could they have told someone else? And why give her the key to her room anyway? Why lock her in a closet only to let her out half an hour later? Her head hurt, and all the exertion of the last few days seemed to fold in on her until she was craving solitude and silence.

She could see the plumeria flowers by the front of the motel and increased her pace, eager to close herself in her room and lay on the bed and do nothing but breathe. The air was thick with the day's humidity, saturated with the smells of flowers and moisture. Heady. Stifling.

A horn honked behind her. She screamed and immediately ducked, covering her head with her arms, certain she was moments away from being mowed down on the crumbling sidewalk. Blood pounded in her ears, blocking out all other sound. She didn't realize she'd lost several seconds to her reflexive panic until someone touched her shoulder. As though they were playing a game of freeze tag, the touch unstuck her, and she shot forward a few steps before she could turn and see who it was. She wasn't thinking clearly, breathing as though she'd just run a mile, and it took her another few seconds to recognize the person standing before her with red hair, wide eyes, and a concerned expression.

"Gayle?" she asked, as though unsure whether she could trust her own eyes. It didn't seem far-fetched for her to be hallucinating right now.

"Sadie," Gayle countered, smiling even though Sadie could read the worry behind the attempt. "I'm sorry. I didn't mean to scare you."

Sadie looked past Gayle to a light blue Honda pulled to the curb, the driver's door still open. Gayle must have hurried to get out of the car when Sadie had freaked out. Sadie put a hand to her chest as though it would calm her, but her heart was still racing. Being scared by a honking horn was just plain humiliating.

"I called and called once I landed in Honolulu," Gayle explained. "But you didn't answer so I called Pete, and he told me the name of this motel. I was so relieved when I saw you, but . . . it was silly for me to honk. I'm so sorry; I wasn't thinking."

She wasn't thinking about what a mess I am, is what she meant. Why had Sadie thought a new hairdo would somehow hide her current state of disability? "No, *I'm* sorry," she said, trying to square her shoulders and look confident. "I was locked in a closet over at the church, and it kind of freaked me out, ya know?" Why did it sound like a reasonable explanation until she said it out loud?

Gayle blinked. "You were locked in a closet at a church?"

"Well, a storage room, I guess. It was full of boxes and no light and there were prayers and stuff but the lid wouldn't fit under the door and the cardboard wasn't strong enough and there were so many clothes." She took a breath but could feel her heart racing again just by talking about it. "And then they slid the key to my room under the door so now I'm going to my room." To lay on her bed and calm herself down. How would she do that with Gayle here? She thought about what Dr. McKay had said about the difficulties of losing her personal space, and for a moment, she regretted ever telling Gayle she could come.

Gayle was looking at her as though she'd lost her mind.

"I'm not making any sense," Sadie said, shaking her head. "I'm sorry. Uh, why don't we go to my room and we can talk."

"Sure," Gayle said, failing to hide her concern. "Let me just park the car."

Sadie nodded, shifting from one foot to the next while she waited for Gayle to come back. She felt calmer by the time Gayle returned and tried to keep the conversation normal by asking about her flight as they walked to Sadie's room.

Gayle chatted amiably, recounting her travel adventures, which included sitting next to a Hawaiian man who taught her some words while they crossed the Pacific Ocean.

"*Wikiwiki* is my favorite," Gayle said, then turned to Sadie. "It means hurry up."

Sadie smiled and nodded; she knew that.

"I'm going to teach it to the grandkids when I get back—they'll love it. And then there was this drunk lady . . ."

Sadie nodded in all the right places, asking probing questions when appropriate, hoping it would convince Gayle that she wasn't completely deranged. Just slightly so.

"I told Pete I'd let him know what was going on when I arrived," Gayle said after finishing her recitation. She pulled out her phone. "I'll text him to let him know you're okay."

Sadie knew she should use Gayle's phone to call him herself, but she wanted to use her own phone, once she'd had a chance to calm down completely. Plus, he was still at his conference and would need to call her back at his convenience anyway.

It wasn't until they reached the door of her room that Sadie remembered her ponderings on why someone had given her the room key in the first place. What if the key wasn't for her room after all?

But when she slid the key into the card reader and pulled it out, the light above the key slot lit up green. She was relieved she'd escaped the closet before eleven o'clock, when she assumed her card would stop working all together.

"So, how long are you staying here?" Gayle asked. "You checked in last—" She cut off with a gasp at the same time Sadie froze just inside the door of the room, looking at what had been done in her absence.

The stack of papers she'd left on the dresser were in pieces all over the floor; the contents of her shoulder bag were likewise scattered. Something dripped off the edge of the desk where she'd left her laptop. Sadie hurried toward it but stopped when she saw the wet keyboard and the pool of caramel-colored liquid surrounding her computer. She touched a button in a halfhearted attempt to wake up the screen, but it was dead. Ruined. Her finger was sticky, and she was tempted to taste it before rethinking that idea. It could be something foul, though it smelled sweet, like soda.

"What happened?" Gayle said, stepping far enough into the room that she could shut the door.

"I don't know," Sadie said, looking at the pill bottle from Dr. McKay lying empty on the floor, the pills scattered and crushed into the carpet.

"You didn't do this?"

Sadie looked over her shoulder. "I'm a mess, but I'm not insane," she said, offended. "Why would I do this?"

"Sorry," Gayle said. "So, it wasn't like this before you got locked in the, er, closet?"

Sadie shook her head, biting her tongue to keep from being defensive despite the fact that she'd reacted as though to a bombing when Gayle had honked her horn earlier.

"Who would do this?" Gayle asked.

Who *would* do it and who *could* do it felt like equally difficult questions to answer.

Sadie scanned the floor for her phone. It had been in her bag when she left. At first, she didn't see it amid the chaos and hoped she'd put it somewhere else and just didn't remember. Then she saw a familiar metallic red piece of plastic. She bent down and picked it up, realizing it was half of the protective cover she'd been talked into buying when she last replaced her phone. A quick scan found the other half, and then she spotted the phone itself partially under the bed, the screen broken and the keys either crushed or missing. Not far away lay the ice pick Sadie had used to help pick the storage room lock and left in the hallway, proof that whoever locked her in had also ransacked her motel room.

Sadie tried to swallow the thick lump in her throat. She knew her emotion didn't have anything to do with the phone itself, but everything to do with someone violating her space and making such a threatening statement toward her. She turned her phone over in her hand and tried to remove the back cover. The damage to the phone had jammed the cover on, and she had to hit it against the dresser in order to get it off.

"What are you doing?" Gayle asked.

Sadie didn't answer. Instead she removed the battery, relieved to find the SIM card still inside. She used her thumbnail to pull it out of its casing, then dropped the ruined phone back onto the floor. She held the card tightly and scanned the destruction again, wondering if there was anything salvageable. She picked up her wallet and opened it to find the card compartments empty.

A slower scan of the floor provided clues to the multicolored pieces she'd seen amid the white paper. Someone had cut up all her cards—credit, health insurance, library. She reached down and picked up a piece with part of the Colorado state seal—her driver's license. Next to that was a green sliver of paper that Sadie feared was the last of her cash. Whoever did this had brought scissors. They were intent only on making her miserable, not profiting in any way.

"They destroyed everything," Sadie said, looking at Gayle. "My license—my cash." She looked at the papers strewn across the floor. "Everything."

"Why?" Gayle said, venturing a step forward before stopping again. "What would the point be?"

"To get back at me for something. Or to make me leave."

"You need to call the police," Gayle said. "Whoever did this is crazy. You're going to report it, right?"

Immediate arguments began running through Sadie's head: calling the police would mean she'd have to explain what she was doing in Kalaheo. She couldn't expect the police to find out who did this if she hid information. She'd have to tell them everything. It would mean giving a statement, explaining why she hadn't reported Charlie's appearance on her doorstep sooner. And she'd have to stop her own investigation, such as it was. She'd never find the answers to Charlie's questions.

Charlie's questions. She looked at the shredded papers on the floor. Like everything else she'd brought from Puhi, the list was gone. She thought of the confrontation she'd had with Jim earlier that morning. He'd predicted she wouldn't call the police about him locking her out of her room. He'd known she wanted to figure things out on her own, and he'd been right. But that was when the fire for this mystery was still burning within her, when she thought she was making progress and feeling stronger for the efforts she was making. That strength was gone, sapped by the sticky heat of the storage room and shredded like her driver's license and credit cards. Regardless of when it had abandoned her, the passion that had fueled her thus far was gone, and she was left with a horrible feeling of foolishness for having started something she was incapable of finishing.

"Yes," she said, nodding. "We should call the police."

Gayle didn't need to be told twice, and she hurried over to the phone, picking her steps carefully as though not wanting to disrupt the debris. Sadie vaguely noted her friend picking up the phone and talking to someone while she stared at the spot where Charlie's list had been.

I've failed you, she thought, feeling horrible for not being able to help him after all. His letter was now lost in the mess somewhere.

Or was it?

Sadie knelt on the floor and began sifting through bits of paper, looking for the grayish newsprint of Charlie's list amid the bright white paper pieces that seemed so stark against the burgundy carpet.

"What are you looking for?" Gayle asked.

Sadie looked up to see that Gayle had hung up the phone, which could only mean the police were on their way. "Charlie's list."

Sadie recognized a slice of the photo of Charlie and Noelani that she'd printed off the computer and picked it up.

She hoped Charlie had gone to school after she'd seen him at the church. It wasn't her problem anymore, but she kept looking for evidence of his list until someone knocked on the motel room door. Gayle hurried to answer it as Sadie got to her feet. She'd found pieces of Noelani's obituary, Officer Wington's card, and the map Ashley had printed out for her to find the church last night, but Charlie's list wasn't there. Whoever wanted to get back at her or run her off had taken Charlie's list. Why?

"Mrs. Hoffmiller?" a male voice said. She looked up into the somewhat familiar face that instantly reconnected her to the encounter she'd had with Noelani's body. She felt herself tense in response to the connection. Officer Wington. He smiled kindly, as though she were fragile. Maybe he was right. "Why don't we go outside where we can talk?"

CHAPTER 33

Nearly three hours later, Sadie was finally able to call Pete using Gayle's phone during the ride back to Puhi. She wasn't sure he believed she was okay, but she did her best to convince him.

"Do you fly home from North Carolina tonight?" she asked, knowing he'd told her when he was heading back to Colorado but unable to remember.

"Tomorrow," Pete said. "We have a banquet tonight and a final assault weapon firing range in the morning." He paused, then asked, "How are you feeling—really?"

Sadie realized that despite a tightness in her chest, and her PTSD reaction when Gayle had honked, the panic hadn't erupted again—even when she thought for sure it would. "I'm doing okay," she said. "Better than I would have guessed if someone had warned me what today would be like."

"I'm glad you're holding up." He paused, his voice muffled, then came back on the line. "I'm sorry, Sadie, but I've got to go. Can I call you after the banquet?"

"I would love that."

They said their good-byes, and Sadie considered calling Mr.

Olie, but it seemed superfluous now. The police would certainly get in touch with him about Charlie. It was out of her hands. Why did that feel . . . wrong?

"Turn right at the next road," Sadie said, putting Gayle's phone in the middle console.

They reached her condo a few minutes later, and Sadie locked the door three times but hoped Gayle hadn't noticed.

"I'm exhausted," Gayle said. "Is it always so draining? Talking to the police?"

Sadie nodded and passed Gayle on her way to the kitchen. "I'm sure flying for most of the night hasn't helped your energy levels, either."

Gayle shrugged. "I slept most of the way, and I felt fine when I arrived. It's the last few hours that wore me out."

"Well, you're right," Sadie said. "The police do take a lot out of you, and no matter what's happened, I always feel like I've done something wrong."

Gayle sat down on the futon with a loud exhale. "I felt that way too, and all I had to talk about was why I was here and what we saw when we opened the door. Are we done, then? Or will we have to talk to the police some more?"

"It's up to them," Sadie said, opening a cabinet to retrieve two glasses. She was thirsty and assumed Gayle was too. As she passed the fridge, she saw the list of goals she'd made yesterday and frowned. What did it matter now? Despite all her efforts, she'd failed Charlie. She didn't even have his list of questions anymore. "Sometimes they need more info, and sometimes they don't. We may never hear anything else about it."

"So, what, once you give them what you know, you're out of the loop?"

Sadie handed one of the glasses of ice water to Gayle. "Except I usually insert myself back into it," she said, shrugging.

"Do you plan on doing that this time?" Gayle asked in a tone Sadie couldn't define. She almost sounded disappointed that the potential adventure was over. Or maybe she was anxious about Sadie stepping back in. She took a sip of water, looking at Sadie over the top of the glass.

Sadie shook her head. "When I started all this it was with the promise to myself that I could get out if I needed to. And I need to. Whoever broke into my room was making a statement. I'm in no position to egg them on, and I didn't get any information that makes a difference anyway." It was easy to say, but felt horrible to sum up like that. She'd wasted all that time and precious energy on something useless. She went back into the kitchen in hopes of finding something to eat.

"So that Jim guy—he owns the motel?" Gayle asked.

Sadie smiled as she remembered the look on Jim's face when he returned from the charter expedition to find his motel overrun with the Kaua'i police department. They'd conducted all the interviews on the premises and talked to every guest and employee. People not connected to the motel were standing around, trying to get a feel for what was going on. It was Jim's worst nightmare, and Sadie had thoroughly enjoyed knowing she'd been part of that nightmare for him.

Jim wasn't any less tyrannical with the police than he was with his employees. Watching him wave his arms around and demand things be done his way had been Sadie's silver lining. When she and Gayle left, he was just starting to calm down. Sadie hoped she hadn't missed the rest of the show but wasn't about to stick around once the police dismissed them.

"He's a piece of work," Sadie said, shaking her head and pulling open the fridge. There wasn't much to choose from, and she didn't want Gayle to see the deplorable contents, so she shut it and decided to order something from the Polynesian cafe down the street. They delivered and after three months knew Sadie by name. "Did I tell you about the conversation I had with Jim this morning?"

"No," Gayle said, laughing as she leaned back in the futon. "I've hardly talked to you at all."

"Gosh, that's sad," Sadie said, feeling herself relax. Thank goodness. Maybe because she was home, maybe because she'd drawn a line, or maybe because Gayle was here and not mad at her even though she'd stepped into weirdness 101.

Sadie went to the phone on the wall. "I'm just going to order us some dinner, and then I'll tell you everything."

"Oh, good," Gayle said, wriggling in her seat a little bit. "What are we going to eat?"

"Well, my favorite is the Lumpia—that's like a Filipino egg roll, really yummy—and then the Spam-fried rice."

"Spam?" Gayle wrinkled up her nose. "A restaurant serves Spam?"

Sadie laughed; she'd had a similar reaction before she'd tried it. "It's an island," she explained. "With limited fresh meats, Spam is all the rage around here. Konnie, one of the Blue Muumuus, told me she has at least twenty Spam recipes."

"Are you kidding me?" Gayle said, cocking her head slightly to the side and narrowing her eyes. "You're totally making that up. Spam is like the joke of all canned goods."

Sadie shook her head and picked up the phone. "Welcome to the Islands," she said, then dialed the number, excited to share some of the Hawaiian culture with Gayle and hoping it would dim the events of the morning.

Nearly an hour later, Gayle and Sadie had a feast spread out on the table. "Okay," Gayle said, waving her chopsticks—she was totally showing off by not using a fork like Sadie was—"so, the pastor is a creep and his wife is having an affair with a tyrannical motel owner."

Sadie had chosen the wrong moment to take a drink and began sputtering and coughing. She waved her hand through the air as though to wipe away Gayle's words.

Gayle shrugged smugly and took another expert bite of her rice. "Is that about it?"

"No," Sadie said, finding it hard to keep from smiling now that she knew Gayle was teasing. "I don't *know* that Bets and Jim are having an affair."

"But he knows about her marital problems, right?"

"Well, yeah."

"And she went to him for help."

"But why would she go to her . . . lover for help with her marriage?"

Gayle considered that. "You have a point. But why would a happily married woman go to a single man for help? Dangerous ground."

"I agree," Sadie said. "But—"

"And she wanted Noelani to disappear," Gayle said. "Maybe she did it. I mean Noelani's been gone for what, three weeks, and Bets is already trying to pawn off the next honey on the motel, right?"

"Well, she didn't say it like that."

"A spade is a spade." Gayle took another bite, chewed and swallowed, then pointed at the Styrofoam container. "And this is amazing. I can't wait to tell my mom I ate Spam; she'll be so proud of me. She loves Spam."

Sadie laughed and took another bite. They got sidetracked

talking about Gayle's mom, and then her kids, and then Sadie's kids, and then someone knocked on the door.

They both went silent. Sadie tried not to notice the wave of fear that washed over her, but it was a learned response. Gayle either noticed Sadie's hesitation, or she simply got to her feet faster, but regardless, she was halfway to the door before Sadie had overcome her hesitation and stood up from her chair.

"Oh, hello," Gayle said before Sadie had rounded the corner from the kitchen to the living room. Sadie stopped, keeping herself hidden. The possibilities of who could be at the door narrowed substantially if Gayle knew the person. She leaned in to listen.

"Oh, hi. Is Mrs. Hoffmiller here?"

Kiki? Sadie straightened. Gayle had seen her at the motel, but they hadn't been introduced.

"How did you know where to find her?" Gayle asked.

"I got the address from the form she filled out when she registered last night at the motel. I really need to talk to her—is she here?"

"I'm here," Sadie said, coming around the corner and trying to look confident.

Kiki was no longer dressed in her uniform; she wore a sundress with an empire waist that emphasized her pregnant belly. Her hair was pulled up in a sloppy bun, and she had blue rubber slippahs on her tiny brown feet. "Mrs. Hoffmiller," she said, sounding relieved. "I'm glad you're here. I was trying to call before I realized your phone was ruined."

Sadie ignored Gayle's look. She'd tried to convince Sadie to go to Lihue on the way home from Kalaheo and get a new phone, but Sadie had begged off, promising she'd do it tomorrow.

"I really need to talk to you," Kiki said again.

"Come in and sit down," Sadie said, waving her inside. A minute later, after Sadie had made the introductions, they sat across from one another in the same configuration Sadie and Charlie had sat in a few days earlier; Sadie in the rattan chair and Kiki on the futon. Gayle sat next to Sadie on one of the kitchen chairs.

Once settled, Sadie looked at the young woman expectantly, but felt herself tensing with increased anticipation. "Don't you have class?"

"Yeah, I'm skipping it today," Kiki said. "And I never skip."

Which meant that whatever brought her here was more important than school.

"I'm really sorry about your room," Kiki started.

Sadie felt Gayle glance at her, but she kept her focus on Kiki. "Do you know anything about that?"

Kiki shook her head. "I know it sounds crazy, since I was at the desk, but I didn't see anyone go in."

"Aren't there video cameras?"

"Yeah, but they feed into a monitor in Jim's apartment."

"Above the expedition garage?" Sadie asked. Talk about a control freak. He wanted to monitor the motel but not let anyone else see. She wondered if the police had ever gotten copies of the tapes from the last night Noelani had worked.

Kiki nodded. "I can only see what's visible from the office, and I can't see your room from there."

"Aren't you the only person who could make a key that would have let anyone in?"

She hesitated, then nodded. "Yes, I'm the only one who can make a key, but I didn't make one. You heard Jim threaten my job if I let you in, and I certainly wouldn't have let anyone else in. There are a few master keys, though; housekeeping has one, I have one, and Jim has one."

"But Jim was on the expedition," Sadie said.

"Like I said, I don't know who did it, but that's not why I'm here."

If Kiki had something she felt was even *more* important than who ransacked the room, Sadie didn't want to distract her from it. "It isn't? What brought you all the way here, then?"

"The coffee."

"The coffee?" Sadie and Gayle said in unison.

Kiki looked shaken. "The night Noelani used my car—the last time anyone saw her—she'd said she'd pick up coffee for the morning. We were almost out."

"Okay," Sadie said, encouraging her to continue.

"It was in my car when I got it out of impound on Monday."

It was Gayle who put Sadie's thoughts into words. "Why would she have bought coffee if she wasn't coming back?"

Kiki looked relieved that someone understood. "She planned to come back," she said, her voice low. "And that changes everything."

Spam-Fried Rice

Sauce
½ cup soy sauce
4 tablespoons sugar (if using Aloha brand of soy sauce, then reduce sugar to 2 tablespoons)
4 cloves of garlic, minced or pressed
1 tablespoon oyster sauce (optional)
2 teaspoons sesame oil (omit for a less-spicy dish)

Rice
2 tablespoons vegetable oil, divided
5 eggs, mixed
1 onion, diced
1 (12-ounce) can of Spam (light or regular), diced
½ cup red pepper, diced
2 cups of your choice of corn, carrots, or peas (if using frozen
   vegetables, thaw first)
4 cups rice, cooked and cooled (day-old rice works best)

Mix sauce together and set aside.

In a wok or large skillet, heat 1 tablespoon vegetable oil on medium-high heat until hot. Scramble eggs. Remove from pan and set aside. Add another tablespoon of vegetable oil to wok. Heat, then add onion and diced Spam. Cook until Spam is crispy and onion is browned and transparent. Add sauce, red pepper, and vegetables. Bring to a boil, and boil for one minute. Add rice and break up any clumps that have formed. Combine the ingredients and stir until color is uniform throughout. Add scrambled eggs. Mix to combine.

Serves 8.

Note: This dish is delicious, healthy, and quick for breakfast! You can also change it up by adding baby corn, mushrooms, water chestnuts, or bean sprouts along with the other vegetables.

CHAPTER 34

Within a few minutes, all three of them had gathered around the kitchen table, and Sadie had the notebook she'd used yesterday morning before switching to her computer to take notes. She stared at the blank page longer than she needed to in order to gather her thoughts, then she looked up at Kiki, hesitating to dive in completely.

"Why did you come to me?" Sadie asked. If she conducted this interview, she'd be back in the middle of everything. Was she ready for that? "The police are involved now. They're handling the investigation, and everything should go through them."

"I talked to the police before," Kiki said. "When Noelani was first found, they interviewed me, but I didn't make the connection to the coffee until today."

"Did you tell them today, when you figured it out?" Sadie asked.

"No, I came to you." She sounded the tiniest bit annoyed. "You're the first person to ask me about Noelani who seems as though she cares about *her*."

That brought Sadie up short, but Kiki continued speaking. "If you want me to go to the police with this, I can." She looked between Sadie and Gayle. "But I thought you wanted to know what happened to her."

"I did," she said. "I mean, I do, but I don't want to get anyone in trouble."

"Except anyone who might have been the reason Noelani didn't get back to the motel with the coffee," Gayle interjected.

"Well, yes," Sadie said. "I meant that I don't want you to get in trouble for telling me instead of the police, Kiki."

"Do you think something happened to Noelani that night?" Kiki asked Sadie, point-blank. "Do you think someone hurt her?"

Sadie thought about the question. "I don't know," she said, barely above a whisper. "She told her pastor she was worried about staying clean and that she wondered if Charlie was better off in foster care. . . . But she was working so hard. As I started asking people questions about her, they started hedging. People with nothing to hide don't play games like that. Someone locked me in the storage closet, and someone trashed my room. In my mind that means someone knows something they don't want me to find."

"Noelani *was* doing everything right. The more I've thought about it, the more convinced I am that she didn't overdose like everyone says. I think it was something else."

She stopped talking and leaned back in her chair, her dark eyes intent on Sadie's face.

Sadie let Kiki's words wash over her, then looked back at the notebook. "Okay," she said, knowing she was jumping right back in with both feet. How could she not? "Let's start with the night Noelani disappeared. Had you seen her that day, before you came in to cover for her?"

Kiki took a breath. "Angela was out of town; her cousin was getting married on the Mainland and she'd flown out for it. That left

Court, Noelani, and me to run the desk. I worked from six in the morning to two in the afternoon that day and was exhausted by the time Noelani brought my car back from her visit with Charlie."

"What time did she get back?"

"She got to my apartment around six that evening," Kiki said. "I drove her back to the motel and dropped her off. That would have been about 6:15, I guess."

"How did she seem?"

"Distracted," Kiki said. "Worried."

"Did she say why?"

"No, and I didn't really ask. I was on the phone with my sister most of the drive back. When we got there, Noelani thanked me for the car and headed for her room. She worked at ten but said she had some sheets to fold that she hadn't finished that morning."

"I understand her visit with Charlie that day was a last-minute thing," Sadie said, reflecting on what Jim had said about accommodating it.

"She usually got her time with Charlie on Wednesdays," Kiki explained. "But on Friday, her caseworker had told her she could increase to six hours of unsupervised visitation, split up between two days. Noelani jumped all over it, and she set up a time for Saturday, then had to scramble to figure out how to make it work. Typically we work eight-hour shifts at the front desk—six to two, two to ten, ten to six. The three of us had all worked five days in a row, we were all tired, and Noelani had housekeeping in the morning and then the two-to-ten shift Saturday afternoon. She wanted to trade shifts with Court—Court works graves because of her kids—but she still had housekeeping the next morning and the front desk at two o'clock on Sunday." She shook her head. "It was crazy; she'd get no sleep. I told her to put off the visitation, but then Jim approved switching the shifts so long as Noelani could come in at nine. Noelani was determined to make it all fit. She didn't want to miss her chance at the extra visitation."

"What time did she call you about covering for her that night?"

"Ten thirty," Kiki said. "I was scheduled to work at six Sunday morning so I was just getting to bed when she asked me to come in and work her shift for a few hours. I told her I couldn't. She said it was really important."

Sadie was falling into her groove. The knot in her stomach was barely noticeable, and she knew that, at least in part, her ability to continue was due to Gayle's silent support from the chair next to her. "Did she say what *it* was?"

Kiki shook her head. "No, all she said was that it was important and had something to do with Charlie."

"Did something happen at the visit, I wonder?" Sadie mused, writing down the question. Kiki had said Noelani had seemed distracted and worried when she had returned her car.

"She didn't say anything about that, but she sounded really worried. Really . . . intense. When I got there around eleven, she promised me it would only be an hour—two hours max. She'd done most of the side work and said she'd pick up coffee while she was out. She'd given me money for the gas she'd used earlier that day for the visit with Charlie, but I hadn't taken time to fill up my car 'cause I had enough to get to work and back the next day. She said she'd fill it up for me."

"Did she use your car a lot?"

"Not too often," Kiki said. "Just for visits with Charlie. She walked or took the bus everywhere else."

"Do you know what they did on their visit?"

Kiki nodded. "Movie and ice cream, I think. At least that was her plan when she picked up my car. They didn't ever do fancy things. Noelani was saving up for an apartment. She was looking forward to it so much. She lived for those visits."

"What did you think when she didn't come back?"

"I was mad," she said, adjusting her position in the chair. "I hadn't worked a graveyard in months. Since getting pregnant, I'm lucky to get through the day without a nap. I started calling her cell phone at twelve thirty to find out when she was coming back. I bet I called it a hundred times. Jim came in Sunday morning; I was so tired I felt like I was going to throw up. He was so mad." She tightened her jaw again and smoothed her sundress over her legs.

"He told me he wrote you up for it."

"Jerk," Gayle said under her breath before taking a drink of her water.

Kiki nodded. "He runs a tight ship, that's how he says it—'I run a tight ship. Toe the line or walk the plank.'" She lowered her voice as though mimicking his tone.

"Harsh," Sadie said, writing *walk the plank* in her notebook. It was an aggressive term and supported Sadie's opinion that Jim was a ruthless employer.

Kiki continued. "Court was able to take the rest of the morning shift so I could sleep, but then Jim called me when Noelani didn't show up for her afternoon shift."

"Were you worried about her?"

"Not at first," Kiki said, though she seemed to feel bad about admitting it. "Then they found my car out of gas up by Wailua. I had to pay almost $150 to get it out of the impound lot, and although I was still really mad, I was worried about Noelani by that time. She was always real grateful for using my car, ya know, and to leave it on the side of the road like that just felt off."

"Did you think she'd gone on a binge?" Sadie asked.

Kiki hesitated, then nodded. "It was the only theory anyone had, and I thought we were good enough friends that she'd have contacted me if it was anything else. She was so anti-drug, anti-2450; she didn't even drink anymore. She made me promise I'd never smoke another joint as long as I lived. She said you'd never know when you'd reach the point of no return. That's what she called it— the point of no return."

"That meant addiction?"

"Yeah," Kiki said. "She told me how when she started it was just partying and stuff, ya know—kid's stuff. And then she said it was like one day she partied, same as usual, and the next morning she woke up and had meth for breakfast. After that, she couldn't start her day without it. She got into stripping 'cause that was the only job she could get that would pay for the drugs, and that led to more drugs. And now she was trying to clean up the mess she'd made for Charlie." Kiki looked at her hands and paused before continuing. "But then the police found the pot in her stuff."

"Her room was unattended for a little while, though, right? A day or two before it was packed up?" Sadie said.

"You think someone might have planted the marijuana?" Gayle asked, interjecting herself into the conversation.

Sadie shrugged. "Maybe. The chain of custody wouldn't have started until the police had hold of the evidence, and since Jim moved Noelani's things *before* he gave everything to the police, it's possible someone could have tampered with it along the way."

"Chain of what?" Gayle asked.

"Chain of custody. It's a log of who handles evidence and why, where, and for how long. It ensures that if needed in court, the police can prove where the evidence has been and why so as not to interfere with the probative value."

Both Kiki and Gayle looked at her with surprise. Sadie blushed. "I watch a lot of crime TV, or at least I used to."

"Uh-huh," Gayle said, giving Sadie a doubtful look. "And you're hot and heavy with a police detective that probably sweet talks the lingo in your ear for fun."

"What?" Kiki asked, looking concerned.

"The police detective lives in Colorado," Sadie hurried to clarify. "Not here, and he has nothing to do with this." She gave Gayle a hard look. She was messing with Sadie's groove, which was just beginning to feel comfortable again. She cleared her throat and got her thoughts back on track.

"Did Jim get along with Noelani?"

Kiki shrugged. "He didn't *not* get along with her. He treated her like he treats the rest of us."

"Controlling and rude?" Gayle interjected.

"Well, yeah," Kiki said. "That's just how he is, but he wasn't different with Noelani."

"What about Bets?" Sadie said. "Jim's different with her."

Kiki immediately looked down at her fingers in her lap.

"There's something between them, isn't there?"

"I don't know," Kiki said, but she didn't meet Sadie's eyes. "They talk a lot."

"Alone in his office?" Sadie asked. "Like this morning?"

Kiki nodded. "Sometimes she comes over to use the pool, and he'll talk to her outside, but when she's not around, he acts like he's annoyed with her."

"What do you mean?"

"He talks about how she's always interrupting him or that she's pathetic."

"Pathetic?" Gayle repeated. "That's a strong word."

Kiki shrugged. "It's weird 'cause when she's there, he acts like they're friends, but when she's not there, he acts like he can't stand her."

"Have you ever thought they were having an affair?" Sadie asked, though it sounded like a strange question to ask after what Kiki had just said. "Maybe he was pretending to dislike her around people in order to hide it."

Kiki looked uncomfortable. "I've never, you know, caught them together or anything."

"But she could come and go from his apartment without you knowing it."

"And maybe swipe a master key card as well," Gayle added, raising an eyebrow.

She leaned forward, her eyes sparkling a little too much for Sadie's taste. It was important to stay neutral and not jump to conclusions, and yet Sadie had been working off of a theory the whole time.

"What if Noelani saw them together and left that night to confront Bets about it, or to tell Pastor Darryl?" Gayle asked.

Kiki looked a little taken aback. Sadie frowned and directed her question to Gayle. "Why would she borrow Kiki's car to drive half a block away?"

"And there's a back way between the motel and the church," Kiki added. "Plus, what would that have to do with Charlie?"

"What did she say about Charlie?" Sadie asked. "Do you remember the *exact* words she used?"

Kiki looked at the floor, her brow wrinkled in concentration.

"When I explained to her that I had to work in the morning and couldn't come in for her, she said 'If it weren't for Charlie, I wouldn't ask you to do this.'"

"'If it weren't for Charlie, I wouldn't ask you to do this,'" Sadie repeated, writing it down in her notes.

"I asked her what was going on, and she said she didn't want to say anything, just in case she was wrong."

Sadie wrote that down too. "So she was checking up on something she didn't know was true or not," Sadie summarized.

"I guess," Kiki said.

"What about Noelani and Pastor Darryl?" Sadie asked, figuring she might as well lay all the cards on the table. "Jim seems to think *they* were having an affair."

"I don't know about that either," Kiki said, but she shifted in a way that bespoke a new tension.

CHAPTER 35

"Jim said he saw Pastor Darryl visit Noelani at the motel," Sadie said.

Kiki shook her head. "I never saw that, and Noelani never said anything about Pastor Darryl other than the fact that he had really helped her with her relationship with God."

"Is there anyone else you think she would have told if she were involved with the pastor?" Gayle asked. "Did she have other close friends?"

"Not really," Kiki said. "Other than church and work, she didn't have friends. Even she and I never went out or anything like that. When she first started working at the motel, she'd borrow Bets's car for her visits with Charlie. They seemed to be pretty good friends, but it kinda faded out, ya know? Then, a couple of weeks before Noelani disappeared, she and Bets had an argument."

"Like a 'leave my husband alone' argument?" Gayle asked.

Kiki nodded. "I went to get a drink out of the vending machine, and I heard arguing by the laundry room. When I poked my head around the corner, I saw the two of them."

"What were they arguing about?" Sadie asked.

"Bets said something about getting in Noelani's way if Noelani didn't get out of *her* way." Kiki shrugged. "Noelani saw me and told Bets she had to get back to work. I asked Noelani about it later and she said they'd had a misunderstanding—that it was no big deal."

"She didn't tell you what it was about?"

Kiki shook her head. "And I didn't ask. I don't really like knowing other people's business."

Most of the time, Sadie would consider that a virtue. A rare virtue. But right now she wished Kiki had pushed for more information. "Did you tell the police about the argument?"

"Yeah," Kiki said.

"Do you know if they talked to Bets about it?"

"I only ever talked to them that one time, and they mostly asked about the night she took my car and if I knew whether or not she was using again."

"Which is exactly why I think Noelani's past has influenced the investigation," Sadie said, mostly to herself before realizing they were both listening to her. She moved on, wanting to reserve that issue for a conversation with either Bets or the police.

"Did you ever meet Charlie?" Sadie asked, changing the subject.

"Yeah, he's a cute little boy," she said, her expression softening. "Noelani would bring him to the motel for their visits sometimes and let him swim in the pool."

"Jim was okay with that?" Sadie asked.

"Jim liked Charlie," Kiki said. "He'd buy the kid a soda whenever he came over—show him the boat, that kind of thing."

"I heard Jim's ex-wife had kids—was he close to them?" Sadie asked, surprised to find a soft spot in a man who seemed hard in every way.

"I guess. She moved back to Oregon or something. He doesn't

talk about it. Court told me about his stepsons and how hard it was for Jim when they left—she's worked here forever."

"Why?" Gayle asked. "I mean, the guy's a jerk. Why work for someone like that?"

"Well, the checks are never late," Kiki said. "And as long as you do your job, you know what to expect. I mean, I know he's hard on people, but he's fair. He doesn't change the rules on you, or run his hand up your leg or stuff like that. He's decent, if a little rough around the edges."

"He changed the rules on you today," Sadie pointed out. "He wouldn't let you let me into my room."

Kiki colored a bit. "He's never done anything like that before. I mean, he gets mad, but he's never ordered me around like that."

"What about ordering you not to talk about Noelani?" Sadie asked. "He'd told you that after the police came around the first time, right?"

"Well, yeah, but that made sense. I mean, she was an ex-stripper and a recovering addict, but he was giving her a second chance. Then she shows up dead, probably from an overdose. He didn't want that to affect the motel's reputation. We're already *mauka,* and we're not a large motel in a high tourist area. He was just looking out for the interest of the motel."

"Mauka?" Gayle asked.

"Inland," Sadie defined.

"Away from the ocean," Kiki added. "It literally means 'toward the mountains.'"

"*Makai* means 'toward the sea,'" Sadie explained. "The closer to the beach, the bigger the tourist attraction since the beach is the main draw for vacationers."

"Ah," Gayle said, looking impressed by Sadie's knowledge.

Sadie wasn't convinced the motel's reputation was Jim's motivation, but she nodded as though accepting the possibility, and then looked at her notes to see what she'd missed. "I can't think of anything else," she said, looking up at the younger girl with a smile. "How about you, Gayle? Is there anything we missed?"

"I want to know more about Pastor Darryl." She looked at Kiki expectantly.

Kiki shrugged. "I don't know him very well. He would come and talk to Noelani sometimes, but I didn't go to his church or anything. Jim couldn't stand the guy so he didn't come around much."

"I heard Jim and Pastor Darryl were friends before Jim's divorce," Sadie said.

"That was before I ever worked there." Kiki's phone dinged, and she glanced at it.

Sadie thought back to the look on Pastor Darryl's face when she'd brought up Jim. The divorce seemed to be the point where things had changed not only for Jim but also between him and the pastor. Why? And why did Bets still have a relationship with Jim? A close enough relationship that he hired Noelani in order to help out Bets. Yet, Jim said Bets was pathetic, too.

"I better go," Kiki said. "My boyfriend dropped me off before going to the bike shop in Lihue; he's back now."

"Thank you for coming," Sadie said. "I really appreciate it."

"Sure," Kiki said, pushing up from her seat. "If I think of anything else, I'll give you a call. Oh, wait, I forgot about your phone."

Gayle sent a smug look at Sadie, and Sadie sighed in defeat.

"Let me give you *my* number," Gayle said. "And maybe I could get yours. Sadie and I will be together anyway."

They exchanged numbers. Sadie thanked Kiki again, and Gayle went as far as to hug her before she left—she hugged everyone—and then they watched her go down the walk and get into a little brown car before it pulled away from the curb.

They hadn't even shut the door before another car pulled into its place, or rather, a truck. Sadie stepped forward, wondering if it were a coincidence that Mr. Olie drove a truck like that, only to stop when Mr. Olie stepped out of the driver's side of the car. He slammed the door and headed toward Sadie's condo. He walked slow and heavy, as though he wasn't feeling well.

Sadie hurried down the sidewalk to meet him. "Mr. Olie, what are you doing here? Is it about Charlie?"

"Why aren't you answering your phone?" he snapped, his expression fierce.

She started. "I don't have it. I mean, someone broke into my room in Kalaheo and destroyed it." She noted the sweat on his forehead and his labored breathing. "Are you okay?"

"I could use a glass of water," he said.

"Sure," Sadie said, turning back to the condo where Gayle stood on the threshold. Gayle stepped aside, opening the door wider so they could pass through. "Could you get him a glass of water?" Sadie whispered to her friend.

"Of course," Gayle said. She closed the door, and Sadie followed Mr. Olie into the living room. He sat down heavily on the futon and raised a hand to his chest as though trying to catch his breath.

"Are you sure you're all right?" Sadie asked, remembering his history of heart issues.

"I'm fine," he said. "I've been calling you for hours."

From the corner of her eye, Sadie saw Gayle shake her head as she retrieved a glass from the cupboard.

"Like I said, my phone was ruined. I'm going to get a new one as soon as you and I are finished, though." She cast a look to Gayle, who smiled and nodded her acceptance.

"I need to ask you some questions," he said, dismissing the phone situation, for which Sadie was grateful.

"Okay," she said, settling herself into the chair. Gayle brought Mr. Olie a glass of ice water, and he eyed her as he took it from her.

"This is my friend Gayle, from Colorado. She just flew in today."

"I need to talk to you alone," he said to Sadie briskly before taking a long drink of water.

"Oh, she's okay to—"

He glared at her, and she cleared her throat before looking up at Gayle.

"I'd been wanting to check out the pool anyway," Gayle said, but she was not happy. She let herself out the sliding glass door. Once she was gone, Mr. Olie turned to face Sadie.

"The police said you saw Charlie this morning."

"Yes," Sadie said, nodding.

"Tell me about it. Everything."

Would it kill him to ask nicely? All the same, she told him everything, from seeing Charlie enter the church to thinking he'd sat behind her in the chapel to finding the prayer he'd slid into the cross. "I gave it to the police," Sadie said.

"I know," he said gruffly. "You should have called me."

Sadie crossed her arms over her chest. "If not for the fact that I was locked in a storage room where I nearly died of a panic attack only to be let out to discover that my room had been ransacked, I would have."

CHAPTER 36

Well, the police are now looking into the whole thing, and they called me to see what I knew," he said. "I'm in a very difficult position."

Sadie hadn't considered the fact that Mr. Olie had operated behind police lines, so to speak, just as she had. The police hadn't made a big deal about that, yet, but she was a visitor who could be sent home. Mr. Olie was a federal employee. "I didn't mean to get you in trouble," she said. "But things had escalated to a point where I couldn't *not* bring the police in. I'm sorry."

He grunted and took another drink.

"Have they found him?"

He shook his head. "His school is about a mile from the church. He was on the morning bus but didn't go to class."

"Oh, dear," Sadie said, her stomach sinking. "Have you been looking for him?"

"I can't do much," he said, wiping the sweat from his forehead. "But I've been working on other things. Turns out Nat was fired from a job with Parks and Rec six weeks ago for failing a drug screen."

Sadie's heart sunk. "You're kidding," she said. Did everyone here do drugs?

"Just weed, but still, that's why she didn't apply to have him approved to stay there—because he wouldn't pass the background check. He's had clean screens since then, but it doesn't change the facts."

"Will that affect her ability to adopt Charlie?"

"We'll have to take it to a judge and see, but it certainly won't help things. It was a totally different thing before the police knew about Charlie being on the run. Now there's going to be police reports and statements on record."

"Have you talked to Nat?"

Mr. Olie nodded. "He was there, and after I talked to CeeCee and put the fear of God into her, I did the same with him. He feels horrible, and he's really worried about Charlie. His story isn't too different than Charlie's—Dad out of the picture; Mom addicted to crack. Anyway, both he and CeeCee said Nat would have another place to stay by the end of the week. I hope we can still salvage the placement, but I don't know. I've got to find Charlie if I have a chance of making a case that this family is a good place for him." He sighed. "And maybe I'm wrong; maybe it's not a good place. I don't know anymore. And now the police want to know what I know, and my answers may very well take me off Charlie's case altogether."

Sadie hated the thought of Charlie losing what little security he had. "I'm so sorry," she said. "I really felt as though I had no choice but to go to the police."

"If you see him again, call me before you call the police this time."

Sadie tightened her mouth, not liking the way he ordered her around, and yet she really did feel horrible for making things more complicated for Charlie. "I don't know how I'd end up seeing him again," she said. "I'm not planning to go back to Kalaheo, and he doesn't have anyone who will bring him back out here."

"Well," Mr. Olie said, scooting to the edge of the futon, "he seems to keep showing up in your path, so if it happens again, call me."

Sadie wasn't comfortable making him any promises, so she skirted a direct answer. "Do you have a card so I can call you directly?"

"Not with me, but I'll give you my cell number."

Sadie went to the kitchen for the notebook and pen, then took her time returning to the living room; she could hear him struggling to get off the couch. It was quite low, but she didn't want to embarrass him, and she knew he wouldn't accept her help. When she reentered the room, he was standing. He handed her the empty water glass. She was glad to see that the short rest seemed to have helped him and would have asked if he were okay except she was tired of being snapped at. He gave her his number, and she wrote it down in the notebook next to her interview notes.

"Will you call me if you find him?" she asked.

"How do I do that? You don't have a phone."

"My friend has one," Sadie said. "Let me give you her number."

"I left my phone in the car," he said, waving away the idea.

"I'll write her number down for you."

He grunted. Not interested.

"Well, we were about to go to Lihue to get me a new phone," Sadie said. "So you should be able to call me within the hour."

He grunted again, and she clenched her jaw as she followed him to the front door. She nearly apologized again, but stopped herself. She'd apologized enough and still didn't know what else she could have done. She had reached her limit and done all she could. And yet . . . here she was talking to Kiki and promising to call Mr. Olie if Charlie showed up for some reason.

"What are you going to do now?" Sadie asked.

"Prepare my argument for the judge," he said. "We've got an emergency hearing set up for Monday morning, and I need everything in place before then. Of course, if Charlie doesn't show up, it will all be for nothing."

Sadie opened the front door for him, but he paused on the threshold. "Oh, I almost forgot," he said, reaching in to the pocket of his buttoned-up shirt, plaid instead of floral, which seemed a little out of place on an island where practically everyone wore a Hawaiian shirt. "CeeCee gave me this when I told her I didn't think Charlie believed Noelani had died." He handed Sadie a small purple envelope the size of a thank-you card. "She said she found this in his room a few days ago—under his pillow. She hadn't seen it before, but I think it supports the theory that Noelani threw in the towel one way or another. Poor kid. I'll need the note back, but I gotta get going if I'm gonna talk to Janet before she leaves for the day."

Sadie thought he should go home and rest—the day had obviously taken a lot out of him—but wasn't about to say so.

He didn't even say good-bye after handing her the note, just lumbered to his car.

After she watched him drive off, she looked at the lavender envelope in her hand. Charlie's name was written across the front along with a small, hand-drawn flower. Inside the small envelope was a slightly smaller note card. It had white flowers on the front of the lavender card—an odd choice to give to an eleven-year-old boy. Sadie closed the front door and headed back to the kitchen where she sat down and opened the card.

Dear Charlie,

I know it's hard to understand why I would have to leave, but I can't be the mom I should be. I can't take care of you, but I want you to have a happy life. I love you so much, and I know that you'll be safe now. I'm sorry for not being a good mom and for not saying good-bye. Be a good boy and trust in God to make all things right.

Love,
Mom

When she finished reading, Sadie took a shaky breath and read it again. When she finished the second time, however, she felt more confused than ever. What did this mean? Was it a suicide note? Who would give a suicide note to their child? She thought back to the things Charlie had said and wondered if he'd interpreted it to mean his mom was just going away—leaving him with CeeCee. That fit better with what Pastor Darryl had told her except that Noelani had wound up dead in the ocean.

What if Noelani had planned to leave, but then something happened and she'd ended up dead? But then why had she bought the coffee? And why leave work in the middle of her shift and say it was because of Charlie?

She looked at the flower drawn next to Charlie's name and wondered why it reminded her of the mural she'd seen on the wall of the church kitchen.

"Can I come in now?"

Sadie looked up at Gayle, who was peeking through the sliding glass door.

"I'm sorry," she said, coming to her feet. "I got distracted."

"No worries," Gayle said, though she was obviously annoyed as she wiped the sweat from her face. She frowned at her now-wet hand and moved to the sink. "What did the fat man want that was too sensitive for me to hear?"

After Gayle had dried her hands, Sadie handed her the note card and explained what Mr. Olie had told her about Nat and CeeCee. "Why would Noelani give this to her son?" Sadie asked after Gayle read the note. "I can't think of any reason a mother would think that was a good idea."

"Other than letting him down gently," Gayle said. "But, yeah, that doesn't fit. She didn't leave, she died. And if she was suicidal, why announce that to your kid?"

"I can't help but wonder when Charlie got this note."

"What do you mean?" Gayle asked.

"He'd just had a visitation with his mother—a visitation his mom was so excited about that she risked upsetting her boss and making things difficult for her coworkers to make sure it happened. Why go to all that trouble and then send him a suicide note?" Sadie looked at the envelope in her hand. "And this wasn't mailed. Unless it came in another envelope, I suppose. But then CeeCee would probably have seen it and not have discovered it under his pillow."

"Good points," Gayle said, handing the note back to Sadie.

"I don't think Noelani had anything to do with this note," Sadie said, replacing it inside the envelope. She questioned her confidence in that belief but realized that's what she truly thought. "She'd worked so hard in his best interest that to end it with something like this just does not fit for me."

"Who else would send it?"

"Bets said she thought it would be better for Charlie to believe his mother had left and that if her body hadn't been found, that's what everyone would have believed."

"Why would she say that?" Gayle said, looking slightly horrified.

"Exactly." Sadie waved the note again. "Noelani lived with Bets and Pastor Darryl for months. What are the chances there's a handwriting sample lying around their apartment somewhere?"

"You think Bets could mimic Noelani's handwriting?"

"The only person she needed to fool was Charlie. What eleven-year-old boy pays close enough attention to his mother's handwriting to be able to tell a forgery?" She pointed at the flower on the front of the envelope. "And Bets is an artist. She painted an amazing mural on the wall of the church with flowers that, if I'm remembering correctly, look an awful lot like this."

Gayle spoke slowly. "If she sent this, she didn't think Noelani was coming back."

Sadie held her eyes before nodding slightly.

"Oh my gosh," Gayle said, her face paling. "Bets killed her. That's how she knew Noelani wasn't coming back."

"Maybe," Sadie said, trying to rein in the thoughts she could see spiraling in Gayle's eyes. "Assuming she *did* write the note and assuming Charlie *did* receive it between the time his mother disappeared and when I found her body. There are a lot of details we need to figure out before we can make that kind of accusation."

"I want to just drive over there and put this in her face, force a confession," Gayle said.

"I understand," Sadie said with a smile. She could relate. "But she's not going anywhere, and the police are involved so we don't need to act rashly. We do, however, need to find Charlie and connect this note to Bets's painting, if we can. Every bit of connection we find makes our case that much stronger. We don't want to get too antsy and miss an opportunity to line up the facts."

Gayle nodded slowly. "But what if Bets is the one who broke into your motel room? If she wrote that"—she pointed at the note—"then there's a very good reason for her to want to scare you off."

"You're catching on quick," Sadie said, feeling the bubbly rise of excitement that was unfamiliar and comfortable at the same time. "And I guess I need to go get a phone."

"Finally," Gayle said, bringing her hands together as if in prayer. "I told you so!"

"I know, I know," Sadie said. "But it better not take very long. While we don't need to rush into this, we do have a lot to figure out."

"Yes, sir," Gayle said, snapping her heels together and saluting. "I'll follow your lead from here on out." She cut her fingers away sharply, making Sadie laugh.

"Let me put some stuff together, and we can go. I've got some other muumuus if you want to change. Mainland clothes can be really uncomfortable here on the island." She looked pointedly at Gayle's long pants and polyester shirt that would most certainly get sticky and overly hot.

Gayle eyed the pink-and-blue muumuu Sadie had been wearing all day and shook her head. "No offense, but I can't imagine wearing a nightgown in public."

Sadie shrugged. "I felt the same way at first, but remember you're in a different world here. While we're out, pay attention to how many women are wearing them."

CHAPTER 37

Forty-five minutes later, Sadie had her old SIM card in a new phone. It wasn't the same model as Sadie's old phone—they didn't have them in stock—and she frowned as she pushed buttons on the touch screen, trying to figure out how to use the menu. "I hate learning new electronics," she said. "I think I just set a weird ring tone." She tried to get back to where she'd been, but ended up turning on the camera instead and exiting back to the main menu. So overwhelming to be an old dog learning new tricks.

"At least people can get in touch with you now," Gayle said. "And the guy set up your e-mail for you. That's a bonus since your laptop is out of commission."

"Yeah," Sadie said as she finally figured out how to call her voice mail.

She was curious to hear if Mr. Olie was more polite in his voice mail than in person.

He wasn't. He told her she shouldn't have gone to the police and to call him back immediately. She deleted the message and was about to exit her voice mail when the robotic voice that wasn't supposed to sound robotic said "Next message."

There was a pause. "Uh, hi, this is Charlie. You said you would help, and so I saw you at the motel after the church. K. Bye."

Sadie immediately pushed the button to hear the message again.

"Listen to this," she said when it finished, but she couldn't figure out how to put the phone on speaker. With a growl, she told Gayle what Charlie had said.

"How'd he get your number?" Gayle asked as they approached Puhi, passing the flower stand where Nat had said he'd lost Charlie on Tuesday.

"I left it with CeeCee," Sadie said. "But I also gave it to Nat. I told Nat I wanted to help Charlie—I never told Charlie that."

"He was listening?"

"He's sneaky," Sadie said, then hurried to add, "and adorable." She found the log of recent calls and dialed the number Charlie had called from, but it rang and rang. On an impulse, she texted the number to Shawn and asked if he'd do a reverse lookup on it for her; he had an app on his phone that made it a thirty-second job. "Charlie's had a hard life. I hope he can stay with CeeCee. I can't imagine him having to start all over again with someone new."

"Poor kid." Gayle pulled onto the Kaumualii highway, heading back toward Puhi and, further south, Kalaheo. "Was Noelani really a stripper like Kiki said?"

"Yeah," Sadie said, thinking of the pictures she'd found on Facebook. "Sounds like she had a pretty tough life, too." She continued scrolling through the calls she'd missed and realized that she had nearly half a dozen—only Pete's number was one she recognized. Had she listened to all the messages on her voice mail?

"Everything I've heard about her shows that she was really working hard to clean up her act since leaving O'ahu," Sadie said. "I wonder if Charlie's still in Kalaheo. The message was left at 1:33, so it was after we talked to the police. Maybe he's hiding. I think he wants to talk to me. Why else would he have called?"

"When we called the police, you said you were done."

Sadie tried to read Gayle's tone, but couldn't be sure what she meant. "You think I should stay out of it?"

"Oh, not necessarily," Gayle said. "All these people are coming to you, and, like Kiki said, you care about Noelani—you're invested. I'm just reminding you of what you said, that's all. I'm happy to take any direction you feel good about."

"It doesn't seem to be done with me yet," Sadie admitted.

"So, are we going to Kalaheo?" Gayle asked, glancing at Sadie.

"Yeah. I think so."

Gayle smiled, giving Sadie some comfort that she wasn't pushing her to do something she was against doing.

She put the phone to her ear where the robotic voice said she had one more unheard message.

"Mrs. Hoffmiller, this is Nat, Charlie's foster brother. My mom's talking to the police, but I thought I would call you too. The cops said you saw him. Please give me a call."

As soon as Sadie hung up, she called Nat, hoping that between the time he'd left the message, which had been around three o'clock, and now that Charlie had been found.

"Nat," Sadie said when he answered the phone. "It's Sadie Hoffmiller. You left me a message about Charlie."

"Yeah," he said. "You saw him?"

"This morning at the church. But he also called me this afternoon. I just got his message. Have you guys found him?"

"No," Nat said.

Sadie deflated against the car seat. "Oh. I was hoping you had."

"And I was hoping *you* had," Nat said. "When did you see him at the church?"

"Around ten," Sadie said.

"What was he doing there? Did you talk to him?"

"Not really. He was putting a prayer into a prayer box. Did the police tell you about that?"

"No," Nat said. "They asked more questions than they answered."

Sadie told him about the note she'd found in the prayer box. "He's still looking for her."

"Ah, man," Nat said. "Well, thanks for the info. I'll tell CeeCee."

"One more thing, Nat."

"Yeah?"

"Charlie received a note last week, a purple envelope, from his mom. Do you know *when* he received it?"

Nat was quiet. "I just learned about it today. I don't know when it showed up."

"The envelope didn't have a postmark," Sadie said. "So it didn't come through the mail, right?"

"I guess," Nat said. "CeeCee doesn't know when it came either. I wonder if it was a long time ago—like months."

"But why would she send it months ago? This is the first time she's left."

"Yeah, maybe." A silence came between them. "So, you've talked with Mr. Olie, then?" Nat asked.

"A little," Sadie said, squirming.

"Did you tell him about Charlie getting away from me and coming to you?"

Sadie hated feeling like she was disloyal to everyone. "I'm sorry, Nat. I had to."

"Nah, I understand," Nat said. "I just hope it doesn't end with Charlie going to another home. We're the only family he has left, you know. We love him."

"I know you do," Sadie said. "And Mr. Olie knows that too. He's fighting to keep you guys together . . . but the fact that CeeCee didn't notify him when you moved in is a problem." She hoped she wasn't being petty to bring up his culpability in the situation.

"I know," Nat said, not defensive, just . . . sad. "And my stupidity doesn't help. I guess Mr. Olie told you about that, too."

"Yeah," Sadie said. "But he's sympathetic. He knows you love Charlie."

"Could you let me know if you hear somethin'?"

"Of course," Sadie said, knowing full well she was overpromising everyone.

"Thanks," Nat said. "CeeCee's about out of her head with worry."

Sadie ended the call and explained the gist of it to Gayle.

Gayle smiled sadly. "It seems like Charlie has some people who love him."

Sadie nodded. "Yeah, CeeCee and Nat seem to really want him, ya know? I just hope he can stay with them."

Sadie's phone rang—a stupid tinkling of wind chimes. She'd have to figure out how to change that. A wave of trepidation rushed over her when she saw it was Shawn. There was so much she hadn't told him, and so much she still didn't want to talk about. But she'd sent him that number to look up; he was involved now.

"Hey, sweetie," she said, answering the phone. "How are you?"

"I'm okay," he said. "But what are you doing? You workin' a case?"

"Um, sorta."

"You've never *sorta* worked a case before, Mom. What's going on?"

Sadie bit her lip. Shawn had had a hard time since Boston— they'd both been skirting the topic for months—and despite all she'd done on this case, she didn't want to burden him with it. Would it be too much for him to handle? How fragile was he? Having faced her own fragility, the thought of tipping him over was overwhelming. But if she really thought he was incapable, why had she texted him the number Charlie had called her from?

"Is it about Boston?" Shawn asked. That had become almost a code word for them. The city where so many bad things had happened now encompassed all the events and feelings and fears—as though it had been some kind of military secret.

"It's not about Boston," Sadie said, relieved that it was the truth and realizing that amid all this new stuff, Boston had finally faded into the background. "It's something new."

"Well," Shawn said expectantly and perhaps with relief, "tell me about it."

"Okay, but don't get mad."

"Why would I get mad?"

"Because she should have told you three weeks ago!" Gayle yelled, causing Sadie to jolt. She looked at her friend, who stared at the road. "Well, you should have," she said in a normal tone. "And you know it."

"What—is that . . . Gayle? You're still in Hawai'i, right?"

Sadie took a breath. "Yes. I'll tell you everything, but understand that I didn't tell you sooner because I didn't want you to worry."

"That excuse again?" Shawn said, both annoyed and sarcastic. "I thought we were past that."

Sadie sighed and did her best to catch him up on what was

happening. To his credit, he took it well and kept his judgments to himself. "So the kid called you from the number you gave me?" Shawn asked.

"Yes," Sadie said, relieved he wasn't angry with her. "If you have a minute to look it up, it might help me find him."

"I already looked it up," Shawn said.

"Oh." Sadie scrambled for her notebook. "Where's it from?"

"A place called Bartley Expeditions, in a city called Kale-ahh-eeo on Kaua'i. Do you want the address?"

"No," Sadie said. "I know the address." What was Charlie doing there? He must have called while Jim was out with his expedition.

"So what's next? What else can I do to help?"

It was on the tip of her tongue to tell him that was all she needed, but it wasn't true. She didn't have her laptop anymore so she had no way of accessing information. "Can you do a quick background on the owner of that business—Bartley Expeditions? His name is James, James Bartley, and he lives here in Kalaheo above his business. He owns a motel next to it by the name of Sand and Sea. He's been married before and had some stepsons, but I don't think he has kids of his own."

"Okay," Shawn said. "Anything specific I'm looking for?"

"I just want a basic history," Sadie said. "And I'm curious as to when his marriage broke up and why, if you can find it. Are you sure you have time?"

"Do you think we could move to a place where you trust me to manage my time without having to remind me of my responsibilities?"

Sadie blinked. Shawn was never cross with her. Ever. "Um, I didn't mean to imply I didn't trust you."

"Really?" he said with as much of an edge in his voice as she'd ever heard. "Then why didn't you tell me all this sooner? You must not have thought I could handle it."

Sadie felt tears coming. "I haven't been handling it very well," she said. "And I knew you were having a hard time too. I just . . . wanted to protect you, I guess."

"I'm twenty-two years old," Shawn said as though that made him a man of the world. It was still so young in Sadie's mind. "I've faced off with a few murderers, and I do my own laundry. I think I deserve a little more credit."

Sadie didn't know what to say.

"And I love you," he added, bringing the tears finally to Sadie's eyes. "And want to help you if I can, okay?"

"Okay," Sadie said, sniffing.

"I'm on this Bartley guy, and I'll call you as soon as I get any info."

"Thanks," she said. "And I'm sorry."

"It's all good," Shawn said. "I'll talk to you soon."

Sadie put the phone in her lap and stared out the windshield. "Are you mad at me too?" she asked Gayle, who'd been silent since her outburst.

"No," Gayle said. "We love you, and we want to trust you, but you didn't tell us what was going on—and I'm not just talking about Noelani."

Sadie didn't know what to say. She assumed Gayle was saying this to make her feel better somehow, but she only felt worse. Was she a bad mother, a bad friend, and a bad girlfriend for not telling the people she loved about her anxiety? Were they all angry with her beneath their concern? If so, it proved the belief she'd been battling that the expectations other people had of her was how she determined her own value. They wanted her whole and saw a broken version of Sadie as unacceptable. If that were true, then pretending she was okay was her only option.

"Hey," Gayle said softly, poking Sadie's leg to get her attention. "Life has a funny way of teaching us things sometimes. You're always the first responder when someone needs something, you love to help, you love to be involved, you love to encourage and support people to be their best selves. You need to learn to accept the same thing when it's you who needs the help. That's all I'm saying. When you don't tell us you need something, we feel like you think we're incapable, but we're not. We all know we must be pretty dang amazing to have you love us like you do. All we want is to return the favor."

"I don't know what to say," Sadie said, finding it difficult to accept what Gayle was saying.

"How about thanks?"

Sadie looked at her, unsure of how she meant the comment, but Gayle's expression was soft and sympathetic. "Thanks," she said, though it seemed lacking.

"You're welcome," Gayle said. "And, see, now everything is good again!"

Sadie smiled weakly and looked around, recognizing that they were getting close to Kalaheo. She'd planned to call her credit card companies during the drive to request replacement cards, and she opened up her file of information she'd brought from the condo. She was hopeful she could get a few of the cards canceled and new ones on their way by the time they reached the church. Or maybe they should go to Bartley Expeditions instead?

Five minutes later, a customer service rep assured Sadie that her new card was on its way. "Could you verify your most recent charge to make sure the card wasn't used before it was destroyed?" the rep asked.

"Oh, I'm sure it wasn't used," Sadie said, thinking of how short the time period was between her being locked out of her room and the discovery of the vandalism. "And I'll have a police report for you to put on file in another day or two."

"It's standard practice to review the current charges," the woman said. "Can you recall the last purchase you made on your card?"

"Um, I guess it would be . . . oh, yeah, I paid my car insurance," Sadie said, though it seemed silly since her car was in Garrison. "Last month."

"I see that one," the woman said. "What about the charge for Hawaiian Air?"

"Hawaiian Air?" Sadie said, looking at Gayle, who lifted her eyebrows. "When was that made?"

"The charge went through at 8:21 this morning, but . . . yes, there's the confirmation. It was made yesterday afternoon."

CHAPTER 38

Sadie opened her mouth to dispute it, but then caught herself. The charge had been made *before* Sadie's wallet had been shredded. There was only one other person besides herself who'd had access to her wallet before then.

Charlie.

"Is there a way I could look at the specifics of that charge? I, uh, thought I'd used a different card for that reservation."

"I can e-mail you the information," the woman said. "But I'll need you to let me know within twenty-four hours if you're disputing it or not."

"Certainly," Sadie said. "I'll let you know as soon as I verify the info." She gave the woman her e-mail address and then ended the call before toggling to the app for her e-mail. She'd never had e-mail on her phone, but now she was glad that Gayle had talked her into it and that the cute boy at the cell phone store had set it up.

The e-mail from the credit card company arrived a few seconds later. The text was tiny, but she was able to zoom in and then turn the phone sideways to read it.

Gayle slowed down. "Where to? The church?"

"That's probably best," Sadie said. "For now." She looked at the information the credit card company had sent, but all it said was that a purchase had been made for the amount of $82. She grunted in frustration.

"How much was your ticket from O'ahu to Kaua'i?"

"Um, about $90. I just did one way."

"So did Charlie," Sadie said. "Assuming it was him. But who else would it be?" Her anger dissipated when she realized why Charlie was going to O'ahu—to find his mother.

"Kids these days," Gayle said. "I got a new TV last month, and the only person who can get it to play a DVD is Karra; she's two."

"I'm calling the airline," Sadie said, closing the e-mail program and trying to get back to the dial pad. "What if he's already left?"

"I'm sure they wouldn't let him board," Gayle said. "But they won't tell you anything about a passenger anyway."

"They have to tell me. It was my credit card."

"Let me make a call," Gayle said. She pulled into the church parking lot and parked next to Pastor Darryl's Jeep. "That client of mine who helped me change my flight might know a trick or two. If that doesn't work, then we can call the airline."

Sadie nodded, but she didn't like doing nothing. She looked out the windshield at the orange roof of Bartley Expeditions. "I'm going to Jim's," she said, making an instant decision as she reached for the door handle. "Maybe Charlie's still there." Even as she said it, though, she knew that was unlikely. It was four in the afternoon. He'd called her hours ago.

"Wait," Gayle said, the phone at her ear. "Wait for me to make this call."

"I can't," Sadie said. "I can't waste any more time. Make the call and then go to the church. The mural I was telling you about is in the kitchen. See if you think the flower matches the one drawn on the card. And call me with anything you figure out, okay?" She pulled the card out of her purse and handed it to Gayle.

Gayle looked as though she wanted to do anything but agree to the plan, but she nodded. "Be safe."

Sadie smiled. "I will." She shut the car door and hurried through the church grounds, certain she could find the back way from this direction. She was right; the path was much more clear. After crossing through a second hedge into the motel's parking lot, the path split. One headed for a covered corridor entrance to the motel; the other led to the expedition office.

Within two minutes of leaving Gayle behind her, Sadie was at Bartley Expeditions. The garage door was down, but the office door was unlocked. She let herself in and took a moment to absorb the silence, the emptiness.

"Hello?" she called, just to make sure. No one answered. Convinced she was alone, Sadie headed around the empty reception desk, scanning the area for evidence that an eleven-year-old boy had been there. He hadn't left anything behind.

Sadie picked up the phone on the counter and used it to call her cell phone. When it rang, the display showed the same number Charlie had used earlier. Sadie hung up and searched the desk for more evidence, but discovered nothing. She turned back to the phone and found the call log. It showed that her number had been called at 1:33, but within a minute of that call, another call had been placed with the 808 area code. She picked up the phone again and called that number.

"Aloha, Kaua'i bus office," a woman said when she answered. "Can I help you?"

"Um, yes," Sadie said, thinking fast. Why would Charlie have called the bus station? She'd no sooner asked herself the question, however, than she knew the answer. She scrambled for some scratch paper and a pen while glancing at the door, hoping no one would come in during the next two minutes. "Can you tell me what buses I would need to take to get from Kalaheo to the airport?"

A few minutes later, Sadie thanked the women for her time and tapped her pen on the paper full of times and bus numbers. She wondered what kind of progress Gayle was making on Charlie's flight. Despite Gayle's assurances that he couldn't fly by himself, Sadie wouldn't have guessed he could hide from everyone who was looking for him or book the flight by himself, but he had done both those things. Charlie was as streetwise as any kid she'd ever met, and she wouldn't be the least bit surprised if he managed to get on the plane.

Sadie considered calling the police, they might be able to get to the airport quicker than she could, but she'd told Mr. Olie she'd call him first. She dialed his number, which went to voice mail after four rings. She left a quick message with the basics, promising to call him when she knew more. She hung up, feeling better knowing he couldn't yell at her for not calling this time.

Should I call the police now, she wondered? She didn't want to. She turned to the door leading into the garage. Jim's apartment was here. The motel's security cameras fed into his apartment, and, assuming she could get in, she might be able to figure out who had trashed her room. Maybe she could catch sight of Charlie too.

"Hello?" she called again as she pushed open the door leading to the garage. "Jim?"

Still no one answered. The boat Jim had been loading this morning looked like it hadn't been moved at all, still parked right where it had been. What if Jim had made up the expedition to make her *think* he had left? If not for the fact that Kiki had told her about it long before Sadie had posed any kind of threat to Jim, Sadie would have pursued the possibility, but she trusted Kiki. And the police would be verifying the expedition anyway.

She walked around the boat, looking for anything of interest. Maybe the interesting aspect was the boat itself. Noelani had been found in the ocean. Someone hadn't expected her to be found—probably Bets—which meant that the chances were good a boat had been involved. This boat, perhaps.

Sadie thought back to the conversation she'd overheard between Bets and Jim. Jim had said, "I'd be careful who you said that to." What had he meant by that? Bets was pretty open with him about Noelani being gone and wanting to be done with her. Were they in this together?

Sadie rounded the stern of the boat, and her eyes lit on the stairs built into the wall across from her, near the door she'd entered. She looked up the length of them to the door at the top. More important, she analyzed the simple residential lock embedded in the door-knob as she climbed the stairs.

At the landing, she knocked on the door, just to make sure no one answered, and counted to twenty before pulling her lock pick set from her bag—she'd never leave home without it again—and quickly selected the best picks for the job. This lock had to be easier than using an ice pick and a whisk.

CHAPTER 39

It *was* easier to break in with the proper tools. Much easier. She was inside within thirty seconds, in part because she had the picks, but she was pretty sure she was also fueled by the numbing fear of getting caught.

Though some people might not have believed it, Sadie had never liked doing the wrong thing. And yet this didn't feel all that wrong. In fact, it even felt a little bit right. If Jim hadn't locked her out of her room, no one would have been able to destroy her things. The only way she might find out who had been behind that, and how that person was connected to Noelani, was here in Jim's apartment.

As soon as she got inside, she locked the door behind her and texted Gayle, telling her she was in the apartment but not to worry.

Gayle didn't respond immediately, which Sadie chose to believe meant that she at least understood and at best agreed. She slid the phone into her bag and took a few moments to scan the apartment, which was a big studio space with a small kitchen table in the very center of the room. One corner was taken up by an L-shaped desk and dominated by a large LCD TV, a computer keyboard, and monitor.

All in all, the apartment wasn't that bad, for a bachelor pad. There was minimal clutter and no underwear on the floor—something Sadie appreciated. The bed was made, though Jim could have taken a minute to straighten the coverlet so the edges hung parallel to the floor.

The one thing that looked out of place was a loose knit pink sweater draped over the back of one of the kitchen chairs. Sadie walked to it and fingered the yarn, picturing Bets last night, pulling the sides of this very same sweater around herself as she watched Sadie and Pastor Darryl head for the Jeep. It was bad enough knowing that Jim and Bets had met together in his office; knowing that Bets had been here was far worse. Sadie still wasn't certain that what she was seeing was what it seemed to be, but she didn't have the time to figure it out.

The LCD TV demanded Sadie's attention, reminding her why she was there in the first place. That had to be where the video feed was connected. She hurried over to the TV and ran her fingers along the edges until she found a power button. Immediately the screen glowed to life, and Sadie smiled at the eight squares of images that provided her an instant view of Jim Bartley's kingdom. The cameras covered all the common areas of the motel as well as the interior of the reception office. The eighth camera showed the path leading between the motel and the church.

Sadie scanned each frame to make sure Jim wasn't in any of them. She actually thought she'd feel better if she could see him somewhere. He wasn't in any of the frames, however. Where could he be?

A woman Sadie didn't recognize was working the front desk—Court, she assumed—checking in a young couple, perhaps honeymooners. A few teenagers were playing in the pool, but the rest of the cameras were clear. Assured she was safe, Sadie was faced with the task of figuring out how to rewind the video so she could see who'd been in her room that morning. She looked at the computer and took a breath. Technology had never been her forte. Wait, she had her phone!

She quickly dialed Shawn. "Mom, I'm still verifying some time-lines, but I did talk to—"

"I need your help with something else," she said, cutting him off and quickly explaining the situation. "So, any ideas?"

"A few," Shawn said. "On the video display is there a name any-where that might lead us to the program he uses for the feeds?"

Sadie checked. In the bottom of the eighth frame was the word Visatrol.

"Sounds like a cholesterol medication, but whatever," Shawn said while Sadie woke up the computer. She braced herself for a password, but no prompt appeared for one. Maybe he thought the lock on his apartment was enough security. A tab at the bottom of the screen also said Visatrol.

Sadie clicked on the tab and then blinked at the interface. "I just pulled it up, but it's broken up into five different frames . . . Ah, man, I hate this kind of thing. I just need to rewind the videos."

"That's why you're calling me," Shawn reminded her. "Hang on—I'm looking it up."

Sadie was in no mood to hang on, but she didn't have much choice. Her attention was momentarily stolen, however, by a snap-shot tucked under the glass top of the desk. Sadie leaned forward and stared at a younger, happier version of Jim, standing between two young boys. They both wore blue baseball caps that said Bartley Expeditions, and the three of them held a really big, really ugly, fish.

The blue, blue water of Hawai'i behind them created a picturesque scene.

"I'm downloading a tutorial . . ." Shawn commented.

Sadie glanced at the video frames—still no sign of Jim, thank goodness.

"Oh, and I talked to his ex."

Sadie straightened. "Already?"

"I found her number, called her, and she answered."

"Wow. What did she say?"

"That Jim was controlling and verbally abusive to her, but that she stayed as long as she did because he was so good with her sons," Shawn said.

"Shocking," Sadie said. "He was good to the boys?"

"Excellent," Shawn said. "Oh, wait—Okay, I've got the tutorial going. Let me just . . . Okay, yep . . . Look in the lower right section and click on *history*."

Sadie did so, and the section changed to a listing of dates and times.

"The program records in ten-minute increments, so just chose which camera you want, click on the date and time you want to review, then press play. It should replace the current frame of that camera with the past one. You can play it in real-time, slow, or speed view."

Sadie followed his instructions, and within seconds she was watching what video camera five—the one that showed the expedition office—had recorded at 1:20, which was about the time Charlie had called Sadie's phone.

"Got it, thanks," Sadie said. "I'll let you go."

"You don't want to know anything else about Jim?"

She wanted to say not right now, but it felt rude after all Shawn had done. "Sure. What else was interesting?"

Shawn rattled off some facts, like where they had gotten married, when Jim's ex filed for the divorce, yada yada yada, while she scanned through the video.

"She said Pastor Darryl finally convinced her to leave."

"Really?" Sadie said, her attention snapping back to Shawn's voice.

Shawn repeated himself, and Sadie understood why Jim hated Pastor Darryl so much.

"She said Darryl helped her realize that the kids were still front-row to an unhealthy relationship, even if Jim treated them well. I guess the divorce happened pretty fast once she made the decision to leave."

Sadie thanked Shawn again for the information and said she'd call him soon. She tried to focus on the next ten-minute segment from video camera five, but instead thought about what she'd just learned about Jim. It made sense—why Jim was so nice to Charlie and so bitter about Pastor Darryl. The one answer she didn't have was whether or not Jim was in love with Bets. Bets's insecurity regarding her husband's questionable actions was a perfect opening for Jim, if he were motivated by revenge instead of lust.

Sadie looked over her shoulder at the sweater that shouldn't be there and then turned back to the video.

She played through the video fast and when no one showed up on the frame, moved to the next segment. Right away she saw Charlie. The time read 1:31, just minutes before he'd called Sadie. She watched him go inside, looking around as he did so, but he didn't come out until the next section. He was in the office for just over ten minutes—long enough to call Sadie and the bus station.

She scanned through the next two segments just to make sure Charlie hadn't come back. Then she changed to the camera that showed the section where Sadie's room was located and started with the 9:50 video. She played it fast, but had to figure out how to stop it when she saw people appearing and disappearing quickly due to how fast she was viewing the segments. They were only other guests passing by, though. No one attempted to go into her room.

Sadie's phone rang—Gayle.

"I just got your text. You're seriously in his apartment?" she said.

"Yes," Sadie said, still watching the video. "And I'm about to find out who broke into my room."

"Oh my gosh," Gayle said. "This is so insane!"

"I know," Sadie agreed. "What did you find out about the ticket? Anything?"

"Yes," Gayle said, and her tone changed dramatically. "It's Charlie. He's supposed to take the 7:45 flight to Honolulu. I was able to talk to security, and I told them that he's your grandson and is in big trouble for using your card. When he tries to check in, they'll hold him and give me a call."

"You are amazing," Sadie said, awed by what Gayle had accomplished. "Thanks!"

"Do you want me to—"

Sadie nearly missed the flash of someone on the video, and she quickly rewound it to watch it in real time. "Hold on," she said to Gayle.

At first she didn't recognize the woman who stopped in front of room nine, Sadie's room. She had a bag over her shoulder and was holding a fountain drink. She looked around quickly, then slid a key into the door and stepped inside.

Sadie rewound the tape again and watched it slowly, leaning

toward the screen so as not to miss anything. It wasn't until the woman looked around in slow-motion that Sadie could identify her. Mandi? Pastor Darryl and Bets's "roommate"?

"Sadie?" Gayle asked.

"Um, can I call you back?"

"Yeah, but get your *okole* out of there before he catches you."

Sadie paused. "Where on earth did you learn that word?"

"The man on the plane," Gayle said casually.

"What were the two of you talking about?" *Okole* meant rear end; Sadie had never used the word herself.

"Never you mind. Do you want me to stand guard or something?"

Sadie refocused on the task before her. "No, I've got the surveillance in front of me." She scanned the camera frames. Still no sign of Jim. Only camera three was on history mode. "Can you go check out the flower on the card?"

"I'm on it," Gayle said. "Wikiwiki!"

"I will."

Sadie hung up and froze the video image, looking at it closely, wanting to be sure. What was Mandi's connection to all this?

It wasn't until the next ten-minute segment that she saw Mandi exit the room. She still had her drink cup, but Sadie knew the contents were all over her laptop. Once outside, Mandi adjusted her purse on her shoulder, then hurried down the walkway toward the church. She didn't look nervous, which bothered Sadie. Sadie had barely spoken to the woman, and yet she'd trashed her room. Why?

Sadie exited camera three and pulled up the history for the one that showed the pathway to the church. Mandi showed up in the frame, but instead of taking the path to the church, she cut to the path leading to the expedition office.

Jim would have been gone at that time, so what would Mandi have been doing at the office? Sadie switched cameras again and watched Mandi enter the expedition office, only to leave within two minutes, not long enough to do much. She hadn't been carrying anything other than her purse and the empty drink cup.

Movement in one of the real-time frames of the surveillance system caught Sadie's attention, and her eyes snapped to the interior of the motel office. Her breath caught in her throat as she saw Jim and Court talking at the reception desk.

Jim was a hundred yards away from her at least, but having forgotten about him for a minute made Sadie feel vulnerable. She'd learned what she needed to learn, which meant she had no reason to stay where it was so risky. She returned everything to the way it had been when she'd entered the apartment before running toward the door.

She was halfway across the room when she noticed a small white rectangle on the floor by one of the kitchen chair legs—the same chair Bets's sweater was draped over. It looked a lot like the key that had been slid beneath the door of the storage closet where Sadie had been trapped. She looked from the card key to the door—a straight shot. Mandi could have come to Jim's apartment to return the master key by sliding it under the door; the same way she had returned Sadie's room key to her a few minutes later. Again, she asked herself, *why Mandi?*

Sadie opened the door, turning the lock so it would lock behind her, and pulled the door closed before hurrying down the stairs. She was on the bottom landing with her hand on the office door when she heard a voice. Her stomach knotted. She was so close to being out of here, but she was still very much inside.

She looked around for somewhere to hide and ran around to the far side of the boat. She climbed up on the hub of the trailer wheel-well so that her feet wouldn't be visible. The only thing to hold onto was the edge of the hub, necessitating a crouched position that had her legs shaking and her fingers white with strain after the first few seconds. Sadie closed her eyes and tried to lean against the boat as best she could to help herself balance.

"Just play it out," she heard Jim's voice say as the door opened.

She listened for another voice, but when he paused before speaking again, she realized he was on the phone.

"Trust me, it's working out fine. . . . Nobody really cares about who got into that room, but they're looking into Noelani more than ever. And based on what Bets said this morning, you're right about her being in the middle of it."

Sadie's fingers were burning but she heard his feet on the stairs. *One more minute*, she told herself, barely keeping her position as Jim continued.

"Are you kidding, Mandi? This is the best opportunity you've had to date. . . . Yeah, I got the sweater, and I'm heading over there later to *confess*. . . . Believe me or don't, but everything is working out just like it should. And ironically, we can thank Sadie Hoffmiller for that."

CHAPTER 40

Mandi?

Sadie heard the apartment door at the top of the stairs open and shut before practically falling off her perch. She didn't hesitate before running around the boat, through the waiting room, and out of the office. She was banking on the fact that Jim probably hadn't turned on the TV yet and therefore wouldn't see her leave. She took the long way back to the church, though. She didn't want to show up on video any more than she had to, and she used the extra distance to think through what she'd just discovered. Jim and Mandi were working together!

It seemed so far-fetched, and yet it made perfect sense if Jim's goal was to get back at Darryl. What better person to work with than the woman Sadie was pretty sure had a crush on the pastor. Jim was taking advantage of Bets's insecurities to set her up—and using Sadie to do it. It wasn't until Sadie was hurrying across the church parking lot that the final pieces clicked into place. She stopped in the middle of the pavement.

"He wanted me to stay here," she said out loud. That was why Jim had kept her locked her out of her room; it had forced her to stay in Kalaheo. The "why" was harder to figure out. He hadn't been angry about her eavesdropping. He'd simply been plotting how to use it to his advantage. How did Noelani fit in? The only direct tie, or as direct as Sadie had found so far, was Bets.

Sadie dug her phone out of her bag and texted Gayle.

Sadie: Where are you?

Gayle: In the church, helping Pastor D clean up the storage room. I didn't tell him why it was a mess.

Sadie: Do you know where Bets is?

Gayle: Just pulled in from the store. Working on dinner. I don't think she knew what happened in the closet either.

Sadie: I don't think so either. I'm heading her way. Bring PD over when you finish. Did you see the flower?

Gayle: Dead ringer. She wrote the note—I'd put money on it.

Sadie returned her phone to her bag and headed around the church to the pastor's apartment. She stopped at the door, took a deep breath, and knocked loudly while quickly prioritizing her objectives. She had to have her focus be on the most important thing— the note sent to Charlie.

The door opened, and Sadie smiled while lifting her chin. "Hi, Bets," she said before Bets could come up with something to say instead.

"Um, aloha," Bets said cautiously, clearly not thrilled to see Sadie. "Can I help you?"

"Well, I was wondering if I could come in." Sadie was banking on the fact that Bets would be too polite to say no. "It's so hot. Could I get a drink maybe?"

Bets hesitated, uneasy, but then nodded. "Sure."

She stepped back so Sadie could enter the great room area of the apartment that was filled with a good collection of the local Koa wood furniture as well as some upholstered pieces. A countertop separated the living room from the kitchen. Everything was neat and clean. A huge painting of Mount Wai'ale'ale hung on one wall. Above an organized desk set against another wall was a collection of pictures—wedding portraits among them. Bets looked so young and carefree—gorgeous in a simple white dress.

"I love your place," Sadie said, meaning it. It was cozy and neat and . . . loved. The condo in Puhi didn't feel that way, and Sadie suddenly missed her own home. Beyond the decorations, the apartment smelled delicious. "What are you cooking?"

"Kalua pork," Bets said as she passed Sadie on her way to the kitchen.

"I thought that was cooked in a big pit with banana leaves and things."

"We only use the *imu* out back when we're cooking a whole pig. This time I'm using a slow cooker." She opened a cupboard and removed a glass, in a hurry to get rid of Sadie, or so it seemed.

"I'd love to get the recipe sometime," Sadie said. "If it tastes half as good as it smells, my son will love it."

Bets smiled politely, but Sadie could tell she had no intention of giving Sadie anything beyond a glass of water.

"Um, could I also use the restroom?" Sadie asked, stalling for more time, hoping to figure out her next move.

Before Bets could answer, Sadie pointed toward the hallway on the opposite end of the apartment. "Just down there, right?"

"Uh," Bets said, but Sadie was already on her way.

The bathroom was the second door on the right, but she could also see into what she assumed was the master bedroom at the end of the hall. She looked over her shoulder to make sure Bets wasn't following her before hurrying into the bedroom. If there were secrets here, she would find them in the bedroom. Bets wouldn't risk leaving something out in the open with Mandi in residence.

She closed the door quietly behind her, her heart pounding in her chest as she looked around the pristine room—pristine except for one thing. Charlie's list lay face up on the nightstand, just waiting to be discovered.

If Bets had really broken into Sadie's room and stolen the list, she wouldn't have left the only direct tie to the break-in out in plain sight. Clearly it had been planted here by someone else. Sadie wondered where Mandi was right now.

Sadie picked up the list, grateful to have it back. She folded it up and stuck it in her bag, mentally checking off its recovery from her to-do list.

Before returning to Bets, Sadie took a minute to look for anything else that might be helpful—a journal, or something belonging to Noelani—though Sadie didn't know what that would be—anything that might prove her suspicions. But every drawer was perfectly organized and nothing stood out. Sadie knew she'd been gone too long. She took a deep breath; she just needed to do one more thing.

"I meant to bring some note cards with me," Sadie said as she stepped into the living room.

Bets was slicing tomatoes in the kitchen, but Sadie's glass of water was on the counter, waiting for her to drink it and leave. She ignored it and made a show of looking through her bag. "I must have left them at the condo. Do you by chance have something I could borrow? I wanted to write a thank-you card to my hairdresser; she did such a great job."

Bets looked at Sadie's hair before meeting her eyes and putting down the knife. "A note card?"

"You know, stationery, thank-you cards—something a step up from notebook paper. If it's no trouble."

Bets was too polite to say no. "Um, sure." She rinsed her hands in the sink before coming around the counter. Sadie followed her, which Bets hadn't expected. She looked over her shoulder, more nervous than ever but didn't tell Sadie to back off.

When Bets reached the desk, she pulled open the second drawer from the top. It was perfectly organized with envelopes and a few boxes of cards. Bets reached for a box of thank-you cards, then hesitated and reached for a box of stationery instead.

"Those cards would be perfect," Sadie said, ignoring the stationery Bets handed her and stepping close enough grab the box of note cards Bets had avoided. They weren't purple, though, and Sadie dug through the drawer, moving around the perfectly organized contents.

"What are you doing?" Bets said, stepping back. Her voice was panicked, not angry. "I don't like you going through my things." She reached past Sadie and grabbed the box of note cards Sadie still held.

Sadie immediately grabbed the box back despite the fact that the clear cover showed that the cards were light yellow with bumblebees spelling out "Thank you." Bets's eyes went wide, and she tightened her fingers on the box. Her action only spurred Sadie's own determination, and she grabbed the box with both hands, pulling it away from Bets.

As soon as she had full possession, she ran for the kitchen counter, ripping off the top of the box.

Bets was right behind her. "Give me that!" she said, sharp and scared.

Sadie didn't bother wasting the energy to explain herself. She grabbed the first few note cards and pulled them out of the box, dropping them behind her.

Bets inhaled sharply. "What are you—"

And then Sadie saw a corner of lavender stashed below the yellow. She pulled out the last of the bumblebee cards just as Bets grabbed her hair and yanked. Sadie stumbled backward, her scalp on fire. The contents of the box flew upward and scattered through the air, some purple, some yellow.

Sadie reached behind her and grabbed Bets's wrist, trying to unlock her grip. She didn't let go, forcing Sadie to find the pressure point on the back of the hand, between the thumb and index finger. She pushed it with her own thumb until Bets screamed and let go.

Sadie moved her hand up to Bets's wrist as she turned, twisting the arm as she marched her backward until Bets hit up against the desk, knocking one of the picture frames to the ground in the process.

Bets looked from her arm to Sadie's face, shocked and afraid.

"What have you done?" Sadie asked. She hadn't wanted things to get violent, but she needed answers.

"You're crazy," Bets said. "I want you out of my house."

"I'm happy to leave as soon as you tell me what you've done."

"I haven't done anything, I—"

"You wrote that note to Charlie."

Bets's eyes went wide, and she opened her mouth but didn't speak.

"I think you were trying to comfort him somehow," Sadie said, offering the only olive branch she was prepared to give this troubled woman. "But you wouldn't have sent it if you didn't already know Noelani was dead."

The expression on Bets's face melted into shock again. She pushed against Sadie, and Sadie let her go, confident in her ability to reestablish control if she needed to. Bets stumbled a few feet away, pushing her hair out of her eyes.

Sadie moved to the center of the room, blocking the door in case Bets was considering an exit. "You must have panicked when her body was found," Sadie said. "Which means you expected that it wouldn't be."

"You're crazy," Bets said, her eyes frantic. "I don't know what you're talking about."

Sadie put her hands on her hips. "The police will track the stationery back to you. They'll make the same connection I made between the flower on the envelope and the flower on the mural in the church. They'll also confirm that it's not Noelani's handwriting. Even if it was similar enough to fool Charlie, it won't fool the police."

Bets covered her ears and clenched her eyes closed as though trying to block out Sadie's words. Sadie just spoke louder. "You thought she was having an affair with your husband. She was threatening your marriage and—"

"Stop," Bets said, her voice low and husky. "Stop it."

"I can't," Sadie said, lowering her own voice and resisting the urge to accuse Bets of murder right then and there. "Because it's the truth, and the truth can't hide forever. You argued with her earlier in the week. What were you arguing about?"

Bets hesitated, then folded her arms across her stomach and looked at the ground. "Darryl," she said. "She was meeting with him more and more often. Jim told me Darryl had come to her room at night, and I . . . I just couldn't take it anymore."

"You told her you'd get in her way if she didn't get out of yours. How would you get in her way?"

Bets let out a breath, then inhaled as though pulling in strength to continue. "I told her if she didn't leave, I'd tell DHS that her community involvement was a sham and that I knew she was dealing drugs. I told her she'd be arrested, and she would have been."

"You put the marijuana in her room?"

Bets nodded slowly. "Where she wouldn't find it, but the police would if I chose to call them."

"And what did she say to your threat?"

"She said I was crazy." Her eyes narrowed. "I'm not crazy," she said, too defensive. "I'm not! I just . . . I know how easy it is for a man's heart to wander, and she was a stripper! Darryl was . . . he was with her so much. I just . . . I just . . ."

"Did you talk to her again after that? After you threatened her?"

Bets looked at the ground but said nothing.

"You knew she was dead when you sent that note to Charlie."

A new voice spoke up. "What note?"

CHAPTER 41

Sadie and Bets both turned to look at Pastor Darryl standing in the doorway. Gayle stood behind him and caught Sadie's eyes, shrugging like she didn't know what to do. Judging from the ashen look on Pastor Darryl's face, he'd overheard enough to know the seriousness of the conversation.

"What note, Bets? What is she talking about?"

Gayle cleared her throat and held the note over Pastor Darryl's shoulder. He looked at it for a moment before taking it.

"Darryl," Bets pleaded, her voice shaking.

He removed the note from the envelope and read it. Then he looked up at his wife, his eyes confused. "I don't understand," he said, looking between his wife and Sadie. "What's going on?"

"Bets sent that note to Charlie after Noelani died but before her body was found," Sadie said.

"I didn't do anything to her," Bets said, pleading. "I swear."

"Then how did you know she was dead?" Sadie said, drawing Bets's frightened gaze back to her. "You wouldn't have given that letter to Charlie unless you knew his mother wouldn't be coming back to challenge it." She paused. "And I heard what you said to Jim this morning—that you wanted Noelani to go away. I believe your actual words were 'What does it take?'"

Bets's face drained of even more color, and she swallowed.

"What is she talking about, Bets?" Pastor Darryl said, but he didn't move toward her. The distance he maintained did not go unnoticed by anyone.

"I . . . I saw what happened," Bets admitted, tears running down her cheeks as she looked at the floor again. "And I knew Charlie would be devastated. I just wanted to help him, that's all. I thought if he had that letter he could . . . grow into understanding that she wasn't coming back and he'd know that she said good-bye."

"What happened?" Sadie asked again. "What happened the night she disappeared?"

"She called from the motel," Bets said, her voice a whisper. She wiped her fingers across her cheeks.

Darryl cut in. "You told the police you weren't there when she called—"

"Please, let her talk," Sadie interrupted, giving him a hard look. He closed his mouth, and Sadie nodded for Bets to continue.

She wouldn't make eye contact with anyone as she spoke again. "She started leaving a message for Darryl, asking him where Ho'oka Beach was."

"Ho'oka?" Darryl repeated.

Sadie shook her head at him; he lowered his chin as a sign he wouldn't interrupt again.

"She wanted directions?" Sadie asked Bets.

"Yes. I picked up the phone before she finished and asked her why she was going to Ho'oka. Darryl and I . . . we used to go out there and watch the stars at night. It's very . . . private."

"Where was Darryl?" Sadie asked, tensing herself for what might come next.

"In Kapaa, not far from Ho'oka."

When she didn't continue, Sadie turned to Darryl for an explanation.

He cleared his throat. "I'm part of a group of local churches who pray together and plan community projects. We meet once a month, and I always forward my cell phone calls to the house so I'm not interrupted. Bets knows where to reach me if there's an emergency, but she said she didn't get the call and there was no message."

"So you never knew Bets spoke to Noelani that night?" Sadie clarified.

Pastor Darryl shook his head.

Sadie turned back to Bets. "You gave Noelani directions?"

Bets nodded. "She was upset, and I thought . . . I thought she was taunting me by having me tell her how to get there, but I told her anyway."

So she could catch them, Sadie thought to herself.

Bets crossed her arms over her chest and turned away from her husband as she spoke. "Darryl warned me that his meeting would go late, and his cell phone was forwarded so I couldn't call and check up on him. I just . . . I just had to know."

"You followed her all the way to the beach?"

"Almost," Bets said. "She stopped at a convenience store and bought something. I thought maybe she'd go back to the motel—maybe I was overreacting. But then she got back on the highway, heading toward Kapaa. I turned off my lights when she turned onto Paapa Road and pulled off before the final turn into the beach parking lot. I walked the rest of the way. She was already heading toward a truck that had its lights on, pointed at a boat in the water." Bets closed her eyes and ducked her chin. "She was yelling at someone standing on the dock, saying something about Charlie and going to the police. I didn't understand what she could mean. When she turned back toward her car, a man tackled her from behind, throwing her to the ground. Another man jumped out of the boat."

"There were two of them?" Sadie asked.

Bets nodded.

"Then what happened?" Sadie asked in almost a whisper to keep her voice from cracking as the scene took shape in her mind.

"I couldn't have helped her," Bets said, as though justifying her inaction. She lifted her chin and sent a pleading look toward her husband. "I was scared for my life. I ducked behind some trees, but I could hear them fighting. Noelani was yelling at them. One of the men told her shut up and . . . there was a thud . . . and she did." She paused, and everyone in the room was silent. "When I dared look again, the two men were carrying her to the pier. She wasn't moving. . . . I watched them put her into the boat."

"You wouldn't have written that note unless you *knew*, without a doubt, that she wasn't coming back."

"I knew she wasn't coming back," Bets whispered. "Only one man took the boat out. The other stayed by the truck, smoking and talking on his phone. I was afraid to leave, afraid he'd hear me. The boat came back about an hour later, and Noelani wasn't in it. The man in the boat threw some bags onto the dock. The man by the truck headed toward them and yelled, 'You got rid of her?' The man in the boat said she was gone.

"As soon as I felt I could get away without them hearing me, I went back to my car and came home. Darryl came home within twenty minutes." She paused. "When almost a week went by without a word, I sent Charlie the note. I thought it would help him feel better when she never returned. I thought . . . it was the right thing to do. I never imagined they'd find her."

Sadie had to take a deep breath to remain calm. She wanted to ask Bets why she hadn't called the police. She wanted to ask how she could be so callous in regard to Noelani's death but so compassionate toward Charlie's loss. But those were the types of questions that would shut down the conversation, and Sadie needed to keep Bets talking.

"Do you know who the men were?"

Bets shook her head. "I didn't get a close enough look. The only lights were the headlights from the truck and the lights on the boat. I didn't recognize their voices either. I don't think I know them."

"What about the truck or the boat? Do you remember anything about them?"

Bets looked at the ground. "The truck was red, a two-door something or other. The boat, though, had a name on the back. *Serenity*, I think. It was written in silver lettering along the back and reflected the headlights of the truck."

"*Serenity?*" Sadie repeated, sickened by the irony.

Bets looked up at Sadie. "Maybe I should have done something," she said as though just now realizing it. She flicked a look at Darryl. "Even though she was in love with my husband, maybe I should have at least tried to help her."

Sadie shook her head, struggling to even look at the woman who had let another woman die, perhaps in part because she didn't want Noelani around. "She wasn't in love with your husband," Sadie said. "He was counseling her."

Bets shook her head. "No. It was more than that." Her voice shook, and she seemed to be pointedly avoiding her husband's eyes, which, if Sadie weren't mistaken, were wet.

"Jim wanted you to think it was more than that," Sadie said. "But he had his own reasons."

Bets's eyes filled with tears as she shook her head, her chin trembling. "What do you mean? What reasons other than the truth?"

"Melissa," Pastor Darryl said.

Bets turned her head in his direction but wouldn't look at him.

"Jim's ex-wife?" Sadie wanted to make sure they were talking about the same person. Gayle still stood behind Pastor Darryl. Intentionally or not, she was blocking the door.

"He's never forgiven me," Pastor Darryl said.

"Why does he hold you responsible?" Sadie asked, remembering what Shawn had told her over the phone and knowing that Bets needed to hear it too.

"We were all friends," Pastor Darryl said, his gaze cutting between Sadie and his wife. "We all worked with the outreach program together."

"Until you and Melissa started getting so close," Bets said, finally looking up at him, though hesitantly.

"She came to me for help," Pastor Darryl defended. "She needed advice."

"Did you tell Melissa to leave Jim?" Sadie asked.

Pastor Darryl shook his head. "I would never tell anyone what to do," he said. "Only how to seek direction from their Sovereign. Melissa was unhappy, and in time, she felt she received the answer to leave Jim and remove her boys from a disintegrating relationship. Jim was a good dad to those kids, but he wasn't always a good husband. You know that, Bets. You heard them."

"Heard them?" Sadie asked.

"They fought," Pastor Darryl said. "A lot."

"It was none of our business," Bets said, a hint of anger in her tone.

"She came to *me*," Pastor Darryl said. "In my capacity as her pastor. I counseled and prayed with her. I encouraged her to seek out professional counseling or to at least let me talk to Jim so he would understand how serious she was about needing changes. She said she felt God wanted her to simply leave, to end the marriage that she felt was abusive. She was afraid to try to make things better, afraid he would hurt her, and so when she made her decision, she left immediately. I know it was devastating for Jim. I know it broke his heart to lose his family, but for him to blame me is his way of avoiding his own responsibility."

"You could have warned him," Bets said. "You were his friend."

"And I was Melissa's *pastor*," Darryl said, shaking his head. "I've questioned my own actions a hundred times and asked God to confirm I did the right thing. He has answered me. I did the only thing I could do. Melissa came to me for counsel. Jim never did anything to fix things. They each chose the paths they took, not me."

"Was your relationship with Melissa anything other than that of a pastor?" Sadie asked because she felt she had to.

"Of course not," Pastor Darryl answered sharply. "I have never had an inappropriate relationship with another woman. I love my wife." He looked at Bets, who was staring at the floor again. "I have only ever been in love with you, Bets. Only you."

"Just a tip, then," Gayle said from where she stood behind Pastor Darryl. "Keep your hands to yourself so people don't wonder if that's true."

He looked over his shoulder, shocked by Gayle's words.

Sadie shook her head, warning Gayle that now wasn't the time, but Gayle continued speaking. "The whole time we were at the church you were touching me—my back, my arm, my shoulder." She shivered. "I didn't even know you. It was creepy, and Sadie said you did the same thing to her when you first met."

Sadie winced but tried to keep her expression calm as he looked at her in confusion. "The spiritually hungry are often starved for appropriate touch," he said.

"Your interpretation of *appropriate* can send a confusing message," Sadie said, looking at Bets. "And it makes people wonder."

"I don't care what people think," he said automatically. But then he took a step toward his wife, realizing that she thought the same thing other people did. "I have never been unfaithful to you, Bets, not with my body or my heart."

Sadie tried to reroute the conversation, turning her full attention to Pastor Darryl. "I think Jim used Bets in an attempt to exact revenge for what happened with his wife," she said. "Bets went to him for help in getting Noelani out of your apartment, and that created an opportunity for him. He's been feeding her lies about your relationship with Noelani ever since, and he's managed to undermine Bets's confidence in your vows to her."

Bets tucked her hair behind her ear, folding her arms and holding herself even tighter, like a little girl getting scolded. Sadie sensed that she still wasn't convinced of her husband's faithfulness.

"And he's planning to tell you that he and Bets have been having an affair," Sadie finished.

Bets stiffened and raised her head, her beautiful eyes wide. "What?" she said, horrified. She turned to her husband. "Darryl, I never—"

"Mandi's in on it too," Sadie said, making sure the people deserving of blame shared it equally. "She broke into my motel room with Jim's help, and then planted this list in your room." She pulled

Charlie's list from her bag. "There's also a prayer in the prayer box at the church from someone with the initials ACR. I'm thinking—"

"You read the prayers!" Pastor Darryl cut in, horrified. "Those are private."

"For you to read, right?" Sadie countered. "I'm thinking the A stands for Amanda. I can only assume Mandi expected that you'd eventually read her prayer and perhaps pick up on the hints she's been dropping. I also think she gave Bets's sweater to Jim to use as proof that Bets had been in his apartment. Pastor, I don't—" She stopped herself, reminded of why she was there. She turned to Bets. "All of this can be worked out later. Right now, you need to take us to Ho'oka Beach. You need to show us where Noelani died."

Slow-Cooked Kalua Pig

3 to 8 pound pork shoulder, butt, or picnic roast
3/4 teaspoon Hawaiian sea salt per pound of pork
1 teaspoon liquid smoke per pound of pork
1 banana

With a steak knife, pierce pork several times—don't be shy. Rub pork with sea salt and then with liquid smoke. Put in slow cooker. Slice an unpeeled banana down the center and lay the halves on top of the pork, peel side down. Cook pork on lowest setting for 8 to 16 hours, depending on the size of the roast and how low you can set the temperature of your slow cooker.

Halfway through the cooking time, remove and discard the banana, and turn roast. Remove pork from slow cooker 1 hour before serving and let cool for 10 minutes.

Remove pork drippings from slow cooker to a container and place in freezer to allow fat to congeal. Once the pork is cool enough to handle, remove the fat (and bones, if necessary), and shred the meat with a fork. Return shredded meat to slow cooker. Once the drippings have congealed, skim fat from the top with a spoon and discard. Add drippings to the shredded pork.

Serve pork and drippings over short-grain white rice. (Pork can also be served with shredded cabbage that has been lightly sautéed with soy sauce.)

Notes: Hawaiian sea salt is a specific type of seasoning usually found in specialty stores or whole food markets. It's similar in texture to kosher salt, but has a specific flavor. This is a traditionally salty dish, so if your family doesn't eat a lot of salt, cut it down accordingly.

For a quick version of this recipe, use pork ribs, omit the banana, and cook in a slow cooker on low for 6 hours.

CHAPTER 42

After a few minutes of discussion, Gayle and Sadie decided they would follow Darryl and Bets to Ho'oka Beach. The arrangement wasn't Sadie's first choice, but Darryl had said, "Please, I promise you we'll do whatever you need us to do, but let us have some time."

And when Gayle pointed out that she and Sadie may need to leave quickly if the airport called about Charlie, Sadie acquiesced.

Sadie and Gayle spent the drive talking about what they had learned in their separate adventures. Sadie was impressed with how well Gayle had handled Pastor Darryl.

When they finished catching up, Sadie looked at the time on her phone: 5:30. "I hope this doesn't take too long," she said, looking out the window. The green foliage, broken up by an occasional road or house, seemed endless and encompassing. When would Charlie get to the airport? Was he there now? Did he make it past security without them calling her? Was he just waiting for the plane to announce boarding?

"We'll be fine," Gayle said. "Have a little faith."

Faith. Such a big word sometimes, especially when her doubts were circling her like sharks in the water. Things had felt so over-whelming at the start of all this—a few simple words typed into the Google search bar—but they were ramping up, and she worried that at some point the dam that was holding back all her anxiety would break open. Then what?

"So, this is the kind of stuff you've done all those other times you were nearly killed?" Gayle asked a few minutes later, saving Sadie from her thoughts.

"Pretty much."

"So, you kind of stir things up like this? Follow all the leads and see what happens?"

Sadie smiled. "Stirring it up is a good way to put it," she said. "The bits and pieces of the truth tend to rise to the surface, then it's a matter of skimming it from the top and putting it together to create a whole truth."

"It's pretty intense," Gayle said. "I mean, what if you're wrong? What if Bets lied to you and she killed Noelani? What if we're being led to our deaths?"

"Are you trying to freak me out?" Sadie asked, facing her. "I sup-pose Bets could be lying to me, but I can usually tell. The fact is that most people are so shocked by the horrible things they do that they don't know how to hide it once they know I know something." That wasn't always true. There were exceptions to everything.

The Jeep in front of them started to slow down. The right turn signal blinked, and Gayle followed, muttering "Here goes nothing" under her breath.

Gayle made the turn onto a nearly invisible road cut into the vegetation. The ride became a bumpy one.

"Sheesh," Gayle said a minute later when yet another pothole bounced them both in their seats. "People come all the way out here when there are accessible beaches all over the island?"

"Not everyone wants to combat the tourist crowd," Sadie said. "And obviously whoever was in *Serenity* didn't want anyone to see what they were doing."

Bets had said that upon the return trip, the man had unloaded bags of something. Something he found on another beach? In the water? Something that had to be taken to a remote, secret beach in the middle of the night? Something worth killing for?

A few minutes later, the narrow road opened up to a parking area covered with gravel and a layer of red dirt.

Gayle slowed down to park while Sadie looked around to assess the last place Noelani had been. The tree line was about thirty yards from the water. A sandy beach stretched from one side of the boat dock, a rocky shoreline on the other. There was a minivan in the parking lot, but Sadie couldn't see the owner. A sign posted near the dock warned of hazards in the water: rocks and riptides. SWIM WITH EXTREME CAUTION, it said.

Once parked, the four of them stepped out of their respective vehicles and walked toward one another in silence. Bets's eyes were red and swollen, but Pastor Darryl was holding her hand as they all came to a stop.

"Where was Noelani parked?" Sadie asked, breaking the tenuous silence.

Bets pointed toward the left side of the parking area.

"Where was the truck?"

"Just right of the dock." Bets pointed toward the large lava rocks that separated the parking area from the water.

Sadie and Gayle immediately began walking toward the dock ten feet apart, scanning the ground in front of them. There were oil stains and uneven coloring on the ground; would Sadie be able to find what she was looking for? Would blood still be there two weeks later? She had concrete with blood stains from years ago, when Shawn had hit his head on the BBQ while playing football with some friends, but dirt and gravel was different. Dirt was organic, changing, affected by the elements. Had Noelani bled in those last moments on the beach?

"Sadie," Gayle said. "Come look at this."

Sadie joined her friend. At Gayle's feet was a three-inch, asymmetrical black circle, different from the oil stains. Different from anything Sadie had seen. She crouched down to inspect it before scanning the area around it. There was another spot, much smaller and lighter, a few feet closer to the dock. Then another, and another, and another. Sadie's pace sped up as she hurried toward the dock, following the spots. Noelani's blood. It was surreal.

When they reached the dock, Sadie's feet suddenly froze beneath her. She could not move forward. The water lapped against the blackened wood just like it had at another dock Sadie would never forget. The water was murky where it mixed with the sand and dirt. A body had been beneath the last dock Sadie had been on.

Gayle gave her a strange look as she passed her and stepped onto the wooden dock as though it were an ordinary sidewalk. Pastor Darryl and Bets hung back, watching with fearful interest as Gayle took the lead.

"Here's another drop," Gayle said. "The color is different against the pale wood, but it's got to be blood."

Sadie willed herself forward, but she didn't move.

Gayle walked about two-thirds of the way down the dock, then she looked around, as though hunting for the trail. After a few seconds, she glanced back to Sadie. "It's gone. The trail ends here," she said, pointing into the water next to the dock.

"That's about where the boat was," Bets said quietly. Pastor Darryl pulled her close and put his arm around her shoulder.

Sadie stared at the dock, imagining the scene Bets had described: Noelani tackled, thrown into a boat—a boat with the name *Serenity* on the back in silver letters. Noelani had taken a trip on that boat and had not come back. Why? Who had killed her?

Jim had a boat, but Pastor Darryl was his target, not Noelani. Or had Sadie missed something there? Could Noelani have learned about the game Jim and Mandi were playing? Could Noelani have threatened Jim's opportunity to get his revenge on Pastor Darryl? It would have been an elaborate setup, luring her to Ho'oka Beach with a boat in waiting. What of the bags being unloaded from the boat? Jim's boat wasn't named *Serenity*; Sadie didn't recall seeing a name on it at all. Wouldn't Bets have recognized Jim or his boat?

Gayle looked at Sadie. "Are you okay?" she asked.

Sadie nodded. "Yeah," she said, but she took a step away from the dock, away from the water.

The sound of tinkling wind chimes caught her attention, and it took her a second before she remembered it was the silly ring tone on her new phone. She pulled the phone from her bag and looked at the unfamiliar number. It couldn't be the airport calling about Charlie because they had Gayle's number as the contact.

"This is Sadie," she answered, moving away from the group for some privacy—and to increase her distance from the water.

"This is Hannah from the Department of Human Services."

"Yes," Sadie said, her thoughts returning to Charlie. She hadn't seen him for nearly eight hours. Had Mr. Olie caught up to him first? Was that the purpose of this call?

"I was calling to tell you that Mr. Olie is in the hospital," Hannah said.

Sadie gasped and stopped walking. "Oh my gosh," she said, raising a hand to her chest. "Why? What's happened?"

"He was out of the office," Hannah said, her voice low and heavy. "It appears he had a heart attack."

Sadie closed her eyes, picturing Mr. Olie as she seen him that afternoon. He hadn't been well, but she'd been afraid to push the issue. Perhaps she should have.

"Is he going to be okay?" Sadie asked.

"We're not sure," Hannah said. "He's in the ICU at Wilcox Memorial."

"Thank you for calling me," Sadie said, humbled by the sudden turn. "I sincerely hope he'll be all right."

"He asked for you," Hannah said.

Sadie startled. "For me?"

"About an hour ago. I found your number on Mr. Olie's voice mail. Do you know where Wilcox Memorial is? In Lihue?"

CHAPTER 43

S adie stood in the doorway of the ICU room, images of another day transposing themselves over this one until the floor felt as though it were moving beneath her feet. More than two decades ago, her husband, Neil, was the man lying on a hospital bed, hooked up to what seemed like a hundred tubes and wires while equipment beeped and whirred, trying to keep him alive. When she'd finally been shown into the room that night, she'd known Neil was already gone. Only the machines were sustaining him. Everything had changed for her that day. She wondered if Mr. Olie had anyone in his life who would miss him as much as she and her children had missed Neil.

That is not today, a voice in her head said. *Walk.*

She walked, moving over the threshold and focusing on the large form lying on the hospital bed. He'd asked for her, but she couldn't stay very long. When she reached the bed, she took in the gray pallor of his skin and the purple rings beneath his closed eyes. An oxygen mask covered his nose and mouth, and she could hear puffs of air that blew into the mask in accordance with the rise and fall of his chest.

Sadie reached out a hand and placed it on his arm. "Mr. Olie?"

His eyes fluttered open, but it took a few seconds for him to focus on her face and a few more before recognition came to his eyes.

"I heard you asked for me," Sadie said with reverence.

He lifted his hand, obviously weak and waved for her to come forward. She thought he wanted her to lean closer, which she did, but he pushed against her hand and pointed toward the head of the bed, jabbing the air. Sadie wondered what he was indicating and then saw a letter board leaning against the wall. She'd used them before during her volunteer work with disabled adults. Mr. Olie wanted to tell her something and this was the only way he could communicate right now.

She nodded to him that she understood and reached for the board. He relaxed, lowering his hand, his chest laboring to bring the oxygen in and out.

She began pointing at the letters in alphabetical order; he made a brushing motion with his hand, as though telling her to hurry. She started skipping to every third letter, and he seemed content until she landed on U, then he made the brushing motion again, but in the opposite direction. She went back to T then S. At S he raised his hand, palm out in a stopping motion.

"The first letter is S," Sadie said, then went backward on the alphabet board one letter at a time. N. M. L. He made the stop sign again. "Second letter is L."

He nodded and brushed backward. K. J. I. Stop. "Third letter is I." S-L-I? Slide, slick? Was he capable of spelling things correctly in his current state? Slinky?

He brushed forward. J. K. L. M. N. O. P. Stop.

"Slip?" Sadie said, glancing quickly at her legs to make sure hers wasn't showing. Then she looked at him. He nodded as best he could, then hit her board.

"Is that the whole word? Slip?"

He hit the board again, this time on the number grid.

She started going through them, taking note of the numbers he gave her a stop sign on. "Twenty-three," she said when he put his hand down. He nodded, looking exhausted.

"Slip 23?" she said altogether.

He nodded and she blinked. What did that mean?

"I'm sorry, ma'am. Time's up."

Sadie looked at the nurse in the doorway who was putting on latex gloves, then back at Mr. Olie. He was staring at her. "Slip 23," she said again, anxious about her confusion. Mr. Olie had worked so hard to tell her something, and she wasn't getting it. "I don't understand."

The nurse came forward and Sadie looked at her, pleading. "I'm sorry," she said. "Can I stay a few more minutes? He's trying to tell me something." She looked at Mr. Olie and pointed to the letter A. Surely one more word would clarify what he was trying to say.

"Ma'am," the nurse said.

Sadie could feel her anxiety rising. "Just another minute. Slip 23. Okay, is the first letter B, C, D, E—"

"Wait," the nurse said, looking at the letter board and then at Mr. Olie. "Do you mean a boat slip?"

Mr. Olie nodded, the nurse smiled, and Sadie inhaled sharply. He'd found a boat? He'd told Sadie he was preparing for the emergency hearing on Monday. How did tracking a boat *she* was looking for fit into that?

"I'll update his chart first, but he really needs to rest," the nurse said, turning to the computer by his bed.

"Okay," Sadie said to the nurse. She turned back to Mr. Olie. "Where? Where is the boat slip?" Sadie moved her finger quickly below the letters on the board. He stopped her at N, and she started moving her finger again but he shook his head and brushed backward. "The letter's before N," Sadie said out loud.

Mr. Olie didn't stop her until she got to the letter A.

"N-A?" Sadie said out loud.

Mr. Olie nodded and Sadie went forward again. He stopped her at W, then I, L, and I again.

"Nawiliwili?" the nurse said, looking up from her computer work. "Nawiliwili Harbor?"

Mr. Olie nodded.

"Slip 23 Nawiliwili?" Sadie repeated. The words felt like baby talk in her mouth.

He nodded again.

Sadie looked at the nurse. "You're familiar with Nawiliwili?"

"It's a beach, resort, harbor, and shipping port," the nurse said.

"And a boat slip—that's those, uh, parking spots for boats?"

The nurse nodded. "Except they aren't free. The boat owners have to lease the space."

"Do you want me to go there?" she asked Mr. Olie. When he nodded, she turned back to the nurse. "What's this harbor like? Is it safe?"

"Safe?" the nurse repeated, looking at Sadie strangely.

"I mean, are there people around? Is it . . . remote?"

"Nah," the nurse said, waving the comment away. "It's full of people, really busy."

Sadie turned back to Mr. Olie. "Is this the boat she was on?" she asked despite her stomach tightening. She didn't want to go to a harbor and look for a boat, but if this was *the* boat, how did he find it? If only she could get all the information he had, but she could tell he'd given his all to give her this much.

Mr. Olie nodded, then closed his eyes.

"Is there anything else?" Sadie asked.

He shook his head without opening his eyes. The effort to pass on what he'd learned had drained him. Sadie put down the letter board and touched Mr. Olie's arm again. He opened his eyes briefly, and she saw tears in them. He was scared.

Sadie reached for his hand, and he held on to her, though his grip was weak. She gave him a squeeze, feeling her throat tighten as she wondered if there was anyone coming to hold his hand tonight. That the room was empty, and that she was the only person he'd asked for, seemed to answer her question.

She went from missing Neil to being so grateful to have Pete in her life. Someone to hold her hand, to sit beside her and comfort her through the hard times. She was surrounded by people who loved her, and she felt immensely grateful for each one of them.

"Is he going to be okay?" Sadie asked the nurse as Mr. Olie closed his eyes, a single tear rolling down his face.

The nurse didn't answer and Sadie interpreted the look on her face to mean that she wasn't willing, or able, to give a prediction.

Sadie turned back to Mr. Olie and wiped at the tear track on his face with her free hand. "You're a good man, Tate Olie. You've done good things for many people, and this world is a better place for having had you in it. I'll find out what happened to her, and I'll do my best to make sure Charlie is safe. I promise."

His face contorted and though he didn't open his eyes, another tear rolled down his face.

"Ma'am," the nurse said softly.

Sadie nodded that she'd heard, then kissed Mr. Olie lightly on the forehead.

"Be well," Sadie said quietly. "I'll come see you in the morning with an update."

When Sadie entered the waiting room, Gayle stood, and Sadie shook her head in answer to the question in her eyes. "I think he found the boat," Sadie said, sticking to business so she didn't get overwhelmed by the emotion. "At a marina called Nawiliwili."

Gayle was already typing the name into her phone as they both fell in step on their way to the main entrance. "Looks like it's a couple miles southwest of Lihue," Gayle said as they went through the automatic doors. "And you think he found *the* boat? *Serenity?*"

"He must think it's the right boat or he wouldn't have worked so hard to give me the information," Sadie said. "I guess he wasn't twiddling his thumbs after all." She felt horrible for thinking badly of him.

They had reached the rental car when Gayle's phone rang. Gayle answered the phone, settling into the driver's seat. She flickered a look at Sadie, who paused with her seat belt partway over her shoulder. Was it Charlie? Was he at the airport?

"I'm afraid she's not with me right now," Gayle said into the phone. She paused. "I'm not sure where she is. . . . I suppose I could, but I'm not sure I would be that helpful. . . . Yes, I went to a beach with Bets Earlhart this afternoon. She's there?" Gayle looked at Sadie again while she listened to the voice on the other end. "I'm happy to come in and make an official statement," she said, betraying that it was the police on the phone. Why had she said Sadie wasn't with her? "I'll be there as soon as I can." She hung up the phone. "Trade places with me," she said before getting out of the car.

Sadie got out of the car, but when their paths crossed at the trunk, she put her hand on Gayle's arm. "The police?"

Gayle nodded. "Bets and Pastor Darryl are giving them a statement, and we got pulled into it."

"You told them we weren't together."

Gayle nodded. "You have a little boy to pick up from the airport and a boat slip to look into. You know as well as I do that once you go to the police station, you won't be investigating this anymore, and Charlie, especially, deserves someone who cares about him be the one to pick him up. Drop me off and take the car."

Gayle was right so Sadie nodded and went to the driver's door. It felt strange to be behind the wheel of a car; it had been months since she'd driven. They both put on their seat belts, and Sadie carefully reversed out of her parking stall.

Gayle searched for directions to the Lihue Police Department on her phone. "It's not far," she said when the map came up on her screen.

"You're sure you don't want to come with me?"

Gayle shook her head. "You can do this," she assured Sadie, with more confidence than Sadie felt. "And I can help set the scene with the police before you get back."

Sadie dropped Gayle off a block away from the police department so no one would see her in the car. They swapped phones— not only did Gayle's have the map from the airport to Nawiliwili Harbor, but it was the only number the airport security had.

Sadie watched Gayle walk to the corner and then turned the car toward the airport in Lihue.

CHAPTER 44

No one from the airport had called before she arrived, so Sadie parked her car and headed for the terminal.

Once inside the small airport, Sadie walked around, looking at every occupied bench and the face of every person beneath the height of five feet. She wished she had the name of the person in security Gayle had communicated with. After checking the main terminal, she stood in front of the windows that looked out over the road used for passenger pick-up and drop-off and took out the note where she'd written the times for the bus to Lihue.

Charlie had made the call at one thirty—four-and-a-half hours ago. Surely the bus didn't take that long to get here. Maybe Charlie had changed his mind. If so, she'd have to wait until his flight left to make sure. Or maybe he just hadn't arrived yet.

She watched hotel shuttles and taxis come and go. She watched sunburned tourists wrestle their luggage toward the ticket counter. One man limped in with one arm in a sling and multiple abrasions on his face and shoulder. Surf accident, no doubt.

When the white-and-green bus pulled up to the curb, Sadie held her breath and moved closer to the doors. She argued with herself about the chances of Charlie being on *this* bus, but it was the time closest to the flight he'd arranged, and he wasn't at the airport yet.

Five or six people stepped off the bus—adults, one toddler with her mother. As each one disembarked, Sadie became more and more tense. What if he wasn't here? Where would she look next? And then a little dark-headed boy with a light blue shirt and brown sandals stepped off the bus, a school backpack on his shoulders. He looked up at the signs and moved forward, holding the straps of his backpack and trying not to look nervous.

She didn't move toward him right away. He was coming to her.

As he entered the building, Sadie stepped in front of him. It took half a second before he recognized her. He took one step backward, as though to run, but Sadie grabbed the strap of his backpack and turned him around before marching him out of the airport, hoping security wasn't going to chase her down.

He tried to pull away, but Sadie didn't let up on her grip. "I've already told them what you did," she said. "They won't let you board the plane."

He stopped fighting.

"I have to hand it to you," Sadie said. "I didn't even consider you'd taken a credit card. You went for the one in the back of my wallet, didn't you? The one I didn't use much and therefore wouldn't notice."

They crossed the taxi lanes and had reached the public parking lot before Sadie turned and looked down at Charlie. He didn't look up at her, but she was grateful for his surrender.

"Charlie," she said, gently, though she didn't let go of the backpack. "I'm not angry with you, but I need you to come with me, okay? The police need to talk to you."

He immediately looked scared, and Sadie hurried to continue.

"You're not in trouble. But there are a lot of grown-ups who haven't been doing good things, and the police need to talk to you about it. Will you come with me?"

He looked at her, still not quite trusting her. It made Sadie sad to think of how many times this little boy must have been let down by people he trusted.

"I got your message," Sadie continued. "You heard me tell Nat I wanted to help you. I meant that, and even if it doesn't feel like it, I'm trying to help you now."

"I need you to help me find my mom," Charlie said. "That's the help I need. I think Mom is on O'ahu. She didn't go to any of her friends in Kaua'i, so maybe she went back to where we used to live."

"I see," Sadie said, exhaling. Should she try to convince him that his mother was gone? The idea made her wince inside. She couldn't do it. "I met a really nice police officer who wants to help you too," she said, totally passing the buck but needing Charlie to come with her. "Will you let me take you to him?"

"I'll be in *pilikia*."

Sadie had heard the word before but didn't know what it meant. "What's that?"

"Uh, trouble I guess. I'll be in trouble."

Sadie shook her head. "No you won't. All we want to do is help, but we need your . . . *kokua*." *Kokua* meant cooperation, and the police certainly needed that from Charlie.

Finally, Charlie nodded, and Sadie smiled before leading him to the car. When he slid into the passenger seat, Sadie told him to put on his seat belt, which he did without argument. She'd said she was taking him to the police, but she was planning to go to Nawiliwili first. Then she'd go to the police with *everything* she knew. She could hand it over and walk away. Well, maybe she couldn't walk away from Charlie. She wondered if going to Nawiliwili was in part a chance for her to have a little more time with him.

"Can you tell me about the last visit you had with your mom?" Sadie asked as they left the airport. She might as well learn what she could while they were together.

"Why?" he asked, caution in his tone.

"I'm just curious," Sadie said. "What did you guys do?"

"We went to the beach," Charlie said.

Kiki had said she thought they'd gone to a movie and ice cream. "Did you go to a movie?" Sadie asked.

"We was gonna, but it was too much money. And I like the beach."

"You went home after the beach?"

"We got a shave ice. I got cherry lime, and Mom got mango."

Mmm. Sadie loved shave ice.

"And *then* you went home?"

Charlie nodded.

"Did your mom seem okay? Was she happy?" Kiki had said Noelani seemed distracted and worried when she dropped off the car after the visit. Whatever had motivated Noelani to leave work later that night had something to do with her son. Maybe he knew what it was without realizing what he knew.

"She's always happy when she's with me," he said, looking at her as though daring her to question it.

"Well, of course she was," Sadie said with a smile so he would know she didn't doubt it. "But sometimes adults get worried about stuff—stressed out."

"She wasn't stressed out," Charlie said, shaking his head. "She was happy."

"Did she drop you off or walk you to the door when you got home?"

"Kinda both."

"What do you mean?"

"I wanted her to see the tree house 'cause Nat and me'd finished it, but she went to make sure it was okay with CeeCee first."

"I bet she liked the tree house."

Charlie nodded. "We played spy."

"Spy?" Sadie said, a tingle erupting in her chest. "What's that?"

"A game Mom made up. We laid real still in the tree house so no one would see us."

"Who might have seen you?"

"Nat," Charlie said. He smiled at Sadie. "He was a spy for Russia, and we had to listen and not get caught. He was talking on the phone. Spy talk."

"What did he say on the phone?" Sadie asked. A sign for Nawiliwili came into view, and she began to slow down.

Charlie shrugged. "I don't know."

"You don't remember?"

Charlie shook his head and looked around. "Are we going to Nawiliwili?"

"You know this place?" Sadie asked, turning into the marina's parking lot.

"They keep boats here."

"Yes, they do," Sadie said, parking the car and looking out over the marina. Big boats were on one side; smaller boats were pulled up to docks on the other side. She looked over the water, a churning feeling in her stomach. Maybe she should leave and let the police follow up on Mr. Olie's discovery. But she was so close. What if the police missed something? What if they didn't think it was important?

If she could get a picture of the boat in Slip 23 and show it to Bets, she might be able to identify it. The slip was leased, which meant that there would be records that could lead back to whoever had put Noelani on the boat.

Sadie pulled out Gayle's phone and texted, well, herself, and told Gayle where she was and what she was doing. Chances were she didn't have the cell phone with her if she was being questioned right now, but Sadie wanted to make sure people knew where she was. Just in case. She didn't want to explain to Charlie exactly what she was doing, but she also didn't dare let him out of her sight.

"We just need to run to the dock and take a quick picture of a boat, okay?"

"Why?"

"Just 'cause," she said with a smile and a shrug like it was no big deal.

He scrambled out of the car, and they headed to the pier. When they arrived, Sadie stopped and took a deep breath as she stared at the water. This pier was wider than the others she'd encountered and probably had steel beams holding it to the ocean floor. It was safe and secure.

"Auntie?"

Sadie looked at Charlie in surprise at the unfamiliar greeting. She'd heard other women called that, but no one had ever addressed her with the informal endearment. She liked hearing it, though; she liked that Charlie would use it for her.

"You okay?" he asked.

Sadie smiled. "I don't like the water very much," she admitted. "It scares me."

"It's just water," Charlie said.

Sadie chose to borrow some of his bravery. She put out her hand. "I know you're too big to hold hands, but I'm not."

He frowned at her hand, but took it reluctantly. Sadie gave his hand a squeeze and finally felt capable of stepping onto the dock. It didn't shift beneath her feet, and she felt better.

She began reading signs that directed her to the right section of slips. The sky was the color of orange sherbet as the sun set, warning Sadie she didn't have much time if she wanted a decent picture. The motion of the waves against the side of the stationary dock gave her a sense of vertigo. She held on tighter to Charlie's hand.

There was a locked door with metal grating around it to keep the slips secure, but when a man came out talking on his cell phone, Sadie told Charlie to run forward and catch the door before it closed. He was fast and nearly silent; the man didn't even notice. That boy could get himself all over the island—catching a door was elementary.

Sadie looked around to make sure no one was watching them. A few people were around, but they were all involved in their own activities and paying no mind to the haole lady and her little brown companion.

The boat slips were basically slots cut into an extra-wide pier, providing docking access on three sides of the boats, which were backed into each slip. Black numbers were painted on a three-foot cylinder at the head of each slip; most of the cylinders had hoses coiled around the base.

"Eighteen, nineteen, twenty," she muttered, counting them off as she moved down the dock. Most of the slips were occupied with some type of watercraft, everything from small speedboats to larger boats that seemed to be a tight fit. "Twenty-one, twenty-two." She stopped and stared at the numbers on the cylinder, afraid to look at the boat itself. "Twenty-three."

She lifted her head and looked at the blue-and-white boat gently shifting on the small waves within the inlet. The name *Serenity* was spelled out in flowing silver letters on the back of the boat and seemed to hypnotize her. There was no "serenity" in any of this, but *this* was the boat Bets had described, *this* was the boat Noelani had been thrown into and possibly out of three weeks ago.

"This is Nat's boat."

Sadie's stomach sank as she looked over her shoulder at Charlie. Maybe she should have left him in the car after all. She didn't want to know it was Nat's boat, even though she'd suspected it since learning about the game Noelani had played with her son in order to listen into Nat's phone call. He must have said something about a time when he would be at Ho'oka Beach.

Sadie imagined Noelani processing whatever she'd overheard as she got ready for her shift that night. Maybe she considered calling the cops but rejected it based on the last meeting she'd had with them. Plus, she'd want to know whatever she overheard was valid before going to the police.

Sadie imagined Noelani working and watching the clock, knowing she would miss her chance if she didn't act. The choice may have been a split-second one. She called Kiki but didn't want to tell her what she was doing in case it was nothing. She called Bets for directions. She bought the coffee on her way out of town so she wouldn't forget, and maybe as a way to tell herself that she was on a fool's errand and that she'd be back at the motel in no time, feeling silly for overreacting.

"Auntie?"

Sadie forced a smile at Charlie. "I just need to take a quick picture."

Why would Nat have a boat like this anyway? Maybe it wasn't his boat at all and Charlie was mistaken somehow. She could be jumping to conclusions.

Charlie pointed to a triangular flag attached to the stern. It had black-and-yellow zebra stripes. "That flag used to be on my bike, but my friend Rhett said it looked like a girl flag so I didn't want it no more. Nat didn't think it was girly, though."

Sadie felt her stomach drop even further. Nat *was* involved. A sense of urgency sent her scrambling for Gayle's phone in her bag. She tried to figure out how to use the camera and tried *not* to imagine Noelani's crumpled body lying inside the boat.

Sadie finally got the camera figured out and had lined up the shot when Charlie jumped onto the boat as though he'd done it a hundred times, which he likely had.

"Charlie," Sadie scolded, finishing the picture and dropping the phone back into her bag before moving toward him. She immediately saw the water within the slip and pulled her hand back, afraid she might lose her balance and fall in. "Come back here. We're not getting on the boat right now. It's time to go."

Charlie looked at her from where he stood on the back of the boat. "Why did we come here then?"

"Uh," Sadie said, not wanting to tell him. "Just come with me, okay." Sadie stepped as close to the edge of the dock as she dared and held out her hand again. The water seemed dark and menacing, and her breathing became shallow. "Come on," she said. "Please."

Charlie looked confused, then turned his back to her and headed toward the bow. "Do you think my mom came on this boat? Did Nat give her a ride somewheres?"

Sadie swallowed, then she took a deep breath before stepping onto the boat, immediately grabbing the railing on either side of the step-in with both hands. The boat shifted beneath her weight, and she felt sure it was going to flip over completely. She didn't breathe again until she was all the way in the boat, trying to calm her heart rate by taking deep breaths. She couldn't see Charlie anywhere. There was a covered driving area toward the closed bow with seats on either side of a narrow set of steps that led down to an open door.

"Charlie," she said, using a softer tone since her sharp one hadn't worked. She headed for the stairs, holding on to something with every step she took even though the boat barely moved beneath her. "We shouldn't be here. It's not safe."

Charlie didn't answer her, and she headed down the steps and ducked to enter the narrow cabin door. The cabin consisted of cushioned seats set up in a horseshoe around the wall of the boat. The seats were piled with fishing equipment, life jackets, and some articles of clothing. Charlie stood in the middle of the cabin, holding a cell phone in his hands. It was purple and black. He looked up at Sadie with a hopeful expression on his face.

"She *was* here," he said, his eyes lighting up. "Maybe Nat knows where she went!"

Sadie didn't know what to say; she'd say anything if it meant getting Charlie off this boat. Yes, his mother had been on this boat, but not like he thought.

"That's your mom's phone?" Sadie asked once she found her voice.

Charlie nodded, a huge grin on his face. "It was right here." He pointed toward a box of what looked like odds and ends on one of the seats. "I bet Nat gave her a ride or something."

CHAPTER 45

L et's go ask him about it," Sadie said, waving toward the door, her
heart in her throat. "If we hurry maybe—"

The boat rocked slightly, and a moment later Sadie heard a
voice. "—yeah. Midnight pick up. Quadrant six," the voice said.
Nat's voice. Was someone with him?

Charlie looked even more hopeful and took a step toward the
cabin door. Sadie grabbed him, put a hand over his mouth, and
pulled him to the side of the door where she peered out between the
hinges. Nat's back was toward the cabin. He was alone but still talking. He must have had a Bluetooth earpiece or something because
both of his hands were free as he stowed a bag under one of the seats
near the back. Charlie started wiggling.

"Charlie," she whispered right in his ear, causing him to go still
in order to hear what she had to say. "You have got to trust me right
now and stay still. Please. I've helped you every way I can, and I
promise you that I'm helping you now. Please stop fighting me."

He stayed still, but she knew he wasn't convinced.

"Yeah, just grabbing a few things now," Nat said, turning toward
the front of the boat.

She hoped his comment meant he wasn't staying on the boat. If that were the case, she and Charlie could just wait until he left and then get off the boat. Confronting Nat, especially with Noelani's phone in Charlie's hand, wasn't safe.

"No crazy wahines this trip," Nat said. "You can bet if one shows up I'll take her farther out to sea so she doesn't come in with the tide this time. . . . Who'd have thought they'd ever find her, yeah? I've got to get this run over with quick, the 5-O are looking for Charlie. . . . Right. . . . I know it's important or I wouldn't be doing it. . . . Yeah, it's my last run. . . . Just time to move on is all. . . . Six bags? You'll be at Malai'i to pick up? . . . Good. . . . Yeah. Nobody's camping out there right now . . . the road is really bad. . . . Just get there early enough to take it slow."

She felt Charlie stiffen. How much did he understand? She removed her hand, looking at his scared face in the fading light that was coming through the windows at the top of the cabin. She feared he understood more than she would have liked. She put her finger to her lips and he nodded slightly, then she turned back to the door, and, while Nat's back was to them, she slowly closed the door until it rested against the doorframe. She didn't dare risk it clicking into place.

"I'm on it, brah," Nat said, his voice muted through the door.

With the door mostly shut, Sadie hurried the two steps across the cabin toward Charlie, taking him by his shoulders. Words were at a premium. "We're going to wait for Nat to leave," she whispered. "And then we'll get off the boat so we can talk about this, okay?" She prayed that Nat was getting off the boat. His phone call didn't give her much hope, but she couldn't conceive of what she'd do if he went out to sea.

They moved to an empty section of the seats, and Sadie held

331

him close to her, the fear stretching between them as they waited for the vibrations of Nat's footsteps to disappear, proof that he'd left the boat.

As quiet and careful as she could, Sadie took Gayle's phone out of her bag and sent the picture of the boat to her phone. The phone made a beep when the message was sent, and Sadie spent another precious minute figuring out how to turn off the sound. In case the police had taken her phone from Gayle, she also texted Pete, explaining it was Sadie, not Gayle, and that she was in a boat docked in Slip 23 at Nawiliwili Harbor and asking him to tell the Lihue police . . . quick.

A moment later, Sadie's worst fear was realized. The engine growled to life, and the boat began moving forward slowly. Time to come up with a new plan. Charlie started to shake and tremble against her. Sadie dropped the phone back in her bag, smoothed his hair, and shushed him. They nearly lost their balance when the boat turned. Charlie held on to her, and she moved with him, willing him to calm down. It seemed like a very long time before he finally did. By then the boat had picked up speed, and Sadie felt sure they were heading toward open water.

Charlie pulled back and looked toward the door. "I want to go home," he whispered. "I want CeeCee."

"For now we need to stay here, okay, and be quiet."

"We can jump off," he said quietly. "I'm a good swimmer."

Nausea enveloped Sadie, and she shook her head quickly. "We'll just wait," she whispered, hoping that the messy cabin meant that Nat didn't come down here very often.

"Will Nat . . . hurt us?"

Nat had said he and Charlie were brothers. Charlie must be

so confused. "If we don't bother him, he'll never know we're here," Sadie said.

But what if he came down? Sadie moved Charlie off the bench they were sitting on and pulled up one of the cushions. It lifted in her hand like a lid, and she peered in to see that the compartment was full of more boat gear—life jackets, a tarp, and some lightweight fishing net made from string. She started pulling the items out one by one and putting them on the floor. It was getting dark, and she'd soon be out of light. She reached a child-sized life jacket and waved Charlie to come over from where he stood a few feet away, watching her.

"Let's put this on you," she whispered.

Charlie shook his head, looking at the darkening windows. "I can swim."

"You should always wear a life jacket on a boat," Sadie whispered, already sliding it over his arms. "Just in case."

"But I don't—"

She gave him a "don't argue with me" look, and to her relief, he stopped. She helped him buckle the jacket, then instructed him to climb into the compartment she'd emptied.

"Will Nat hurt me?" he whispered again as she helped him step inside.

"People do strange things when they're surprised." She thought of Noelani confronting Nat in the parking lot of Ho'oka Beach, a surprise that had led to Noelani's death. When Charlie was situated inside the storage area, Sadie stuffed a few of the life jackets around him, asking if he were comfortable. He shook his head, and she realized that was a silly question to ask.

"Don't close me in," he whispered loudly, sounding frightened at the prospect.

He'd be safer if she could cover him, but she couldn't imagine shutting herself into a box like that so she grabbed a towel from the cushions. She was about to drape it over him when she noticed a dark stain on one end of it. She pulled it closer to her face and felt a new wave of nausea as she threw it to the side. She couldn't say it was blood, but what if it were? She picked up a different towel and inspected it before draping it over Charlie, making him look like a pile of clothing. She kept the towel off his face but instructed him to pull it over himself if he needed to hide. He nodded.

"Where are you going to hide?" Charlie asked.

Sadie looked around the small space and forced a smile. "I'm too big," she whispered. "But I know karate so I'm okay."

"You do?" he breathed with a touch of awe.

Sadie nodded and pantomimed some standard moves. He had managed a smile by the time she finished. She winked at him in the increasing darkness. "I'm going to look around," she said, nodding toward the small windows that let in the last of the light of what had likely been a spectacular sunset—every sunset was spectacular here.

Charlie nodded, and she carefully made her way around the horseshoe of padded seats, moving things out of the way in order to open the bins and inspecting all the items she came across. In the box where Charlie had said he'd found Noelani's phone, Sadie found a stack of papers. She had to hold them close to the window to see what they were, but she was able to identify a map of the ocean, with little squares drawn and labeled with letters and numbers Sadie assumed were longitude and latitude lines. A few of the squares were highlighted.

Sadie wished she knew how to make sense of it all, but she guessed the map might mean more to someone with more knowledge than she had. What she *could* determine was that Nat used his boat for something Sadie feared was illegal. In case the papers might make sense to someone else, she folded them up and slipped them into her bra, making sure Charlie didn't see her.

The motor on the boat stopped, creating near silence save for the waves lapping at the sides of the boat. She'd been able to ignore the fact that she was separated from the depths of the ocean by thin sheets of metal and fiberglass, but hearing the water so close made her stomach tighten. She initiated her breathing exercises as she tried to push away the thoughts of Noelani's hair flowing with the current. She stopped when she felt the vibration of footsteps on the deck.

"Why did we stop?" Charlie whispered from his hiding place.

"Shh," Sadie said, watching the door as the steps continued. With the boat at a standstill, Nat didn't need to stay in the driver's seat. Sadie moved carefully toward the area behind the small door. In case he opened it, she'd be hidden and perhaps he wouldn't realize she was there. Maybe he wouldn't come down, though. Maybe she had nothing to worry about.

The first footfall on the steps leading to the cabin seemed to stop her heart, then it raced ahead to make up for the lost beat.

Nat fairly skipped down the other two steps, throwing open the door. He turned on a small light and began shuffling through a box. Sadie knew she wasn't fully hidden by the door, and the bright pink and blue of her muumuu would easily attract his attention if he looked her way. Charlie worried her more, though, and she hoped he'd stay quiet and still.

Nat cursed. Was he looking for the papers Sadie had taken? His movements became more frantic. He cursed again, and Sadie's anxiety kept increasing, making it hard to breathe, hard to think. She closed her eyes in hopes of getting herself back in control; she had to be able to think clearly right now.

Suddenly, everything went still. She held her breath, imagining Nat turning off the light and heading back up to the deck. The silence continued, and then Sadie felt the protective shield of the door move away from her.

She opened her eyes and met Nat's gaze.

"What are you doing on my boat?" he demanded.

CHAPTER 46

Nat folded his arms across his chest and stared at her. Though small for a grown man, he was still bigger than she was.

"I didn't know it was your boat," Sadie said truthfully and forced a smile that she worried looked as fake as it felt. She wanted to look toward Charlie, to assure herself he was safe, but stared straight at Nat instead.

"Why are you on it?"

"I like boats?" She hadn't meant for it to sound like a question but it did.

"Don't mess with me," he said, the edge in his voice rising though fear was there too, robbing him of some of his intimidation. "What are you doing here?"

"Could we go up on deck?" she said, fanning at herself. "It's kind of stuffy down here."

Nat hesitated, but then stepped to the side so she could get around him. He didn't close the cabin door when he followed her out. She went up the stairs and toward the back of the boat, trying to ignore the way her chest tightened when she looked at the blue-black water surrounding them.

They were floating in the middle of the Pacific Ocean, and though she could see a line of lights, shore perhaps, it was very far away. The sun was down and the night was gray. A breeze ruffled Sadie's hair and muumuu, but it wasn't cold. Yet. She didn't have time to look for any other nearby boats as she focused on the man standing across from her, staring her down with his arms folded over his chest.

"Why are you here?" he asked for the third time, his patience clearly at an end.

"Someone thought Charlie's mom had been on this boat," Sadie said. "I was—"

Nat dropped his arms, reacting much more than Sadie had expected. "She's never been on this boat," he said, defensive. "Who said that?"

"I . . . don't know," Sadie lied. "But I must have misunderstood, right? Totally got on the wrong boat."

He narrowed his eyes at her. "Why were you hiding?"

"Um, I was, well, checking out the boat, and then I heard you get on and I got scared so I stayed down there."

He watched her for a few seconds, and then opened his mouth, pausing for a minute before he spoke. "You heard me get on," he said as even more fear crept into his expression. "What else did you hear?"

He was talking about the phone call, but she shook her head. "Nothing," she said.

He stared at her. "No good," he muttered, his voice low as he ran his hands nervously through his hair. He took a deep breath.

Sadie watched him closely, jumping when his head whipped back in her direction.

"Why are you looking for a boat? Who thought Charlie's mom had been on one?"

Sadie shook her head.

Nat lowered his chin and raised his shoulders. Moments before he moved, she realized he was coming after her. She screamed and dove to the side, crawling toward the steering wheel while waiting for him to tackle her at any moment. There wasn't anywhere for her to go except the cabin, but then she'd be leading him to Charlie. She scrambled to the other side of the boat and got to her feet, holding on to the side as she turned to face Nat, only realizing then why he hadn't come after her.

He hadn't been coming toward her at all. Instead, the bag he'd brought on board earlier was at his feet, the zipper undone. In his hand, Nat held a pistol.

Sadie looked from the gun to Nat's face and tightened her fingers on the side of the boat. Her heart jumped to her throat.

"Tell me what you're doing here!" Nat yelled.

"You don't want to do this, Nat," Sadie said.

"Tell me what you know! How did you find my boat?"

"Someone saw you," Sadie explained, hoping her cooperation would diffuse his rising panic that could quickly lead to a jittery trigger finger. "Well, they saw the boat." She spoke slowly, formulating a plan.

"Who?" he yelled. If they were anywhere but in a boat on the ocean, Sadie would have expected someone to come running from the yelling. Then his expression grew more concerned. "The person who wrote that note to Charlie," he said, almost breathless with the discovery. "Who was it?"

"The police are coming," Sadie said quickly. "They know where I was going." Assuming Pete or Gayle had gotten the messages she'd sent. Her bag was still over her shoulder and her phone was still inside, but she'd turned off the sound and didn't know if they'd tried to call her back.

"It was an accident," Nat blurted out, regret lacing the panic. The gun, however, was still pointed at her.

"What was an accident?" Sadie asked because she couldn't help herself. Maybe it *was* an accident.

"Charlie's mom. She just . . . just freaked out." He wanted her to believe him, and Sadie realized that she wanted to believe him too.

"Did you know she'd overheard you? Did you expect Noelani to meet you at the beach?"

"No! Why would you think that?"

"Because CeeCee wanted to adopt Charlie."

"You think I'd . . ." He took a breath and shook his head slightly in disbelief. "Why does everyone think this has anything to do with Charlie?"

"Noelani was his mother," Sadie said, remembering that Charlie wasn't far away. She lowered her voice, not wanting him to overhear any of this. "Of course she would be concerned if she knew you were involved with something dangerous."

Nat's phone rang. He put his hand in his pocket but spoke into the Bluetooth earpiece still connected to his right ear. "Yeah," he said nervously. "I'm running late. . . . I know. . . . Right." He hung up and put the phone back in his pocket, obviously concerned by the content of the call.

"You're meeting someone?" Sadie asked, thinking back to what Bets had seen and heard the night Noelani had died. This boat had come to Ho'oka Beach, where Noelani had confronted two men. The boat then left and came back carrying bags of something. So Nat was ferrying something, drugs probably.

"You shouldn't have come here," he said.

"I'll go back into the cabin," Sadie said, pointing toward the door. "And I'll stay down there until you finish. At the dock, I'll go and forget about any of this."

"You'll go to the cops. You'll ruin everything."

"Ruin what, exactly?" Sadie asked carefully.

"A job," Nat said, running his hand through his hair again and clenching a fist anxiously. "That's all this is, a job, and a temporary one at that. Tonight's my last run. I just needed to get through a rough spot. No one was supposed to get hurt. No one was supposed to die."

"Drugs, right?"

His eyes narrowed and his shoulders straightened defensively. "It's just weed. It's practically legal."

"So you're transporting it across the ocean in the middle of the night because it's legal?"

"Shut up!" he yelled, the veins in his neck standing out. "We panicked, okay. I didn't even know it was her until she came straight at me, talking about Charlie not being safe and how she was going to the cops. I just . . . I just panicked and then she hit her head and . . . she wasn't moving. I had no choice but to take her out in the boat; she was supposed to disappear forever. She should have minded her own business."

"She did what any mother would do—try to protect her child."

"She was a druggie," Nat said with disgust. "He's better off without her."

"She was doing everything she could to fix her mistakes and—"

"You think those kind of things can be fixed?" he cut in, waving his arm around, the veins in his neck bulging again. "My mother was a crackhead. I was six years old when they took me away. She said she'd fix it too—never did." He shook his head, his jaw flexing. "Why should Charlie's mom be any different?"

"Should?" Sadie repeated, latching onto the word. So much was being said, more than she wanted Charlie to hear, but this confession was the truth Charlie had been hunting for, even though it was horrible. "So because your mom couldn't do better, Charlie's mother shouldn't have had that chance either? Charlie shouldn't? Noelani was doing everything she could to get him back. You took his mother away."

He straightened his arm, pointing the gun at her head, and she felt her heart rate increase as she held his eyes—full of sincere regret, but with enough desperation to override his conscience. If he killed Sadie on this boat, Charlie would live with that the rest of his life, too. She'd already said too much.

"It was an accident," Sadie said, putting her hands up in surrender. "I'll help you explain it to the police."

He shook his head. "You won't be able to talk anyone out of anything. I'll go to prison."

"Noelani's death was an accident," Sadie repeated. "But my death won't be. Just let me go to the cabin. I'll help explain what happened. I can help you."

"No, you can't," he said, looking even more desperate. "Like I said, some things can't be fixed."

Suddenly, something clattered along the bottom of the boat. Sadie looked in the direction the object had come from—the cabin—and felt her breath catch when she recognized the purple phone.

Charlie, she thought, but didn't say it out loud. *Don't come up here.*

Nat kicked at the phone with his shoe. He recognized it an

instant before turning to look into the open door of the cabin. "Someone's with you," he said. He took a step toward the cabin, and Sadie hurried to block his way.

"No one," Sadie said, though it was ridiculous to say out loud. "No one else is here, just me. I dropped my phone."

He didn't even look at her as he pushed forward, intent on the cabin door.

Sadie grabbed his arm, pulling him back. He pushed her off, and she kicked the back of his knee, causing him to lose his balance and fall toward her, catching himself on the driver's seat, which swiveled beneath him.

It was the opportunity Sadie needed. Driven by instinct and the need for survival more than conscious thought, she grabbed the wrist of the hand holding the gun and jabbed her thumb into the same pressure point she'd used on Bets, forcing Nat to drop the gun.

He grunted in pain, then looked into her face. She saw the change in his eyes. Until that moment, he'd been unsure how to deal with her but hadn't seen her as a threat. Suddenly, that had changed and his whole face tightened as he grabbed her chin and threw her to the side.

She hooked a foot around his, causing him to stumble again as she tried to brace her fall. Sadie moved toward the gun which had fallen on the far side of the boat, but Nat grabbed her arm, wrenching it behind her. She screamed, trying to hit at him, but he had her in a hold and marched her toward the edge of boat. Her whole body froze as he bent her over the side.

Not the water. Anything but that.

"You shouldn't have come here," he said. "I'm sorry you did. This should never have happened."

"N . . . n . . . no," Sadie said, pulling against him, unable to breathe as she stared at the water lazily rolling beneath her. Something else clattered across the deck behind them. Sadie was still pulling back as hard as she could and tried to turn her head to see what it was.

She didn't get the chance to see what Charlie had tried to use to distract Nat this time. In a final lunge of strength, Nat grabbed Sadie around the waist and threw her over the side of the boat.

CHAPTER 47

Sadie screamed for a split second before the glassy blackness swallowed her whole. Instantly, she began fighting for the surface, but it felt as though a vacuum was sucking her toward the bottom of the ocean. She clawed at the water, grabbing for a stability that didn't exist.

Her lungs felt ready to burst when she finally broke through the surface, gasping and thrashing and gulping for air. She could still feel the pull toward the bottom. She opened her eyes, looking for Nat but he wasn't at the edge of the boat, waiting for her to surface. Which meant Charlie's attempts at distraction had worked.

"Nat!" Sadie screamed, taking swift strokes to the boat and smacking the hull with her open hand. "Nat, you coward! Come finish what you started."

"You should have let it be," he said, appearing instantly above her. "You're *pau!*"

The moonlight glinted off the metal of a pistol, and Sadie yelped before diving back into the water—suddenly the better option. She hit the side of the boat with her head and came back up for air, trying to find something to hold onto, but the slick hull offered no options. Still, he wouldn't shoot her if she stayed by the boat, would he? He wouldn't risk missing and sinking the craft. She kicked furiously in order to keep herself up, wondering how long she could tread water. Maybe she really was pau—finished. But then what? What about Charlie? What about her children and Pete and Gayle?

"Who else is here?" he yelled, half to her and half into the boat.

That meant Charlie hadn't revealed himself. Sadie moved toward the front of the boat, hoping that would make it harder for Nat to grab her or shoot at her. She tried not think about the miles of water and countless creatures below her. She still could barely catch a breath.

Something hit the side of the boat, and she looked up to see Nat leaning over the side, a paddle in his hand. He whacked it against the hull only a few feet away from her. She should probably have some kind of comeback, or at the very least encourage him to give up the rest of his secrets, but the only thing she could think about was keeping the panic out of her brain. Survival, that was her only thought.

Survival—and Charlie.

She heard a splash on the other side of the boat and looked up in time to see Nat look across the boat as well. Had Charlie jumped in the water? Sadie swam around the front of the boat, afraid to call for Charlie but aching to hear the reassuring sound of his voice.

When she reached the other side of the boat, however, she saw a torpedo-shaped floatation device. Sadie's arms and legs were already burning from the short amount of time she'd spent fighting the water, and she started swimming toward the floatation device, but Nat's voice pulled her up short, making her realize the risk she would take by swimming away from the boat. She stayed where she was, trying to blink salt water out of her eyes.

"Who came with you?" he demanded, then turned toward the interior of the boat. "I'll kill her!" he yelled, looking around the boat. "And then I'll kill you too." His voice was not that of a confident mercenary, though. He was scared. Terrified. But desperate.

He lifted the gun and fired a shot into the air. Sadie swore she could feel the shot reverberate through the water. The preserver floated farther away from the boat. Maybe Charlie would figure out a plan if she could get Nat to focus on her. Putting her life in the hands of an eleven-year-old boy wasn't her first choice, but she had so few options right now.

"You're going to prison," Sadie said, cringing to talk about this where Charlie could hear, but she had to keep Nat's attention. "Regardless of what happens to me, the police will catch up with you." A wave splashed her in the face, causing her to sputter and spit.

"She shouldn't have been there."

"She didn't want her son living with a drug dealer!"

"She should have minded her own business," he said. He put one foot on the side of the boat to steady himself, but kept the gun at chest level. He continued to turn his head between Sadie and the boat, as though not sure where his attention should be.

"You're still a murderer," Sadie said.

His head snapped toward her, and he pointed the gun in her direction as his eyes narrowed. She took a breath and let gravity pull her under the water so as to take away his target. She kept one hand on the side of the boat as she moved closer to the front again. When she broke the surface, she had to gasp for air, both to fulfill the sheer need of her body demanding oxygen and to stifle the anxiety she was beginning to think would drown her before the ocean did.

She couldn't see Nat but she heard him run to the other side of the boat, giving her an opportunity to swim for the life preserver. She was feet away from it when something slashed through the water in front of her a split second before she heard the gunshot. She reeled and headed back for the boat, but managed to catch the thin nylon rope attached to the preserver with her arm first.

Another shot entered the water beside her, and she felt a slash on her ankle but told herself it couldn't have been the bullet. However, her ankle began to burn, which brought on a whole new fear. Now there was blood in the water. Did sharks swim at night? She whimpered as she pulled the nylon cord closer so she could grab the life preserver.

The life preserver, though it kept her afloat, made it harder to stay next to the boat, and it was almost more work to keep her position than it had been to keep herself above the water. There was another splash, this time on the other side of the boat, and she heard Nat run across the boat again.

"Nat?"

Charlie's soft voice cut through the air in a way the bullets and the splashing and the terror never could. Sadie craned her neck to see what was happening on the boat, but she couldn't see over the side. Nat was silent, and, realizing Charlie had just created the perfect distraction, Sadie began swimming as silently as she could toward the back of the boat.

" . . . are you doing here?" she heard Nat say as her head bobbed in and out of the water.

" . . . true? . . . killed my mom?" Charlie asked.

Sadie rounded the back of the boat and found the ladder. She gripped it with both hands and pulled herself up smoothly until she could catch the bottom rung with her bare feet, only then realizing she'd lost her slippahs and her shoulder bag to the ocean when she'd been thrown overboard. Her breathing was heavy and thick, but she tried to mute it as much as possible as she lifted her head high enough to see over the back of the boat.

Charlie stood at the top of the stairs that lead to the cabin, looking at Nat who stood with his back toward Sadie. Nat was still holding the gun, though it was pointed away from the little boy who'd just asked for a confession.

"I . . . I . . . I'm so sorry, Charlie," Nat said, back to the man Sadie had met that first night. The man concerned about Charlie. The man who called Charlie his brother. "It was an accident. I didn't mean for it to happen."

"You took her on this boat?" Charlie asked, his chin quivering. "You put her in the ocean?" His voice broke, and Sadie's chest tightened, but she started climbing, slow, smooth, and careful. The paddle Nat had swung at her earlier was on the row of seats on the right side of the boat. Sadie reached the top of the ladder but remained crouched, ready to jump back into the water if need be.

A quick glance down showed blood running from a three-inch gash on her ankle where the bullet must have grazed her. She looked away from the rivulet of watery blood that trailed down the edge of the boat and ignored the searing pain.

"It was an accident," Nat said again. "She . . . she shouldn't have been there."

Sadie took a step onto the once-white cushion of the seat, bloody water pooling in the indentation she made with her foot.

"Why did you do that?" Charlie asked.

Sadie reached for the paddle. Just as she grabbed the handle, Nat saw her. He turned fast, but this time she was faster. She wrapped both hands around the handle and brought it down hard on the wrist of the hand holding the gun. He screamed, and she lifted the paddle again, ready to hit him in the face.

"Get in the cabin, Charlie," she yelled. "Right now!"

She had no idea if Charlie followed her instructions. She swung for Nat's face, but he dodged. Sadie immediately swung again, this time at the back of Nat's knees. He fell, hitting his shoulder against the steering wheel. Sadie jumped off the seat toward him, but slipped on the slick bottom of the boat with her wet and bloody feet. In an attempt to get her balance, she pitched forward, which happened to bring her down hard on Nat's back as he tried to stand. It was very WWF, and a happy accident that seemed to punch the air out of his lungs.

She didn't waste a second of his shocked stillness. She grabbed his left arm, twisting it behind his back and pulling his wrist nearly up to his neck. He cried out in pain, but Sadie just shifted her position so she was sitting squarely in the middle of his back, bracing her right foot against the side of the boat. She'd never been so grateful for the extra twenty pounds she'd been trying to lose for the last ten years.

"Charlie!" she yelled. "There's some fishing net in the cabin. Get it for me, quick!"

"But you said for me to go—"

"Net! Now!" Sadie yelled, pulling up on Nat's arm even harder when he tried to roll her off of him. Her arms were shaking in an attempt to hold him, and the breeze off the water felt icy on her wet skin. Her adrenaline had kicked in, and the panic attack she feared would be the end of her had not taken control. "It's by the seat you were hiding in. On the floor. Hurry!"

Nat yelled at her, swearing, demanding she let him go. She

pulled up on his arm again. Though she wasn't devoid of sympathy, she knew what Nat was capable of, and she wasn't taking any chances.

"Lucky for you," she said between clenched teeth as she strained to hold him still. "I'm fully prepared to show you more mercy than you showed Noelani."

A moment later, Charlie's head appeared over the top stair. He looked scared as he handed over a bunched-up wad of net. Sadie leaned forward, digging her elbow into Nat's back to hold him still long enough so she could let go with one of her hands and grab the net. It was made of thin strings, and when she shook it out, it proved itself plenty long for her to use as a rope.

"Do you know how to drive this boat?" Sadie asked Charlie as she tried to figure out how she was going to tie up Nat with only one hand.

"Kinda," Charlie said, but he looked at Nat with sad, scared eyes.

Sadie leaned down, close to Nat's ear. "You really want him to watch you fight me? You said he needed to learn how to be a kane. Now's your chance to show him that a real man accepts the consequences of his actions."

She felt Nat's resistance decrease and his muscles go soft beneath her, but she still wrapped the net around his wrists before tying them off and rolling him over. She tied up his feet as well.

Nat looked at Charlie, tears filling his eyes but apparently without justification any more. He turned his head, and Sadie felt in his pockets for his phone. He didn't fight her. She left Nat lying in the middle of the boat as she limped to join Charlie who had started the boat and was driving forward without realizing the harbor was somewhere behind them. Her chest was tight. It was hard to breathe, but she did everything possible to keep from losing it in front of Charlie.

Sadie put one arm around Charlie's shoulders. He'd started to cry but was trying to keep a brave face despite his trembling chin. With her other hand she dialed 911 on Nat's phone. Her hands began to shake.

"Yes, I'm in a boat off the coast of Kaua'i and don't know how to get back to Nawiliwili Harbor. Oh, and I also need to report a murder."

CHAPTER 48

Monday afternoon, less than seventy-two hours since the Coast Guard had guided her to the harbor, Sadie pulled up with Gayle to the temporary shelter where Charlie had been staying while the police finished their investigation.

An hour earlier, Charlie's new caseworker at the DHS office had called to tell Sadie she'd been granted a visit before Charlie would be returned to CeeCee's care later that afternoon. Charlie had been asked if he felt comfortable returning there and he hadn't hesitated, which relieved everyone—CeeCee especially.

Mr. Olie was still at Wilcox Memorial but had been able to explain that he'd spent Friday reviewing everything he knew about both Charlie and his foster family in order to present the best argument possible to the judge Monday morning. During his search, he'd come across a record of a boat CeeCee's late husband, Yogi, had owned. With Sadie's questions about Noelani fresh in his mind, and questions about Nat not much further behind them, Mr. Olie had tracked the boat to Slip 23 at Nawiliwili Harbor before the symptoms he'd been ignoring all day caught up with him.

Sadie had gone to see Mr. Olie on Sunday to update him on what had happened after he had passed the slip number on to her.

"I couldn't have done it without you," she said when she finished the story that still felt a little unreal. "I'd have never thought of Nat."

Mr. Olie had only grunted, but she'd decided that was his way of saying "Thank you so much. You're wonderful!"

"Charlie Pouhu," Sadie said when they reached the reception desk. "I have an appointment to see him at two o'clock." She'd made the recipe for Aloha cookies Tanya had taped up inside one of her cupboards. She and Gayle had eaten too many but she still had enough to fill two plates with what was left. One plate was for the receptionist, who accepted them with a soft "Mahalo." The second plate was for Charlie; Sadie still felt bad that the first thing she'd ever fed him were brownies from a mix.

A few minutes later, Gayle squeezed Sadie's arm before Sadie was led down a hallway and into a common area full of furniture, books, and a TV.

Charlie sat alone on the couch watching cartoons. Sadie sat down next to him. He glanced at her but then ducked his chin and kept watching TV. What she wouldn't give to read his thoughts. Then again, maybe it would be too hard. He'd lost his foundation too many times in his young life, and Sadie was connected to the latest one. His reticence wasn't hard to understand in light of all that had happened.

After a minute of waiting for him to say something, she broke the ice. "Howzit," she said, trying to get him to smile by using the pidgin greeting she'd heard the local kids use.

"Hey," he mumbled.

She handed him the plate of cookies. He pulled back the plastic wrap and quickly ate two cookies while still watching his show.

Sadie pulled his worn list of questions out of her bag and unfolded it on her lap. He glanced at it, straightened slightly, and then looked back to his show, more intent than ever.

"You left this at my house that night I found you in the courtyard," Sadie said. "And I wanted to get it back to you."

He didn't say anything.

"Charlie," she continued softly. "I know how to answer these questions now."

He looked at her then, his expression guarded. The sounds of an animated explosion came from the TV.

"Can I turn that off?" she asked, pointing at the TV.

He nodded almost imperceptibly, and Sadie picked up the remote and clicked off the show before returning her attention to the note.

"Number one was how did I know your mom." She smiled sadly at him. "I've gotten to know your mom through her friends and through you and through the good changes she was making in her life. She was a strong woman, Charlie. I think I would have liked her very much."

He looked down at the plate of cookies.

"Number two was if I told any lies to the police. I didn't. I told them exactly what happened that day I found your mom, and I've told them everything else, including how you helped me on the boat with Nat. I wrote the name of a police officer on the paper." She turned the paper toward him, now filled with her handwritten answers as well as Officer Wington's contact information. "He said that anytime you want to know more about what happened, he can talk to you about it. I know you haven't always trusted the police, but Officer Wington is a good man."

Charlie looked at her again, having dropped some of his guard.

"The third question was if your mom had a new boyfriend." Sadie shook her head. "She only wanted to take care of you, Charlie, and she didn't want anything else to get in the way." Emotion was creeping up on her, and Sadie had to pause to clear her throat. "Four. Was Mom taking drugs? No, Charlie, she wasn't. She had been clean since she lost you, and she was doing everything she needed to do to get you back. When the two of you played spies in the tree house after your last visit, she heard Nat talking on the phone and knew he was doing something bad. She tried to stop him. She died doing a good thing, Charlie—trying to help Nat and trying to help you. Nat didn't understand that, but he didn't want to hurt her either. When he told you he was sorry, I think he really meant it."

Charlie's expression softened, but he ducked his chin even lower, reminding Sadie of how much he'd really lost. His mother, Nat, and a little more of his innocence. The loneliness was familiar to Sadie, who had lost so many people she loved—people she couldn't have imagined living without. But she *had* lived on, and she believed that life had a way of offering you new opportunities when others were taken away. She didn't know how to explain that to someone so young. Hopefully, life would show him that was true. She moved on to the fifth question.

"She did talk about you that night, Charlie, and when things got bad, I have no doubt she wanted to be with you more than anything in the world."

Charlie blinked rapidly against the tears forming in his eyes, and Sadie stopped fighting her own, wiping them quickly with the back of her hand.

"The last question, Charlie, was about when your mom was coming back." Sadie took a deep breath and put her arm around Charlie's shoulders. To her surprise, he leaned into her. She kissed

356

his hair and then rested her head against his. "She's not coming back, Charlie," Sadie said, her voice cracking. "But she didn't leave you on purpose, and she loves you as much now as she ever has."

The emotion finally broke through and Charlie began to cry. Sadie held on tighter and closed her own eyes, tears dripping down her own cheeks. She thought about all that had happened, here in Kaua'i, back home in Garrison, in Boston, Oregon, Miami, England. So many tragic events that Sadie had been a part of it, but none of them had felt quite like this. More than ever she wanted the magic words that would make sense of this for Charlie, make sense of it to her, but there was no quick fix for the heartbreak that had happened in this tropical paradise.

They cried together for what felt like a long time, but then Charlie straightened and looked at the list Sadie still held on her lap. She passed it to him and he took it.

"Charlie, I don't know why bad things like this happen, but I do know that while this is a horrible thing, you have good things in your life too."

He looked doubtful and rubbed at his red eyes.

Sadie continued. "I have two children. They're both adopted, and I love them so much. CeeCee loves you like that, and I know she'll take really good care of you. She wants you to be happy. Mr. Olie and your new caseworker want to help you any way that they can, and even though you don't know me very well, I hope I can send you some letters and postcards. And maybe you can send me some too."

He shrugged, but didn't look up.

After a few seconds, Sadie reached down and lifted his chin so he was looking at her. "Life is a gift, Charlie, a wonderful journey full of amazing things. You're very young to have had to go through such a horrible tragedy, and I'm so very sorry for it, but . . ." She let the word hang between them. She forced a smile as she dropped her hand. He didn't look away. "It's because of you that everyone knows the truth now. It's because of you that your mom was working so hard to be better. It's because of you that us grown-ups are looking around and seeing what we can do better too."

He blinked at her. "Pastor Darryl said my mom's an angel now," he whispered.

Sadie nodded, wanting to give Pastor Darryl a hug—an appropriate one.

"And she isn't sick anymore or sad or anything. She's all better now, right?"

"Yes," Sadie said. "And she's watching out for you, Charlie. Even though she isn't here, every time you think about her and remember the good things, she's there, feeling it with you and loving you still."

"How do you know?"

"Because I have angels too," Sadie said, her voice barely a whisper. "I feel them sometimes, and I dream about them, and I know that they come to me when I need them. People don't go away just because they die, Charlie. I believe that with my whole heart."

Charlie sniffled, trying to maintain a brave face and nodded, a look of hope on his face. Maybe one day, the hope that what Sadie was saying was true would become a belief of his own.

"Oh, Charlie," Sadie whispered. "One day you're going to be a grown-up man, and when you have a child of your own, you will remember what it felt like to be loved by your mother. I hope you'll look at the choices she made—good and bad—and choose a road that will give your child what you have missed out on without denying them the beautiful things your mother gave you."

She knew he didn't really understand what she was saying. She hoped one day, though, he would remember her words and that they would mean something then. She wrapped both arms around his small shoulders, pressing her cheek against his hair. That he'd seen so much sadness in his young life was tragic; she hoped the worst was behind him and that he'd have the chance to experience joy as life marched forward.

She wondered if the hard times for her were behind her as well. It was hard to think it was possible, but she did know there was joy ahead, too. She needed to find a way not to get lost in the pain. Her children would help her, as they always had, and Pete and Gayle would help her too, and in his own way, Charlie would be a part of that as well.

"There is a wonderful life yet to be lived by you, Charlie Pouhu. Don't let it pass you by."

Aloha Cookies

½ cup butter
½ cup shortening
1 cup sugar
1 cup brown sugar
2 eggs
1 teaspoon coconut flavoring (optional)
1 teaspoon butter flavoring (optional)
1 teaspoon vanilla
2 cups flour
1 teaspoon baking soda
1½ teaspoons baking powder
½ teaspoon salt
1 cup quick oats
1 cup coconut (sweetened or unsweetened)

1½ cups macadamia nuts, chopped
1 cup white chocolate or regular chocolate chips

Preheat oven to 350 degrees. Cream butter, shortening, and sugars together. Add eggs and mix well. Add flavorings and vanilla and mix well. Add flour, baking soda, baking powder, and salt. Mix well. Add oats and coconut. Mix until combined. Add nuts and chocolate chips. Mix until well blended. Drop by 1-inch balls (or use a 1-inch scoop) onto a greased cookie sheet. Bake for 10 to 12 minutes or until just barely browned. Cool two minutes on cookie sheet before removing to cooling rack.

Makes 5 dozen cookies.

Note: Gayle prefers this with the coconut and butter extracts. Tanya prefers milk chocolate chips.

THE STORY BEHIND THE STORY

TOP SECRET

Scan the QR code or visit the website below to access a special bonus chapter of *Banana Split* and learn more about Noelani and Charlie.

www.ldsliving.com/story/67270-banana-split-secret-chapter

Acknowledgments

There was a time when the only people who knew what I was doing while I was hunched over the computer for hours on end were my husband, my kids, and my sister, Crystal. These days I wonder how I ever did this without an auditorium full of people helping me move forward and cheering me on.

Shadow Mountain once again did an amazing job with their production. Thank you to Jana Erickson for supervising all the details, Lisa Mangum (The Hourglass Door series, 2009–2011) for smoothing out my words and making me sound so good, Shauna Gibby for another mouthwatering cover, Rachael Ward for the fabulous typesetting, and everyone else who operated behind the scenes at Shadow Mountain to make this book what it is. I have an amazing pit crew—thank you so much.

Thank you to my writing group: Nancy Allen (Isabelle Webb series, 2008–2012), Jody Durfee, Becki Clayson, and Ronda Hinrichsen (Trapped, 2010). Thank you for your continual guidance and help as I honed the story. I don't know how I ever did this without you guys.

Much thanks to my beta readers: Curtis Moser, Tina Peacock,

Melanie Jacobsen (*Not My Type*, 2011), Krista Jensen (*Grace and Chocolate*, 2013), my sister, Crystal White, and my aunt, Sandy Drury. My eyes were crossed by the time I sent the manuscript to you guys and you provided priceless feedback. Susan Law Corpany (*Lucky Change*, 2010) was a priceless Hawai'i resource for me—mahalo.

Sadie's Test Kitchen Bakers were once again amazing: Whit Larson, Annie Funk, Michelle Jefferies, Laree Ipson (Grandma Jensen's Caramel Sauce and Homemade Hot Fudge), Don Carey (*Bumpy Landings*, 2010), Megan O'Neill, Sandra Sorenson, Lisa Swinton, and Danyelle Ferguson (*((dis)Abilities and the Gospel: How to Bring People with Special Needs Closer to Christ*, 2011). They are the brilliance behind the recipes and work so hard to ensure everything in this book is as good as we say it is.

To my amazing family, who have now seen me through fifteen published novels, thank you for every bit of the beauty and magnificence you bring into my life. I often say I couldn't do it without their support; it is not a rote phrase meant to gloss over their contributions. From brainstorming ideas with me to fixing their own dinner to encouraging me when I lose my faith—thank you Lee, Bre, Madi, Chris, and Kylee for making the entirety of my life so worthwhile. May I give you wings the way you have given me mine.

And once again and always, thank you to my Heavenly Father who loves me and has given me such remarkable blessings.

Enjoy this sneak peek of

TRES LECHES CUPCAKES

Coming Fall 2012

CHAPTER 1

I t was the cold that woke her.

Sadie reached for the plush blanket, as soft as kitten's fur, so she could pull it up to her chin and settle back in for a couple more hours of sleep; the fire she lit in the evenings always burned out in the early morning hours, inviting the autumn chill back in. But instead of finding the comforting softness she expected, her hand brushed across rough stone and rubbed gritty sand beneath her fingers. A breeze passed over her, rippling the silky fabric of her blouse that afforded no protection from the cold night air.

She wasn't in her apartment. Why not?

Then she began to remember.

Her body tensed as equal amounts of confusion and memory swirled together, like two children trying to talk over each another as they both explained their version of events. From the bits and pieces of her recollections, she knew she was in the New Mexican desert. She'd been at the Balloon Fiesta, the annual hot air balloon festival in Albuquerque. She'd been selling cupcakes—Lois's Tres Leches Cupcakes to be exact—but then . . . then something had happened. Someone had brought her here, far away from the tourists and balloonists and anyone else whom she could call to for help.

The Cowboy.

But he'd been sent by someone else. Langley? Standage? She wasn't sure. But she knew the Cowboy had brought her here to kill her. He said she'd crossed a line.

What line?

Why couldn't she remember everything?

She must have made a run for it. How had she gotten away? They'd come after her—the Cowboy and the man he worked for. And then . . . then . . .

What had happened then?

Sadie attempted to sit up, but her head spun, causing her to lie still again. Then she rolled to her side and used a rock, gray against the blackness behind it, to pull herself up, though her joints and muscles screamed in protest. As her eyes traveled up the side of the hill above her, she could make out the scraggly silhouette of brush against washed-out desert dirt. She looked toward the bottom and saw that the hill she was on continued for several more yards, ending in an arroyo. She'd come to a stop at a ledge of sorts near the middle of the incline. Perhaps the rock she'd used to help her sit up had stopped her. None too gently, it seemed.

Once sitting, she put a hand to her throbbing forehead and gasped in pain at her own touch. She pulled her hand back. Even in the minimal light of the crescent moon, she could see the contrast between her pale skin and the dark smudge on her fingers. Knowing the stain was blood made Sadie's throat tighten and her hand shake from something other than the cold. Where was she?

Fear began to take over. It was hard to breathe, and her body seemed to involuntarily curl in on itself though her back and hip protested. Everything hurt. *What had happened?* How long had she been here?

"She went this way," a voice said from somewhere above her, the words carried to her on the wind. Another voice answered the first, but Sadie couldn't make out what was said. She didn't need to. What she needed to do was hide. Quick. Though she couldn't remember everything, she knew that if they found her—whoever *they* were— she'd never get back to Santa Fe.

Sadie knew firsthand how well the desert could hide a body.

Discussion Questions

1. Have you read other books by Josi Kilpack? If so, how did this book compare?

2. What did you think about the opening chapter? On a scale of 1 to 10, how intense did you feel the scene of Sadie finding Noelani's body was?

3. At the beginning of the book, Sadie agrees to go snorkeling with the Blue Muumuus simply because she doesn't want to reject another invitation. Have you ever felt pressured to do something you would never have considered otherwise? Was it a positive or negative experience?

4. In this book, Sadie is involved in an internal battle with growing anxiety and depression. Have you or someone you know struggled with this? Did Sadie's journey feel authentic?

5. The police seem eager to attribute Noelani's death to a drug overdose. Do you feel that law enforcement tends to dismiss or gloss over drug-related crimes? Why? As a society, do we tend to be less-sensitive to victims of drug-related crimes?

6. Was there a particular scene or element of the book you particularly liked? Disliked?

7. Mr. Olie says that CeeCee is one the best foster parents he has in the program. What qualities does she possess that make her a good foster mom? Do you think the foster care program helps or hinders a child's development?

8. Have you made any of the recipes in any of the books in the Culinary Mystery series? If so, what did you think? What additional recipes would you have included in the book?

9. How did you feel about the revelation of whodunit? Was it a satisfying ending?

10. Did you use the QR code or visit the website www.ldsliving.com/story/67270-banana-split-secret-chapter to read the "Story behind the Story" of Noelani and Charlie? If so, what did you think?

11. Did you read the first chapter of *Tres Leches Cupcakes*? Do you have any predictions as to what will happen in that book?

About the Author

Josi S. Kilpack grew up hating to read until she was thirteen and her mother handed her a copy of *The Witch of Blackbird Pond*. From that day forward, she read everything she could get her hands on and accredits her writing "education" to the many novels she has "studied" since then. She began her first novel in 1998 and hasn't stopped since. Her seventh novel, *Sheep's Clothing*, won the 2007 Whitney Award for Mystery/Suspense, and *Lemon Tart*, her ninth novel, was a 2009 Whitney Award finalist. *Banana Split* is Josi's fifteenth novel and the seventh book in the Sadie Hoffmiller Culinary Mystery Series.

Josi currently lives in Willard, Utah, with her wonderful husband, four amazing children, one fat dog, and varying number of very happy chickens.

For more information about Josi, you can visit her website at www.josiskilpack.com, read her blog at www.josikilpack.blogspot.com, or contact her via e-mail at Kilpack@gmail.com.

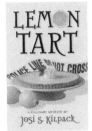

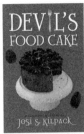